ANOTHER LIFE

&

OTHER STORIES

EDWIN WEIHE

ANOTHER LIFE
&
OTHER STORIES

A PLEASURE BOAT STUDIO BOOK

Design & Composition by Shannon Gentry
Cover Photograph by Noreen Weihe
Author Photograph by Honor Weihe

Library of Congress Catalog Card Number: 00-101770
Weihe, Edwin.
Another Life & Other Stories / Edwin Weihe

ISBN: 1-929355-01-7

Published by Pleasure Boat Studio
8630 Wardwell Road
Bainbridge Island ·WA 98110-1589 USA
Tel/Fax: 1-888-810-5308
E-mail: pleasboat@aol.com
URL: http://www.pbstudio.com

Pinted in Canada
First Printing

for Noreen

CONTENTS

GIRL IN THE COAT

Parker's best defense was to get out of Larry and Sylvia's house as early and painlessly as possible—he had an important seven a.m. flight to Chicago, in fact—but as soon as his wife Mary rose to help Sylvia clear the dinner plates, Larry started right up, his face engorged with blood. He had been drinking like a sailor since five, and now he was going to spout off whatever the hell he wanted. That meant going after Parker, testing his patience. Parker braced himself, actually gripping the edges of his chair. He understood this was hostile territory: their little madhouse, Larry's empty Merlot bottles marching up the table. The three kids were upstairs with Jennifer, the sitter.

The twin boys, aged six, were both terrors, and Parker's attention wandered ceilingward to their screeching and the slamming bathroom door and finally little Emily awake and crying and poor Jennifer doing whatever she could, against impossible odds, to get her back to sleep. Parker suspected there had always been this storm of noise and terror upstairs, even before the children. The twins had arrived late in the marriage, like burglars through a broken window, and by the time the fact had fully registered, it was really too late to do anything but hand over whatever they wanted. Five years later, when it was obvious both Larry and Sylvia were at the ends of their very separate ropes, they sleepwalked back onto the crime scene, and—surprise, surprise—*Baby Emily* appeared, and, as Larry described it, mere anarchy was loosed upon their house.

And so Larry, too, looked up at the water-stained plaster.

"I'm sinking here, brother. Throw me a line."

"What's a nice girl like you doing in a place like this?" Parker said.

Larry considered the question. "Except I'm not so nice," he said finally. "Someday I'm going to toss them all overboard."

"Look. The kids are wonderful."

"Back at you. Only yours are praggaly out of the house."

"I'm sure they'll be praggaly out for another ten years."

"You know so damned much."

"I don't know anything," Parker said, glancing out the window.

"You know how to fucking defend yourself."

"Looks like it's raining again."

Larry held his palms up. "I think you're right," he said.

He picked up an empty Merlot bottle, then put it down again. Upstairs, one of the twins had wedged his foot in the bathroom door and Parker could hear the cracking noise of the door bending against the weight of a shoulder. Sylvia went into the hall and shouted to Jennifer to please change the baby and bring her down.

"I'll tell you, I wish to hell I was going with you," Larry said.

"Why not? We used to have a helluva time."

"Yeah, I was up for it then."

Sylvia and Mary came back into the dining room with decaf coffee and little plates of something chocolate, a dense little cake that would keep Parker up all night if he was foolish enough to eat it. They sat down.

"Look, why don't you go?" Sylvia said. "If I need help around here, I can always call in the National Guard."

"Careful now," Mary said, ducking a little. When she did that, Parker noticed her blouse opened. "Jennifer's boyfriend— isn't he in the Guard?"

"That one's adrift, right up here, let me tell you," Sylvia said, tapping her forehead. "She's in his place now, she moved in, like a trailer or some sort of *hideout* up on cinder blocks over in Rosewood or somewhere, and he won't let her drive. He doesn't want her going anywhere he can't see."

"I think she's only eighteen," Mary said. "She was at the university last year. She's really very sweet. She was in Parker's freshman class, wasn't she, honey? I don't think she did very well."

Parker did not remember. "There's so many," he said.

"No point in going to this conference if you're not armed to the teeth with a paper," Larry announced, pounding the table. "Isn't that right, Parker? And Parker *has* a paper. Tell everybody what your paper is on."

"It's not important," Parker said.

"Of course it's not important. But *po-lice* tell us what it's about. Unless it's a dark secret. Is it a dark, furry little secret?"

"Yes, why not tell us, honey?" Mary said. "I'm always so proud of Parker's work."

"It's on Conrad," Parker said, folding his arms. "'Conrad and the Sanity of Style.'"

"The thing is," Sylvia said, "this madman—Taylor's his

name—is violent, I know this for a fact. One night he came here to pick her up. Remember, Larry?"

"Shit," Larry said, and lifted a forkful of cake. It fell just as it neared his lips. "Shit and more shit."

"Well, thank you for keeping up your end of the conversation," Sylvia said. "Anyway, they argued right out there in the car for like an hour, and then I saw the car actually rocking—you know, *rocking*?—and I saw her climb over into the back seat."

Larry stabbed the fallen cake until he finally got hold of a small piece of it. He pointed it at Sylvia, and then, in turn, at Mary and Parker.

"Maybe they were humping," Larry said.

"I know she tried to have another boyfriend once. She's *nineteen*, by the way. And no angel, I'm sure of that. Anyway, Taylor found out and this poor guy like suddenly *disappeared*. Can you imagine? The guy just fell off the map."

"She's very good with the children," Mary said.

"She isn't, really. They're going to kill her if the boyfriend doesn't."

They were quiet for a moment, listening, and then they looked at each other. Larry drew a deep breath.

Mary sighed. "It's another world out there, it really is," she said.

"You busy yourself half the year getting up the goddamned little paper, then drag it to Chicago or wherever, and what for? So that some dyke post-colonialist, for chrissakes, will cut it down and terrorize you in front of thirty-five of your colleagues? No sir. Let's be perfectly frank, all right? All you're hoping for is just maybe your proud little wife, assuming she hasn't bothered to actually *read* the bloody thing, might come up with a blow job."

"Now you're really going overboard, Larry," Sylvia said, turning away.

"Man in the boat. Man in the goddamned boat. You see? I just rub Sylvia the wrong way. *Isn't that right?*"

As Sylvia gave him the look, Mary whirled around, a little too abruptly, to greet first Jennifer and then Emily, who hung bow-legged like a little monkey from Jennifer's short, pink skirt. Larry stared at the both of them as though he had never seen them before in his life. Then he turned to Mary.

"Now this one, your husband, his hands are clean. Not once in my mammary has he had to really defend himself against anything."

"But Larry, didn't I just overhear you say to Parker...," Mary said.

"Mary. Immaculate Mary. Listen. Your husband here. He's a goddamned rock. What's that island?"

"What is he talking about?"

Larry's eyes rolled around the dining room.

"I have to say, I really...love your house."

"This is *your* house, Larry," Mary said.

"It's a solid, steady house. Real sweet view of the water all around and around."

"We've done everything we can to make it a pleasant home," Mary said. "Where you and Sylvia are always welcome."

"No, listen. *Don't let anybody in.* Got it?"

"Sure," Parker said. "Just calm down."

Sylvia swiveled around to face Jennifer. Jennifer had let go of Emily, who was about to fall on her face in the living room.

"I do hope you've put wax in your ears," she said. "Like what's-his-name. Odysseus."

"But he didn't," Parker said, lifting himself with some effort from his chair. "He listened."

"The goddamned rock of Gibraltar," Larry said. "Hey, I love you, man."

"I love you, too," Parker said, and then it occurred to him how wrong Larry was, that, in any case, it was only his life that was a rock.

Mary smiled warmly at Jennifer and then watched Parker turn his back on the dinner table and wander off into the living room. He set Emily back on her feet, watched her stagger a step or two, and then, taking her firmly under her arms, lifted her up to his face like he might a newspaper.

"She loves you, man," Larry said, but he had already turned away.

Parker tossed Emily into the air. It was a little toss and the child went up and returned happily as Sylvia and Mary and Jennifer stood watching. He tossed her up again, higher, so that at the top both arms flapped like plump little wings. She was not so happy as before, and searched now around Parker's shoulder. Jennifer stepped up behind Parker, and she was smiling gleefully when Emily flew up again—now inches from the ceiling, her round, bird-eyed face frozen in terror—and she, Jennifer, wished she were up there too, her legs dangling, safe beyond the reach of gravity.

"*What are you trying to prove?*" Sylvia exclaimed.

"Honey?" Mary said.

Little Emily, screaming bloody murder, was caught, and then quickly Sylvia took her, turned her head away from Parker, and rocked her.

"You could have missed her," she said, a hiss escaping her lips.

She carried Emily back into the dining room and stood for a moment over Larry. Emily went silent, as if she were quietly suffocating, then suddenly she was screaming to wake the dead. Larry's gaze was fixed on something outside the window.

"No," Jennifer said. "He couldn't."

"Honey, you have your flight to get up for," Mary said. "Remember?"

"I'm afraid Jennifer's going to need a designated driver," Sylvia said.

It was Mary's idea that they swing by their house on the way out to Rosewood. She had a black wool coat she'd worn just twice in three years that she knew would be exactly right for Jennifer and she desperately wanted her to have it.

"It's perfect for traveling," she said.

When they arrived, Mary hurried inside with Jennifer in tow while Parker waited in the car with the windshield wipers ticktocking. He could guess what Mary was up to, her casual little chat about how much more appreciated college is when you've been out awhile and the importance of having clear direction in your life. Clearly he was taking the early flight to Chicago, but for some reason now, the wine perhaps, he couldn't actually picture himself going, or the conference room where he would deliver his paper, or what idea or issue or new ground his paper addressed. Everything, in fact, was just a blank when Jennifer emerged from the house in the black coat. Mary was right behind her. Jennifer ran around the car and got in next to Parker.

"Doesn't she look absolutely *new* in it?" Mary said, resting her arms on Parker's open window.

"Oh my God, thank you so, so much," Jennifer said.

"I'll do my bath thing. Okay, honey? Don't worry. I'll wait up."

"I'm all right," Parker said. "Better get out of this rain."

"Really. Just count on it."

She kissed Parker through the window.

"'Night, Jenny," she said.

"*I love your house*," Jennifer called after her.

Parker backed slowly out of the driveway and then he and Jennifer headed across town toward Rosewood.

It was a dark evening, without traffic. For a while, the blur of green lights stretched out before them like a carpet. Jennifer was quiet. She held tight to the lapels of her new coat as if she were bracing herself against a great wind. He could see that her eyes had teared up. Parker smiled to think what the coat must mean to her. He had no memory of it himself, of Mary wearing it or even purchasing it, and so it unsettled him a little, not unpleasantly, that this mystery, dark and woolly, had entered the house without his knowledge, and, in fact, became known to him only now as it departed.

"It smells so new," Jennifer said. "This coat."

She put her face down into it, brushed her eyes with it.

"I guess it is new, practically," Parker said.

"I love your wife," she said. "She's so generous and good."

"I can tell she's very fond of you, too."

"So beautiful. We had such a great talk once, about all kinds of things. All I could do was stare at her, how beautiful she is, what a beautiful face she has. I was still in school then. I liked your course. I really did. But I guess I did terrible on the final."

"Look, I'm sorry about that."

"It's not your fault. Things were getting pretty mixed up in my life. Taylor was in it. He's been my boyfriend. It was the wrong decision. I couldn't think right. I don't blame anyone but myself. I really don't."

"A nice girl like you…," Parker began, but Jennifer was shaking and sobbing now, so he stopped.

"Could you just pull over a minute? Please?"

"Sure."

There was no safe spot for another block, but right after the next red light, which was interminable, he turned into a closed service station and pulled in under the roof behind the line-up of pumps.

Jennifer had stopped crying.

"You okay?" Parker said.

"I would never do anything to hurt her," she said, turning to him. "I really, really want you to believe that."

"Of course I believe it. Why shouldn't I?"

She moved toward him suddenly and kissed him. It was a tear-wet kiss, near his mouth, and his hand had gone up in defense, so he touched the coat, too. It was softer than he had imagined.

He was about to say something clever when she kissed him again. Her whole body now moved up behind it. Her tongue flapped around in his mouth like a bird. Then after a long while she sat back and hid her face in her new coat.

"I'm so, so sorry," she said.

"Don't be," Parker said. "I mean, it's all right."

"Is it?"

Parker looked away from her a moment, then started the car, and pulled back into the street.

"I'm not going there, you know—where I'm living," she said.

"You're not going to Rosewood?"

"I'm going near Rosewood, to a friend's. I've been taking my stuff over to her place since last weekend. I have to leave something. You know, just a couple of things hanging around. Taylor'd know if I took it all."

"But isn't he expecting you back tonight?"

"Sure he is. But I'm moving on, is what I'm doing. Be sure to tell your wife that, okay?"

"I'll tell her."

"I know she'll be happy about it."

"Where do we go now?"

"Just go straight out to the end of this. It's not far."

Parker found himself driving carefully now in the heavier rain, with both hands on the steering wheel. Again, he found the slow rhythm of the traffic lights and for nearly a mile moved miraculously from green to green. Jennifer had turned her face to the wet window, but now she sat up straight, carefully unbuttoned her black coat, and opened it wide away from her skirt. Then she lifted up, slid the skirt back to her hips, and, in a smooth, reverse motion, pulled her dark panties out over her knees. She wiggled them until they dropped.

"Now where?" Parker said. He turned up the windshield wipers.

"Go left," she said. "Then I'll tell you when."

Her friend's place was a basement apartment in a one-story, shingled house. It squatted there in the pitch dark.

Jennifer turned to him, but he couldn't see her face clearly.

"Better turn out the headlights a minute."

"It doesn't look like your friend is home," he said.

"She'll be back. She's already gone every place she's going. Now, will you just do this one thing?"

"What is it?"

She reached out to him, turned him toward her, and pulled his hand down between her thighs. Parker still could not see her, but he could feel her now, and so he stared intently into the dark where she was supposed to be. He could hear her deep breathing.

"Just do it up and down slowly like this," she said. "I know it's only going to take a minute."

In a minute her breathing went shallow, and she moved quickly toward him and kissed him with such urgency and force, the car rocked. He could feel her tears against his face again.

"Now I can't ever go back," she whispered.

She sat back and jerked her skirt down a little.

"Anyway," Parker said, "I mean, what the hell. Why should you?"

"Now just give me one more minute, will you? Please? I'll be right back."

She got out and, the coat pulled up onto her head, ran around the side of the house. Once she was inside, a light low against the driveway went on.

Parker knew he could leave if he wanted and his worst crime would be letting someone else help her on her way to a new life. In any case, what exactly did she have in mind? She was moving on, but where? To what? He could not imagine it any more than he could remember her failure in class. And yet, he wanted to save her somehow. He wanted her to have more than a new coat. He would talk to her, if that's what she wanted. He would give her whatever she needed. He could give her his ticket to Chicago. That would take her far away. She would be out of reach of all the bad decisions she had made in her life. She was still young enough to begin again. If necessary, he would take her wherever she was going. He would not let her fall.

Parker was still smelling her on his fingers when Jennifer appeared like a large bird-shadow with two leaden wings dragging on the driveway. He got out and opened the back door for her.

"I have these two bags full," she said. "It's really all I need."

"And where are we going?"

"To the bus station. There's an eleven fifty-five I've got to be on."

She pushed the two bags into the back seat, got in beside Parker, and soon they were heading back downtown.

"Know something funny?" she said. "I've never been on a bus."

"Really?"

"I mean on a real Greyhound bus going someplace far. Have you?"

"No."

"I suppose a certain kind of person rides one."

"I don't know."

"I just hope there's no creepy types on it that might touch me if I'm sleeping."

"Most people are nice. Just imagine everyone sitting around you will be like Mary."

"Now that's a pretty great thought. Thanks."

"You're welcome."

"Maybe I'll imagine you're there too."

At the bus station, Parker pulled up behind three taxis.

He carried the two suitcases up to the entrance door, where Jennifer caught up with him and stopped him. She took the suitcases from him.

When she turned to him, he saw she was sobbing again, the tears flowing wildly down her face. He had never known anyone to cry up a storm like that, and for a moment his astonishment gave way to envy.

"I'm sorry," she said.

"Why?"

"For what I did. I've never done anything right my whole life. That's a fact."

"It's not," Parker said.

He reached out to touch her face. She gulped her tears, then laughed.

"Even those children hated me."

"It's all right. They're only little terrors," Parker said.

She smiled, and turning on this, without another word, lugged her two suitcases through the wide door and into the station.

Back home, as he washed up in the downstairs bathroom, Parker looked hard at himself in the oval mirror. His face seemed unanchored from the rest of his body. Then he heard Mary say something from the bedroom. He dried his hands thoroughly and went up.

"Was Taylor waiting?" she said.

She was sitting cross-legged on the bed in a blue nightie. The way she was sitting, her white knees flared out and up like a young girl's, the wedge of white panties, and perhaps the nightie itself, which seemed new, reminded him of when they were first married.

"I guess he was," Parker said. "I don't know."

"Did you walk her to her door?"

"No."

"Maybe you should have," she said. "It's just that I worry about her. She should be doing something different with her life."

"I'm sure that's occurred to her," Parker said. "Tommy home?"

"He's at Bernie's for the night. I don't know what their plans are."

Her thoughts seemed to turn in that direction as Parker undressed.

"Bernie's a good kid," he said.

"Carrie's home."

"Good."

"She's so quiet lately. I can hardly get a word out of her. I ask her something, something inconsequential, really, and she acts like I've just invaded her privacy and turns away. What could be going on with her?"

Parker went into the bathroom.

"Honey, are you showering again?"

"Look, she's sixteen," he said. "That's all."

"With so many secrets?"

"There's nothing to worry about. All right? Everybody's safe."

"Who said we weren't?"

Parker closed the door and stepped into the hot shower. The shower smelled of Mary's soap. It was a clean, familiar, lilac scent which, in bed, rose off her soft skin and hovered over the two of them like ether until their books snapped shut and the lights went out. He was thinking this, standing trance-like under the flood of water, when suddenly he remembered that Jennifer's panties were still on the floor of the car. They had dropped effortlessly—down her calves—out of view.

He turned off the shower, stepped out, and dried himself quickly before the steamed-up mirror. Then he slowed. That the panties were indefensible went without saying. Jennifer had marked the car with them. But in the morning, early, before sunrise, before suspicion, they would be gone, gone anywhere, out the window, and he would go on with the rest of his life.

"If you really want to know," Mary said.

Parker had stepped into his pajamas and was struggling to tie the strings.

"What's that?"

"Here. You're tired. Let me do that."

She scooted to the edge of the bed and gently wrestled the strings from his fingers. Then she reached inside his pajamas and held him.

"Your two bags full," she said. "This is what they need, if they only knew."

"Who's that?"

"Poor Larry. Sylvia. Both of them."

"I think they've already tried it."

"I know I'm right."

Parker let the pajamas drop to the floor and climbed onto the bed. Mary kissed him quickly, playfully pushed him over onto his back, then straddled him and kissed him again. When she sat up the straps of her nightie were down around her white elbows.

"I like this," he said about the nightie.

She ran the fingers of both hands through her hair and

then reached over and switched off the bedside light.

"Honey, you always do, every time," she said. "But I just can't help thinking."

Parker tugged a little at the sides of her panties.

"Let's get these off," Parker said.

"If Sylvia only knew," she said, lifting up her leg. Parker felt her push the panties down with her thumbs and then stretch one side out along her thigh to her knee.

"Wait a minute," he said.

"If she could only just cast everything else aside. Everything. If only she could cast out all her little resentments, just cast them right out the window."

"Hold it."

"Darn these things," she said.

"This is not going to work."

"If she could only banish her foolish, foolish worries, and just look at him, in the light of day, look into his eyes and truly know him for the first time."

Parker clenched his teeth and ripped the panties from her leg.

"Honey, *my God.*"

"I'm sorry."

"*What's that noise?*"

Parker sat up quickly. Mary swung over onto her pillow. Someone was pounding on the kitchen door.

"Honey, maybe it's Tommy. Maybe it's the *police*."

Parker pulled on his pajamas and went to the head of the stairs. In a moment, Mary was in her robe beside him. The pounding was harder now and they could hear a male voice. They went down.

The young man outside stood close to the kitchen door,

his large blue eyes searching around inside. Parker and Mary stared at him through the small panes of glass. He was tall and wiry, his wet blond hair slicked back and tied tight in a pony-tail. He was not at all what Parker had imagined.

"What does he want?" Mary said. "*What do you want?*"

"He's looking for Jennifer," Parker said.

"Taylor?"

Hearing his name, Taylor rocked back from the door as if from a precipice. For just a second, Parker thought he looked boyish, vulnerable. Then he rocked forward again and pressed his face against the glass.

"They said you took her," he said. "Have you got her?"

"My husband drove her home," Mary said.

"No, ma'am. He didn't do that."

"Honey, you said you drove her home."

"I took her where she wanted to go."

"But where was that?" Mary asked.

"Oh man, oh man, I'm going to kill somebody if I don't find her quick."

"No you're not, Taylor," Mary said firmly, as though to a child.

"Listen," Parker said. "You better move on."

"Move on *to what?*" Taylor said, his voice cracking. He shook the door violently. "That's what you say. With this here house. *With this wife.*"

And with that, he drove his fist through the glass. Mary jumped. "Stop it!" she said. "Just stop it!" But when Taylor's bloody hand reached around inside for the doorknob, Parker suddenly took hold of it, as though he wanted to shake it, and pulled back with all his weight.

Taylor's face, red and astonished, broke through the window panes, splintering the frame and sending glass out across the kitchen floor.

"Oh my God, let go of him," Mary said. "You've hurt him."

"*You come in if you have to,*" Parker said. And he yanked hard again so that Taylor's whole body jackknifed over the window sill.

When Parker finally let go, Taylor groaned, straightened, and fell back outside onto the ground. His face was starting to bleed. Parker and Mary looked down at him through the shattered door.

"You were only defending yourself," she said. "Defending *us.*"

Taylor crawled off a few feet, managed to stand up, and backing away, disappeared around the side of the house.

Mary stared after him. "Sylvia tried to warn us," she said.

Parker was already on his way upstairs. Carrie stood in her bedroom doorway and, still half-asleep, held her hand up as if to wave.

"Dad?"

"It's all right," he said. "Go back to sleep."

He dressed quickly and went back down.

"Parker, there's blood on your hand. Where are you going?"

"Call the police if you want."

"But honey, what's there to be afraid of?"

Parker headed for the bus station. It was already midnight, and so he hoped Jennifer's bus had already come and gone and that she was safely on her way. He reached around on the floor, found the lace-bordered panties she had left there, and put them safely into his jacket pocket.

A ridiculous and frightening possibility suddenly occurred to him—that she was still pantyless, stark naked under her short skirt, and had sat in the public bus station for more than a hour like that and was now riding the bus with God-knows-what sitting right there beside her.

Only one taxi now sat outside the station, its driver dead asleep behind the wheel.

Parker stepped out into the rain and hurried inside. He was surprised to see, at this late hour, so many people waiting. In fact, there were twenty or more sitting in the rows of blue plastic chairs and standing around the coffee machine in the corner. Jennifer was not there. He walked over to talk with the woman at the ticket window.

"I'm wondering if there was an eleven-fifty bus?" he said.

"It's gone," she said without looking up.

"Right on time."

"Yep. Just about."

"You don't remember if there was a young woman on it, do you? She might have been wearing a black wool coat."

The woman looked up.

"What's the matter with your hand, mister? It's bleeding on my counter."

Parker pulled his hand back, searched around in his pockets, found the panties, and wrapped them around his open palm.

"Where exactly was that bus going?"

"That bus? That bus was going as far west as a body can go without drowning."

He nodded and walked over to the window. The rain was now whipping against it. Yes, and a hundred points between, he thought to himself. She could jump off at any one of them, her skirt lifting in the warm breeze. He stood there, staring vaguely in the direction of his car. Christ, he had come all the way out here again. He was a fool. They would be right about that. He could not defend himself. He held his wrapped fist up to his mouth. His face was burning. Now he could not see anything outside the window. Even his car seemed to have raced away into the dark.

"Hell, you look like an honest guy," a man behind him said.

Parker turned and came eye to eye with a long-faced man wearing a Mariners cap.

"And that's saying something in this frigging place," the man added.

"You also missed the eleven-fifty?"

"I've got to sit through the whole night before there's another."

"You didn't happen to see a young woman in a dark wool coat?"

The man stared at Parker's wrapped hand.

"Jesus, I wish to hell I had," he said. "Listen, this here's my bag. This is what I'm washed up on, okay? It's just about the whole thing."

He rested his foot on a large, army-green duffel bag that sat on the floor between them. The two of them stood there, heads bowed, looking down at it.

"If you would just watch over it for a minute," he said. "Make sure nobody steals it? You know the type. Just for ten minutes or so while I'm doing some business right over there."

He pointed across the room to the door that said "Men" on it.

Parker waited alone with the duffel bag until he felt something, like an old anchor, finally snap loose and sink within him. He reached down and lifted the bag. Though a whole life was in it, the man said, it was much lighter than he had imagined. How could that be? He looked around, as if he were daring the room. Nobody moved. The bag firmly in hand, he backed out of the station door into the rain and carried it quickly to his car.

Miles out of town, heading west, Parker still could not say where he was going. But he knew there would be much to explain if he did not make it. He smiled to imagine himself a kind of gangster. He had just killed somebody. The corpse was rolled up in his trunk. And he was heading out into the night to find some place to put it.

ALL CLEAR

We were watching a ball-game, the Red Sox killing the Mariners, when suddenly Rhonda showed up. "Anybody starving?" she said. She was dressed for a hot summer evening. Jimmy sat up surprised and—he was almost twelve—looked her over. He put a huge handful of yellow corn curls into his mouth and turned back to the TV.

Rhonda dipped her moony glasses and gave me the eye, like this wasn't her fault, and leaned against the front door. Her leather overnight case dangled from her finger like Grace Kelly's in *Rear Window*. She had seen the movie about a hundred times—including once already with me—and that was the part she loved best: James Stewart help-less in a chair with a broken leg in a big white cast like an elephant tusk, and Grace Kelly sweeping in unexpected with everything she needed in a little dark thing the size of a jewelry box. Not to worry, she said. She was completely in charge. Only Rhonda was not exactly Grace Kelly. What she had were great breasts, better than anything I'd ever seen in magazines. She'd got them when she was fifteen, and now she was thirty-seven and she still had them. They were something she'd always have. And she loved me, she said and said, but I could take all the time in the world I needed, and she would just drop over weekends and Tuesday nights and cook something nutritious for a change and give me something real hard to think about.

"It's still Tuesday, right?"

"This is my kid Jimmy," I said. "Come on, Jimmy. Say hello to Rhonda."

Jimmy said "hi" without moving anything, even his lips.

"It's a great pleasure to finally meet you," Rhonda said. "Your dad, he's always going on and on about you, you know? So now you're suddenly here, finally."

"I'm probably leaving soon," he told the TV.

"Thing is, his mother called," I said. "It's a real emergency. She needed to drop him off for a few hours."

"Look, are you boys hungry in this heat? I could fix something. Is there something I can fix?"

"We can always eat, right?"

"I'm sure your mom's just fine," Rhonda said.

In fact, Margaret had sounded desperate. I was thinking it was about her sister. She had had a lump removed a month or two back. Maybe now she was in her death throes. Anyway, Margaret needed to drop the kid off immediately. She needed me to keep him overnight, just this once. She really sounded desperate, like only she could. She settled for eleven o'clock. I don't know. I never kept him overnight. It was too strange. This place, when the lights went out, I didn't want to be seen sleeping here by anybody I knew.

It was after eight before Rhonda finally got something together and brought it in on trays, first Jimmy's, then mine, with napkins and tall glasses of ginger ale, and set them on the low table between the couch and TV. The game had just ended pathetically—a shut out, eight-zip. Jimmy, who had been staring at the screen for an hour, down to the last whiff, like he was waiting for a goddamn miracle, suddenly brightened and sat up and announced he wanted to go home immediately.

"For chrissakes," I said.

"Is there something else the boy would like?" Rhonda asked.

"We can eat this, okay? This is good. What is this?"

"You don't like it either?"

"I haven't tried it. We just want to know. Right, Jimmy?"

"I'm going home," he said again. He stood up.

"Your mother's having an emergency," Rhonda said.

"It's no big deal," he said, stepping away from her. "She just thought Dad was free, is all."

"Look, I *am* free."

"Why would she think that?" Rhonda said. She sat down.

Jimmy leaned against the front door. He smiled at me all gums and little teeth, like mine, like he was perfectly grown up and wanted to tell me something.

"I can stay by myself," he said. "Like when Mom has to work late, I just lock myself up. When she gets home, she gives a signal."

"I don't know," I said.

Rhonda slipped her sandals off and put her feet up.

"You gentlemen do whatever you like," she said.

Driving home, I asked Jimmy if he wanted to take the wheel of my new car. It was still light enough and I figured we could go up to the Garfield High School parking lot where he could squeeze in in front of me and go around a few times. I told him maybe the car would be his some day if he played his cards right. But he only grumbled something under his breath, and when I asked him straight out what was it, he said he was too big now to squeeze in, and anyway, his mother was teaching him.

"She's teaching you? I taught *her*, for chrissakes. When we were kids, I taught her lots of things."

After a while, Jimmy said, "Did she sit on your lap?"

I laughed. "That's funny to think about," I said. It really was.

We pulled into the alley and cruised slowly behind the McCormick's house, and then the Smith's, Shakley's, and Appleford's. Finally I eased off into the narrow spot beside our fence. Jimmy jumped out even before I cut the engine and pushed the door shut gently. We went in through the gate and out across the unmowed lawn to the back door. Right away he searched under the dark mat for the key.

"Is it there?"

"Sometimes she puts it in different places," he said.

"Yeah, I know what you mean."

While he tried the three empty planters, I felt around in the dirt below the railing, and then up above the door, but no luck.

"I'll try out front," he said. "Maybe there's a window open."

"Better not be," I said after he had already disappeared around the house. That would be like her.

I went the other way, under the magnolia, and around to the north side of the house. Sure enough, the bedroom window was cracked open. A thief could climb right into the house and help himself to anything he wanted. There was a light on, too, dimly. I put my face close to the corner of the glass and looked inside.

Margaret was stretched out on the bed, naked. I could see clearly the bony angles of her hip, and the silhouette of her thick hair. A man was with her. He was close up against her, his face moving behind hers. It was nobody I knew. I had to watch for a minute. It was strange, looking into my own house like that, like it was a picture, but not in a magazine. He probably hadn't done anything yet. He was only kissing her shoulder and pulling her hair back away from her ear. He was combing it with his fingers.

When Jimmy suddenly came up behind me, I almost jumped through the glass.

I pulled him away with me around the corner of the house, under the tree, and out across the back lawn to the car.

"Was anybody there?" he asked.

"That was real smart," I said, and yanked him tight against my face. He stared hard at me like there was nothing I could do to hurt him. "Real goddamned wise."

I opened the car door and shoved him inside. Then I went around and got in and started the engine, gunning it, and hit the shift. We lurched back and struck something. Something clinked on the pavement.

"Fuck you fuck you fuck you," I said.

I found the gear and we jumped out of the alley and back onto Second Street. I spent the next mile and a half chasing green lights.

"We going back to the other place?" Jimmy asked. I had forgotten he was there. He was looking away from me, out the window.

"We're not going anywhere," I said. It was a relief to say it. I tried to picture a road we could speed down with the windows wide open.

After a couple of miles I pulled into a car wash. All the stalls were busy, which is pretty strange when you think about it. I got out to look at the back light and figure the damage. Jimmy wandered over to the Coke machine and pulled on the coin return a couple hundred times. When I checked my watch, it wasn't even nine o'clock.

We drove out to Albert's Diner. I figured we were both hungry. The place was a fake railway car and we had it all to ourselves.

Right away Janice said to Jimmy: "Listen, are you with him? This guy? You better be careful."

"Meet Jimmy," I said. "He's real hungry. And smart."

Jimmy hardened and looked up at her. Janice was thirty-three, a little overripe, and was more or less married to this guy who owned the diner.

"We just had an accident," he said.

"Oh my my. What happened?"

"I broke a tail light, is all."

"Is all? Such a nice new car? That's a man for you. He can go bang bang bang something and not think anything about it."

"Who says I'm not thinking about it?" I said.

"Excuse me—what did he say?" she asked Jimmy, looking his face over carefully. "Is your dad talking again? Doesn't he have such a sweet way of talking when he wants to? He can talk up a real storm before he shuts up for two whole months."

"All right, all right," I said. "Can we have a couple of your cheeseburgers?"

"Now this is a heckava sweet looking boy. Who would have guessed. Such a sweet face. And you're real smart, too. Right? Smarter than this guy."

"I'm fourteen," Jimmy said.

Janice took her own face in her hands. "If I had a fourteen-year-old kid, I'd want him to look exactly like me, his mother, so that it was just like looking in the mirror. And on a real hot night like this, I'd just drop everything and we'd go skinny-dipping in the lake and forget everybody. You hear what I'm saying?"

"The kid's twelve," I said.

Albert stepped out of the kitchen. He was taking off his white apron. When it was off, he wiped his forehead with it and the back of his neck.

"The grill's closed," he said without looking at me.

"Are you kidding?" I said. "We just ordered a couple of burgers."

"Yeah, well, maybe tonight I'm just a little anxious to get home, if you know what I mean."

"But we're starving to death, right, Jimmy? Are you in business here or what? Is this a going concern or what?"

"Just look at the clock," Albert said, gesturing to the Coca Cola one over the coffee machine. "What's that tell you?"

It was nine-forty.

"There's time, all right," I said. "There's plenty of time left to cook up a couple of goddamned burgers."

"I'm desperate to get out of here," Janice said with her back to Albert. She pulled her blouse away from her skin.

Albert went back into the kitchen.

"Nobody's going anywhere," I said after him. "We don't care what time it is."

"What I'm thinking," Janice said, learning toward both of us, her blouse sticking again, "is maybe we could find a couple of beers out at your place."

"Now?"

"That's what I'm trying to tell you. This is an emergency. It's got to be right now or something really terrible is going to happen, I know it."

Albert stepped into the kitchen doorway. His thin blond hair was freshly slicked back.

I stood up. "Nobody's leaving here," I said. "We'll help ourselves if we have to."

"I'll fix the burgers," Janice said.

"Tonight we'll just call this Jimmy's Diner. What do you think, son? We'll just make this our own place where we can eat any time we goddamn want."

"Look, it's no trouble," Janice said, and she slipped past Albert into the kitchen. Albert stood there in a face-off but it was Jimmy he was looking at, and then he turned back into the kitchen.

I took a minute to sit down, but when I did, Jimmy swung off his seat and walked out of the diner.

"Wait a minute. We're just settling in here."

The screen door whined and then banged shut.

Janice came out of the kitchen.

"Hey, the burgers are coming right up. Where's everybody going?"

We drove over to Echo Lake.

A narrow park with a green bench and a lamp ran a hundred feet along the beach. A fat man and a willowy woman who were walking their terrier came into the light and went out again. Only the first sixty or seventy feet of water was visible, then it got dark quickly, and you had to know the lake went out another six hundred feet into it. A stand of trees was on the other side, and just short of it an old float with a ladder you could swim out to if you were strong enough. When we were kids, there was a rowboat left on the beach. In those days, before anybody knew anything about real life, a guy and the girl he was really crazy about would row out late at night with a flashlight.

Jimmy had a great arm and threw stones out into the lake so far you couldn't hear them hit. After about a thousand stones, he turned around and asked me was it time yet, was it all clear?

"Will you just quit it about the time?" I said. What I meant was, there just wasn't any point in thinking about it. "Look," I said.

"There's nothing to look at," he said. He scooped up a few stones.

"The hell there isn't," I said. "Now listen. You listen to me."

But he was already slinging the stones low over the water.

I took my shoes off and my shirt, and slipped out of my pants down to my boxers. I was in pretty good shape, actually. I came up quickly behind Jimmy and ran past him and plunged into the water. The cold down deep was a welcomed shock. It felt good to strain my whole body against something. I swam under as long as I could and came up in the dark.

"Hey, come on!" I said.

Jimmy just stared out into the lake. It felt strange, being way out there where he was looking. Then he wandered over to the bench, undressed, and, holding his arms, he came back and waded a few feet into the water. In his white jockeys, he looked younger, his body narrow in the shoulders and long-legged and fragile like his mother's.

The willowy woman reappeared, by herself now, and hesitated a moment on the beach in the light. When Jimmy saw her, he took a couple of quick steps deeper into the water and dove in.

I watched him come up, brush back his short hair, and go under again. When after a while he had not come up, I swam in a few feet to wait for him. The woman on the beach was walking back and forth and looking out at us. Then suddenly behind me the water broke and I whipped around and saw Jimmy, his white skin breaking in and out of the darkness. I could hear his fast breathing. I swam out to him and he said something to me.

"Yeah, she's gone," I told him.

He whipped some water at her.

We swam out. Jimmy pulled ahead of me and went under a couple of times and then came up where I wasn't looking. My head kept jerking around like a crazy hen. The kid was a swimmer.

But after a hundred feet we stopped and treaded water. I could not quite see his face, but I could hear him and knew he was finally out of breath. I swam over close to him and after a minute he rested his arm on my shoulder. He hung onto me a long time without saying anything or hardly breathing.

When I stopped hearing him and there was only the darkness, I heard something else far out into the lake. I knew right away what it was. It came to me so unmistakably, I felt as if I had risen from the water and was standing on it. It was the rowboat banging, banging, banging against the float.

"Somebody's out there," I said.

"What is it?"

"Out there on the float. They rowed all the way out."

"Who did?"

"They're still doing it," I said. It unsettled me how amazed I sounded. "It's still being done."

"But what do they want?"

"Everything," I said. "Don't worry, it's all right."

But he had already pushed off and was swimming away from me with clean, strong strokes. On the beach, he dressed quickly over his wet jockeys and headed for the car. He would be starving to death by the time I got him home. Now she would say I never fed him.

When he had disappeared into the parking lot, I turned on my back and floated in the dead quiet until finally I remembered Rhonda. She came slowly into view. I couldn't imagine she was desperate enough to have waited. Fact is, I had not thought about her all evening. Not once. If I stroked her hair, if I combed it with my fingers, if I moved my lips against her ear, how would she ever know?

I stayed out there awhile, then swam in.

LOVE SPOTS

Norman waited out by the car in the half-dark and at first May did not see him. She hesitated at the doorstep between the brass coach lamps. A warm, expensive light bathed both her angry face and the gold party dress. She looked ravishing in it.

When she had finally spotted him, she came quickly down the walk, her arms held out for balance. In the ovals of light along the edge of the brick he could see clearly the clicking heels and the long rise of her calves. She stopped only once to glance back at the house, her father's white colonial looming up behind her.

"Hey, do you have any idea what time is it?"

"It's the dress I've got an idea about."

"Really?" she said. She searched his face. "You like it?"

"I'd like to get under it," he said.

May glanced back at the house. "But honey, it's only eleven o'clock. Mary Simon just *arrived*. For godsakes, people are just *arriving*."

"We arrived at eight."

"I've been looking forward to this for a month, and now

45

what are we doing? We're stomping out."

"Who's stomping? We're out, that's all."

"Charlotte, right there at the door, she's saying to me,
Hey, why are you stomping out?"

"Is there a goddamned law against leaving?"

"There should be because they're very nice people."

"Your father's people. They like to look way down on
everything, including that dress."

"Oh, they're not. And anyway, this thing hasn't even *relaxed* yet."

"Believe me, it's relaxed," he said, and opened the door.
"Now will you get in?"

"No."

"Just get in, all right?"

It was a new car, even smaller than the last, and she looked
awkward getting into it. The gold dress climbed quickly all
the way up her thigh. Norman shut the door securely, then
ran around the front of the car, his hand sweeping the black
hood, and got in.

"We'll be home before Rose," May said, her arms folded.

"Who's talking about going home?"

Her head fell back against the headrest and she closed
her eyes as Norman eased the car out into the street. He was
excited. He felt released. He drove straight out across the city.
Soon he was racing down Elliott Avenue along the Sound.

"Keep an eye out for the cops," he told her.

May lowered her electric window and leaned into the
fresh air.

"Anyway, where the heck are we going?"

"Up to Discovery Point. Remember?"

"Now? Tonight?"

"Hey, you might even enjoy it."

May sat up. "We can't get there from here," she said. "You have to go back to Wayne Road and wind up along the ridge."

"Christ."

"It's going to rain," she said. "I saw a flash just a minute ago. If it rains, we just as well head back to the party."

"We can make our own party."

"Oh Norman, do we have to?" she said, her voice suddenly plaintive. "We already have a perfectly nice one."

The narrow road above the Sound climbed the ridge. It irritated him that he had forgotten it because once he was up there he knew it like yesterday and remembered perfectly the first time May went with him. They had driven without a word nearly a mile along the dark border of evergreens.

The road suddenly widened into the clearing.

"This is it," he said, and he hesitated at the edge of it. It was lighted now, a blaze of light from tall, aluminum poles bright as swords, and it was paved, too. Cars were parked in numbered places up against the steel railing. He pulled in where he could and cut the engine and headlights.

"This is somebody's assigned spot," May said. "From those condos."

Norman looked over his shoulder. Back where the abandoned Navy barracks had been, now there were stern rows of boxes, each vaguely aglow, stacked three high. He frowned and turned back to the clean windshield.

"We were on the top of the world up here," he said.

"You were on top of me, was the idea."

In moonlight, you could see far out across the Sound, across the immense dark of the water, to the islands. You could pick whichever you wanted and re-name it whatever you felt like. Then you had to make love. It had been impossible to sit there long without wanting to. Now the wall of lamplight cut them off.

"It's safer now," May said.

"Maybe out there," he said, and turned to her. There was a veil of light over her face. "In here it's real dangerous."

He leaned over and kissed her hotly under the ear.

"Norman, there's two of you, I swear to God," she said. She turned her mouth to his and let him kiss her the way he wanted to, never mind the lipstick, and he tasted like the scotch.

"Okay, now what are you doing?" she said, coming up for air.

"How do we get you out of this?"

"Honey, couldn't we just kiss? Do you think we should?"

"Why shouldn't we?"

"Well, you can just reach in if you really have to. You have a license, you know. If your hand's not icy cold."

"What the hell's the trick with this?"

There's no trick. Just don't *rip* anything, okay?"

"I'm not ripping."

"Honey, it's a simple hook, all right?"

"Okay, okay," he said. He sat up. "I'm slipping."

"You're married, Norman."

"You want to listen to the radio?"

"We could go back to the party." She ran her hand up along his thigh. "Just for a little while. You're fine. Look, don't I know? This isn't such a good place anymore"

Norman stared at where he remembered the Sound was. He wished they could go driving into it to know it was there. He gripped the brake handle beside him, held it for a moment, and pulled up and pushed the button to release it.

"I wonder," he said, "if you can buy a car with a bench seat anymore. Like that old Bel Air with the torsion-air suspension. We stretched right out on it. You had one foot on the seat, the other on the ashtray. Jesus, remember the ashtray? It got so bent up we couldn't close it. And the whole car rocking and rocking. Remember?"

"I remember the cop with the flashlight tapping on the window."

"They still have them on the pickups. You can tell, the way the girls sit in the middle of the window."

"Sure, we could get a pickup," May said.

Norman backed the car out and swung around to face the road. He threw it into first and, with a little squeal of the tires, pulled out.

He drove back into the city. Soon they were up on Capitol Hill cruising slowly along Fifteenth Street toward Volunteer Park. They had not been up here at night in years. May glanced over Norman's shoulder at the young men who sat in cars parked with their doors open along the wide street. Other men on the lookout stood near the park gate, gesturing and smoking cigarettes.

Norman slowed so they could look up the lamplit drive into the park.

"Remember the place up in front of the old museum?"

"Afterwards, I sat up on the camel," May said.

"Between the humps."

Another block beyond the park they passed the high steel fence of the cemetery. Norman glanced in the rearview mirror and whipped left onto a dirt road. May held his arm. The fence stretched into the dark. At the end of it, he turned sharply right and ran into an iron gate.

"*Watch it*," May said.

Glass had broken. Norman threw the door open and stepped out to look at it. It was the right-turn fixture, shattered. He picked up a piece of it, turned it over and over as though he could do something about it, then tossed it aside. Then he slipped through the bowed bars of the gate. Straight ahead a narrow gravel path cut through the cemetery. The headlights lit up the pale gravestones in the beds of grass.

May lowered her window and stuck her head out.

"Norman? What's the damage?"

Norman waved to her to come out.

"I'm not going out there," she said, throwing open the door. She tiptoed on the gravel up to the gate.

"Come on," he said.

"I'm not ruining this dress," she said. She took hold of the bars. "Now where are you going? *Norman?*"

Norman had disappeared off the path of the headlights and out into the trees.

"We're going to get caught," she said. "Norman? *You're not leaving me here.*"

Suddenly Norman was in the light again and running toward the gate. He held his fingers to his lips.

"*Shhhhhh*," he said. He was out of breath.

"Where'd you go?" she whispered.

"Remember the Fitzgeralds?" he said. "Malcolm and Emily and David II?"

"Fitzsimmons," May said.

"And the Wallots. Weren't they glad to have us? Weren't we the goddamned life of the party?"

"It gives me the creeps," May said.

"You ran all around here, remember? With your dress up? Laughing and singing. Raising hell."

"I don't know what I was thinking."

"White cheeks in the moonlight."

"It's because you made me crazy, Norman. Now you're just making me mad."

"My party girl," he said, and he grabbed for her dress through the bars. She backed out of reach.

"I'd like to be—if we can please get out of here? Look, it's not even twelve yet."

Norman squeezed through and they got back into the car and closed the doors. When he leaned over to kiss her, she held him tight. His face was hot.

"I suppose we could have made Rose here," she said. She stroked his hair. "Now I'm thirsty. Aren't you just a little bit thirsty? Honey?"

May was right. It wasn't even midnight. He drove back on Fifteenth past the grand old houses May always admired and then slowly as Fifteenth became Boston Street.

"This could take all night," she said.

"Listen, didn't we do it once in somebody's big old garage? Drive right into it? In broad daylight? I remember the sun pouring through the roof boards. Didn't you jump out and close the big doors?"

"Yes, I think the sheriff was hot on our tail. You wanted to make love right there in the car."

"You can get away quick in a car."

"She climbed up to the loft."

"Who did?"

"Mona Wilde. Mona Wilde and Elmore Gatz in *Outlaw of Love*. We saw it four times."

At Boston and Tenth they waited at the green light and watched it turn red, then green again. Her arms folded, May looked out the window.

"What else were they in?" he asked.

"If we hurry back, we can have one last drink at Daddy's."

He drove out across University Bridge, down the hill and out along the canal road. Near Fremont, the traffic increased suddenly, backing up as far as the shipyard. He turned off and cut up into the neighborhood of old saltbox houses huddled under the bridge, high above. He slowed at the dark cul de sac beneath the bridge where it hit the hill. He looked up. He could hear the fast cars overhead singing on the grate.

"I've never once been to this place," May said.

"You have."

"Not here, not in my right mind," she said. "You have to be pretty drunk to come to a place like this. Look over there, near the piling."

Two men rolled in blankets and brown coats lounged against the concrete. A woman was with them. She turned her round face into the headlights and raised high a paper bag.

"I think she knows you," May said.

"Me? How could she?" Norman said. "But I can see those two switching off when they want to." He put his arm around May and pulled her close.

"Don't," she said.

"Why not?"

"Don't you see? She doesn't have a house. If she had a house, that's where she'd be, in her own bed."

"You were here a couple of times."

"If I was, it was because we didn't have a nice bed. I would have remembered this poor place."

"You remember the ceiling on the Bel Air? You were always sliding down to get a look at it. In that gauzy skirt you weren't wearing a stitch under? You couldn't get enough of it. You were mad for it. And you must have seen the bridge up there. You were looking right up. You must have seen it. You must have heard the singing on the grate."

"*Don't*, honey," she said. She straightened her dress. "And I never wore any gauze dress, I can promise you."

Norman slumped against the door. "What the hell," he said. "We can have that last drink at O'Connor's."

He had remembered O'Connor's when they first came into Fremont and hit the heavy traffic. O'Connor's was in a row of busy bars and restaurants here on the north side of the canal drawbridge. An anxious young crowd was gathered outside the bright doorway. As they cruised past, luckily a red Porche pulled out of a place and Norman deftly slipped into it. Things were looking up.

He kissed May quickly and put his hand way up her dress.

"Get out," she said. "Will you get out?"

He kissed her again and ran around the car to open the door.

"Honey, will you wait a minute?" May said. "Will you slow down?"

Her high heels clickedy-clicked down the sidewalk until she reached the crowd at O'Connor's. She could see that Norman was all hyped now, his head jerking around like a rooster with all the good-looking young women, not one of them over thirty.

"Norman, look at me, will you? The way I'm dressed? I'm supposed to be at Daddy's in a nice living room, standing by the piano."

"Baby, you look fabulous."

In fact, several couples in the crowd were looking right at her. May had the only gold dress. A couple of the women there could have worn one if they had wanted to.

"We'll never get in," May said, her arms folded. Norman wrapped his arms around her.

"Okay, Lady. This is a stick-up."

She bumped him away. "Now stand still," she said, "so we don't lose our place."

Every few minutes they moved up a little closer to the window. Inside, it was packed solid. Norman remembered the famous story about the corner booth and the couple who made wild love under their raincoats.

"Remember that photo booth?" he said. "That little black-and-white I showed your father? Our two faces grinning at the camera?"

"Now that *was* funny," she said. "You'd made a little what-do-you-call-it, a love spot on my neck. Think he saw it?"

"Baby, that wasn't the half of it. You were bouncing on my lap with your skirt up."

"My God, I couldn't have."

"We were still crazy then."

"Some of us wise up," May said.

The crowd moved abruptly. Norman and May caught up with it and finally reached the window. Norman cupped his hands around his eyes, like binoculars.

"It's different, all right," Norman said. "People actually seem to be breathing in there."

"I don't know how with all that smoke," May said.

Norman turned away.

"I'm thinking maybe we won't get in there after all," he said. "What the hell time is it anyway?"

"What?"

"Christ, it's past midnight."

"*Is that Rose?*"

It was Rose, all right. Norman took a breath and turned back to the window. Rose was standing only fifteen feet away, practically within arm's reach, in a tight circle of friends. She looked pretty grown up.

"Those men are at least thirty," May said.

"You think so?"

"Norman, she's *seventeen*. What kind of place *is* this?"

"Sometimes she looks older," he said, staring at her.

May rapped on the glass with her ring.

"Don't do that!" Norman said.

"*Rose!*"

"She can't hear you."

"Look at her. She can't *be* in there."

"Talk to her in the morning."

"We'll talk to her tonight," May said.

"Look, why should she spoil it?"

"Spoil it? Spoil what? *Rose!*"

Now May rapped hard with her knuckle. A large man just inside the window turned and looked at her as if she had just appeared from the fog. Norman yanked her out into the sidewalk.

"Come on, baby. We're out of here."

When he turned her toward the car, she stepped out of one of her high heels and, retrieving it, almost popped out of her dress.

"Who does she think she is?" she said, hopping three

steps. "Aren't there laws? Don't they know she's *illegal*?"

"Look, all they can do is throw you out," Norman said, calming her. "She's just trying to live. Now can we go someplace and forget about it?"

"We're going home," she said. She was already ten feet ahead of him.

"It's early. She won't be home for hours."

He caught up with her at the car.

"So there," she said. "You got a ticket. Now do you see what I mean?"

He unlocked the door and she slid in quickly, never mind the dress. It rode up to expose the narrow band of lace of her stockings. Coming back around, he yanked the ticket from under the windshield wiper, crushed it in his raised fist, and, after looking both ways, fired it across the street.

"I'll tell you one goddamned thing," he said, dropping his hand on her knee. "This is *our* night."

But May had turned her face to the window and he could hear her little noises, and he thought, Here we go.

"You're the most beautiful thing I know," he said without looking at her.

She turned to him and pulled him close to kiss him. He could feel her tears on his face. "Let's just go home now," she said.

"What's home, for chrissakes," he said.

"Honey, don't say that. Home is where we have our own nice bed. It's all ours. We can do whatever we want. I'll wear the pretty black for you, okay? With the lacy lace? And we can do anything you want. I know you want to. I can feel you do."

A horn blasted and they both jumped. Norman whipped around. It was two teenagers sitting high in a white four-wheel.

When he gave them the finger, they blasted again. He threw open the door and jumped out.

"Norman, *don't*."

The girl was driving. Her blond boyfriend sat very close to her so that Norman saw their two heads together in the closed window like in a photo.

"You can't park here," he told them. "It's *illegal*. You hear what I'm saying?"

When he rapped on the glass, the girl turned, cupped her ear, and shrugged. The round face beside her barked something at him.

"Look, who bought you this anyway? *Dad?*"

He took his time walking back to the car. It had started to rain. So that was it. Now it was raining.

"So did you scare them?" May said. "Did you scare them half to death?"

"Just stop talking. All you want to do is talk."

He pulled out into the street and, without looking, made a sharp U-turn. May righted herself and looked at her watch.

"It's too late for anything," she said.

"I know a spot."

"Norman, I swear to God."

"Just keep shut, will you? I'm taking you."

"How far is it?"

It was a place he had once heard of, down by the lake. When they reached the Arboretum he turned onto Lake Washington Boulevard and wound through the park. May was silent and stared up at the dark trees passing overhead.

"There's moonlight," he said as they slowed for the steep curves. It had already rained. Much more seemed gathered on the edge of the clouds. He cleared the film of water from the windshield. The north lake was very wide at first, and gray, but it narrowed as they neared the end of it. Just across, the slopes of Seward Park rose into the woods.

Finally he pulled into the strip of parking lot near the swings. There were no cops around. He drove through slowly and at the dead end of the lot eased up over the lip of the curb and continued across the lawn into a bowed opening in the trees. In a hundred feet they stopped in a clearing on the edge of the water.

He cut the lights. The moonlight cast a gossamer of white across the close water.

"Doors all locked?" she asked.

"The car's tight," he said, and he turned the ignition key. He lowered his electric window. "Can you hear the water? Seems like it took us the whole evening to get down to it."

"It's nice."

He reached over and put his arm around her and drew her as close to him as the divided seats would allow.

"I guess we could use that pickup," she said.

He kissed her quickly twice, and then long and sweet like old times, and he could feel her soften, her head thrown back, and her eyes, with some of the light in them, following his own like she was afraid to let go. He felt her reach down and slip off her high heels. He took one from her and tossed it into the back seat.

"Careful," she said.

"It's this dress that got us into this," he said.

"So you say."

"With its little hook."

She reached in and unhooked it for him and pulled the whole top down carefully, rolling it, and tucking in the edges.

"Let's not ruin anything," she said.

They kissed for a long time, like she liked. When finally he touched her knee and started up her thigh, she lifted, pulled the gold dress up, first as far as it wanted to go, then with a wiggle, up over her hips so that, for safety, it finally bunched up around her waist. Then she removed her stockings.

"So," she said, and kissed him.

He reached between her thighs to touch the white lace. "We'd better get these off too. Heck, you needn't have worn them."

"I would never, never... not," she said. Then she kissed him deep and hard so that their teeth clicked, and all the time easing the panties down with her finger. And suddenly Norman remembered it was Veronica Chapman, his sister's friend, who had worn the gauzy dress.

"Oh Norman, I don't think we fit anymore," she said as she quickly calculated the inches between door and steering wheel.

He pushed off his shoes, undid his belt.

"We'll have to climb back," he said.

"You think we should?"

He went back first, climbing between the seats, bumping the interior light. Then he scooted over and rubbed his head. May came after. It surprised and awed him that she was so utterly naked both up to the bunching of gold around her waist. So much wifely flesh and weight too, graceless and beautiful as she settled back against the door. Then she raised her knees and eased forward a little just as she remembered you had to. In the small car he loomed over her like a house.

It was when he bowed to kiss her belly that May saw the two men standing at the edge of the water.

"*Somebody's there*," she said. She sat up, swung her legs around, and yanked the dress up over her breasts.

"Just be still," Norman said.

The two men talked awhile, then came toward the car. They walked like they were stepping on shells. The younger one's head was sharply outlined, large and shaved close. The other wore a short jacket lashed with stainless zippers. Norman watched their approach with more curiosity than fear, as though they might be men he knew.

May touched the lock button.

"We're locked in," she said. She held her hands between her legs like a child. Norman grabbed the hem of the dress and pulled hard to bring it down over her hips.

"Honey, *don't*. You'll tear it."

When the two men reached the car, they peered inside, and then the older man lit a cigarette. The younger man, who was no more than seventeen, Rose's age, with small, curious eyes, first tried the door, then pressed his thin face against the glass and tapped his fingers.

"Hey, pussy, pussy," he said. "Looka here, Oscar. It's Dad here was gonna do it to Mom. Practically caught them right in the act. Can you beat it?"

He began rocking the car. Norman tried to get up, banged his head on the ceiling, and fell against May. She reached around and held tight to him. The car rocked and rocked until there were tears in her eyes.

Finally Norman broke loose and grabbed the front seat. "You guys get going, hear?" he said. He pulled himself forward.

The younger man laughed, and then as he walked casually around the front of the car, he ran something metal and sharp along the black hood.

"God*damn*," Norman said.

"Please just make them go away," May said.

But the younger man had already reached through the open window and grabbed hold of the steering wheel with his large fist. Norman lunged for the window button, pushed it, and the window rose and tightened against the man's arm.

"Oh!" he howled. "It hurts so good!"

He let go and reached around in the air with thick probing fingers. Past him, through the windshield, the lake suddenly vanished. Rain flooded the glass.

"Holy shit!" the younger man shouted. "We got to get in here where it's nice and cozy. *Open this fucking door, Romeo. We're drowning out here.*"

With his free hand he reached around the windshield and ripped off the wiper. Oscar smiled and shook his head. His short, gray hair was soaked flat against his skull.

"All right, goddammit," Norman exclaimed. "You've had your fun. I'm coming out."

"*No, you're not doing that,*" May said. "Just let them do what they want."

"Hey, Oscar. She says she's ready now. She's primed. Didn't I tell you?"

May looked up at Oscar who had put his arm on the roof of the car like he was embracing it and was looking in at her, studying her.

"Will you please help us?" May said.

"*Jesus, May,*" Norman said, more to the window than to her. "Let me deal with it."

"What's that?" Oscar said. "*May? Is that you?*"

"What?" she said.

"You know her?" said the younger man.

"It's just got to be," Oscar said, searching May's face. "Don't I know you? Help me now. Wasn't it nineteen hundred and seventy-two?"

"Say something," Norman said.

"He's just making…"

"Seventy-four? The Lucky Star, wasn't it? Don't I have that right? Don't I remember that correctly? Didn't we take a ride out to my place? Out on Cherry? Can you believe it, May, I'm still there. I never moved. But you could move. You were a real bouncer, is how I remember you. A real trampoline woman."

"You can tell she's the one who takes charge. Right, Oscar?"

"He's crazy. I don't even know where the Lucky…"

"Now listen, partner. You tell me. It's the two of us now. Isn't she a bouncing fool? May, weren't you the crazy one? Don't it bring back those olden days, the way it were? I don't think I've had a real bouncing up and down on since. No, not like that. When was it? Try to remember, will you?"

"May?"

May lunged across Norman at the window.

"*Shut up*," she said. "*You just shut up.*"

She had hit the wet glass so hard with both fists, Oscar actually jumped back. The other man, his hand still on the steering wheel, howled with laughter.

"Jesus, May," Norman said to himself.

"*Everybody shut up*," she said.

Reaching around on the floor she came up with one of her high heels. She lunged forward and struck hard with the spike at the thick fingers on the steering wheel. The fist jerked back to the glass. She struck again and again until she hit.

"Hey! Hey! *Bitch!*"

He pulled hard until he was out.

May climbed up into the driver's seat and started the engine. It roared. Oscar raised his arms into the rain and fell back. Finally she found reverse and swung the car back and around, then jammed it into first. The wheels spun. The two men jumped away, back into the downpour, as she raced blindly away from them through the opening in the trees. The car flew off the curb into the parking lot. Norman held tight to the headrest.

Then they were back out on the road along the lake. Now the rain made a fine sheet of gray on the driver's windshield.

Norman's whole body shook. He searched around for a seatbelt. When he looked up, he did not know where he was.

"How can you see a damned thing?" he said.

"It's all right," she said, her hands gripping the wheel.

He climbed through into the front seat. May looked strange, her white thighs, the tuft of dark hair beneath the gold belt. He searched around the floor until he found the lace panties.

"You need to get dressed," he said.

"It's okay."

"Can you see anything at all? Maybe I'd better drive."

"It's clear enough."

"I'd better."

"Okay," she said. "All right. I'll pull over the first good place."

THE MORNING ROOM

Cherry read it in the newspaper first, that Arlen Browne had been involved in a terrible accident. Arlen and his wife Rita lived right next door, over the laurel hedge, in what was, before her own time, the Adamson's house. They were nice people. No kids.

"Let me see that," Rich said.

"Oh, it's our Arlen Browne, all right. With an 'e'."

She held the rose-patterned coffee cup in both hands. The coffee was cold because down in the kitchen the very first thing he did was pour it, then pour his own and sip it and carry it out with him when he searched for the newspaper. On the way back, usually he paused in the doorway to glance at the weather report.

"Jesus, he hit a goddamned jogger. In sweats. They don't even have an I.D. on him."

"Someone will be looking for him."

"No I.D. Amazing. I mean when you think about all the madmen out there, miles from their houses, without a stitch of I.D. No wallets, dogtags. Nothing."

"I'm sure Arlen feels just sick about it."

"Says it occurred only a hundred feet from a crossing. That's suspicious."

"Well, there's a designated trail, isn't there? He must have veered off. Usually there are warning signs. Still, at night, in the dark. You know, I read someplace that's how *everything* began? This atom made just a little jog—you get it? like to the left?—and banged into another atom, and there was this terrific bang-banging chain reaction. Suddenly everything was *here*."

Rich looked hard at her. He wasn't really sure who the hell this woman was he married. It had all happened so quick. Bang, bang, you're married. Christ, when she said crazy things like that, he wasn't even sure who he was or where he was. He folded the newspaper carefully, like the paper boy, and sent it flying.

"There's no witnesses," he said. "Nobody knows a thing."

Balancing the half-full cup, one of a pair her sister had given them as a wedding gift, Cherry pulled aside the comforter and carefully sat up. The coffee had been cold, but the thought nice. Now it would be nice if he called Davey, to get back to that too, settle that. Just pick up the telephone. *Somebody* has to pick it up.

"Will you call Davey, then?"

"Let's mind our own business."

"He's just a freshman, thousands of miles away."

"He'll call when he needs money," he said, and she watched his eyes wander off into the wall.

When she had disappeared downstairs in her yellow robe, Rich got up slowly and dressed slowly, this day with its chance of showers in the afternoon already anticipated, a list of things at the office, churning in his head.

He glanced out the window. The Browne's house, over

the hedge, was set off by the flat lawn and the trim bushes in island-like clumps. Small pink and white flowers would spring up soon. The house itself was white, boxy, ugly. Only the new addition struck you. Arlen told Cherry there had been a garden there once upon a time, but the Adamsons had ripped it up and laid out the concrete patio, which was scarred like a gravestone with initials and handprints, and was already cracked. So the house, he said matter-of-factly, was really *wanting* an addition, which Rich thought was a ridiculous way of putting it. Now there was this new, glass room, like a goddamned light bulb, sticking right out in the morning sunlight to eat their breakfast in. Well, maybe the house was wanting to say, *Thanks! Oh, I wanted you so much!* Everything was pretty amazing, like the fool joggers without I.D.'s. Figure this. This poor bastard brings in an architect and a contractor, who cost an arm and a leg, and then carpenters and electricians at thirty bucks an hour, and just a week after it's finished, even before all the tools and ladders are taken away, he just happens to kill a perfect stranger, somebody in gray sweats and no I.D., not even a clue. All the wanting and planning and then *that* happens.

That night Cherry eased into bed with a full report from Karen Miller who lived across the street in the brick house. Karen and Rita sometimes talked.

"Karen says poor Arlen's got enough troubles. Now this."

"What troubles?"

"Rita troubles. You know how she is. The way she goes around."

"Excuse me, I don't."

"Remember I saw her walking around naked in her

kitchen one afternoon? Not even an apron?"

"You should try it sometime."

"Rita steps out, all right? So what I'm telling you now is what Karen said, that Arlen is taking this new thing, this horrible, horrible accident, *very* hard."

Rich was undressing. When he was down to his shorts he said, "So is somebody claiming now it was *his* fault?" and he went right into the bathroom. In a minute the deafening shower came on.

Cherry had news about the incident, but it was Davey she wanted him to talk about. The kid had refused to come to their little wedding, which she would not accept blame for. Though she had not actually seen him, in person, she felt as close to this boy as if he were rattling around inside her, just as he must be rattling inside his father. And she worried about him, too, like his real mother did. She had seen a photo of her with Davey, a baby in her arms. Her rope of black hair for him to touch. She looked just like a child herself, like a child holding a child. My God, who knows who really starts these things. Which party is guilty. Davey was only ten. And he chose his mother. What could be the terrible sin in that? He had to choose somebody. Now he was eighteen and in a nice college in New Hampshire and refused to come home to anyone for Thanksgiving and Christmas. Didn't that prove he felt something, that he was holding something back? What you do in a situation like this is simple enough. You *say* something. You *speak*.

"So listen," Rich said. "Have they got an I.D. on this guy or not?"

"She says they don't, not yet. But he was wearing a brand new wedding ring. There was nothing inscribed on it yet. It means they just got married. Like *us*. You know? *They* were brand new, like the ring, and now he's dead. Karen says it's just the thought of that that's killing poor Arlen."

He had come out of the bathroom in his white pajama bottoms and now he was buttoning the top up to the collar.

"I'm tired of hearing how poor he is," Rich said.

"Now the police are going around to houses near the crossing and down along the trail and showing people a sketch of the man."

"They have a sketch? Of a *corpse?*"

"Poor Arlen wouldn't look at it. Karen says he sees the man too clear in his mind. He sees his face turned right at him. Looking straight *at* him. He says he'll never forget that face as long as he lives."

"The hell he won't."

"He stood there just before he was sent *flying.*"

"He stopped?"

"Like a squirrel, I guess she meant. You know how a squirrel or deer or, you know, a raccoon or something…?"

"*What?*"

"Freezes in the headlights."

"I wouldn't mind seeing it," he said. "This sketch."

The two of them lay flat out in bed. Everyone in the world was in bed, Cherry thought. Husbands and wives, lovers, a father alone in a house, a woman alone in a house, still together, right here in the same world. Such secrets! Arlen and Rita, too. Such whispered troubles.

"And what about his *wife,*" she said suddenly. "Isn't she still waiting for him? Standing at the window waiting for him to just jog on home? Can you picture her? Standing at the window? She must have called somebody. The police."

"Some don't," Rich said.

"She wouldn't expect him to just disappear like that, would she?"

"*Who knows?*"

"All right. I'll shut up."

"Look, you don't have to shut up."

But if just possibly Cherry was still talking, Rich was not listening. He was trying at quarter past nine to go quickly into a deep sleep like he always did with sweet Sarah Lee, like the cupcakes. Afterwards with her, he always took a nosedive, everything stopped forever, all the goddamned lights went out, and good night, good night, down he went. So he tried thinking about her, about her legs and her belly and strawberry hair and nosediving. This was not the way with Cherry. With Cherry, when she finally quit talking, he might have to lie awake all night with nothing on his mind and only the time ticking away. This is why he was always a little afraid to make love to her. She was like a black coffee at midnight.

A̲t dawn, the carpenter's kid came into the Browne's yard and took away a small rattling ladder and the long two-by-twelve they had rested the table saw on and part of a roll of wire the electrician had left.

Arlen was in the kitchen, passing back and forth in the window, watching the kid. Rich watched from the upstairs window until both the kid and Arlen were out of view, then went downstairs.

He sipped the cooling coffee and went outside and searched around under the bushes for the paper. Already he was starting to think about the day, calculating the long drive to Portland. It would be better to fly if he could. If he could only go flying over everything he hated: the morning clutter getting out of town, and the rush hour in Tacoma and Olympia, and the damned patrol cars with their radar and clocks!

He shook the newspaper open with his free hand. Across the hedge a door closed. Possibly he and Arlen had come out at the same time, Arlen to talk to the kid. Arlen and Rita Browne were alone. The carpenter had a kid. Everybody, it seemed, became somebody else to somebody else. Davey's mother, who became somebody else, married now these eight years to somebody else. To a burglar who slithered under the side yard gate and in through a crack in the house. She married the burglar so there would be somebody else to father the boy, so that the boy would have another father and would learn things and grow up and be nice and cheery, just like she was so determined to grow up. Good for her, whose lying face he could not even picture. Good for her and her big burglar and little burglar. And when he was three thousand miles from home and needed money, he knew damned well who he had to call.

He glanced at the weather forecast. So it was unfair in Seattle, but there was good running room farther south in Portland where an unseasonably warm wind was blowing over a sweet belly and wild strawberry hair, where there were many things to learn and grow up into and be nice and cheery.

Rich shut the newspaper and went back inside to take up Cherry's coffee.

Cherry sat up in bed and switched on the lamp.

"Oh, it's nice and hot, honey," she said.

"Good," he said, and dropped the newspaper on her lap. She immediately folded back several pages.

"Here it is, like I told you. The sketch."

"That's the guy? That's like a kid."

"He really doesn't look that dead, does he?"

"It doesn't look like anyone," he said. "I mean, it looks like anybody. It might as well be me. They'll get a lot of crazy calls."

"Now it's like a real person. Poor Arlen. He's the one who's suffering so. Can you imagine what it must feel like to kill some perfectly real person?"

"What are you asking that for? Why are you asking me? Christ."

"You see?"

"What I see is he didn't choose it. All right? So forget it." She shut up for a minute and finished reading the story on page four about the accident. There wasn't anything else new in it.

"What did you say about Portland?"

"I've got to go down there on business. I might need to stay over."

"I'll be watching for you if you don't."

"I'm saying I might have to," he said, and he put his empty cup on the bedside table and got up and went into the bathroom.

Cherry's coffee was getting cold in her lap. She put aside the folded newspaper and stared at the closed bathroom door until it could have been practically anybody's door and listened to the shower running until she couldn't hear it. When Rich finally emerged in his underwear and slippers, she said, "At least you can call Davey. If you call him, then you can come home tonight."

"What are you talking about? Is that some kind of ultimatum?"

"I meant…"

"What the hell?"

"I *meant*, then you'll be happy and *want* to come home."

When Rich returned late the next evening, Cherry was upstairs in bed, listening. She listened to the front door close, the coat hanger in the hall closet, the refrigerator, the long silence before the click of the light switch. He came up on feet light as a ghost's.

"Anyway, that's over with," he said. "The deal in Portland."

"Wrapped it up?"

"That's what I said."

"Good for you."

He pulled his tie free, broke the knot, hung it up with all the others on Davey's tie-rack: school-made, shellacked, inherited, father from son. Trousers back on their hanger. He stood with his back to her in the face of the open closet. In his shorts. In his white body.

She took a deep breath, held it, exhaled through pursed lips, like they said to do in *Redbook* if you ever wanted to sleep. And if you just figured calmly, if you just calmed right down, it was all easy enough. She had done all the figuring in his absence. She had added it up. The boy was just caught up in the middle of it, like they always are. His mother chose him, took off with him, and left the husband. It wasn't Davey he wanted back at all. It was her. She was why he raced all the way to Portland, just to spite her. And he would run right over Davey, who was perfectly innocent.

"So now what?" he said. He stood in the steamy doorway, drying his hair, staring at her. "You having trouble breathing?"

"It's to relax. *Redbook* says."

"Nobody's come in to claim the dead guy? You know, the sketch?"

"Nobody. Nobody's claiming anybody," she said. "So Karen and I are thinking poor Arlen needs to be cheered up a little. We're thinking, tomorrow we'll drop on over. You know, bring him something, a gift or something. To cheer him up."

"Sounds like a whoopee party."

"You can only think about things so long."

"Sure, go ahead. Throw him a goddamned party."

Cherry inhaled deeply.

"Karen has theories," she said when all the air was out.

"Wacko Karen."

"She says Rita and the unidentified man might have actually known each other. And Arlen, perfectly innocent of the whole matter until last week, found out. Then he learned of the man's odd habit of jogging at night far from his home. He waited for him there where the trail crossed the road."

"This is a red herring if I ever heard one."

"Everything's a red herring to you."

"It said the guy *wandered*. Wandered *off* the trail. He came out of nowhere a good hundred feet from the crossing."

"Just maybe there's something new to report. Maybe there were no footprints anywhere. Between the bushes. In the dirt beside the road. In fact, what if he was hit right there at the crossing, then carried back?"

"What are you trying to say?"

"*Carried back too far to make any sense.*"

"You're saying a crime's been committed?"

"Why not? The police are investigating. *And* the newspapers. Everything will be brought out into the light. All the secrets. Everyone exposed. People called into testify. Nobody will escape. Karen says it will be like the Last Judgment."

"You know what I think? I was away too long."

"I waited for you."

"I just left you here too damned long, okay?"

"Yes. Like she left you."

"Now who are you talking about?"

"Davey's mother."

"His mother *what*?"

"If you want her back, then get her back. Go ahead. Try and get her."

"Are you stupid? Are you crazy? Are you finished?"

"No."

Rich looked at his wife incredulously.

"Davey's mother is a fat woman who lives in Denver, Colorado, with her husband *Don*. You know that. I don't think I'd recognize her if she showed up on the front page of the goddamned newspaper."

"I can pack up. I can go someplace on a bus."

"Oh, move the hell over," he said, hopping into bed with her.

"*I won't.*"

"Come on, Cherry. Move over."

Cherry poured her own coffee at six a.m. and went out to find the newspaper and brought it back to her coffee at the kitchen table and sat down slowly. Her body ached from the lovemaking. Why shouldn't it? Something comes into you and then it deserts you. That's funny. He comes, she welcomes. He leaves, she's left. But they are left too. Something leaves them, too, and afterwards they also ache.

She read what was there on page four of the paper, then looked through the window out across the lawn to the laurel hedge. Poor man, she thought. We will bring him gifts.

Rich stood in the doorway.

"You hear that phone ringing over there?" he said.

"I don't hear it," Cherry said.

"Who the hell's calling at this hour? What do they want?"

Cherry looked up from the newspaper.

"The body has been positively identified," she said.

"Who?"

"They need to notify the next of kin first."

"The wife," he said. "The bride."

"Yes. That's right. Now the mourning can begin."

They sat together awhile in the kitchen, drinking coffee and waiting, like in a Trailways depot. Then Rich left her there and went off to work.

The day flew past him like telephone poles. Everything felt speeded up, as if all the coffee had finally got to him, and he lost track of time. When he arrived back at the house, it was well past the dinner hour.

He wasn't hungry. He opened and closed the refrigerator door, looked around the kitchen, turned the lights out, then went upstairs. He took a long shower and climbed in between the fresh sheets. He switched off the lamp. He stretched out across the wide bed.

After a while, he tried the *Redbook* exercise. He inhaled very deeply, held it, then exhaled very slowly through a narrow crack in his lips until he was sure all the breath had gone out of him. Then he held there, too, not breathing, and focusing his mind on it in the huge silence. It was pretty amazing, actually, like he had brought the whole world to a stop. He inhaled again, drawing the room's soap-smelling air deep into his lungs until he was afraid they would burst, then let go again as slowly as he could manage, until his head felt a little light, and then very light, like now his whole body could lift right up off the bed and go anywhere. He held to that. He was starting to get the hang of it—his arms were thrown wide for balance—when he heard voices outside from across the yard.

He caught his throat and sat up.

He threw off the sheet and went to the window. There were dim lights in the Browne's house, in the south end of the living room, the dining room, the narrow hall to the kitchen with its two windows over the sink. Arlen, in silhouette, passed in and out of view. Then Rita. And there was wacko Karen. Cherry, too. He was not sure he had ever seen her at such a distance. At such a distance, in this other house, she did not seem herself. The woman behind her had turned away. He thought of poor Sarah Lee in Portland and he pressed his face against the cool glass.

Davey came into view. *Davey*. He was leaner now. Tall, too. His mother, her hand on his shoulder, moved with him in and out of the window frames.

All of them poured into the dark of the morning room. There they moved around like shadows, their arms raised and reaching, searching the walls and ceiling. It was when he was sure they were all finally there, inside the glass, that he was drawn back to the kitchen window and the girl with the thick braid of hair, now framed there like an old wedding photograph. Her eyes, he knew, were dark and anxious.

He hurried down to the kitchen and stepped out into the backyard. Slipperless, in his white pajamas, he moved quickly out across the wet lawn. He could not even feel himself breathing. Now he was light with longing, light enough to fly. He was almost flying, in fact, when he burst through the deep cut in the laurel hedge and into the dark clearing. Suddenly, the morning room switched on, a burst of light. Blinded, he froze in it—threw out his hands against its unwavering arrival.

HER BIRTHDAY SUIT

This morning the painter slapped Baby's Breath and then Desert Dusk and then Seashell on the face of our house, and Marian and I tried to decide. The chips, she says, never tell the truth. You have to get the real thing onto the real house and stand back, in several lights if you can manage it, and then compare and make a decision. This is our anniversary. Twelve years of wedded bliss. The house job is more or less a gift to ourselves. The painter, a likable young man my son calls Dad, stands with his arms folded and tries to make up his own mind, as if he's the one who has to live with it.

Max, who is not yet four, is racing back and forth in the front yard, throwing and failing to catch his red beanbag frisbee. He throws with all his might and the frisbee flies wherever it wants: behind him so he almost falls over backwards trying to follow its course, or out across the lawn where he runs to retrieve it, or more often than not, straight up into the blue so that it dive-bombs down to him and he throws up his arms in defense. He has been doing this since the painter arrived at seven-thirty. Marian is definitely irritated. She's standing there drinking her black coffee and trying to decide about the paint while the red frisbee buzzes only inches above her head, rattling the china, as it were, and then goes sailing over the white picket fence.

"I'll get it," I tell her.

"Will you just wait a minute? We've got to decide this. So which is it on the right? Is that the Seashell?"

"Hey, I like it!"

"That's the right shade? It captures everything?"

"Honey, it's great."

"How can you tell in this light?" she asks, her glance arching from me back to the paint. "It could be anything in this light. So what's it going to be when you get home at five?"

I don't know, I don't know. Now the painter's on the spot. I figure he's real close to a decision. "And what about the windows?" she says.

"Save them," I tell her.

"*Trimmed with what?* My God, do people get divorced over things like this?" she asks the painter.

"Yes ma'am, it can happen," he says, and then he's gone out through the gate to retrieve the frisbee. When he's got it, he throws it back over to Max who, seeing it coming, ducks to let it sail, lifting a little on a swell of air, into the rhododendron.

"Jesus, you guys!" Marian says. Yes, she's irritated. She's sure I'm going to run straight off to work and leave the whole matter to her, and she's right, I will, if I can possibly manage it. The thing is, what's it matter if the house is Baby's Breath or Seashell or Desert Dusk, since after a certain point the shades just take off on you anyway, where before any one of them might have held the place up fine. But Marian is determined to solve this and get it right, despite the fickle light, and even if it means dragging me down with her. The poor painter, too. Surely she realizes he has another life besides this one.

When the two of them have approached the wall of the house, stand there rather formally before fresh paint, staring like the couple on a wedding cake, I begin my slow getaway toward the car. It's not serious, really. After twelve years, to the day, Marian knows the point when I'm spineless, as uncertain as clay, and burdens like these fall to her. The boy sees me and whips the frisbee wildly back over his head. It flies up like a flame to the house, catches the edge of the gutter, and seems to stick. *Oh no.* We stare together. When he turns back into the sunlight, his face glares like a coin.

I am supposed to go straight downtown. In fact, if I remember right, there are people actually waiting for me, with things to talk about, things to be gone over. Downtown is dead ahead west on Madison Street that goes all the way into the Bay. Trouble is, any rush hour is your worst nightmare. For months now the workmen have been tearing it up and patching it up and tearing it up again, so everything's deafening with jackhammers and stinking of hot tar. Everybody's jammed into the hour glasses. Who needs it? And so to kill time I just circle back a few blocks into Madison Park, to visit the bank machine. This is my anniversary. I will need hard cash for the flowers and haircut and dinner.

These early summer mornings in Madison Park, just stand anyplace and the senses go flying, whirl about in the air like Max's frisbee. They go out to the hot smell of the bakery, and the flower tent at Bert's, and around the corner to the lattes at Starbucks'. Heels click on the sidewalk. Small plates clink.

Chairs scrape as they're brought forward or pushed back. Car doors opening or closing. Even in the hushed moment, when you imagine a blue skirt's being smoothed, everybody's about to be late. The shops open early now, at nine, and parking spots go fast. At a quarter past eight, my own car is running in the No Parking zone. I let it run.

Overhead a jet traces in a sort of white a frame of sky, like the window trim, I am thinking. The crisp new money feels cool in my hand.

The woman getting out of her car across the avenue reminds me of Sondra Ross, the actress. My eyes zoom in on her. Oh, it's the red hair, I'm sure. Also, the dark, reddish brows that almost meet. And the way she suddenly lifts her chin and then turns a little so that she's both looking at you and pointing the way you're supposed to follow, as she did in the one with Kevin Kline, or the other guy. It's not Sondra Ross, of course. Why should it be? This is only a smartly dressed woman, now in her thirties, who might own that little shop she's parked in front of, or the one right next to it, Park Travel, with the bright, stuffed parrots in the window. But she *is* looking at me. She is, if I read her right, pointing the way to something.

I am thinking now this morning's course may be altered. It's really not too late for either of us. Her car door shuts. She goes to the shop without the parrots, finds her key, swings the glass door open. And holds, in the balance. I think she's thinking, Well, *why not?* Who's going to catch us like this, out of school, this one little time? I picture this: Myself in a flash right there with her in the doorway. My hand firm against the silky small of her back. And the deep, warm kiss like she wants. Like we both want. Silence, big eye to big eye, like two whales.

All decisions infinitely postponed. Then herself slipping away into her little shop, with its scent of sachet, and the door closing behind her. Myself in reverse motion crossing the avenue to the running car.

The avenue takes me straight downtown. I let it. Already I am thinking that tomorrow, at eight-thirty sharp, she could be there as I come away flush from the machine.

All morning at the office I suffer various shades of guilt. After all, this in my anniversary, and if there is any day in the year when infidelities should rest and memories awake, this is it. Marian is very big on anniversaries. She celebrates the day we met, the first time we made love, the day we saw the little shadow of Max on the ultrasound at Providence Hospital. In time, really, everything becomes an anniversary. Not just the marriage, with its photograph of wedding dress and tux, but the divorce, too: a guy and a woman thousands of miles apart on February 3rd, say, raising a glass. And do not think my Marian will forget this day when the paint is finally decided. The one anniversary, you see, will only remind her of the other.

I do worry about these things piling up, the endless procession of high-priced meals and raised glasses. And the decisions about where to do it and what time exactly! All those damned reservations.

Around noon I phone home. I let it ring. I know she's there. It is only a matter of letting the line hang in the water long enough, then *whoosh!* She's hooked. Out from the yard. Up from the laundry room. Meanwhile it rings and rings and rings.

"Come on, come on," I say.

Finally it stops. The receiver is dragged from its rest.

"Marian?...Honey?"

These are the fragile five or six seconds, stretched endlessly at the movies, when the knife's at your wife's throat, or when her tongue's ripped out, or when she's dragged herself, over the jagged terrain, from the bloody tub.

"Honey? *Marian?*"

Nothing.

"Max? That you, monkey?... Hey, monk. Will you talk to me?"

I know his breathing. I know his boy's breathing, his lips wet against the receiver, his eyes staring down into it. He's no talker. Still, I listen to him. I'm happy I called.

After a while, we've fallen into the same rhythm. We could sleep now if we needed to. Instead, I begin to worry.

"Max?... Where's Mom?... Will you tell Mom?... Max?... Hello?... Is the painter there? The nice man who's painting the house? Is he there?... Where's Mom?... Is she outside?... Is she upstairs?... Is the painter there?... Max? Is the nice painter upstairs?... Max, honey?... Jesus, where's your mother?"

"*Who's this?*" Marian wants to know.

"Where were you?"

"Is this my anniversary boy?"

"The same," I say, and I remind myself that, after all, this is her anniversary, too. My anniversary fool.

"Well, we've decided," she says.

"You have?"

"It's the right thing."

"Is it?"

"Yes, we've compromised."

"What sort of compromise?"

"So where's Mr. Who-Cares? Not back in his little cell?"

"How about if I don't like it?"

"How about if you move to New Mexico?"

"When?"

"Not before you settle on the restaurant tonight."

"Oh my God, no!"

"*Yes*, my darling. *And* make the reservation. The sitter's coming at seven sharp. And don't let Michael cut your hair too short, all right? Last time you came out of there looking like one of those what-do-you-call-em?"

"Guys on death row?"

"Monks."

My appointment with Michael is right at five. He's been cutting my hair for six or seven years now, and I like him because he has no serious ambition and takes three days off each week to play semi-professional soccer. He shares the salon with two other stylists who subscribe to the various glossy magazines of their profession, and to *Vogue* and *The New Yorker*. Michael, may God forgive him, still keeps the latest *Playboy* handy and, once I'm strapped in and wrapped in a rose-red sheet, I settle into it.

The strap is for kids and high-fliers, he says, but in my own mind I am sitting in an electric chair somewhere in New Mexico, somebody down the hall is waiting to flip the switch, the Governor is out to a real fancy restaurant with his wife. And Michael leans over to me and says:

"Any last words?"

"Cut it short," I tell him.

We talk. He asks about Max, whose head he shaves every fourth Wednesday, and I confess to him in some detail about the woman I kissed in the shop doorway this morning, and how God awful I've suffered for it already, and about the affair my wife is having with the painter. Then I ask him could he please recommend an expensive restaurant.

"It's my anniversary," I tell him.

"Well, there's Campagne down at Pike Place. It's good."

"Really?"

"Expensive. The Painted Table is practically next door. Incredible bread."

"The bread's good?"

"Cost you an arm and a leg. And up the street is the Georgian Room. Sell your house. You can't go wrong."

"Thank you," I tell him, and flip the page.

"Hey," he says. "Can you guess who that is? Can you believe it?"

He means in the magazine. And no, I can't believe it. There's a whole page on Sondra Ross, in black and white. Photos taken by a friend, it says, when she was only seventeen, living in Encampment, Wyoming. Boy, some friend.

"You know something, she looks pretty much the same, don't you think?"

"I didn't recognize her," I tell him, "in her birthday suit."

"They do this, I don't know, every two or three issues: dig up old snapshots of some famous actress in a compromising position. I've got a theory on it."

"People love anniversaries. My wife does."

"It's like what that guy Warhol said about everybody getting to be famous for fifteen minutes. You see, I think *Playboy* has this huge file cabinet and inside there's a snapshot of every woman in America in a compromising position."

I want to laugh, but there's a current of something burning through me.

"Everything's got to be captured," I say.

"Hell yes. Sooner or later," Michael continues, "every woman's snapshot will surface."

"Every man's, too."

"Hey, you think?"

Frankly, I don't know where Marian and I will end up tonight. I don't know what will happen. Something expensive. And Sondra Ross? Out of the blue like that? We should be happy just to alter our days.

The flowers are still possible. Necessary, you might say. Otherwise Marian will die. I remember now, sometimes at rush hour there's a girl hawking them up on Sanctuary Drive. The police keep her moving. Even *her* picture was in the paper once: this girl on the run, hugging the curb, roses held out to an open window.

GREEN LAKE

A new girl in the café, she's called Emily like my sister, brings my cappuccino holding the white saucer in the silver-ringed fingers of both hands as if she might snap it in half. She believes I am reading, she doesn't speak, she slides the coffee to the edge of my book. The dark aroma commingles with the light, rose-watered scent of the freshly scrubbed skin, then the bluejeans, frayed and unwashed, *obligatoire* in this café, and cinched by the red-beaded belt. She smells seventeen. Still, she has done the beast with two backs, if I can trust my nose at this handy elevation, and likely within the hour, though of course this is none of my business.

My business is to drink coffee and read. It allows me to hang my head all day long without arousing suspicion or curiosity. As a child, I had a child's sort of accident, a sudden blow to the upper vertebrae, so that my spine, at the base of the skull, where my kneeling father held it, under this camouflage of bohemian locks, curls now like a shepherd's staff, and keeps my chin more or less glued to my chest, like a good middleweight's. So it's my position in life to be a reader. My little destiny. I'm sure, in fact, that if I were to sit here only a moment or two over a blank table, the first Good Samaritan would stop and quickly shove a book or newspaper or menu, something printed, for chrissakes, under my nose. Only Rosanna, as I recall, ever thought to push the book away, and put in its place, between us, a small mirror, oval and teak-framed, like the artisans sell at Pike Street Market. First she leaned over it to do her mouth with a kind of vermilion, then held a dark point to her eye, then blushed her cheek like sunrise on water. I saw her like that, the parts of her in little, oval worlds of their own.

And so I wait awhile here at this window table. It is my spot, Nancy tells me, if I arrive early enough to claim it. Several years ago, in a different frame of mind, on a Saturday evening as a guitarist improvised on the corner platform, I carved by candlelight my initials in the hard wood, and I can feel them still vaguely here, mine among the others. On winter days when outside the pavement is ice against my face, I may dig in here, reading and sipping, from morning until well into the night. In summer, I'm out by eleven. It's the glare that bothers me, uproots me from my spot—window light that knifes across the page and lifts the words, as though onto a glass slide, separating black from white, and lets them hang there suspended, anxious, like loose souls, so before long you discover your eyes caged and pacing the way they do when you're dreaming. You expect the next breeze from the door to whirl them out into the street.

"You should be out in this," Nancy said. "This gorgeous Sunday. Take your book, why don't you?"

"So that's a new girl," I said. "Emily Claire."

"Just Emily, from Portland. She's seventeen."

"Where's Rosanna? I was supposed to meet her."

"Were you? Well. They're playing her demo on the radio. I've heard it twice already this morning. You know—her demo?"

"Yes."

"Well, they're playing it *ad nauseam* on the radio."

"Is she coming in or not?"

"She is and she isn't," Nancy said. "You know Rosanna. You can never tell where she is exactly."

"I don't care where she is," I said.

"You're a sweet fellow."

"As long as she's here when she said she might be."

She stood silent, playing with the beads of cotton from the frayed border of her apron. It was a short apron, coffee stained, and protruding a little over a generous abdomen, the check pad staring out of its pocket.

"Who am I to talk," she began. "When I was seventeen I had no worries. When somebody wanted to ground me with worries, I'd just hold my fingers up like this, crossed, and fly away. Into the blue. I had my own life. Freedom! Now I'm exactly thirty-six and I have Frank. You've seen Frank. Frank is exactly what I've been trying to avoid my whole life. When I ran into him three years ago, he was crazy with little ticky worries. He'd sit all day biting the hair on his arm. Now he's bloated with them, like a black cloud hanging over me, about to burst. And all he thinks about is doing it. You know? I'm talking morning, noon, and night. Getting loose of his worries. Making little worry deposits, in me, on me, on anybody else who'll sing along. Forgive me."

"What for?"

"It's really not your business."

"And Rosanna? Will she perform here evenings or not?"

"The Demo Queen? Ask her when she comes in," Nancy said.

"Is she coming in this morning?"

"I'm the last to know anything."

It is contrary to my condition, my head hopelessly hung, but just once I would like to look straight into a woman's eyes—you know, into those lakes of longing.

Blood on the pavement will concentrate the mind. I hadn't noticed it coming in, perhaps Rosanna had blinded me, but there it was at the door, and inside the door, dry blood, but fresh too, bright as nail polish. Do not be surprised by this. There's more blood around than you think.

Book in hand, I followed it to the crosswalk where it seemed to pause a moment and collected, as I did, while waiting for the light. Listen, I know what people think when they see a fellow with his face hanging over the pavement, that he's some filthy scumbag scrounging for cigarettes and money. That's why I wear a decent pair of Oxfords, shining up at me, so anybody'll think, Hey, he's only deformed, poor man! And why not a fine pair of shoes since I spend a good part of my waking day, upright or horizontal, looking at them? Still, there's blood on the curb, too. And in the street, despite the laws and condemnations, the refuse: the sales slips and gum wrappers, cigarette filters, fliers for poetry readings, bottle caps and can tabs, chain links, a nail file, a postage stamp, sometimes a photograph or just a bit of a photograph so that all you have is a foot or knee or hand in a pocket. Only a week ago, in fact, I found a letter. All the i's had little circles over them, like halos. What she wanted was her key back. The guy had her key.

"Don't touch me! ... All your promises! ... Just put it in an envelope," she said. Now she had a post box. She wasn't going back until he gave it to her. Oh, if the key wasn't returned she was going to run him over in the parking lot or on the street when he was crossing and had his head in the clouds, and back up over him and then spin out, burning rubber over his thick skull, and she didn't care if she got consecutive sentences or what. It was a two-page job compressed into a ball the size of a left testicle. In the crosswalk equidistant between curbs.

Now this condom in the gutter. What people will throw off, like skins, into perfectly public places. Well, I come across quite a few right out in the open, in the middle of sidewalks, and hanging limp over the curb, or on a bush like an ornament. How do they get to such places? Thrown from speeding cars, I suppose. Parachuted from windows so high up I can't imagine them. Perhaps there's great merriment in the clouds and all the condoms and nail files and wadded letters are just raining down.

It might explain the blood. Going with the light, I followed it across, then picked up another drop on the sidewalk, and took a left, veering off like an errant atom into the thick grass.

Sunday explained the bells. I suppose they come from St. Matt's, though that's some distance, and thankfully down wind. Sometimes in a wave of quiet, on a day like this, or an evening before the lights come on and the brown shades go down along the sidewalk, I hear somebody's whistling, a chord or two, and next thing I know I'm humming along.

The bright, thick grass gently slopes toward Green Lake. I could smell the water. Now there were real voices and the confusion of radios and dogs barking, close.

Soon I was down among the girls in their shorts and tops. Nymphs on the lawn. Nausikaa and her maids. Hurray! Then a shadow raced at me across the grass, a whoosh of wind over my head. I dropped in self-defense. Dark birds attacking? How many? Two red dogs came bounding after, and leapt, their long red tails whipping my shoulder.

"Are you hit?" cried the first voice coming toward me.

Then her legs—sunlotioned, reeking of coconut, shimmering with fine, grain-golden hair—stretching up into bunched white shorts, a sailor's rope for belt.

From behind, another girl approached. "They almost took his crown off!" she exclaimed. Her voice crackled like static.

"Oh, did they hurt you?"

"Safe," I said, waving my book.

"Well, what's the matter with him anyway?" demanded the other girl, hanging back. "Is the guy hung over or what?"

"I'm afraid he may be hurt. It's all right to say so."

My thumb shot up to the back of my neck.

"Jesus," the other said. "They hit him, all right."

"Poor sweetie."

"Somebody's going to get sued around here!" she yelled, moving off toward the faraway guys. Their answer waited, coiled, then whirled through the air, close enough to uncurl my hair. In a second the dogs were snarling and barking, fighting over the frisbee.

"He can't look up, is all," said the golden girl. "That's right, isn't it? You can't look up?"

"I'm hooked on this," I said, jabbing the ground.

"He's hilarious," giggled the other.

"Poor man," she said, drawing closer. "My name is Dolores. She's Candy."

"Give him our phone numbers while you're at it."

"Shut up, will you? He's so sweet. Like he's proposing or something."

"Get a dog, Dolores."

Dolores leaned over me and whispered. A rabbit ear of her bandeau brushed my nose.

"Can you smell me, mister?"

"Yes," I said.

"What do I smell like?"

"Like flowers on a mountainside."

"Honestly?"

"Jesus, Dolores. What's going on?"

"He wants to see me if you don't mind," she said sharply over her shoulder.

"Is this really necessary?" Candy said, her voice breaking. Then she shouted back to the boys: "The guy wants to see Dolores!"

"Dolores?" one of them shot back. "What's she up to now?"

"It's true, isn't it?" Dolores said, pushing my book aside. "You do want to?"

"What?"

"Want to look at me."

My downed knee slid back, and my body arched achingly at the waist, my curious eyes straining heavenward.

"They don't know a thing about me," she said.

Now Candy is laughing so hard I have to hope she'll choke to death. I stood up and searched the ground for the best way free, then took off way around them, and headed out across the hill.

"Duck!" shouted one of the guys.

Duck? The frisbee had already struck the small of my

back. The sting raced up my spine. Then the snarling dogs were close. In only a few steps and one small leap over the languid limb of another nubile, I was clear and running in my fashion, peeping around my shoulder for the galloping mob.

It's good to run, normally. There's the rub. I stopped, turned slowly like a divining rod, found the scent of the lake. The breeze picks it up, carries it ashore, through the evergreens. My nostrils flared. But with my first step waterward, I fell—book flying—hard into the grass.

This fellow had tripped me up. He lay beside me with thin arms outstretched, palms up, eyes closed, as if he were counting to ten thousand. *All-e all-e in free!* The sun was pouring into him.

He slept an unshackled sleep, like he owned the whole park. I lay a moment beside him, still as a corpse in the warm grass, and stared at shoes smudged with green across both toes. Only peace I wanted. A soft bed.

I closed my eyes like my friend's. At first the noon light was enough to shine through and make the dance of shadows. Soon I found the dark. My mother came in. Yes, my own mother, like she is. Her face, in a cave of thick brown hair, looked up, yearning. *Up.* Father too, his head like a brown eraser atop a long blue tie. And Emily, her mouth agape. Then others appeared: Nancy, her face ablaze with sunlight, and girls dancing on the lawn, and three small children, their faces waiting like dinner plates, every blessed head raised and raiseable!

Quickly I opened my eyes. Yes. Blazing sunlight. Money in the bank. Stretching a little, I nudged my neighbor's hand.

I searched through my parted shoes for the lake. Looming there, in the way, were three round boys, their shaved heads showing through, like boulders. A Great Mother swooped down behind them.

"You don't need to see this, hear me?" she said. And then: "Is this your book, sir? You should be ashamed of yourself!"

She yanked them away. The view opened wide to the parade of joggers, skaters, bikers on the marked path which lined the lake, and the crescent beach just beyond, and the crouching bodies, still more heads bowed. Then the shimmering water. I could see far out, the red rowboats with their gold oars in the air, and hear the hum of a radio.

I rose, gathered up my book, and headed down to it.

At the shore, the three boys were skipping stones. Behind us, the woman squawked at them to stop. Far out on the lake someone's radio was playing Rosanna's demo. I sat down, put aside my book, took off my shoes and socks, rolled up my trousers. I waded out. The warm water rose up my leg. When I was waist high in it, soaked through to the groin, my feet in the icy bottom, I stopped, stood still, listened. I could hear it, all right. No doubt the station was playing it all day long. The song came over the water and all around me the surface went mirror still. I could see myself reflected in it, my face framed in its riot of dark curls, floating in a white sky, my head cut off, suspended. Myself, it seems, sprung free. *Where?* Then the water wrinkled wildly and I went as quickly as I had come.

"Walter! Billy! Did you hit that man? You, Eddie Beale!"

I listened awhile, then turned back. The beach, in the glare, seemed as blinding as a blank page. Then the three boys appeared, squatting, their round, heavy heads bowed, scrounging for flat stones.

OFF SEASON

1.

Tom Foyer has had his eye on my sister since the ninth grade. In those days she would come out to the field with a gang of girls to watch the Spartans practice after school. They would sit six or seven rows up in the stands with their knees wide apart and skirts always tucked down between, except Ellen, who never thought about it. Whenever we were at mid-field, Tom would look over at the wedge of pink her white legs led up to, and then cut out into the flats for a pass, no matter what the call was, only to get a better look at her. I would flip him one now and then, putting it just off his fingertips. I was trying to tell him something. I was trying to tell him Ellen would be out of reach even if he chased her a thousand miles into the desert and the best he could expect was to go flying on his face. But he never understood it. Instead he cut out into the flats almost every play, even when he should have been blocking, with Randy Bean and Gil Muffet, for me on the keeper.

Saturdays he would drive out to the house with Randy and Gil and sometimes Gil's brother, Red, and after tossing the ball awhile, we would all lounge around on the little island of white wicker chairs in the yard. It's a big yard with a sycamore tree and a falling-down barn and the driveway turn-around between, and hardly a blade of grass anywhere. But that's where we would spend the whole day hatching up something for the evening, and then unhatching it, so that every hour we would have to start up again. Of course Gil always wanted to go to the movies. That is because he had a girl to meet him there in the dark in the two seats where the arm pulled out. Nobody knew her from school. In fact, nobody knew her from any- where, not even Ellen. They would neck and eat popcorn like there was no tomorrow. Afterwards, reeking of hot butter, he would meet up with us at Good Riley's, and it would only be ten o'clock, the whole evening still looming before us.

The rest of us wouldn't be wasting our money at the mov- ies, thanks to Ellen. While we were talking plans she would come out the screen door in her night shorties or slip and sit on the steps and brush her hair out. Her hair was the color and tangle of a peanut shell and hung to her waist, so Satur- days she would spend the whole morning just trying to straighten it, which was hopeless. It wasn't going to do what she wanted it to, and pulling it only turned her face onto her bare shoulder so it always had a kind of dreamy-eyed, lying- down look on it. It was the look that got Tom. He was helpless before it. He would ease himself out of the wicker chair and shuffle over to her like James Dean and ask her what *she* wanted to do, did *she* have any plans. Well, what she and her gang of friends, all morons, did on a Saturday night, or even in what town, was an unsolved mystery, but one thing was certain: she had already seen the movie. Without missing a brushstroke, she told us the beginning-to-end of it, every scene, the best of the dialogue, who starred and co-starred, and if it was in glorious technicolor or some other kind of color. That killed it for us, except Gil, of course, who was happy to know what he was missing.

Around noon Mother would come out, and seeing Ellen was getting too much attention, would tell her to get inside and get dressed and do things she'd made a list of. Then she would ask the rest of us was there anyone who wanted a hot dog while she was cooking them. Then she would bring us Cokes. I don't think the guys ever ate anyplace else or had anything better for a real family. They really liked Mother and thought of her as somebody's older, good-looking sister because she was still lots of fun, always teasing and joking, and no different here in her own yard from what she was at the diner, where she worked evenings.

Sometimes she would sit with us with her arm on my shoulder and say what she would do on a Saturday night if some come-along man would rescue her from the diner. She would dress up and go to a really nice place like the famous Alderwood Inn, which was almost in Crook County, and have a margarita in a stemmed glass as wide as the loop of Venus. After that she would find a pottery garden like they have along the road. She liked best the flamingos standing on one leg, and the turtles, and the patient angels on the birdbaths. Then, after a long walk along a lake in the moonlight or under fast-moving clouds, she'd come back, she said winking, to a loving bed.

"With *Mr.* Jenkins?" Gil wanted to know. My father, he meant.

"Would you have a better idea?"

"He's got a gang of better ideas, don't you, Gil," Randy said. He threw his head back and chugalugged his Coke.

"Truly, though," she said, running her long fingers against the grain of my hair, "home is the best place, like the movie says. It's just got to be. Where else can you be yourself and have what you really want? Like you boys, all together right here, holding tight to these chairs all Saturday long. This is where you should be the most free, though I know you may never feel free unless you run off someplace."

"We can make you as free a woman as you can stand, Mrs. Jenkins," Gil said. "Just say the word."

"Dammit, I *am* a free woman," she said. "There's nobody tells me anything without a good tip on the table."

Then she laughed the way she did sometimes clear across Good Riley's, or like I remember it now when she read to Ellen and me, her trouble-in-pairs, she called us, and something struck her funny, in the book or in her own thoughts. It was a throaty laugh that hung on like a sigh until a little birdsound flew out of it and always surprised us, and made us laugh so our legs jiggled together. Sometimes Father, laying down his book, would call upstairs was there something the matter.

Father was a meat man, as Mother called him, and worked long hours at the Wright Meat Packing Company just south of town. I'm sure he was the biggest man I ever saw in my life, with knuckleless hands, round and white like the ball joints of a dinosaur bone, and he could carry half a steer. I saw it many times, his face flat against his shoulder, like Ellen's when she combed her hair out. There was a time as a boy when I liked going with him on the hot summer days to horse with the crew of muscle men in the cold lockers with the hanging carcasses everywhere, hard as marble, and only the smell of things freezing. Father himself wasn't much of a talker. But sometimes at night, if I begged him, he would read to me from a book by William Wordsworth. It was strange to hear the words come out of such a big man's head, like a ventriloquist was doing it, and I knew he preferred to read to himself without moving his thin lips.

After Mother left, after she surprised us and walked away from Good Riley's and right into somebody's car, people said, and with a small suitcase, I stuck it out in high school, and then in September left Ellen with Father, and went off the hundred and twelve miles to college. Mother always said that would be a real turning point in her life. Well, something else had turned her sooner. That first year I didn't go home much, but some weekends Ellen rode up on the bus, for the dances. She might wear one of Mother's things if it fit her right. I didn't have to tell anybody she was my sister because she could look as old as any college girl if she wanted. Then in late May, Father had his first stroke and was confined most of the summer to his room upstairs. Tom, who saw it as a chance to make a place for himself at the house and horn in on Ellen, came by every day, and he and I built Father a long table that ran across his bed and the armed chair, and Ellen, playing waitress in an old apron, would put out his food and help him eat it, and the three of them would sometimes play cards on it or read the newspaper, like they were at Good Riley's.

Ellen actually took a job there after her school had started up again and I was back at college. I was against it, but she said she would do what she wanted, which was the same as Mother. It didn't matter. I was only gone a month when the call came.

I arrived home at the end of a cold morning rain. Most of

Father's crew showed up for the funeral. The minister said he was a man of quiet fortitude. Afterwards, Tom, Randy, and Gil hung around until late afternoon. Bundled in sweaters, we sat out on the wet wicker chairs and I talked about what college was like. Tom asked me was I going back, hoping I would. I wasn't. Ellen wondered how we could put a notice of Father's death in the *Evening Register* so everyone in the state would know. She boiled up some hot dogs and carried out coffee from the house. We talked until the rain started up again, then Randy and Gil said they were either going indoors or leaving, and went out to the car. Tom stood around, hanging over Ellen like a guardian angel, until finally she told him to scoot. After he left, we had the whole place to ourselves.

2.

Winter months only Tom came out to the house. He would bring Ellen home from Good Riley's in the late evening, and for a while he came inside to say a hello and hang around the kitchen. Then he stopped. I suppose everybody figured he had finally got somewhere with her and now they were a pair of some kind. Even Tom might have imagined it. That was all right. Mother always said people would think what they wanted.

Then an afternoon in April Randy and Gil suddenly showed up. I was upstairs patching walls in the extra room. It was the smallest room we had upstairs and, looking northwest, there was no real light and Ellen and I always thought it was only good for hiding out in. We called it the extra room, even when Mother had her sewing machine in it and had set up a small writing desk she'd bought for eighty-five dollars at an estate sale. Mother had the idea she was going to start up a correspondence with my great-aunt Paulina and several long lost cousins she had known as children, maybe even hook them all together on a party line, and that way bring our little family together with everybody else, with connections we didn't even know. She said she was afraid of what might become of us if we didn't, and he got all teary about it. But I never saw her actually write anything, and pretty soon the desk was stacked with magazines and bills, and the room stayed dark.

Now these two stood in the doorway shoulder to shoulder. You could see they were trouble-in-pairs, like Mother would say. They had come straight into the house through the screen door in the kitchen and right on upstairs, like they owned the place.

"You guys must be looking for work," I said.

"We're too busy looking to find it," Gil said.

"There's sandpaper here."

"Jesus, is this the football?" Randy said. He took it from a cardboard box in the corner and stretched his fingers across the laces. Then he bent over and hiked one to Gil.

"I'd forgot all the goddamned rooms you've got up here," Gil said, and he stepped back into the hall. Randy followed and I could hear the bedroom doors opening. "You think Tom remembers how much house this is?" Gil called out. "You know, you could get some real money for it."

The football flew down the hall and hit something. Then the two of them were in the doorway again.

"You guys trying to wreck this place?"

"You could sell it and go all over the world," Gil said.

"Maybe I will."

"Of course your mother's the real traveler in the family,"

Randy said. "She sure did head out on us, didn't she?"

"Now Ellen," Gil said. "Maybe she'd like to take off, too."

"It's not likely any time soon," I said. "You got that?"

"Oh sure," Randy said, catching Gil's eye. "But maybe you haven't heard about Harvey's cousin."

"What the hell's to hear about?"

"He was in town once already in September, just after you went back to college. Right away he was nosing around the diner."

"Around Ellen, he means," Randy said.

"Like he smelled there was nobody else around."

"Tom was there," I said. "Anybody could see Tom was there with Ellen. He could have handled it."

"Back in September maybe all he could handle was his own dick. Maybe by the time he looked up, the cousin was gone. I'm thinking he had a seasonal job somewhere. You know?"

"Like the mating season," Randy said.

"I might have come down if there was a problem," I said.

"Yeah, well, we figured you were probably much too busy getting your college education."

"The thing is," Gil said. "He's back."

"Is that right?" I said.

"That's right."

"What for?"

"Could be he just hasn't guessed her situation."

"And our poor old buddy Tom hasn't been around to point it out to him," Randy said. "It's like Tom's hiding under some bed, figuring maybe you're going to shoot him."

"What's done is done," I said. "Why would I want to shoot a friend?"

"Sure, that's right," Gil said. "Anyway, Ellen's been a Hail Mary since she turned fifteen. It could have been any of us that caught her."

"Still, I've never seen a guy disappear so goddamned fast," Randy said. "Old Tom Cat, he come in the dark and he go in the dark."

"No, sir," Gil said. "All these years he never once deserved her."

"He must have deserved her once," Randy said, cocking his arm like a quarterback. "He must have deserved her once real good."

I put the putty knife down.

"Hey, anyway," he said, backing off into the hall, "Harvey's cousin, he'd have to be blind not to see she's showing."

"For what he knows," Gil said, "she could have put away too many coconut pies."

"So, what are you morons trying to say?"

"Now we're morons," Randy said.

"What we're saying," Gil said, "is this guy, he's showing up every night and sitting with her at her breaks, and they're like this already, a real pair."

"He's Prince of the Late Shift," Randy said.

"And drinking coffee like he's going to be up the rest of his life. After closing, they go off somewhere in his car. He's got one of those old foreign jobs."

"Black as an umbrella."

The three of us standing there took up most of the space. I tried to picture Mother sitting up at her small desk and writing those letters in fine penmanship to all her long lost relations. She was afraid, is all. Afraid it was just us. She wanted to reach out as far as she could and pull everybody in around us. Maybe she pictured a whole flock of people out in the yard sitting around. It would have been a miracle if anything connected before all the bills piled up.

"Well, that's water under the old bridge," I said finally. "Who needs any more trouble." And I led them out of the room, which was feeling claustrophobic, and down the stairs. "Thanks for telling me."

"Sure," Gil said. "Why shouldn't we?"

They were probably wanting lunch, like Mother had made for them practically every Saturday of our growing up, but I steered them safely through the kitchen and out across the yard to Gil's car. Randy still had the football and I know he wanted to steal it, but I got him to throw it to me, and then I tossed it into the wicker chair.

"Look," I said. "Maybe Tom should be in on this after all."

"Worse that could happen is somebody gets killed," Gil said.

"Just find him and tell him. All right? He might want to do something about it."

"Sure," Randy said. "Who knows? We came out here figuring you'd want to take care of this yourself. You're still her brother. Isn't that right?"

"Ellen needs to think what she's doing," I said.

"She should have done that before she ate all those pies."

3.

First I heard the car on the road coming up to the house as far as the sycamore. Then the engine went off. They were going to be there awhile. I got up and stood at the window.

The moon threw a pale sheet over the yard and the wicker chairs, and clear out to the tree. The guys were right about the car. It was black like Mother's first car when she was only seventeen and drove with her friend Carla all the way to the Minnesota border and back. It was the damnedest car she ever had, she said. Faster than the Impala. I can hear her talking and talking. Now Ellen was in a car just like it, going nowhere.

A light flashed inside, then two firefly glows of cigarettes. Now that was funny. I know for a fact the last time she smoked a real cigarette we were thirteen and eleven and had gone a long way from the house with two packs of Chesterfields, one pack for each. The place was well onto the Adams' property where there was a stand of trees and behind them a ravine where the roots had snaked through and you could sit on them and smoke. There were half-buried things to look at: an old Pontiac and a refrigerator with no door, and a trailer rake snarling at you with bent teeth. You could just toss in your beer bottles if you had any. Everybody did.

Ellen couldn't keep her cigarette lit at first. I taught her to suck hard on it two or three times until the tip of it glowed red hot, then she could sit back and not worry about it. She grinned, closed her eyes, and said no matter what else, she was going to smoke cigarettes the rest of her life and would I please, please bring her a pack whenever I had one. I didn't tell her how I got them. She smoked three or four cigarettes, lighting the one with the other like I showed her, and always blowing the smoke out in one *whoof* without inhaling it.

Then we heard somebody coming, and suddenly Mother was standing up there on the edge of the ravine, tall as the trees behind her. We dropped our cigarettes. She came down, stepping carefully on the ladder of roots, and picked up the one opened pack of Chesterfields and tossed up a cigarette for herself and then a pair of them which she held out to us and poked at us until we took them, and then she lighted the three cigarettes on one match which she said was bad luck. Of course we had never seen her smoke. She told us that when she was our age she had been a considerable smoker and was happy to share her experience with us. She taught us how to inhale. She taught us to drag hard like they do in the movies and pull the smoke down real deep and hold it and then let it shoot out our nostrils. Before we knew it we were blowing real smoke rings, and Mother told us about Montana sunsets which she said the smoke reminded her of and were pink and blue and purple like you were floating, you know, just off the surface of the moon. We must have gone through both packs before my head disconnected from my body. My head went way out away from my body and was anchored to it only by my throat that was like a long telephone cord waving around in the air. Pretty soon I could actually hear everything from my stomach coming up through it. Then I threw up the sandwich and rice pudding I had for lunch, and the wheatcakes we had for breakfast and all the little blueberries with them, and everything left from the day before and the day before that all the way back to before I could remember. And then I threw up all the meals I'd eat in the days to come, so that just the sight of food made my head swim. Mother rocked me in her lap, rubbed my head with her long fingers. She kissed my eyes that wouldn't stay still. Later, when I asked Ellen was she all right, where did she go, she said if it mattered to me at all she had been flying all week, circling just above the yard, and watching me in my slow recovery from a low branch of the sycamore.

I know I never touched a cigarette again, and Ellen

wouldn't either, unless somebody forced her. The firelights in his car had gone out. Ellen could talk up a storm if she wanted to. She was like Mother in that. After half an hour I went downstairs, turned on the yardside lights, and made some iced tea. I sat with it at the kitchen table, waiting.

I was thinking, if she wanted to go off with somebody's cousin and live happily ever after, maybe that was the answer. Of course not even Randy and Gil knew if he was just another moron tomming around, only after whatever she'd show him. Well, she could show him about the family way, all right. She could show him that if he wanted to know.

She had been there that summer afternoon up on old Sooter's Bridge. There was a dozen of us—Tom, Randy and Gil, Red, Harvey, John, and four or five guys from another high school—jumping all day from the stone bridge which had a historic marker on it, and swimming just under it in the black water before it suddenly turned white in the shallows and wound down through the trees. We'd brought Cokes and bags of chips and planned to stay until maybe Father passed by on his way home from the plant and gave us a lift in the pickup.

Instead, Mother and Ellen showed up in the Impala about four. More than half an hour they stood up there on the bridge and watched us jump. Tom did beautiful swan dives like in the Olympics, for Ellen's benefit. But the other guys became more daring than usual, and crazier. They did flips and belly flops and kamikazes, and pretended they'd been hit by enemy fire and screamed in agony and fell all dramatically. Tom was madder than hell. Some fool was going to get himself killed, he said. Mother said so too, and kept shaking her head. After a while, she and Ellen walked down to the lower bank. Randy shouted up to Mother to come on in, the water was stimulating, and she laughed and said it really it was the hottest day so she didn't mind if she did. Of course she hadn't brought a swimsuit. Randy and Gil had banked on it. So she sat down and slipped her bluejeans off and unbuttoned her white blouse, and then only in her white underwear and bra scooted to the bank's edge and sprang into a very nice dive into the crowded water. I swam up close to her, so everybody backstroked away to give her plenty of space. I had never seen her swim, not really, and she swam like a queen in small, splashless strokes, the water dividing smoothly along her raised neck. Then she turned on her back and kicked up a storm, which is all everybody needed. The shouting started up, and the wild laughter. Bombs fell from the bridge. Everybody moved in as close as she'd let them.

I don't think anybody actually saw Ellen undress. She had taken off everything but her white panties, and now stood poised and oblivious on the edge of the bank. She was fifteen and she'd changed. The guys out there with Mother stopped and treaded water. On the bridge, Tom stared in wonder. And nobody leapt from it, but just stood there like soldiers at attention. Until finally Mother shouted to her:

"*Ellen, for godsakes honey what are you thinking of!*"

She didn't answer, didn't dive either, and nobody spoke.

"There's nothing you can put on?" Mother said. "You listen now, I'm coming out!"

I swam up behind her toward the bank, but Ellen didn't move and still nobody else moved, I think because they had never seen a real girl like that, as beautiful. And just as we reached her, she suddenly dove right over us, and even now I sometimes see her sailing across the ceiling just before I switch off the light, and into the water like a knife.

She stayed under a long time and finally came up only ten feet short of the river's far side just as Father pulled onto the bridge in the pickup. Four of his crew were with him, in the back. They stood up to see what was happening. Father got out, looked over the edge, and what he saw first, of course, was what everybody else was looking at, which was Ellen on one side of the river standing in water up to the dark hair that showed through, and then Mother climbing up the other side with her underwear waterloaded and hanging down on her thighs, and me just behind. And he was like some mountain god about to roar, when suddenly the crew behind him in the pickup started hooting. The rest of the guys joined in. Mother and I could hear it right behind us as we hurried up the path to the Impala.

"What about Ellen?" I said.

"Let *her* deal with him."

We leapt into the car and sped away from the bridge like bandits and up the road. In two miles, Mother turned east onto the good road and pressed the accelerator to the floor.

We were a sight. I was shivering in my wet bathing suit, though I wasn't a bit cold, and Mother was driving eighty miles an hour in her underwear and bra and wet hair matted against her face. I started laughing and then she started too so that the little birdsound escaped, and pretty soon she was doing ninety.

"We're never going back," she said. "We're riding off into the goddamned North Dakota sunset, we really are. So what do you say? We'll establish residence, then you can start up at the great University of North Dakota. Jesus, *yes*."

"But how are we going to get out of this car?" I said.

"We'll just walk out. We'll walk right out in broad daylight if we have to. Over there everybody does it. You can do what you want there. People leave you alone. You can do whatever the hell you feel like and really it's all right, it's fine, it's just fine."

I could see her eyes welling up.

"What's the hurry?" I said.

"Honey, life's too damned short."

We were doing better than one hundred ten miles an hour, and I knew she was going to let it go as fast as it could go, until the engine blew the hood off or we flew off the road. Everything was going by so fast, we might as well have been in Montana already. I told her we were going to get ourselves killed, or maimed. She started crying, and then laughing, and then she slowed down.

"Look at me," she said. "You know, mothers used to tell their daughters to mind their underwear in case of a horrible accident and strangers standing around looking up their dresses. My own mother actually told me that, I swear. I guess men will see whatever they can just as long as it's not buried yet. You know how men are. Boy, if Grandma could see me now."

"It doesn't matter what anybody sees," I said to her, grinning, and glad we slowed. "You can be falling right out of your underwear as far as I'm concerned."

"Well, thank you very much for that. Now let's explain that to your father, all right?"

When we got home, we slipped inside through the kitchen and there was Father, seated at the table, waiting. He was cleaning a pistol I know his brother had given to him, but I'm sure Mother had never seen it. My father was such a big man, the kitchen chair had all but disappeared beneath him, and the pistol looked small and ridiculous.

We felt ridiculous standing there before him, me all skin and bone, Mother in her underwear, like outlaws before the judge. First thing he wanted was the keys to the Impala. She feigned like she was going to drop them in her bra. Suddenly he raised the pistol to her face.

"Well, what is it?" she said. His hand was shaking. "I'm not one of your boys, you know."

She gave him the time he needed to shoot her, then walked on by. He hadn't a thing to say to me, so I followed her upstairs where she went straight into my room and threw herself on the narrow bed and cried. I switched on the reading lamp and read to her from a magazine, to calm her. Still, she wouldn't calm. I rocked her in my lap. Of course I was seventeen and could take good care of her if I needed to. After a while, the two of us fell asleep together.

When I wakened, it was night, just like now. The house was still, just like now. Mother was sitting up, staring at the door. It was cracked open and Ellen's face was in it. At first, it looked like my own. Then Father appeared behind her and moved her out of view.

"Stay away from those two," he said, and closed the door.

I had an idea where the gun was now, and so I finished my tea without rushing it and went back to the TV room. There, behind Father's chair, were the four shelves of books he called his library. I had to pull every one of them off before I found the pistol, which was strapped into a leather holster. I checked the chamber. There were two bullets in it.

I went back through the kitchen and out into the yard. The black car hadn't moved its position. With the window light behind me, I was silhouetted up against the white house with a pistol hanging from my arm, and should have scared the bejesus out of them.

I waited to give them the time they needed, then raised the pistol slowly and fired a shot over the car. It hit a low branch on the sycamore tree.

The headlights went on. Then the engine. A door flew open and Ellen stepped out. She marched across the yard right past me and into the house, banging the screen door behind her. The black car pulled around the circle, its lights cutting across me, and then back out of the drive. I followed it down the barrel of the gun until there was only the two back lights, like flames, finally snuffed out in the distance.

I went back inside, turned out all the yardside lights, and went upstairs. Ellen was safe in her room, the door shut behind her. Maybe she was packing a suitcase. Maybe she was crying. Maybe she was waiting for me to tell her again about what we were going to do.

I still had the pistol in my hand. It had taken on weight. Before I went in, I stepped back into my room and slid it out across the bare floor and under the bed.

4.

Gil drove Ellen home one night after work—I saw his car from the window—and the next afternoon he and Randy showed up and tossed the football around in the yard. Both had played line for the Spartans, blocking and tackling as the mood hit them, but today they were real hotshots. Today they were hiking and throwing and leaping and watching the numbers change on the scoreboard.

After a while I came outside with cold Cokes.

"Jesus, we thought you'd locked yourself in," Gil said. "You have something to pump up this ball with?"

"I've got a pump but no needle," I said, and I tossed the ball out to Randy who turned the wrong way for it.

When he came back he said, "There's something definitely weird about playing football in the middle of April. All your instincts leave you."

"Right," said Gil.

Then Randy plunked himself into one of the wicker chairs and fell right through the seat of it. The broken cane closed in on him and held him tighter the harder he tried to stand up. Gil was beside himself. He doubled over like he had been shot in the stomach, and when he finally came up for air, Randy had fallen through another chair and was trotting around with it locked to his hips. They had been left out all winter and I suppose the whole bunch of them were rotten.

When I looked away across the yard and up the road, I spotted Tom walking toward the house. He bounced straight up and down like a wide receiver trotting back to the huddle.

Randy escaped the chair and scooped up the football. Talking too fast, he said that Tom came into Good Riley's last night at eight o'clock without saying anything to anybody and sat in the booth next to the telephone. Ellen came over, they talked, he ordered something and she brought it to him. He took an hour to eat it. She came with the bill and he ordered something else.

"You didn't hear what they were saying?"

"It was real private," Gil said. "There wasn't anybody who could have heard anything. They were whispering. All we know is that Ellen wrote something down, and then minutes later she brought stuff out to him."

"Onion rings," Randy said. "Root beer."

"When he finished that, she handed him the bill, but he just ordered something else, and off she went again. The sonofabitch held enemy territory right up til closing time."

"A four-hour dinner," Randy said. "Sixteen courses."

"Harvey's cousin never showed his face. She and Tom sat outside for more than an hour. They were talking, but Tom looked sick, and anybody could see the situation was hopeless. Those two weren't going anywhere. The cousin—he might have been lurking out in the dark. Who knows? Tom hasn't got a car anymore. So Randy and I drove up and offered them a ride. Randy and Tom both sat up front riding shotgun."

"She got delivered safe and sound," Randy said.

"Yes, I saw you drive up."

"There's nothing we won't do for motherhood," Gil said.

"Hey, Tom!" Randy shouted.

Tom was now in range, so Randy threw him a long pass that wobbled badly and fell short. Tom picked it up. I could see he was out of breath. When he was close enough he threw it at me and I caught it.

"That's a helluva long walk, Tom," I said.

"Maybe you've got a car you don't need."

Then Randy said, "So, did you catch up with the cousin or what?"

"He's none of my business anymore."

"Well, he's *into* your business," Gil said, "since you left some business unfinished."

"I'm saying it's none of my business."

I stood my ground, spinning the ball between my palms. Of course I knew Tom hadn't walked all the way out here to fool with those guys.

"Goddamnit, I'm not doing your dirty work anymore," he said to me. "Because I don't care. *You hear me?*" All of a sudden his face was boiling. "Maybe you forgot she's your sister. Maybe you just fucking forgot. What do you guys think? You think he forgot it was his own sister?"

I threw the ball real sharp into his face. Then he was on me. He came so fast and hard even Gil and Randy couldn't have stopped him. Suddenly I was down, and Tom was pounding my nose and jaw, and when I tried to rise up he cracked me with his head. Then I just let him hit me. He was crying and furious and no one was going to stop him. I just lay back and tried not to mind it. When he did stop, it was like a whole team getting off of me.

I sat up and brought him into focus. Randy and Gil were somewhere off to the side of him.

"Let *him* get her back," he said.

"She's gone?" Gil asked.

"Right."

"With Harvey's cousin?"

"One witness says so."

Tom turned away and started out across the yard. I got hold of the football and stood up. He was still in range. I said something to him and threw it at him, a long spiraling ball, and he turned just in time to catch it.

"There goes that football," Randy said.

That was all either one of them said. They drove out the drive and caught up with Tom and he got in, and I turned and went into the house.

I was going to wash my face but it hurt too much, so I went upstairs and lay down. I lay very still with my eyes wide open. Then Ellen came sailing across the ceiling.

When I awoke it was twilight already. My face was in agony. I went outside and finally got the car started and drove out to the highway, going east. I passed a couple of motels, then the Alderwood Inn. My car was no Impala, but I pressed the accelerator flat to the floor and got it up to eighty and then a hundred before I crossed Crook County line and into the desert. I slowed. There wasn't a light anywhere. Not even one house. Of course there's no way to tell which way they go, when they go. And out here, there's no left or right. There's only a dark that won't quit, all the way to Minnesota.

ANOTHER LIFE

1.

My first evening in Paris I walked over to boulevard St-Germain. It was late spring so already many of the cafés and restaurants reached far out onto the crowded sidewalks. There the stream of us either spilled over the curb or suddenly narrowed and jammed up almost to a standstill. Everyone sitting out front at the small round tables was drinking and talking and looking very earnestly at each other and also looking past each other. The French women had strong, beautiful legs and they knew how to cross them. I walked over to rue Bonaparte, looked in at a hotel there, then came back up to St-Germain-des-Pres. I found a table at Les Deux Magots where it is said that Jean-Paul Sartre wrote *Being and Nothingness*. I envisioned him sitting away from the noisy street in the corner, his back turned, his face cockeyed and buried in paper and three packs of Gauloises. There was nothing on the menu I wanted, so after a glass of pastis, I tried to apologize to the waiter, left a ridiculous tip, and got up. I crossed to the less crowded south side of the boulevard and walked back in the direction of St-Michel. I remembered an English bookshop in the area that used to be open at night. But after searching for twenty minutes, I lost interest and ended up in front of the Cinema Odéon.

I stood on the busy sidewalk next to a woman who, like myself, was looking up at the row of six film posters over the ticket window. The woman, in her mid-thirties, was short but very striking, and wore a light, black wool jacket with large pockets she kept taking her hands in and out of. When they were out, they sat firmly on her slender waist, the jacket swept back, breasts thrown forward. She seemed quite anxious, even angry, as if the movie she came all the way across Paris to see—and which film was that, exactly?—was about to begin without her. I was trying to remember the real names of the five American films. Their bizarre French titles made them seem like different films altogether. Once inside, the subtitles, if you looked at them, only confirmed one's confusion. I was reminded that I actually knew someone in Paris, a friend of Ray Walker's, who dubbed films for a living. French to English, English to French. It was difficult to imagine being in two languages—two places, really—at once. I had no ear for any language but my own. When I glanced back down at the woman, it struck me that she and I had stood together long enough now, and close enough, passersby might have mistaken us for the sort of husband and wife who, locked in the same orbit, never have to look at each other. Of course I looked at her. Her dark, Mediterranean eyes—possibly Algerian—paced back and forth like panthers in a cage. Hollywood, it seems, offered her no refuge. Hollywood *or* Poland. And yet it was clear—I could see the bone-white knuckles peeking out of her jacket sleeves—this woman needed to make up her mind, *quick*. She wanted to act, queue up, sit it out with all the others in the strange dark of the theater.

I had an old impulse to rescue her. My former wife, Carol, believed that anyone entering a movie theater alone was certifiably desperate. The fire alarm's gone off, she said. Don't you hear it? *Somebody's burning with loneliness.* In the dark, that flasher loneliness, she knew, would expose itself. It would molest, or commit suicide, or murder and murder again until somebody recognized it, flipped on the lights, screamed for help. One of our several marriage-saving rituals required that whenever the urge was there, in either of us, to slip off alone to the movies, into the gloom of that dark wood, that was the signal we should high-tail it for bed and our own blue movies under the sheet.

I had no such ambitions for this woman at the Cinema Odéon. I had been in Paris only a few hours and had told myself I wanted to stretch out my economy-class legs on the long boulevard. On the other hand, I know now I really had been searching, womanward, and this is where it would begin, with her.

I asked her, *"Vous aimez les films americains?"*

An interminable moment passed until she looked up and said, "Yes, of course. Why not?"

As it turned out, this was pretty much all she could say in English. My French was strictly grammar-book, but I usually made myself understood by a sympathetic listener. I told her with accompanying nose-pinching gestures that I had seen all five American films and they were awful, every last one of them. *"Terrible,"* I said. *"Ennuyeux."* She searched my face, then turned anxiously back to the film posters. The Polish film was about peasants. The bandana'd head of the peasant woman, a mother, was as round and weary as a tractor wheel. Her children, a choir of six, gathered in the lower right hand corner. The woman's husband has been taken forcibly from his workplace at the factory by the police. But thanks to a misunderstanding, she believes he has run off with Katya, who disappears the same day. She waits for him to come to his senses. But three years later, a simple man in the village asks to marry her. He loves the six children as if they are his own. They live happily for two years. Then the first husband, finally released from prison, returns home where the poor woman is now dying of cancer. No, not cancer. Enough is enough, for chrissakes. That he has returned at all, after such an absence, is a sufficient dilemma.

For some reason I first said to the woman, *"Menage,"* and she jumped a little. *Manger,* I meant. Would she like to have dinner with me? When I made an idiotic gesture with my fingers, like a chimp stuffing berries into its mouth, she nodded, glanced back longingly at the posters, and said she was not very hungry—*"Je n'ai pas faim"*—but yes, if I wanted, we could go to a café.

We crossed St-Germain and headed down Mazarine. I had a vague memory of a nice, quiet café near the intersection with rue Danton. Though the woman was really quite short, she walked very fast with her hands jammed into the pockets of her jacket.

Her name, she said, was Edwidge. I had no reason to doubt it. I told her my name was Jack—*Jacques*—and that I was in Paris for only a few days to attend an international conference on Ernest Hemingway at the American University of Paris. She had not heard of the American University of Paris, but she had heard too much about Hemingway, that he was an egotist, a brute, a womanizer, and three or four other things I couldn't translate. For a second I imagined she turned away to spit on the sidewalk.

There was no café at rue Danton—in fact, no rue Danton—but a bistro on rue Dauphine looked lively and interesting, so we stopped there and managed to find the last table, close to the bar. I said something like, "*Voila*, so here we are," and glanced around cheerfully. In fact, the place was crowded and noisy, with a particularly boisterous gang of eight men rubbing up against us at the next table. I was going to apologize when a waiter brushed by us. Edwidge caught his sleeve and I quickly asked for a pastis and she ordered a bottle of Bordeaux.

When the wine came, she asked me was I a *professeur*. I said that I was, but that I was also a writer of *romans*. This didn't impress her one wit. Her fiancé, Jean, she said, spoke eleven languages, including Greek, Croatian, Arabic, and English. I asked, "Is he a translator?" " Perhaps," she said, though I don't think she understood my question. "If he is a translator," I said, "I would be very interested in speaking with him."

The pastis came and, imprudently, I downed a good half of it in one shot. The seductive licorice taste and smoothness made you forget how quickly it would knock you over. Edwidge gulped her Bordeaux and smiled vaguely, her gaze wandering around the room. A hulking, mustached man in the group near us caught her eye and smiled. I took this opportunity to explain to Edwidge that for several years now I had been looking for someone to translate my three novels. I was not happy with any of them, and hoped that a translator would improve them. In fact, what I wanted, I said, narrowing my eyes, were three entirely different novels, novels that I had not myself written, but which had my name on them, three new novels I could really be proud of. Obviously the language would be entirely different. But if the translator also wanted to change some of the characters, any of them, in fact, that would be fine with me. The stories themselves, which were banal and predictable, needed to be more imaginative, more compelling. I explained to her that the right translator—and it may very well be Jean, her fiancé—could give me another life as a writer. "Just imagine," I said, "all new books." On the other hand, perhaps she, Edwidge, not Jean, the fiancé, should translate. After all, she had the considerable advantage of not speaking two words of English.

She had flinched painfully at every mention of Jean, but otherwise I was having a damned good time when the waiter stopped by to fill her wine glass again, take her order for another bottle, and open for both of us a large, hand-scribbled menu. She looked it over with the same expression of cosmic paralysis as she had the six film posters. As she sipped her wine, her breasts rose and fell in a way I was just beginning to fully appreciate. I raised a toast.

"To these beautiful, succulent, melon-ripe globes, under your silky white blouse."

She nodded and I clinked her glass. Now several of the men from the group next door were at full attention. They were staring at her as if I had just ripped her blouse off. She looked back at them, tried out a different smile on each, and then, in an amazing transformation, her whole expression changed. Suddenly she had the wide-eyed, panicked look of someone caught in the cyclopean headlight of a fast-approaching train. Her hand actually flew up in defense.

A sob roared out. It rolled over her and her breasts shook wildly in the silk blouse. The giant man behind her rose, reached out and put his hand on her shoulder. She sobbed and shook and wiped her nose across the full length of her forearm. Then she started in on Jean.

Jean was a beast, she said in so many words. She spoke so rapidly now, all I could do was pick up snippets of it, a word here, a phrase here, a miscellany of dramatic gestures, and paste them together as best I could. The fellows at the next table were let in on it. Those nearest, including the hovering mustached man, turned their chairs around. She had lived with Jean, she said, off and on for fifteen years, happily and also miserably, and they had been officially engaged now for three years. She waved her hand in the air to show everyone the ring. It was gold with a black stone of some sort, possibly onyx. They had a very nice apartment in the 20th *arrondissement* and could walk to the zoo. But a few months ago, Jean began to stay out late. She thought he was drinking with his friends. That was all right, she said. What did she care? She was not going to be a bitch about it. Men will be men. But one night he did not come home. She thought something terrible had happened to him. She waited and waited and thought of killing herself. When he finally returned, he gave no explanation and only hit her, next to her left eye, so that she had to wear some ridiculous sunglasses in the middle of January. Then he disappeared again, for a week, and when he returned he had a young girl with him, a prostitute from Algeria. Jean said he wanted to help her make a new life for herself. The girl moved in. Edwidge could not communicate with her. She was speaking another language, and all she did was laugh and turn her back. She ate everything in the apartment.

The giant man had folded his arms across his considerable chest and was listening sympathetically, occasionally nodding. But two of his friends had smirks on their faces. Edwidge paused a moment when the waiter stopped by to take our dinner order. *"Encore un moment,"* I said. He looked at Edwidge as if she were to blame for something, which I frankly resented, and then turned away.

Edwidge threw back a full glass of Bordeaux.

The young girl—Marais was her name, or Marie—she was only fifteen—was nothing more than a shameless prostitute who paraded *la de da* stark naked around the apartment all day showing off her young figure and exposing herself in front of the window for everyone on the boulevard. Of course it was very obvious—did they think she, Edwidge, was a complete fool?—that Jean and the girl were lovers, if that is the right word for it. Can you believe it?

To my surprise, the giant man appeared to be shocked. His eyes narrowed and he inhaled deeply, like he was about to lose his patience. His friends, the two smirkers, were now shaking their heads.

They, Jean and Marie, tried to be secret about it at first—was she a blind, stupid old woman?—but after a week they didn't care and made love openly, in the kitchen next to the toaster, on the floor behind the sofa, outside the door in the hall when once she locked them out. Marie was young and could make love all day, if that's what you want to call it, and when they weren't doing it, she was eating like some wild animal, and who was going to pay for it?

"Look," I interrupted, leaning toward her. "Did you tell Jean what you were feeling? That you just can't go on with this life? Believe me, the girl's nothing to him. It's just sex. Anyway, she will get tired of him—Isn't he old enough to be her father?—and leave to find a nice boy her own age."

Edwidge snapped something back at me, which sent several of the men into knee-slapping gawfaws, then burst into tears again. She said she was going crazy. Whenever Jean and Marie were making love, whenever they were stinking up the whole apartment with it, she wanted to kill herself, just to show them.

"*Pourquoi pas?*" one of the men said.

Instead, she said, she ran out and went to the movies. She did this every night. She had seen every movie. All the American ones and also the new Polish one, and now she didn't know what else to do. What do you do when you have seen all the movies in Paris?

She was sobbing uncontrollably, and noisily, when the waiter came by again, stood over us a moment, then abruptly picked up the menu and shook it in my face. "Look, nobody's hungry," I said. I shrugged dramatically. "*Je suis desolé.*" He turned away.

The giant man now had his arm around Edwidge, who was shaking, and one of his friends moved up to assist him. I was beginning to feel like a ninth wheel. One of the two smirkers, a skinny fellow with pop-eyes, got up and actually came around behind me, leaned over me, and put his hand on my shoulder. His breath reeked of whisky and cheap cigarettes.

"My friend," he whispered in English. "They are stupid Albanians. Okay? Jean is a *maquereau*. A pimp. This woman is a whore. The girl is their daughter. I'm afraid you won't have good luck tonight."

I let that sink in. When I turned around, the man had disappeared, I assumed down the winding stairs to the toilet.

I found a five hundred franc note in my wallet and quietly slid it under my pastis glass. Edwidge saw this, her tears froze for a moment I will never forget, then turned her face away just long enough, thank God, for me to get up and leave.

I had no idea, really, why the man with the pop-eyes should have made up such a grotesque story, unless he believed, because my French was so terrible, I would fall for it. I never had a daughter, though I had imagined it a thousand times. Carol and I had been so mad with passion, night and day, to have one, a daughter or a son. In Paris, we had imagined everything was possible.

I took a back route to my hotel along St-Andre-des-Arts, then left on Grands Augustins to the quai. The traffic on the quai was merciless—all the race cars were armed with madmen and killers—but after a while I managed to cross over to the Seine. I walked east toward Notre-Dame. In the distance, the two steepleless towers, recently cleaned, were white as ghosts. I stopped at Petit Pont to look at the river. I could see lovers down in the dark, just like in the postcards.

2.

Claire Stewart was staying at Hotel Esmerelda also. She was exiting the tiny velvet-chaired lobby just as I was entering, with a terrific hangover, and we exchanged hurried smiles, though I'm sure she didn't know me from Adam. She had the dark-rooted, frazzled blond hair of a woman who, wakened by a bad dream, suddenly sits up in bed. I had attended two conferences, including an MLA in

Chicago, where she gave incisive, provocative papers—one on D.H. Lawrence which argued he had never brought Frieda Lawrence to orgasm—and most of us were too intimidated to raise a challenging question. She stood by herself, which I admired, without disciples. Like everyone else, I'm sure, I was anticipating her inevitable face-off with Professor William Buchanan. Buchanan was the conference chair, editor of the Hemingway newsletter, and arguably the leading—or most prolific—Hemingway scholar in the western world. "Buck" Buchanan, as he preferred to be called, had persuaded a lot of very innocent people, including himself, that he *was* Ernest Hemingway.

I took the RER out to Pont de l'Alma and walked up avenue Bosquet to the University, where I registered an hour late and, I'm afraid, missed the first round of papers. The book display tables were upstairs in the central foyer. A good many forests had been destroyed and oxygen lost on Hemingway scholarship, and it had gotten worse since the psychoanalysts and deconstructionists had discovered his feminine side and dragged him out of the closet. I suspected the photos of Hemingway, which changed so radically from one book cover to another—Huck Finn on the river up in Michigan to Old Man and the sea—told the real story, which is that Hemingway had many lives and passed into each of them with at least hope and astonishment, and usually with a new wife and beard.

Hemingway had lived in Paris with his first wife Hadley in the early 1920's. Many of the late morning conference papers dutifully focused on the life he had then, and the writing, including *The Sun Also Rises* and some of his finest short stories, which came out of it. Walter Smith and Dave Hendrickson, whose recent books I had thumbed through, argued, from different premises and texts, that Hemingway's fear of women was at root a distrust of the imagination and the life mysteries it probed. Edna Waites, who had managed to get to Paris from some remote Pony Express stop in Texas, revisited the thesis that Hemingway felt women sucked vital fluids out of a writer and abandoned him on a desert dizzy with mirages, which is to say romanticism. A young graduate student from Johns Hopkins—Marianna, her hair in bangs—focused on Hadley's tragic transformation from lover to mother that cost her Hemingway's affection and their marriage. When Buck Buchanan, sitting in the back row with his arms folded, suggested that all of Hemingway's four wives were better off for having married him, Marianna timidly agreed that at least they had more marketable memories.

Claire Stewart gave her paper on Hemingway and Cezanne when Buck scheduled it, just before lunch when everybody was starving to death. Standing at the podium, she looked a little wild, more frightened than frightening. It was the hair, of course, but also the restlessness of sea-green eyes that seemed trapped inside her gold-rimmed glasses. The focus of her analysis was "Big Two-Hearted River," Hemingway's highly symbolic, post-war story about Nick Adams' effort to heal his psychic wounds in the trout streams of his early youth and innocence. There wasn't anyone at the conference, including young Marianna, who hadn't read and taught the story exactly as Hemingway himself said it should be, that it was all about Nick "coming back from the war but there was no mention of the war in it."

Claire Stewart combed through the story line by line, and argued that it wasn't really about the war at all, and that there was absolutely no symbolism in it. The conventional symbol-heavy, war-haunted interpretation rested on western culture's machismo, its boorish insistence on subjugating, shackling, and colonizing human experience, and transform-ing it, against its will, into meaning. The story, if we would only "open our eyes and look," she said with sudden passion, was "painted," like a Cezanne, and we—meaning all of us sit-ting out there with our mouths open and parched—had mis-read it exactly because a *reading* of anything denies us "access to the real."

When it was over, and before anyone dared to ask a ques-tion, Buck Buchanan, still in the back row, stood up, and more or less announced that this was obviously an original and stimu-lating paper which—since it was now nearly one o'clock—we could all chew up—he meant "on," I think—over lunch. Everyone around me jumped up and left the room.

Claire Stewart arranged her papers and slid them care-fully into a beige folder. The folder went into a leather shoul-der bag that she snapped shut. Then those green eyes swept the room and she walked out.

Outside, I looked for her up and down avenue Bosquet. Several of the participants, including Marianna, stood nearby under a tree, gathered around Buck Buchanan, but when I asked them had they seen Claire Stewart, they pointed in four different directions.

"We're moseying over to Chez l'Ami Claude's," Buck said. "All the gals have deserted us."

"I'm here," Marianna said, raising her hand like a shy teenager.

The troupe of us, with Buck taking the lead, walked back to the river, then down the quai under the Eiffel Tower. Chez l'Ami Claude was a busy, homey place. Buck embraced the stout, mustached proprietor, whom I assume he knew. Tables were shoved together. And before we realized it, Buck was ordering for everybody.

When the carafes of red wine arrived and glasses were filled, Doug Silverman raised a toast. Silverman was a hotshot from Tufts and one of four or five unabashed Neanderthals at the conference who, in the wee hours, would be drinking themselves unconscious in several of "Hem's" favorite watering holes in the Latin Quarter and up on Montparnasse.

"To Professor Stewart. I was just about this far—*this far*—from being swallowed up by her cockeyed argument."

"I'm sure with her it's all a matter of inches," Dave Hendrickson said, slyly. The allusion was to the "Matter of Measurements" chapter in *A Moveable Feast* in which Hemingway reportedly examines Scott Fitzgerald's genitals and assures him he's up to standard.

"She's a very demanding scholar," Walter Smith said, raising his own toast.

"Here, here," I said.

Buck raised his glass. Then, apparently dying of thirst, he pretty much threw the whole thing down in one shot.

"Hell, Claire's okay," he said. "She's fine. We've crossed paths a few times. She likes to keep to herself, out there at the old Esmerelda. But Hemingway, he would have liked her. Take my word for it. He would have hunted her down. Would have known where to find her soft underbelly."

"Okay, then," Silverman said. "To soft underbellies whereever we can flush them out."

"Here, here," Marianna said. Everyone turned to her. "I just mean I'm still here, here."

"Yes you are," Buck said. "And thank the Lord. Which

reminds me. There is another thing that demands to be here, and that's the *gateau Basque*. Trust me, you're not going to want to miss it."

Walking back to the University, I asked myself how he knew where Claire Stewart was staying, though of course the obvious answer was that she had made that known on her registration form, just as I had. Still, it didn't sit well. Nor, for that matter, did the duck confit and *gateau Basque*, so after the first afternoon paper—Silverman's catalogue, technical analysis, and interpretation of Hemingway's gun collection, including the shotgun the Old Man blew the top of his skull off with—I slipped away, hurried back down avenue Bosquet, and took the long, brain-clearing walk up the Quai d'Orsay to the Tuileries Garden.

I was looking forward to the Maillols, the extraordinary early 20th-century sculptures, but several I remembered from the gardens only a few years ago were now gone from the grassy squares along the gravel paths, removed, perhaps, to the nearby Musée d'Orsay across the Seine. Instead, there were some lovely girls there, real ones, sitting crossed-legged on their coats or sweaters. Students, I assumed, hair hanging over their books. Half my age, at least. Out of reach. Still, my "falling woman" was there, waiting in her place near the east end of the gardens. She was a Maillol, but I had named her myself: a larger-than-life, voluptuous, horizontal woman, eyes wide, arms and legs thrown out, as if she were falling from a great height. I stood there a long time looking at her. She was so beautiful, so sensual, and, I think, so frightened in her fall—a fall that was not entirely graceful—, my first impulse was to catch her somehow, come to her rescue. Of course I would have been crushed by the weight of her, even had she been made of flesh and blood.

I wanted to touch her, so I approached, stepping lightly on the dry grass. I reached out. My fingers moved over her classical face, the startled eyes, then down along her taut waist and up over her belly and hips. Life there, I thought. Planets, whole galaxies swirling within. Her powerful thighs, also the subtle rise between, were smooth and cool.

"You can be arrested for that," Claire Stewart said.

I whipped around. Claire Stewart stood, her feet crossed, at the edge of the gravel.

"Really?" I said.

"I was thinking of 'aesthetic arrest,' of course. As Aquinas meant it."

"Well," I said, tip-toeing off the grass, "that's very generous. Thank you."

"So tell me—it's Jack, isn't it?—is she the one you came to Paris for, or only a reminder of the one?"

"I'm afraid she's only a hunk of matter in space and time," I said.

"And yet, no matter the police, it says, 'Touch me.'"

I smiled. She was right, of course. I had needed to touch its private parts. Might have probed further if she hadn't brought the cops in.

"So who is she?" Claire Stewart asked again.

"Hilary," I said. And Hilary's name just sprang out like that. "A girl, a young friend of my wife's, I happened to meet up with here in Paris."

"You were lovers?"

"I wanted to marry her."

"Paris is where things begin for people."

Yes, I thought. Carol and I also began here, honeymooned here, marked this place with memories. In the geology of memory, that was the deeper layer. And Hilary—she might be here now, in Paris, somewhere on this cool, late spring surface of the city.

"So tell me, what began here for you, Claire Stewart?"

"This is actually my very first time in Paris," she said. "Which still amazes me. I'm not even sure where the Musée d'Orsay is."

"Thataway," I said, nodding toward the river.

"I want to see the Cezannes. Will you show me?"

"I can't imagine I can show you anything."

"My god, you're not afraid of me like the others?"

"We're all cowards—even Buck Buchanan."

Claire Stewart laughed, just the throaty laugh I would have expected, and put her gold-rimmed glasses away in her leather handbag.

"Buck's all right," she said. "He's all cock, of course. Cock and big hairy balls. But that's his charm."

"It is?"

We headed up past the Musée de l'Orangerie and out of the park into the Place de la Concorde, crossed the river, then walked back along the Quai Anatole France. Claire Stewart was chatty and animated, really more generous with her conference colleagues than I would have expected, or they deserved, and, I assumed, genuinely curious about my history here, a history I judiciously abbreviated or embellished, depending on how painful it was to tell it. I finally told her about Carol, how we met, Carol's enormous promise as a writer—more promise than I had, or have—what Paris feels and smells and tastes like to those who come to it very young and very wide-eyed and naïve—as it was for the young Ernest and Hadley, I said—and it really was a moveable feast for lovers if they ate only the best of it, and left early.

"So where's Hilary?" she asked when we reached the Orsay. "You don't have the look of a man who's married."

"What look is that?"

"Panicked, like someone in a free-falling elevator," she said. "You have the forlorn look of a fellow who's suddenly free to choose his own bed."

"I fear I may be already lying in several beds."

"And Hilary?"

I shrugged, as if I were trying to nudge a boulder off my shoulders.

"She ran off with somebody else."

"We'll do that," Claire Stewart said, searching for her glasses.

The Cezannes were up the long escalator on the top floor of the museum in a mostly empty room between the Renoirs, which had attracted a large, noisy crowd of tourists Claire Stewart and I managed to navigate through, and, on the other side, the wild and wise Van Goghs.

"Of course I've seen several of the still-lifes elsewhere," she said. "But these really do take your breath away."

"And freeze your heart, some say."

"Poor Jack," she said, without taking her eye from a painting, an arrangement of apples and bowls on an old table. "Do they really freeze your heart?"

"Oh, it's still tick-tocking," I said.

"People think Cezanne was an intellectual painter, perhaps because intellectuals seem to appreciate him most. But he really was quite the contrary, you know. He only wanted to paint the body of the world, the body naked and new, so new it was still being born. The world's body before we dressed it and hid it in ideas and emotions. Lawrence was a madman and hypocrite about many things, but he was right about Cezanne, about these apples of Cezanne's. They are simply and radically there to be seen, touched by our eyes, tasted with our open mouths. That's why, in the 1890's, he stopped painting women. He knew that he, and we, could not see a woman's body except through the lens of our ideas about it. Without the lust of ideas, I should say. The mother, the daughter, the lover, the cradle of civilization, the beautiful, the whore, the doting face in the vanity mirror, the sniveling, weak-willed, pathetic little wacko at the other end of the dinner table—all these women, or images women fulfill and are enslaved by, have held us back not from freedom, dignity, or even greatness, which are only more ideas, but from being, from being right here, for godsakes, in this world, as real and substantial a piece of matter as a hunk of clay or, you see there, Jack, one of those apples. Don't you want to touch it? Don't you want to lap your tongue around its redness? Well? Don't you wish you could, right here and now, before the thought-police swoop in and nab you?"

"Yes," I said. And that was all I said.

In the Van Gogh room, a young woman, dark-haired and slender, drifted in and out of view. I suppose for a second I had a vague idea it was Hilary, that at least it could have been, though I quickly realized it would have to be Hilary some years ago when we had found ourselves suddenly together in Paris, in another life. Still, I took a few steps away from Claire Stewart—perhaps left her hot and hanging, I realize now, as Mr. Lawrence had Frieda—and wandered across the threshold into the Van Goghs. The young woman was in the corner in front of one of the self-portraits. Her dark, short-haired head tilted first left, then right, like a metronome. Her legs were slender, long, promising. I could not see what I could not see. What intimation of matter under that black skirt and blouse, under a silk camisole, under demi-bra, the black, lace-bordered *culotte collante*?

When Claire Stewart suddenly approached me, I said, "I have an engagement tonight, I'm afraid."

"You do? Not another woman, I hope."

"Only an old friend."

"Well, there's so much more to see here," she said. "Thank you for bringing me along this far."

"Entirely my pleasure."

"Yes."

I turned back into the Cezannes, then quickly through the Renoirs and out to where I had stepped off the escalator. The escalator was only coming up, so I found the stairs and took them all the way down two at a time.

I decided to find dinner over on the Right Bank, some small place along rue Saint-Honore, but once there, I found myself racing down it, in and out of the late, after-work crowd, finally to Rivoli, then clear out past Hotel de Ville. I turned up rue Vieille du Temple into the old Jewish quarter and the Marais, and after only a few minutes' search, found the restaurant on rue des Rosiers.

Nothing had changed, not the thick, white tablecloths or the rich, eastern smells from the open kitchen. Carol and I had wandered into this place our first long night in Paris, and back again our last. I felt I deserved now to be here again, this time around alone at a small table far from the door. If in Paris I was going to allow myself to remember, to search and remember, she would have to be there too, waiting for me. She had the prior claim, after all. I ate slowly. I tasted. I looked at people. I smiled a little when eyes met mine. I told the waiter, as best I could, that years ago—and so on and on. And all I could think of is how I had hurt her and deserted her and left her to fall alone for—what was it?—almost a year, until she met Homer Corn. Homer Corn, for chrissakes. What could be more ridiculous? Homer Corn from Nebraska. State Farm Insurance. That he was there—I picture him a starry night in an open field, racing back and forth like a lunatic, his gaze heavenward, searching—that he was there with his hands up when she came flying out of the dark.

It was only a ten-minute brisk walk across the tip of Ile Saint-Louis behind Notre-Dame, over the bridge, and down the Quai de Montebello to hotel. The young man at the desk buzzed me in, I attempted a few pleasantries, and then he informed me, as though I had at some point inquired about it, that Madame Stewart had been up in her room for more than an hour.

I asked him what room she was in.

"Quarante-trois," he said. "*Quarante-trois*."

I took the ancient two-person elevator up to the fourth floor. An elderly couple—they looked Dutch—stood in their rumpled night clothes outside their door. When I approached, the woman nodded at something down the hall, then the two of them stepped back inside and carefully closed the door. Claire Stewart's room was two doors away, and a terrific noise was coming from it. Inside, something was banging, banging against the wall, and a woman's voice moaned and cried, cried and moaned, then shrieked suddenly and shouted *Jesus* so that a chill shot up my spine. Then deep, throaty groans I couldn't swear were Claire's or any woman's. Of course my first impulse was to break in the goddamned door—there had to be at least two people in there—and find out what was going on. And I was about to do just that, or something close to it, when that moan came again, long and rolling like a sea tide, a wave about to crash against some Mediterranean rocks, and I suddenly understood, and stopped. I stepped back, as if from a precipice, and took the steep, winding stairs down to the third floor. I unlocked my room and slipped inside.

I am not certain that Claire Stewart's room was directly above my own—I think we both had shallow, wrought-iron balconies overlooking Notre-Dame—but the racket was pouring through the ceiling and, I was convinced, shaking my fragile old metal bed frame. I lay there with my teeth on edge, thinking of that pompous Buckeroo Buchanan, Mr. All-Cock-and-Hairy-Balls, standing up in the back of the lecture room, making his goddamned point, and promising, if I remember right, to chew her up after lunch. Well, it was already a couple of hours past dinner.

After a while, I just couldn't stand it and went down to the lobby.

"Going out?" the young man said.

"Yes. I'm dying of thirst."

"Key?"

I slapped my key on the countertop, went out, and walked up into the Latin Quarter to search for an Irish pub I knew, Finnegan's Wake. It was at the Place de la Contrascarpe that I ran into the Neanderthals. The four of them were out of it. They had drunk themselves up and down rue Mouffetard, picked up two Sorbonne co-eds for fifteen minutes, and lit a small bonfire of twisted newspapers just around the corner in front of Hemingway and Hadley's first real Paris apartment. I gathered the fire blew out of control for a minute and took away half of Silverman's left pant leg. He shook it proudly. I asked them could they remember where Finnegan's Wake was. They could indeed. Finnegan's was home base.

I followed them into Finnegan's where they went straight to the bar, addressed the bartender by name, and ordered six pints, which included, I assumed, one for myself. I stood up there with them and watched the dark beer settle slowly and magically, the rich, creamy, sweet head rise to the top.

We carried the pints back around to a table in the corner where Buck Buchanan was seated. Of course I was shocked to see him. Waves of guilt rolled through me, too. I had condemned him for being back there in Hotel Esmerelda, nailing Claire Stewart on the cross of the real, and now that I realized he was here, I found myself wishing he wasn't. Who was I to deny love or lust to anybody? Including Buck Buchanan here, puffing on his fat cigar.

"It's one hundred percent Havana," he said.

3.

I woke, if I had slept at all, at six-thirty and walked up boulevard St-Michel in search of a cup of coffee. There are ten thousand cafés in Paris, but at that hour of the morning the city is like a ghost town—the cafes all hung over and boarded up, the shops asleep behind aluminum fences, the kiosks closed like umbrellas and double padlocked. But around seven, the sweeping starts. The sound of it fills the cool, wet-smelling morning air: the old brooms swishing the tiled café terraces, sweeping the sidewalks, the lime-green brooms rasping the water-flooded gutters down to the dikes of old rolled carpet by the sewers, the whirling brushes and vacuum of the lime-green midget trucks. Nearer eight, the traffic now thick and honking on the boulevard, doors squeal and are latched open, shutters bang against walls, awnings roll out. Waiters stand with hands on their hips out on the sidewalks.

I found my first coffee at a patisserie and carried it and a *pain au raisin* across the street and into the Luxembourg Garden. I walked down to a view of the circular pool and fountain. The green metal chairs were everywhere in the neat rows that would not last the morning. The Palais du Luxembourg rose majestically to the right. Everything was there. I walked along the marble wall, then down the north stairs, and finally settled into a chair under the canopy of trees at Fontaine de Medicis.

Our honeymoon summer in Paris, Carol and I came to this fountain every morning to write. I would have preferred, frankly, to read the *International Herald Tribune* out by the pool where the toy boats were in the late morning and where the pretty girls from the Sorbonne. But she would say, "Dammit, mister—writers write," and open her canary yellow notebook, uncap her fountain pen, and immediately begin to scratch away. I loved to watch her. She was like those girls on the grass in the Tuilleries, her head bowed, the strands of blond hair sweeping the page.

"Okay, so what are you writing?"

"Whatever comes out of me," she said, without looking up. "Whatever I can give up. Won't hurt you to try it, Jack."

"I'm thinking about it."

"No, it comes from right here," she said, her free hand pressing her belly. Then she touched lower. "Here, too."

"Nice place," I said. "May I inquire about visiting hours?"

"Maybe after lunch, my poor mad boy."

"And where should I say I'm going?"

She smiled. "You can call it Minnesota," she said.

She had grown up an only child in Minnesota, and the memories came from there: her old house with the grand porch, her mother and father, the aunts and cousins, all the kids she knew, real events which had been fixed, to the last detail, in her imagination—a train killing a cow on the tracks, a girl-friend whose mother shot herself, a boy she loved who joined the army, the violence of sex in her uncle's bedroom. By lunch, she often had most of a story finished, a good story too, which she would later read to me in bed.

One afternoon that summer, George Whitman himself, proprietor of the Shakespeare & Company bookshop, sold us a copy of Hemingway's *A Moveable Feast* . We brought it up here to the gardens and, facing off in our green metal chairs, our bare feet locked around each other's waists, we took turns reading each chapter aloud.

A Moveable Feast is Hemingway's memoir about his life, his and Hadley's, in Paris. The best parts are about food, but there are also wonderful chapters on F. Scott Fitzgerald, Ezra Pound, and Gertrude Stein. Gertrude Stein, in fact, lived very close to the Luxembourg Garden on rue du Fleurus. When Hemingway and Hadley visited her, her companion Alice B. Toklas would steal Hadley away to another room so that Stein could have Hemingway to herself. In the end, she and Hemingway had a falling out. When he last visits her apartment, unannounced, he overhears Stein upstairs whining and pleading to Alice. We are supposed to imagine Alice's sexual domination of Stein, the self-proclaimed genius. Of course it is almost certain that Hemingway made this up, just as he had made up the "Measurements" chapter about poor Scott Fitzgerald. But when you first read *A Moveable Feast*, none of this matters. If it did not actually happen this way, you are convinced it should have.

We managed to finish *A Moveable Feast* at dusk, just as the park was closing. Carol talked Hemingwayeze all the way down St-Michel. She said we should pretend to be Ernest and Hadley, which meant eating better, and visiting Shakespeare & Company regularly, and making friends with important artists of the day. It also meant my finding a special place all my own to write in, and every day counting the words, and imagining true stories that came from my youth. I said that I liked the eating best, but otherwise she had it all backwards. Because she, not I, was the promising young writer, she should be Hemingway and I should be Hadley. Hadley, I said, was out for a good time. She really *wanted* to be off in the kitchen with Alice, eating brownies. I will wear a dress, if you like, I said. And I will wait at home all day for you to finish writing great literature, and then we will go out to the cafés and have a splendid time together.

"Then, Jack," she said, "*you* will have to have the baby."

"Hey, I don't mind," I said. "I'll do it. It beats the hell out of writing books."

But on the way back to our room on rue du Cherche Midi, she put her arm through mine and said the whole idea was terrible.

"In the real story," she said, "the baby spoiled everything. Suddenly they were three, and when they were three, Paris changed and they changed. It's so sad, you see."

"Then we won't let it happen," I said.

"That was also when Paulette showed up. Remember? Hadley herself brought her into their life."

"So let's forget about it."

"Oh Jack. If there are three of us, that won't spoil it, will it?"

"Which three are you talking about?"

In early September, the Parisians who had been on *vacances* in the south returned to Paris. Now it was a different city, with bustling streets and people hurrying to work. Carol and I said goodbye to a few new friends, spent a last evening in the Marais, and headed back to Iowa.

We had both completed the Writers' Workshop Program at the University of Iowa, but decided now to stay on at the University at least another two years. Carol, who had already published five stories in prestigious literary journals, had been awarded a post-graduate fellowship. I managed to slip unnoticed into the English Department's doctoral program and was asked to teach introductory literature courses. We were very busy and very happy, and, like other students in their late twenties, looked forward to a grown-up life someday—meaning life with a real salary—when she would write all day and perhaps teach if she liked, and I would teach all day and write if I had to.

One afternoon, after lunch, in the late spring of our second year back in Iowa, Carol and I sat across from each other at a crowded study table in the university library. It was her masochistic idea that in this "dreamy hour," she called it— when Hem and Hadley were going at it, remember—we needed the rigid discipline of a silent, public place, something as close to a maximum security prison as we could manage. While she kept pen to paper, I lay back in my torturous chair, *Canterbury Tales* upright on my stomach, my feet propped up between her thighs.

"Don't do that," she said.

"Do what?" I asked for everybody at the table.

"It's really all your fault, mister," she said.

"Of course it is."

Carol looked up, cleared the hair from her face.

"I'm late."

She went back to her story, the paper burning up under her pen. I pulled my feet back onto the floor and sat up.

"Maybe we're just a little early," I said.

In the days that followed, Carol worked with a strange urgency on a new story, as if she were afraid she would lose it if she did not get it out on paper. She said it was like writing down a dream, but in fact it was memory. She called it "The Play House," and it was about the play house her father had built for her in Minnesota and the woman she had actually discovered there, early one morning, sleeping in it. The evening she finished it, she sat cross-legged on the bed and read it to me. At the end of it, I felt sure I would not myself write fiction again. All the weight of it fell from my shoulders. And she, at that moment, was as beautiful as I had ever seen her.

But in the night her period came.

When a child, even an imagined one, dies, the memory of it can grow inside you, and want to be born again.

We worked at it all that summer. That summer, too, we moved to the West Coast where I found my first job as a college teacher. Carol taught an evening fiction writing course in the college's extension school, and wrote during the day. The dozen stories she had written our final years in Iowa were still "out there," swimming around in literary America, searching for journals to take them.

When "The Play House" came back the sixth time, she sat with it in her lap in bed and cried for a long time, until the tears gave way to bitterness.

"I don't know what's wrong with me."

"There's not a damned thing wrong with you," I said, rubbing her feet.

"What they want is for everything to be nice and cozy," she said. "Cozy stories they can curl up with and stroke like cats. Well, I wrote those already and life's not like that. I know it."

"Maybe sometimes it is."

"It's not, Jack. And you would know that if you were writing yourself."

"Hey, come on. I am writing. I'm doing the book on Paris."

She sat up and pulled her feet up under her.

"Real writing, for godsakes. The writing we were finally doing *in* Paris."

"Oh sure, I remember now. The kind nobody wants."

She gave me the look, as if I were an idiot, then turned away and looked out the window. There was nothing out there but the side of somebody's house.

"I don't care about them anymore," she said. "I really don't."

A few days later she began a novel. I knew she was ripe for it. She had the talent for it, but also the grinding discipline and courage she would need for the long haul. And indeed the chapters came. They came quickly at first, then slowly and painfully, and finally in secret.

What I remember is that it began in Minnesota, in childhood. But her heroine, she said, was not herself. She was a girl she knew in school, who came every day on a country bus from a long distance, a village where she lived with her aunt and uncle. One night a woman the uncle had known returned to the village after nearly a ten-year absence. The uncle at first told terrible stories about her, the girl she had been before she left, and the aunt repeated them and embellished them. The stories were wonderful. They were terrible and cruel and funny, and the more the aunt embellished them, the more vividly their young niece imagined her and wanted to be her. Later, she found photographs of the woman in a wood box in her uncle's workshop. The woman, then in her early twenties, raven-haired and beautiful, was always alone in them—posing dramatically on a rock by the lake, her head thrown back like a movie star, or looking up from a game of cards, or glancing back over her shoulders. In one of the photos she was naked in the distance, walking away on a narrow, wooded path, in autumn. The girl had never seen a picture like that, and she was certain it was now fixed in her memory. The story, I knew, would not end in Minnesota. Wherever the woman had been for ten years, who she had been, that would be in there, too. Also, the man—or was it a woman—who held the camera.

Late one night, when she had stopped and the pages had been slipped into a box in a drawer, she sat awhile at the end of the sofa, and I came to her very carefully like a cat and lay my head in her lap.

"Your little heart's beating fast, Jack. I can feel it."

I turned and pressed my face into her belly.

"And you have a perfect, soft body. Dark smell, too. Your nice secret."

"It's not so perfect. I don't care what they said. If it doesn't work."

"Your secret drawer," I said.

"Stop it," she said, and I rolled over. "So what did they

do to you, mister?"

"Well, a very nice, very plump nurse escorted me to a small, white room—a Sahara desert in the eye of a sandstorm, it seemed to me—where she sat me down and handed me a glass jar and what I assume was the hospital copy of *Playboy*, some three years old. Of course I told her that I only read the articles. And she said, 'Keep reading the articles until you're finished,' which I thought was pretty damned funny."

"Who was she? This other woman."

"That's the thing," I said. "It was really, truly eerie. She looked exactly like you."

"Oh, I'm sure."

"Except for the black Stetson."

"Maybe you should invite her over. Isn't she the perfectly healthy woman the doctor was telling us about?"

When she got like this, she would fold her arms and stare straight ahead like a driver speeding past a hitchhiker. And I don't know where she went, where she was going, so solitary, in such a hurry, although sometimes, though less and less often now, she found her way back to her desk, to the pain and the writing that went into the drawer.

At the end of our fourth year on the West Coast, we moved out east to another university and a better job. Research for my book on the expatriate American writers in the Twenties had twice taken us back to Paris. Each time we returned, Carol took up her novel again, and eventually she took it up yet again when we had settled into our new house. I too, at her urging, began writing fiction. I suppose I had found, without searching, a small, shallow vein of melancholy that I could mine, though the digging was still hard and tedious. Whenever I managed to finish a story, Carol read it aloud in bed.

Afterwards, if I asked her, she might show me new sketches from her drawing class—finely rendered leaves, rose petals, plump vases and jars that reminded me of Cezanne—and, sometimes, when we were lucky, we would lie awake a long time in each other's arms.

Several of my little stories made it into magazines, so with Carol on my back, I began a novel. It was not a very long novel and I finished just hours before it was scheduled to kill me. When it was published and reviewed well enough, I began another. By the end of our third year on the East Coast, I had published three books. We celebrated with a trip to Paris, our last together, as it turned out. The truth is, I never took the writing very seriously. I had not written a paragraph I was particularly proud of—certainly nothing I myself enjoyed reading aloud—and I labored in the deep shadow of Carol's own work, the published and unpublished writing I had seen, and the secret pages which came now, like her life, one day at a time.

The two long weekday evenings when Carol was at the studio, I sat at my desk in its dark corner, a vaguely round light over my notebook, and usually managed to fill a dozen pages. But whatever I was writing that particular evening—I can't remember now, really— it could not hold me in place. It had let go, or I had let go, and I drifted up, out of reach of whatever story it was, or might have been, and then held there, suspended in space, levitated, like someone who had died. Where was old Gravity when I needed her? I looked down, like a man hanging over the basket of a hot air balloon, and tried to name everything I saw. But the words would not come, and whatever images there were receded, then vanished into thin air. Nothing materialized. Nothing mattered.

I stood up, backed away from my desk as if there were a loaded gun on it, and went out to the back porch. My yard was out there, on the other side of the screen. That's something. There were trees, too, and a goddamned birdbath. Which proves what? I found the light switch and flipped it on. There now, the whole yard vanished. I sat down in the white wicker chair. Carol kept her drawing materials next to it on the long birch table we had made from a door. Pads of paper: sketches of the trees, the birdbath, the far brick wall and vines I could not see. A dark, polished wood box of charcoal pencils. A new carton of pastels. A metal sharpener. A cosmetic brush. A charcoal dusty cloth. An old hardbound drawing book, closed. Pages torn from magazines. A pile of photos. Tools. Things. The world could be touched by the eye. Even in the dark, touched.

I leafed through the photographs. They were taken at the studio, I assumed. Still-life arrangements on an old table. Apples and pears. Bowls and bottles. Then a photo of a woman, naked—a nude, I should say—her back to us, hands up behind her short, dark hair, standing against a vague background. A young model. Then I saw that Carol had sketched her in charcoal on several pages of the drawing book.

I was still looking when Carol returned home at ten. I stood up, tried to kiss her, and asked her how her class went. She looked tired, her eyes swollen.

"Not tonight," she said. "It's Thursday."

"But you went out," I said.

"Just to the movies. You looked like you wanted to work."

"Well," I said, sitting down again. "That explains it. I almost went mad."

"I don't want you to go mad," she said.

ANOTHER LIFE & OTHER STORIES

"And who's this?" I asked, picking up the photo. "She reminds me of somebody."

"So you've been snooping through my things."

"I needed your things. If you'd rather, I'll rummage through your lingerie drawer."

"She's a student in the class. She needed the money. She was married once. Now she's desperate to go to Paris. You know, to paint or something. To live. I said to her, why not? I gave her Ray and Evelyn's number. She's so sad, Jack. When I listen to her? She breaks my heart."

When Carol went up, I stayed out on the porch awhile. I was thinking of the fountain in the Luxembourg Gardens—not the Medicis, but the grand pool with the spouting fountain in the middle. In summer, in late morning, the old lady puts the boats out, and children carry them over to the pool and push them far into the water with sticks. The sailboats are of every color, and ancient, and the sticks are ancient too, worn smooth, and everything is exactly the same as it was when Hemingway came to the gardens, and even before Hemingway. And the small boats, leaning this way and that in the breeze, sail in toward the fountain until the fountain rejects them and sends them back to the edge.

The lights out, our cold feet touching, I asked her, "Why's she so sad? What's her story?"

"If you have to know," she said.

"Tell me."

"In Maryland, where she was born, where she grew up in a very ordinary sort of way, she knew a boy who was mad for her, and when she was sixteen, they married secretly and ran away to Virginia Beach. But she would not let him make love to her until there was a proper church wedding, with her mother present. Of course this was strange. She says as much herself. She didn't care a whit about church or her mother, but in truth, she was afraid of the boy. She was afraid of his madness, of what might happen to her if she surrendered. They each found a job—he in a movie theater, she at a Buick dealership not far from the beach—and she, at least, was happy for a time. The boy saw all the movies that came to town and described them to her in great detail so that she never had to go herself. After they had been married like this, in this strange way, for six months, a man at the dealership who worked in service came on to her and before she knew it they were in a motel making love. The affair, she said, was short and very noisy, like a string of Chinese firecrackers, but in that time she loved this man heart and soul and could think of nothing in her life but him.

"At home, at night, the mad boy beside her, she felt guilty and sad and kissed him very tenderly, which of course only made things worse. In the months that followed, she met other men: a fellow who lived with his mother and raised llamas, a man who slept in his truck, a university student who was going to be a famous astronomer, a body builder who was afraid of the dark, the red-haired husband of the woman she worked with—and she loved each of them so wholeheartedly when she was with him, making love, or afterwards resting in his hot arms, she was certain it would last forever. But when an affair ended, like just another sad little story she had written, and for a time she was alone again with the boy she'd married, she felt very empty, here inside, without any life at all. On those days she began to let the boy look at her when she undressed and eventually touch her soft skin and then the places he longed for—though naturally this only made her more and more anxious for another lover, someone she could throw her whole aching body around and be with as if no other life were possible. Eventually there were other affairs that only began and went nowhere, and then somehow the word about her got around, and soon—though she searched the whole horizon—there was no one left to love. There was only the foolish, mad boy wide awake beside her in the dark. But one morning, not long ago, she woke and the boy was gone. He'd run off with another woman. Well, she said, a man will do that. Just a few months ago, the papers came from the lawyer."

"She's some lover," I said.

"But she couldn't *receive* love. She couldn't let it in."

"But why not?"

"I think she was afraid of what it might cost her."

"What did she want?"

"Oh Jack. Don't you see? She wanted more than one life."

4.

Late afternoon I woke in an empty lecture room. As far as I could tell, in fact, the whole building was deserted except for young Marianna. She was sitting on the stairs, gathering her papers.

"Hey, I found out you write novels," she called after me.

I stopped and looked back up at her. She sat with her arms around her knees, her eyes fixed on me from under the curtain of dark bangs.

"Let's keep that a secret," I said.

"I don't mind. It's just that it's pretty cool knowing somebody who writes primary sources."

I smiled. We went out to the street together. I found my

little red map book. I needed to figure out the best metro connection to the Bastille.

"First time in Paris?" I said.

"*Oui*. Do I look it?"

"You look very French, in fact."

"Honestly? Like how, exactly? How do I look French?"

I looked up at her, her guileless brown eyes.

"And is the gang here still showing you a good time?"

"Well, sad to say, the fellas have abandoned me. I don't think girls are allowed in the bull ring."

"The hell with them," I said. "And what about the women? Claire Stewart, for example. Professor Waite."

"Women are okay unless you is one."

"Yes, I see what you mean."

"So where are you off to?"

"Well, I'm having dinner at seven with dear old friends in the Bastille."

"Honestly?"

"Honestly. He's an American painter. My wife and I met them our first trip to Paris."

"Professor Stewart said you weren't married."

"That was many years ago, when you were in about the fourth grade."

"You'd be mortified by how much I learned in the fourth grade," she said. "Anyway, I might go dancing tonight. Three very nice Frenchmen asked me just this morning on Pont Neuf. Do you know the little park there?"

"Yes, of course. But you'd better think about what you're doing."

"Maybe I'm tired of thinking," she said.

"But these are men you just met?"

"They're young men, I should say. Eighteen or nineteen. But very funny and very sweet. They want to meet on the bridge tonight at ten. The problem is, I'll need a new dress. *And* shoes. I didn't even think to bring shoes to dance in. So that's where I'm off to now, if you have to know."

She brushed around me and started up the street.

"You want to be careful," I said. But I'm not sure she heard me.

Ray and Evelyn Walker lived in the 11th *arrondissement* not far from the Bastille. At the time they acquired their open-plan apartment, a converted welding shop, in the late sixties, the Bastille district was still populated by artists and artisans, and on rue du Faubourg St-Antoine, for example, and in the courtyards behind the large doors, you could still find the cabinet and furniture makers and even a few potters.

They had escaped with their three small children from Philadelphia where Ray had been a successful and unhappy orthopedic surgeon. In Paris, they tossed the children into the French school system, Evelyn found a teaching position in a bilingual school in the 15th, and Ray barricaded himself behind a five-lock door, let his hair grow long and wild, and taught himself to paint.

The locks took some time to unlock—I could still remember the exact order—then the door pulled open, and I found my way through heavy curtains into the large main room. The intense early evening light, which poured into the room from two walls of ceiling-high windows, had the immediate and strange effect of lifting everything, a cluttered ark of objects and people, like an airy sea swell. In the studio corner, Ray rode a short stool, his face two inches from the painting, his fine-pointed brush gently stroking the canvas as if he were afraid he might hurt it.

"Imagine you were here only last week," he said without looking up. His hair, grayer, was tied tight in a ponytail. "You remember where the Bombay is."

I went to the freezer and found the bottle of gin, which I put on the kitchen counter next to a covered bowl. I lifted the lid of the bowl and peeked in at a large quartered chicken, coated with mustard, that was marinating very nicely.

The gin poured like syrup over two ice cubes into the short glass.

"Want one?"

"You know I never mix art and the appetite," he said, dropping his brush into a jar of paint thinner. He swished the brush around, shook it over the floor, then wiped it carefully. At the kitchen bar, he pulled himself onto the edge of a high stool. The Bombay was waiting for him.

"This is still the best there is," I said.

We touched glasses.

"Jack, you look awful," he said. "Evelyn will tell you the same thing when she gets back from the market."

"I can't wait."

"Of course we're sick about Carol. My God. What else can you say? That poor fellow she finally married—Howard Corn—he sent us a nice letter."

"Homer," I said.

"Sure, that's right. Homer Corn. Can you imagine?"

"I figured he would contact you himself."

"Evelyn had one helluva cry over it. I should warn you. She's still damned upset. And angry."

"I know she was very fond of Carol."

"How old was she exactly? We were trying to remember."

"Carol was thirty-nine," I said.

"Okay. That was Evelyn's guess. For some reason, I thought she was much younger. Maybe that's how I remember her. And so how long's it been since you were here last? I mean, you two together."

"Five years. Time flies."

"I can still see her standing right over there by the window, checking the street for car thieves. You know, she had this thing about break-ins."

I put another two cubes of ice into my glass, poured the Bombay over them, and carried the glass over to the studio. Several unframed paintings hung over his work table. Above them was a long row of filed paintings that formed the wall between the studio and the bedroom on the other side.

All the paintings, including the unfinished one on the large wood easel, were of children, rendered in bold colors and finely outlined, caught, or fixed eternally, in a mosaic-like pattern. There was never a background of any kind. The children ran, jumped, leapt, skipped, whirled, danced, swam, and slept, and they did so somewhere outside of time in a pictorial space that held them, as a hand might, from ever falling. Carol loved them, perhaps for the most obvious reason, and Ray had generously given her two of his favorites. But when I looked at them too long, they frightened me.

"As you can see, I'm still trying to paint," Ray said.

"I would think you'd had enough of children."

"They keep coming. I turn my back a minute, and before I know it, there they are, like a hard rain."

"I wish my own work came as easily," I said.

"Maybe that's the problem with it, Jack."

I glanced out the window and down at the street.

"Is there a problem with it?" I said.

"I'm doing some writing myself now, okay?"

"Bully for you."

"Started two years ago. Pounded out fifteen stories for a little collection. I'm not sure what I should do now with the manuscript. Thought you might take it and pass it along to your publisher."

So it was clear now this was the price of the dinner.

"Sure, I'd be very happy to glance at it," I said.

"Did you know that I'd wanted to be a writer before I even thought about painting?"

"You must have wanted to be an orthopedic surgeon somewhere along the line."

"That was the last thing I wanted, the very last, and it was a mistake. I backed off of that because I wanted to paint."

"And before that you wanted to write," I said. "So now you're doing that."

"Exactly. I should have stayed with what I loved first. That's the only true love, you know."

"What's next? Or should I say, what's *before*?"

"Who knows what our first dream was. Whatever the hell it was, I can tell you this: We should have stuck with it and had no others. Because the others—what you wander off to—they only take you away from yourself. Okay? And if you keep going down that long road to as far away as you can get, you know where you end up?"

"I can't imagine," I said. I crunched down on an ice cube.

"You end up spent, Jack. Spent beside a slut young enough to be your own daughter in a cheap room in Paris."

I glanced in the direction of the door. Various locks were turning. Finally the door banged open, scraping the tile floor, and Evelyn slowly emerged from the curtains. She lugged two nylon grocery bags into the kitchen area and turned on the oven.

"Hey, guess what the cat dragged in?" Ray said.

"Hello, Evelyn," I said, going to her.

"Oh dear Jack," she said. "I didn't see you."

She kissed me three times, as they do in Provence, then hugged me for what seemed like an eternity. She was very thin, but strong, with strong, long-fingered hands. Her hair, a reddish brown, very thick, was braided. It hung like a frayed rope clear to her waist. Still holding me, she stepped back and searched my face.

"Jack, you look awful," she said. "What a dreadful trial this must be for you."

"She's not talking about the Hemingway conference," Ray said.

"Jack knows what I mean," Evelyn said.

I didn't want to get her started, so I retrieved two more ice cubes from the freezer and poured another double-shot of the Bombay.

"So what's your problem with Monsieur Hemingway?" I said to Ray.

"You mean besides his being an over-rated writer, a grandstander, an egotist, and a womanizer?"

"Yes."

"That's why he killed himself," Evelyn said as she pulled up a large baking dish from under the counter. She put it next to the covered bowl. "I hope you're hungry, Jack."

"I'm starving," I said. I pulled myself up onto a stool. I liked to watch Evelyn cook. "So how are the children?"

"They're all doing just fine," she said. "Ben's married now

162

and they have a nice little house just outside of Lyon."

"You know what happens to kids, don't you?" Ray said from the studio. "You feed them, shelter them, love them, even educate them, and how do they thank you? They grow up and become capitalists, doctors, or PhD's on boondoggles in Paris."

"They don't get down to the farm much anymore, which is a terrible shame," Evelyn said. "And naturally I can't get Ray out of wherever he is."

"Which is neither here nor there," Ray said.

Evelyn placed the marinated chicken quarters skin up into the baking dish. Then she scraped out the remaining mustard in the bowl and spread it over the chicken. She peppered it and poured what smelled like vermouth over it, and slid it into the hot oven. Then she poured herself a half-glass of red wine.

"But Ray's right, I guess," she said. "The children grow up and they don't have time for the farm, much less the garden. It's a lot of hard work, let me tell you. I remember how much Carol enjoyed it. She could kneel out there for hours, weeding and pruning. In the evening she'd write in that notebook of hers, filling page after page. Whatever she was writing, it began out there. She'd rooted it out somehow. The writing, I think, was the nurturing. God knows she should have had children, Jack. It's a shame and a crime that she didn't. We talked about it, as women do. I know she wanted them with all her heart."

"She was perfectly healthy," Ray said. "She'd been checked out A to Z. Am I right about that, Jack?"

"Right as rain," I said.

"Yes, I am. So there wasn't a thing in the world wrong with her."

"Look," I said, turning on the stool. "Where's that manuscript you were going to show me?"

"Jack's going to peddle it to his publisher."

"Yes," Evelyn said. "I suppose you're in a position to do that now."

"I'd really like to help," I said.

When Ray came back with the manuscript, I thumbed through it and read the story titles aloud. Evelyn said her personal favorite was "You Can't Go Roam Again." Ray lifted the manuscrit from me and read the whole, long story very seriously, as though it were Joyce or Proust. My stomach was growling noticeably when finally Evelyn put some fresh green beans into a pot for steaming. Then she took the chicken out of the oven, and I watched her scrape the mustard off and put the chicken back into the baking dish. Then she transferred the chicken pieces to a white serving platter, which she covered.

"Since we're reading things here," Ray said, "you might want to look at this."

"What's that?"

"The letter Homer Corn wrote to us."

Evelyn gave him a look, then turned back to the baking dish. She skimmed the fat from the cooking juices and then set the dish on a burner. As the juices came to a quick boil, she whisked in some crème fraiche, then lowered the flame to let it simmer. She cut the flame under the green beans.

I breathed in everything—the green beans, the chicken, the simmering mustard sauce.

"'Dear Evelyn and Ray,' it begins. Well, it's dated up top. 'January 3rd.'"

"Sweetheart?" Evelyn said. "Do we really have to? Now?"

"Listen, we're going to do this. This has to be done."

"Sure, why not," I said.

> Dear Evelyn and Ray—I have the saddest possible news to tell you. As you know, Carol has been very ill with cancer these past four months. On Friday last, she passed. Because you were so fond of her and she of you, I want you to know that Carol did not suffer and died very peacefully in her sleep. It was one of her last wishes that someday soon I will visit Paris and have the opportunity to meet two of her dearest friends. As you know, Paris was such a special place in her life! It held so many wonderful memories of her youth and so much that truly inspired her as an author. The two of you, dear Evelyn and Ray, were truly part of that inspiration. She spoke of you even to her last days in this world.
>
> Very truly yours, in sorrow,
> Homer Corn.

Evelyn, her eyes welling with tears, removed the baking dish from the low flame and spooned the mustard sauce onto the chicken. With tongs she plucked the fresh green beans from the pan and dropped them on a white plate.

"*Even unto the last days in this world*," Ray said. "I assume the cancer was ovarian. That was it, wasn't it, Jack?"

In fact, I did not know.

"We'll have him here to dinner if he does come to Paris," Evelyn said to Ray. "Do you want to cut the bread?"

"I'll do it," I said.

"No, you're the goddamned guest," he said.

"Please, Ray," Evelyn said.

She put three plates out on the bar, and flatware and blue napkins.

"She was a beautiful woman, okay?" Ray said. "That's all I want to say. Beautiful and very gifted. I'm sure that's something you appreciate, Jack."

"Yes, of course," I said.

"You were a beautiful couple."

"Thank you."

"In a beautiful marriage."

"Yes," I said, and I could already feel the other shoe dropping.

"And you blew it."

"Yes, I suppose I did."

"You were in the best place a person can be in this life. Then you blew it. And for what? A mixed-up twenty-year-old slut child right out of the sandbox."

"She was twenty-one," I said weakly.

Ray's face was red, his eyes needle sharp.

"For this, this *whoever*, you abandoned the woman who loved you."

"Look," I said, eyeing the chicken. Evelyn's head was bowed over it. "Her name is still Hilary, and it's a lot more complicated than you're making it."

"The thing is, we're as guilty as you are," Ray said. "Maybe more."

"That's nonsense. And do we want this food to get cold or what?"

"When she first arrived in Paris and called us, as Carol told us she might, we were very generous with her. Let her sleep in the back room—same bed you and Carol slept on many times, okay?—and Evelyn showed her around Paris and helped her find her own little place over in Montparnasse. We played it straight."

"Hilary was always very grateful to you both."

"But I could tell from one look at her she was trouble."

"Aren't you smart," I said.

"I don't have to be that smart, Jack."

"It makes a good story, a nice cautionary tale."

"*We were right to let her in,*" Evelyn said with sudden passion. "Right to help her. That's what Carol wanted. Carol was such a generous person. She always put others before herself."

"The mistake we made was telling you where she lived."

"We could have said we didn't know."

"But you asked, and we told you. So we played our part in Carol's death."

"Why?" I said. "Because you gave me Hilary's goddamned address?"

"There's no reason to swear," Evelyn said. "No reason to make things worse. It's dreadful enough that poor Carol's gone."

With this, Evelyn began shaking and sobbing, her face in her hands.

"Look, if it's any consolation," I said as I looked down at the three white plates. "Hilary ran off with another man."

"No doubt another woman's husband," Evelyn interjected bitterly.

"I guess we got a postcard from her," Ray said. "Seems that he took her first class all around Europe."

"Why complicate things further?" I said. "Apparently she's now left him too."

"Of course she left him," Evelyn said. "Nothing's dear to her."

"She's a flitter," Ray said. "Rootless. If she were ever to

call us again…."

"Actually, I thought she might have," I said quickly.

"Hilary?"

"I thought she might have made her way back to Paris."

"Why should she?"

"We all come back."

"Not all," Eveyln said sternly.

"Once you've left," Ray said, "you can't come back. People try to. But it can't be done."

"If she called here…," I said.

"We will not make the mistake of helping her again," Evelyn said.

"You're all alone, Jack."

"Well, so I am."

"*You deserve to be alone*," Evelyn hissed. Her whole body was shaking so hard she had to hold on to the refrigerator.

"Jesus, Jack," Ray said. "I guess you better leave."

I inhaled deeply, stood up, and followed Ray through the curtains to the door. He unlocked the five locks and I sprang out into the narrow hall and swung down the winding stairs. The locks locking again, a bolt banging shut, echoed after me.

Out on the street, alone and angry, I looked up at the Walkers' window just as a stone-black object came whirling down at my head. I turned and it struck me hard on the shoulder.

It was Ray's manuscript. I picked it up and crossed the street. Near the end of the block I stopped near a busy café and slammed the manuscript into a large green trash barrel.

I had almost reached the metro station when I decided to go back. It was, after all, at least something in this life I could go back for. Naturally it was buried at the bottom. I jack-knifed over the rim, my feet off the pavement, and in the pitch dark picked through whatever there was until I got my hands on it. When I straightened up, the whole barrel toppled over into the street. I glanced over at the café. A guy and his girl had come out to watch.

5.

Down in the metro, in the warm tunnel-driven stench of the platform, I waited among the teenagers. It was Friday night and they had swarmed into the station in packs. The wiry, black-jacketed boys went back and forth at each other, taunting and laughing. They banged the candy machines. They scratched dark triangles into the lingerie ads. The girls stood apart in their micro skirts, chattering. Their lips were bright red.

A man near me sat against the wall, his head between his legs. The woman with him stared up at me. In my mind, I had been composing a letter to Evelyn, and because it was going nowhere, I wanted to say to this woman, *Really, it's not my fault. I can explain.*

When the train arrived, I pushed inside and stood tight against the glass door. I reeked from the trash barrel. At Bastille, the door sprang open. I stepped aside, let the car empty, then quickly found a seat to myself. From the window, I glimpsed the bare, stick-thin legs, then the high-gloss shoes, as they disappeared up the stairs. They would roam the streets until midnight. Go dancing on rue de Lappe.

Bastille, I realized too late, had been my connection. I glanced at the metro guide. Now I would have to wait until Strasbourg St. Denis. I could make the change there and get on the line to Montparnasse—then, for chrissakes, not forget to jump off at St-Michel.

Montparnasse had been Hilary's first Paris address. But that late afternoon, now nearly four years ago, when I arrived at the place on rue Notre-Dame-des-Champs, the concierge told me she had stayed there only a few weeks and had moved to the Right Bank with a girl working at the corner café. The girl, I quickly discovered, was no longer there. But when I explained to a young waiter that I was Hilary's father, he gave me an address up on rue Montmartre.

At rue Montmartre, no one in 3C answered the buzzer at the street door, so I waited until someone exited, and slipped inside. The tiny elevator was out of order. In the back, just inside a cluttered courtyard occupied by what looked like a tile maker, I found the worn, wood stairs. A terrible thumping noise came down from them. As I went up, the stairs narrowed and wound tighter, and also the thumping grew louder, and now there was a man's threatening voice.

I stopped a step short of the third floor. Only a few feet down the narrow hallway a short, wavy-haired man was pounding his fist on 3C. Except for his occasional allusion to "Fernande," I hadn't a clue what he was shouting. After he shook and pulled at the doorknob, his small black shoe came flying up at it, banging it repeatedly, but to no avail. Naturally I was alarmed, but there was also something pathetic about this little clown of a man, his boyish face so twisted with anger and frustration, he really seemed on the verge of tears. After watching him only a minute or two, I stepped confidently up into the hall and waited there, quite impatiently, staring at him. He stopped his pounding, stood a moment with his arms nervously folded, then turned and, his eyes fixed on mine, as if he recognized me, slipped past me. He spun so quickly down the winding stairs, I don't think his feet touched anything.

I tapped on 3C.

"Hilary? Are you in there? … This is Jack. *Carol's husband?* … I'm staying with Evelyn and Ray over in the Bastille. … Look, there's no one out here but me. That fellow's gone. … Hilary? Are you all right?"

A voice came through the door.

"I'm okay," she said. "Meet me at Café d'Or. Can you?"

"Yes. Are you sure you're all right?"

"Around the corner."

"Yes, of course," I said. "Don't worry. I'll be there."

At Café d'Or, I sat outdoors at a small round table and ordered a *demi*. The beer reminded me how hungry I was. As far as I knew, Hilary had no way to recognize me, so I watched out for a slender young woman with short dark hair—a description, I soon realized, that fit half the French women coming up the sidewalk. After half an hour, when I had memorized the bar menu, the waiter brought me a *pastis* and asked me did I want anything to eat.

"Jack?"

Hilary slipped into the chair next to me and asked the waiter for a Jameson's on ice. She was wearing sunglasses and her hair was still very short and dark and her face, the high cheekbones and very full mouth, was more beautiful than I had guessed it would be. She tossed the sunglasses onto the table. Her left eye was blackened a little, though because her eyes were already so dark, a deep, flawless brown, and her brows dark and thick, it was hardly noticeable.

"Was that the guy who did that to you?" I asked.

"Dion? He couldn't do anything to anybody," she said.

171

"God, I can't believe you're Jack. The writer?"

"In the flesh."

"How'd you know where I was?"

"A very nice waiter gave up your address," I said. "I told him I was your father."

"Well, my poor father had a horrendous time with me—once he actually put a pistol into his mouth—so I'm pretty sure you'll want to be somebody else. Besides, Carol told me all about you, so I know you're not old enough."

"I am, nearly."

"Well, okay, *Papa*. Now tell me everything about Carol. God, I miss her. She's like a big sister to me. Or mother, if that makes you happy. Always so sweet to me, worrying like a sweet mother. And she's all right?"

"Yes," I said. "Why not?"

"You'd tell me, wouldn't you?"

"Yes, of course," I said. "So, how do you like Paris?"

"It's okay. I mean, nothing's like you imagine it."

"Paris usually is. But you've settled here?"

"God, I'm never really settled anywhere. And thanks to Dion and that bunch, I need to move on real soon. Oh, I'm sure Mrs. Walker is *very* disappointed in me. She dragged me all over the Left Bank to find me the first place."

"Don't worry about her."

"She really dislikes me. I felt that right away. They're in their own little place right up here, you know?"

She tapped her forehead and, finding something funny in her glass, smiled.

"And you? Where are you?"

"Me? I'm right here," she said, holding her open palms up close to her body. She had full, beautifully shaped young breasts, and for a second I imagined that is what she had meant.

"With me," I added, cheerfully. "Are you hungry?"

"Famished."

"Do you want to go across the river?"

"Yeah. I'd like that."

We had to walk up boulevard des Italiens near the Opéra before I could stop a taxi. The driver took us all the way to Place de la Concorde, which was fine with me, and then across the river and back along the quai. Hilary seemed glad to be in a taxi. She had a warm smell that was in her hair and came off the black sweater.

"Who the hell's Fernande?" I asked.

"I met the guy once and he gave me this," she said.

"Sounds like a son-of-a-bitch."

"He was showing off to the likes of Dion and that bunch, guys who work for him. He has a ton of money. He swoops into Paris like once a month and thinks he has to hit some-body. So while he's around, I've got to watch out."

"Why you?"

"God, that's a bad French movie," she said. "You don't want to see it."

While we waited on the quai, jammed up in traffic, she asked me what I was doing in Paris, and I told her about my research on the expatriate writers and artists here, the little book I had written, and the three novels. She said she would like to read one of the novels sometime, and then I told her this was the first time I had been in Paris without Carol and she was asking me how that felt, when the traffic jam eased and the taxi shot forward half a block, then cut abruptly onto a narrow side street. The driver, whose pig eyes caught me in the mirror, was determined to make up for lost time. Laughing, Hilary held tight to my arm.

At Chez Maitre Paul's, I ordered a ridiculously expensive bottle of Bordeaux. I really didn't know one Bordeaux from another, but this one was bound to be excellent. When the waiter brought the *montbeliard,* a smoked sausage with potato salad—there was enough of it for three or four people, I think—Hilary dug right in, and, in fact, I don't think she said another word until our order was finally taken for the main courses. She chose a chicken dish in a sauce of *vin jaune*, I opted for the saddle of lamb with *Choron*, which I explained to her was a bearnaise sauce spiked with tomatoes. And while we ate, slowly but steadily, each mouthful thoroughly savored, Hilary told me about Dion.

"Dion was watching me in a café. He stood at the bar with his pals, Ramon and Charles. Charles is okay. He has a nephew he's always bragging about. But you want to watch out for Ramon. Somebody kicked him in the head when he was born, and maybe before he was born. Really. I was sketching something in a notepad, somebody's scooter leaning against the wall. After Charles and Ramon took off, Dion came over real sly-like and sat down and asked me was I an artist. He speaks pretty good English, actually. And it didn't bother me. You've seen Dion. He's just this little guy with this big wave of hair. He'd seen a James Dean movie when he was a kid and everything just stopped for him right at that moment. Anyway, he looked at my sketch of the scooter and said he was an artist, too. His mother even sent him to an art class for a couple of months, but now he didn't have any time for it. I told him sometimes I modeled at an art school. He bought me a drink. He told me when he had time he drew flowers and things, scooters, lots of things, and stared for a long time at the scooter leaning against the wall. Then he asked right out would I model for him for five hundred francs. Of course I knew what he meant. I was curious to see if he had any talent, and besides, at that point I really needed the money.

"So the next day I went to his place, which was a real shithole, if you'll pardon my English. Like one room, with a sink and gas burner, and this little bed and one chair. His clothes were in a cardboard box. I mean, I really felt sort of sorry for him. I said to him, Look, Dion, do you really have five hundred francs? Because that's a lot of money, when you think about it. At home, in the class Carol was doing, I made like nine-fifty an hour. But Dion, he reached into his pants and whipped out the money and handed it to me before I even did anything. So he sat on the edge of the bed with this pad of paper, which I could see was brand new. There was nowhere to undress, not even a closet. So I just took every-thing off quickly and sat there thinking I was in a doctor's office, and Dion started drawing just like he'd seen artists do-ing it in the movies. He was very serious and kept drawing and didn't say hardly anything, but I could tell he was ner-vous. After more than an hour, he turned the pad of paper over on the bed and went out and down the hall to pee. Natu-rally I had to sneak a look at what he was doing. And it wasn't anything, of course. Like a child. I mean, really, the poor guy couldn't draw a stick. But when he came back to the room, I let him keep drawing for another hour. You know, I figured it was his money. Maybe he'd worked real hard for it. Besides, something strange happened. That's what I wanted to tell you.

"After I knew he couldn't draw, I realized, what the heck, I couldn't either. You know? I wanted to. I really tried to. But I don't have a speck of talent, is the problem. Carol knew that.

Naturally, she didn't say it. But she knew it, and because of the way she is, she still encouraged me, and hey, I ended up in Paris, didn't I? But like I said, I wasn't a real artist either, and there we were, me sitting on a chair naked as a jaybird, and Dion scratching away, both of us with nothing but time on our hands. That's when I told him I ached and needed to move. Change my position. I remember he flipped to a new page. I don't know why, but my heart almost burst when he did that. Little Dion. His little pencil poised and all. I pulled one leg up so my foot was on the edge of the chair and then held my hands up behind my neck. Like this. More like a pose? The thing is, I wanted the poor guy to really see me, my cunt and everything. I just let him look as much as he liked. I didn't feel ashamed and I wasn't afraid of him, wasn't afraid he would do anything but look—take me in the only way he could. We could see each other, is all. You know? Neither one of us could draw a stick."

"So that's our good friend, Dion," I said. "The guy who tried to kick your door in."

"You're a writer, so maybe you don't understand."

When I looked at her, her brown eyes, she glanced down and touched her mouth with the white napkin.

"Yes, but I can't draw," I said.

"No?"

"No."

After dinner, we stood outside a moment on rue Monsieur le Prince. I told her that just around the corner, on rue de l'Odeon, Sylvia Beach had operated her famous bookshop, the original Shakespeare & Company. James Joyce's novel, *Ulysses*, was privately published there, and many famous people, including Hemingway and Gertrude Stein, were regular visitors. But when we walked over, and there was only a crystal shop at the famous address, she looked very disappointed.

"It's not here," she said.

"Well, the memory's here," I said, and I pointed up at the plaque above the window.

"I'm afraid to go back," she said.

"The past?"

"My room," she said. "I was thinking of Fernande."

"Then we'll find a hotel. Do you want to do that?"

"Won't Evelyn and Ray be waiting up for you?"

"So I'll call them."

We walked down to St-Germain, past the busy Cinema Odeon, then up the boulevard to St-Germain-des-Pres. We had a drink at a café near the church, and afterwards I pointed out Picasso's Apollonaire sculpture in the church courtyard and explained something of the history behind it. Hilary held my arm and pushed in close to me.

"Let's hurry, Papa," she said.

We found a reasonable hotel just around the corner, on rue Bonaparte, and rode the elevator up to the third floor. It was a large, quaint room, with 19th-century furnishings, including an ornately carved armoire and mirror, and a formal, stuffed chair. Neither of us said anything. In bed in the dark, with the windows wide open to the shallow wrought-iron balcony, you could see the gray-metal rooftops across the Left Bank, the chimneys reaching into the pink sky.

Early the next morning Hilary left me in bed and returned to the Right Bank. When she failed to call by noon, I decided to cancel the room. I sat around in the lobby for three hours. When I returned from a sandwich stand up the street, there were no messages, so I headed over to rue Montmartre.

When I arrived at her apartment, I found the door cracked open. Inside, three men stood over Hilary, who sat on the edge of her bed with her arms resolutely folded and legs crossed. She was angry, but what could she do? When the largest of the men—Uncle Charles, I figured—waved me back, I held my ground.

"What's the problem here?" I said. "Maybe you fellows better leave."

Dion turned and looked me up and down.

"Maybe you will shut your face," he said.

"Oh, be quiet," Hilary said.

"I can telephone the police," I said. "Is that what you want? How would you like it if I called the goddamned police?"

The one in the sleeveless shirt I knew must be Ramon whipped around and came at me with both fists tight to his hips. Then the flats of his hands suddenly flew up and I was out in the hallway on the floor. It had been at least thirty years, back in the sixth grade, I think, since I had last been knocked off my feet, and I had never before been thrown down a full flight of stairs. It is nothing like in the movies. I have no idea what happened back in Hilary's room, but when Ramon arrived at the bottom of the stairs, he stepped on my hand, then he and a squealing Dion swung down out of view. Uncle Charles finally appeared and actually pulled me back onto my feet. Hilary draped my arm around her shoulder and we went back up again, one step at a time.

I sat on the edge of the bed a moment, my head between my legs.

"God, you could have got yourself killed," she said.

My body felt as if it had just been tossed off a train.

"I'm all right," I said. I slowly sat up. Hilary was throwing clothes into a canvas suitcase.

"Charles says I must get out of Paris for a few weeks."

"Now?"

"I'm afraid of Fernande. Honestly."

"Look, why don't I take you where you're going."

"You want to be with me?"

"I can make sure you get there," I said.

We took the 11:05 train out of Gare de Lyon. It was a slow train, heading south to Marseille, but we had 1st-Class tickets and, when a young man got off at midnight, the whole compartment was ours. Hilary's suitcase was in the rack overhead. I had brought nothing but myself.

I suppose in another life, in the one I had been living, this could not have happened. But back at the Hotel Bonaparte, or at Maitre Chez Paul's—or was it, in truth, in that moment of unwitting complicity, when Evelyn Walker gave up the address on Montparnasse? Or earlier still, in the nude photograph on the porch table—I felt a body shift, as if I have been nudged, and turned, in pitch dark, and was now moving off in a new direction.

We sat across from each other by the black window. Outside, everything was whipping past us, but we couldn't see it.

"If I don't face forward on a train, I get nauseous," Hilary said.

"A writer always faces the caboose."

"Is that really true?"

"Whatever I say is true."

After a while, when she had drifted off for a moment and suddenly awakened again, Hilary got up and kissed me, her mouth warm and lively.

"I speak in tongues," she said.

First she lowered the shade over the window, then drew the dark curtain across the compartment door and closed the latch. She pulled her black sweater up over her head and unhooked her bra in front.

"No one will bother us," she said.

"Maybe the lights?"

"No," she said, and sat down. "Not yet."

"Are you ever shy?"

"It's who I am. I want you to see me."

"I do see you."

She wiggled her skirt up around her waist and pulled off her black panties. She put her fingers down between her thighs.

"I was dreaming about you, Papa," she said. "Do you see?"

"Everything about you is beautiful," I said.

"This is where the train is going tonight, *Monsieur Writer*. Are you afraid?"

"Should I be?"

Still, I turned out the light.

We went into the speeding dark. And finally it didn't matter if we were racing to or away, into the future or memory. There was only the sensation of movement in place.

Then, suddenly, one tap on the door. *"Christ,"* I said. Hilary held me hard inside her. "Shhhh," she said. Now several taps more, quicker. Then some madman out there pounding so that the whole compartment shook. Finally it stopped. We held very still and listened. Hilary's hot breath flooded my ear.

"Stay with me," she said.

We got off in Avignon. It is a lovely city, and there in the very early morning we had coffee and warm croissants by the carousal in the empty plaza. Hilary looked disheveled and sleepy and sexy, and she held her cup to her lips with both hands.

"You're such a mystery to me," I said.

"I'm not."

"But you are."

"I don't want to be. I don't want to be one of those women that men only imagine."

I smiled. "I don't think you need to worry about that," I said.

"I do worry about you, Jack."

"Me?"

"Because you're a writer."

"But I'm not a very good writer."

"I want you to see me and touch me. My face and all the parts of my body. Please don't ever make me something else. Will you promise not to make me?"

"Now you're the one who's afraid."

"I have to be in at least this one place, Jack."

"Where?" I said.

"Where you were with me last night."

Mid-morning, after I had mentioned that Avignon was a famous university town, we returned to the station and took the half-hour train farther south to Arles. There we found a small hotel near the Roman coliseum, ate a very fine lunch of tomatoes and mozzarella at the café next door, and walked around the city. I explained to Hilary that Van Gogh had lived in Arles and many of his most famous paintings were painted here, and that Gaugain had visited him, that there were lovely Gaugains from Arles too, and that is where poor Vincent had cut off his ear.

"Yes," Hilary said. "He was mad for a prostitute."

"Tonight I must make some phone calls," I said. "I'll need to tell people when I'll be back."

"But I can make you never want to go back."

"Then let's do that right now," I said.

"Yeah, let's do that."

Near midnight I went down to the café and telephoned Carol. It was only six o'clock there and she said she had been cleaning the house. Her voice did sound a little breathless, in fact. I explained to her that my research in Paris was going well and I wanted to stay on awhile, perhaps through the summer.

"You should stay as long as you need to," she said.

"And you'll be all right?"

"Of course."

"There's plenty of money in the account."

"Yes, you've done that. Thank you."

"I might travel a little," I said. "Who knows?"

"That does sound wonderful right now," she said. "But you want to call Evelyn and Ray. Will you? They're very worried about you. And all your things are still there. You were in such a hurry."

"I wasn't."

"I'm glad you were, Jack. I really am."

"And you're going to be all right?"

"Really, I'll be fine. Please, let's not worry about each other. Can we not worry about each other anymore?"

"Christ," I said.

"I have to go."

"Where?"

"Is that okay, Jack? Please?"

After a moment, we both said something at the same time, and hung up.

I ordered a demi and sat with it awhile, then returned to the hotel. Hilary was sprawled across the small bed, naked and asleep. I watched her as I undressed. Suddenly she sat up and covered herself. She was not yet awake.

"*Don't let him,*" she said. "*I don't have it.*"

"Who?"

"Take me away," she said.

We remained in Arles to see the festival. First, the bulls ran through the ancient streets, and, in the late afternoon, charged to their death in the coliseum. The queen, chosen from a dozen dark-haired Arlesian girls huddled together on a balcony in the plaza, was crowned. The old dramas and dances on the Roman stage played all week, and then the grand parade, with colorful costumes from all over Provence. Evenings everyone ate and drank and danced in the small squares. Then, when it was suddenly over, and the tourists were gone, and the streets had been flooded and swept clean, Arles was like a small, Roman town again.

Every morning Hilary and I wandered the cobblestone streets, or traced out the spots where Van Gogh had placed his easels, or bicycled across the Rhone into the hot, flower-scented countryside. Once we rented a scooter and rode south into the Camargue to see the wild horses and the pink flamingoes. We ate and afterwards made love and slept wholeheartedly. Then summer ended. After I telephoned my university, explained how indisposed I was with a rare happiness, was forthwith granted a leave-of-absence, we packed our bags and—after a visit to Cezanne's studio in Aix—headed into Italy.

We spent the fall in the mountains just north of Lucca

where Michelangelo, Hilary said, had "found his marbles," and south of Florence, in Panzano, and finally, in early December, in a stone house on a precipitous hillside north of Orvieto. Hilary visited the markets, walked the wet paths beside the vineyards and talked with the farmers and their plump wives and beautiful children, read by the window the English bestsellers she found abandoned outside a bookshop, took long, steaming hot, mineral-reeking baths, offered herself so unabashedly and scandalously, filling every room she found me in with those insistent female smells as old as the race—in truth, it was quite impossible to work, to do anything, in fact, but lap my tongue around it, as Claire Stewart had said, and take it all in.

Still, the work called me. Not, I know, as it had called Carol, and, I hoped, would call her again, quickly now. But as something to occupy me, perhaps in the same sense as Paris had been occupied by the Germans. I needed jeeps and tanks and supply trucks and personnel carriers to enter my veins, and barking officers to tell me what I could and could not do. But Hilary, like the movement of resistance underground, kept these occupiers off guard and anxious, and me still free to love.

In late December, and perhaps feeling a vague sentimentality about the dark and promising season, I asked Hilary—who sat beside me on an old wall, bundled in a blanket—if she would marry me.

"Marry a jaded middle-aged man?" she said.

"Who adores you."

"But Papa, I'm a healthy young woman and you can get it up only four or five times a day."

"I have tons of money," I said.

"Then yes, I will," she said.

But soon after the New Year, Hilary's mood suddenly turned. She was restless. The rain had become too much for her, she said. Besides, she now felt guilty that I was unable to work.

"I want to go back to Paris," she said. "Can we? Now?"

"We can get married in Paris," I said.

"Yes. In April, like the song."

In fact, I was happy to return. I had seen enough of Italy, and all we had done, when we thought we were really in it, was stare at it, without really touching any of it and feeling it. I missed the clamoring friction of Paris, and I missed the food and the gardens, and I wanted to work again.

And so back in Paris we found a comfortable little place on rue Saint Placide, just around the corner, as it happened, from the room Carol and I had had on rue du Cherche Midi. I had a good desk to work at, Hilary studied French nearby on Raspail, at the Alliance Francaise, and most evenings we walked up to the cafés and the movies on Montparnasse.

Spring briefly visited in early April. For a week or two the days were warm and flowers in the Luxembourg Gardens were blooming and students from the Sorbonne came over and lounged around with their heavy books in the green metal chairs. I went there on a Sunday afternoon to write and even managed to fill a few pages in my composition book. But then the old lady arrived pushing her cart ofboats. Soon children hurried to the pool. I loved the way the boats, searching for the center, leaned so close to the water. It was always "against the current," as Fitzgerald said.

That was when I spotted Charles. He stood by the fountain hovering over a small boy I assumed was his nephew. I had no idea he knew I was there, staring at him, until he suddenly turned and walked right up to me and spoke to me.

I understood nothing he said and when he realized that, he stopped, looked around, and spoke more slowly. I gathered he meant to tell me that he knew Hilary was back in Paris, that she was a very amiable young woman, very innocent, *"Vraiment,"* he said, then something about Fernande. When he mentioned Fernande he jerked his head in the direction of the Right Bank, and whatever he said, something was *"terrible."*

"Look, what is it?"

"Elle s'est fait avorté."

"What?"

When the nephew called him, he said something else, that he was very sorry, then returned to the fountain. He looked back at me several times to see if I had moved.

When Hilary returned from the Alliance, I waited until she had eaten something and complained childishly about her diction instructor. Then I asked her why, after Christmas, she had been in such a hurry to return to Paris.

"You're not happy here?" she said.

"I was very happy here until I met up with your old friend Charles."

"Charles? Where was he?"

"What the hell does it matter where he was. He told me you had an abortion. Is that true?"

"Maybe that doesn't matter either."

"The hell it doesn't," I said. "Was that my child?"

"It was ours," she said.

I raised my hand to slap her, but stopped. Her eyes welled up and she turned away and went into the bedroom. I let her cry in there a moment before I went in and sat next to her. Her body was shaking.

"Why did you do it?" I said. "We could have had a child, for chrissakes."

She turned over and wiped her hand across her nose.

"Oh Jack. I just couldn't imagine it."

"What? A child?"

"It was too strange. It terrified me, you know? I dreamed it was coming to take my body away. And I was so afraid. Where would I go? Where would I be? Where could you find me if you wanted?"

"But you're here, always, with me. Right here and in my heart."

She sat up and pressed her hand to my heart.

"Inside here?" she said. "That's where I'm going?"

"You're here already."

She put her arms around me and held me. Her own heart was thumping against mine. I stroked her hair. We were like that a long time, until I could again let go of everything I wanted. Then she kissed first my neck, then my face with her wet lips. I kissed her also. She pulled her sweater up over her head, unsnapped her bra and let it fall away, then drew my face against her warm body. "I'm so sorry," she whispered. "It's you I want inside me. Here. Can't you tell? It's you, Papa. I want you."

I woke in the middle of the night. I felt emptied out, an empty, white pool on the bed. Hilary slept flat on her back beside me. I touched her hot skin, brushed the back of my fingers over the black triangle of hair. Then I got up, found my balance, and went into the other room.

I telephoned Carol.

"Who's this calling?" a woman asked.

"I want to speak to Carol."

"She's gone to Minnesota last summer. You'll have to reach her there. All right?"

"Yes, I will," I said.

After I hung up, I thought about Minnesota and about Carol's returning there after so many years, now a mature woman, mysterious to every one she had left behind in her childhood. Perhaps someone had truly remembered her and welcomed her. The better part of me hoped so. And I thought it was time now for me to return home, Hilary and me together. You could not spend your whole life in Paris, even if, like Evelyn and Ray, you made yourself believe you were actually in it.

I slept in. When Hilary did not return in the afternoon, I went down to a café to look for her. She wasn't there, so I walked over to the Alliance Francaise, but she was not there either, and someone I asked said she had not seen her. She was gone that night and also the night after while I waited by the phone. The third day I walked around the Left Bank and looked for her. In the early evening I took the metro up to rue Montmartre.

It was the only lead I had. It was never clear to me that the apartment there had been really hers in the first place. Nothing over there was clear, in fact. But I managed to get in and climbed the winding wood stairs and knocked on the door at 3C. There was no answer, but I sensed Hilary was inside, or did I need to imagine it, imagine her sitting on the edge of the bed, waiting for me to stop. I knocked again harder, and the harder I knocked the more certain I was, and soon I was thumping the door so that it bent under the assault, and I shouted "*Hilary*" again and again until I thought my heart would break, and stood back and kicked furiously at the door-knob.

"*Ass-ole*, she's not there anymore," someone said, and I turned to see it was Dion, standing on the stairs. He looked ludicrously short, by at least a step or two.

"You know where she is?"

"You are a fool, man, because Fernande, *he* took her. She went away with Fernande."

"Where?"

"Anywhere he wants."

"You tell me or I'll kill you," I said.

"*Ass-ole.*"

I wanted to kick him down the goddamned stairs, but he was too quick and flew off, the echo of his high-pitched laughter whirling down the well.

Hearing this yet again, I missed the connection at Strasbourg St. Denis and was already nearing Madeleine. I waited another station, got off at Concorde and followed the signs to Line #1, direction Château de Vincennes. There were lots of hot young couples in the passageways and up on the platform, waiting impatiently. I stood there sweating, feverish, trying to imagine them: after the cafes and the chatter, after the bistros, after the street roaming and the ice cream, after the dancing until their bodies were on fire, then, finally, love's desperate promiscuity, on some starlit savanna in the world's first place.

Then, as the doors snapped shut at Louvre Rivoli, I saw Marianna in a red dress hurrying across the platform oppo-site. Was it ten already? It was like one of those visions of the end. I jumped off at the next station. Ray's manuscript still tight under my arm, I climbed back out of the metro into Place du Chatelet and into the white, evening air.

6.

Marianna was waiting up on the Pont Neuf. The Seine divided at Ile St-Louis and Cite, and a breeze came down it, converging with a *swoosh* at the bridge, and lifted the back of her dress. Men on the crowded bridge stood at the railing, looking at her.

She wasn't surprised to see me.

"Sir Jacques to the rescue," she said, smiling.

"So where the hell are the guys?"

"I'm a little early."

"They'll think you're anxious."

"Boy, I *am* anxious. Do you like my dress? Say you love it. Will you?"

"It's nice," I said, and it really was.

"That's good, because it cost *beaucoup, beaucoup* francs."

"Look," I said, Two young men at the railing had moved closer to us. "It's going to cost you a lot more if you don't get it off this bridge."

"I'm not afraid."

"You should be," I said. "There are dangerous types around here. You could be kidnapped and taken someplace far away."

"I've dreamed of it."

Just then one of the tourist boats, its spotlights sweeping both banks high up to the penthouses and rooftops, slid like a giant water monster silently under the bridge. Marianna waved to it.

"A smaller boat departs up by Notre-Dame," I said. "Do you want to do that?"

Suddenly she put her arms around me and kissed me. She smelled all perfumed and warm. The two young men watched us, then moved down the bridge.

"What will my wretched suitors do if I'm not here?"

"Be lonely and forlorn," I said.

She took my arm and we walked over to the Left Bank and down along the quai toward Notre-Dame. At St-Michel, where a huge crowd had gathered near the fountain, I explained to Marianna that, because I had rescued my friend's manuscript from the bottom of a trash barrel, I needed to stop by the Esmerelda to change my clothes.

"Must have been a great visit," she said.

"I missed a fabulous dinner."

At Hotel Esmerelda, we met Claire Stewart just as she stepped into the lobby ahead of us. It startled her seeing us together, but she recovered quickly, surprised Marianna with a dramatic embrace, then sprang back to admire the dress.

"It's truly, truly astonishing," she said. "The girl in the red dress. It's every man's fantasy, isn't it?"

"I guess guys are pretty visual," Marianna said cautiously.

"Visual? Yes, that's the guys for you. Like old lions out on the Serengeti. They envision the scarlet flesh at a thousand yards. *Bang*. You know, their eyes, they shoot you like a camera."

"Actually, the shoes cost more than the dress."

"Oh, I believe it. And the lingerie?"

"I'll just go up for a minute," I said to Marianna. "You okay?"

"Jack dear, she'll be just fine until she wakes up."

The clerk dropped our keys together on the desk and Claire turned and scooped up hers quickly. We both stepped over to the elevator.

"I *am* awake," Marianna said, catching up with us.

I pulled the elevator gate open, then the door, and the three of us squeezed in. We went up.

"Push me, will you, Jack? Marianna, how old are you exactly?"

"Twenty-three," Marianna said, her head bowed.

"Twenty-three," Claire Stewart repeated. "Well, I must say, you write very well. We were all quite impressed."

"Thank you for saying so," Marianna said.

"Jack, you stink. You haven't been rummaging around in trash, have you?"

"I'm going to change," I said.

"Every man says that. But who bothers to believe it?"

Marianna and I stepped out at the third floor.

"Enjoy your evening," Marianna said to Claire Stewart.

"Oh, don't you worry," she said as I closed the gate.

At my room, I fumbled interminably with the lock until the door jumped open.

"What's her problem anyway?" Marianna asked.

"I have no idea," I said, and stepped inside. Marianna entered slowly, carefully looked around as if she were making a decision about it, then slipped past me to the French doors, which she opened to the balcony. I plucked a clean shirt and pair of khakis from my suitcase and took them into the bathroom and shut the door. Inside, it was as cramped as a confession box.

"Jeez, you really have a view here," she called to me.

"Jeez," I said. I managed to pull up my trousers without

falling over.

"And nobody can see you. You know? Except the Cathedral, of course. *God.*"

"What?"

I tucked in the shirt, yanked up my zipper, threaded my belt through most of the loops, turned the doorknob, and practically fell back into the room.

Marianna stood out on the balcony in her underwear.

"Jesus," I said. "Will you get back in here?"

She turned and stepped back into the room.

"The lingerie *was* more than the shoes," she said.

"That's right, that's right," I said. "The less you can see, the more it costs you."

"Claire is going to tell everyone at the conference that you got me into bed."

"Sorry about that."

"Boy, I'm the one who's going to be sorry if it's not true."

She unhooked something, pulled everything down, and crawled across the bed.

"Look, this isn't going to work," I said.

"*You* look. Let me make it work."

"I mean I can't do it."

"You're not missing anything, are you?"

"That's just it," I said, and sat down on the bed. "I'm shot all to hell."

She turned to me and put her arm on my shoulder.

"With what?"

"Memories," I said. "Loss."

She kissed me very softly under my ear and sat back, upright against the bed board. Her open hands lay flat by her side. She had small, perfectly shaped, pink-tipped breasts, like a teenager's, like I imagined the girls in the metro, and a tuft of silky hair.

"God, that's what *I* want," she said.

"You haven't found anybody?"

"I got involved once before with a guy I met at a conference. In San Francisco, last fall. His name's David, an Assistant Professor at N.Y.U. He wrote a book on Wallace Stevens that everyone was raving about, so the afternoon I arrived I started reading it. I didn't know jack shit about Wallace Stevens, but the book made the poetry really interesting. So the next morning I spotted him at breakfast, sitting alone—I recognized him from the book jacket photo, of course—and plunked myself down across from him. I told him how much I admired his book. He was very handsome. Maybe a little shy, but I could tell I had aroused his interest. We talked about 'Sunday Morning,' which is the only poem I knew first hand, and the eternal-place-versus-time theme. Do you know Stevens?"

"I know that, in Key West, Hemingway knocked him flat."

"Seriously?"

"He'd criticized Hemingway's work, I think. So what happened with David?"

"Well, I asked him if the escape into aesthetics wasn't just as bad as religion, and he said that as a matter of fact, he addressed that very question in the paper he was giving the next morning. So we talked about that awhile as we walked around Union Square and looked at the department store windows. In the afternoon, we kept talking about it on the boat ride around the bay. He said he liked some of my ideas and would consider them in the final revision of his paper, which he said he'd probably be up half the night working on. Naturally it was *me* I wanted him to be up half the night working on, so on the way back to the hotel I asked him all sorts of inane questions about Stevens' personal life: Did he have girl-friends? How quickly did he get involved with a woman? Did he write in bed? How large was he really? I mean, I could see from a photo in the book that Stevens was a pretty big guy—but you know, how big exactly was he? And the woman who was lounging around on Sunday morning—was she somebody he knew, had a trampoline jumping affair with? Was she at least a brunette like myself? He said that after dinner he needed to work on the paper—there were some details he was still pretty worried about, as well he should have been, and so, playing the dutiful wife, as I was already imagining myself, I told him yes, by all means, and that maybe afterwards, no matter how late, he could drop up to my room on the elev-enth floor. When he looked at me, into my eyes, across a piece of German chocolate cake, I sensed his vulnerability—he was also pretty young and had been tenured less than a year—and I assured him I really, truly loved his paper, which I was dying to hear. So after dinner I left him and went out to find some-thing to wear. You know. Something irresistible in real silk. I didn't care what it cost."

"So what happened?"

"What happened is, midnight came and went. You know how it does that. I got undressed, down to the thing I'd bought, and sat in bed, just like this, with my thighs spread like one of those vanishing point drawings, and I started thinking about his Wallace Stevens paper, fantasizing about all those sensitive details he was working on, and I was still doing that pretty much full throttle when I heard this loud door thumping out in the hall. Right away it occurred to me that David, *my* David, had lost the room number or something—or my God, *I* had given him the wrong number—and now the poor guy was in a hot sweat banging and banging on the wrong door. So of course I jumped up and went out to see. And what it was, was this crazy drunk guy three doors down, locked out, his face blood red and flooded with tears. I watched him kick at the door. He saw me. I was just about ready to invite him over when his door suddenly opened and he fell inside, like he'd been *swallowed*."

"Jesus. So where was David?"

"The next morning, at the conference, I stood up and argued that by the end of 'Sunday Morning' the woman was doing a Molly Bloom on herself, and then I proceeded to rip his paper to shreds, detail by detail by detail, until the sonofabitch was pretty much flat out cold behind the podium. Oh Jack, dear Jack, will you *please* look at me? I bought the dress, the shoes, all the etceteras. What else does a girl have to do to get loved around here?"

I held her for a minute. Smelled her sweet skin, hair.

"Listen," I said. "You can always review my next novel. All right?"

She wiped her tears.

"I may just do that, you know."

"Let's find something to eat. Are you hungry?"

"Yes," she said.

We ate at a place I remembered off Place St-Michel, Les Carpentiers, where the matron admired Marianna's red dress. Afterwards, we walked all the way up the boulevard past the Luxembourg Gardens, then cut over to Montparnasse.

We had a cognac at Closerie des Lilas. Hemingway had written some of his best stories there, including "Big Two-Hearted River," the subject of Claire Stewart's paper on

Hemingway and Cezanne, and there were the obligatory
Hemingway mementos, including a brass plate at the bar and
an oil painting behind it. What I remember most about the
Closerie des Lilas of the early twenties was speculation that,
right after the Great War, this is where Hemingway saw so
many of the dismembered veterans, the legless, armless,
sometimes faceless men, most of them too young for such
loss, who made Jake Barnes and his genital wound so plausible and real, before it had been abstracted into symbolism.
Hemingway knew about absence. And now he too was ab-
sent at Closerie des Lilas. And with him Baudelaire, Verlaine,
Apollinaire. At the open door with Marianna, just beyond
which the lilacs were no longer on the terrace, I could feel
the warm draft in their wake.

"I don't suppose Hadley came here often," Marianna said.

"It was his place to work."

"Yes, he had many nice places," she said.

We walked up rue Notre-Dame-des-Champs. The saw-
mill above which Ernest and Hadley had lived was long gone,
and, I knew, most of what had been on the street was gone,
and at the end of it his good friends Ezra and Dorothy Pound
were gone.

Hilary's first place in Paris was still there.

Back on Montparnasse, we looked into the Dome, Se-
lect, Rotonde, then continued on to La Coupole which had
changed so radically, poor Sartre would not have recognized
it. After a coffee, we cut over to boulevard Edgar Quinet and
looked into the Montparnasse cemetery, which was locked and
dark.

Marianna held her face to the gate. It glowed with per-
spiration.

"Who's there? Anybody we know?"

"Sartre, of course," I said. "Baudelaire, de Maupassant, Tristan Tzara, Man Ray, the photographer. Samuel Beckett, I think."

We stood there, looking in.

"That's the thing," I said. "What threatened her most."

"Who's that?"

"A young woman named Hilary. I had half expected her to be back in Paris."

"She'd left?"

"She'd left with somebody else," I said boldly, and then I realized I had confessed much the same to Claire Stewart.

"So what threatened her?"

"What threatened the woman in 'Sunday Morning,' I suppose. Knowledge of the body's transience—the body that is time itself, where she lived on sand. Overhead, the consequent nightmare hovering like crows. Also, waiting nearby, the starry-eyed tempters: faith, hope, love."

"Love, too?"

"Hilary was afraid of the imagination."

"Now I'm really jealous of her. I too have a body, as you know."

"Yes, I've smelled its salt smell," I said. "In another life, I would have sailed upon it like Odysseus."

When Marianna put her arm through mine, I glanced back over my shoulder and saw, across Edgar Quinet, three men standing together in the dark. Because one of them was short, I immediately thought of Dion. Dion and his two cronies. On the other hand, they had no business with me nor I with them. It was only a way of remembering that she had been with them, and now she was gone.

We walked back to Montparnasse. The district was so crowded it was hopeless trying to get a table anywhere, so we crossed the boulevard and took a side street back to the Luxembourg Gardens. We walked along Vaugirard, past an apartment Scott and Zelda had briefly occupied, around the north side of the park, then past the Theatre de l'Odeon to rue Racine and Marianna's hotel. Marianna led me past it a few feet to the closed book store on St-Michel. It was Friday night and the boulevard was crowded and deafening with cars and music.

Three young black men stood on the corner. They were nodding their heads to the noise and eyeing Marianna as if she were on fire. When I took her arm, she turned to me and threw her arms around my neck and kissed me, a long, hot-tongued kiss, like the one on Pont Neuf, which buckled my knees.

"Those are the guys," she said.

"Who?"

"There. Those three guys. They still want to take me dancing. Come on."

She pulled me over to them and introduced me as a famous novelist from America. Only one of them, I think, understood any English, and she called him Nairobi because that was where he was born. The three men smiled, their teeth white as ivory.

"Marianna," I said, taking her aside. "Are you sure about this?"

"Look at me, Jack. You wouldn't want me to go to waste, would you?"

"No, I suppose not," I said. "In any case, I can always find my way back to Professor Stewart."

"You won't. Promise me."

I smiled at the three young men and then Marianna went off with them, just like that, across St-Michel to rue des Ecoles. I watched the last flicker of her red dress round the corner into the Latin Quarter.

7.

Saturday morning the Hemingway conference ended, but I never made it over to avenue Bosquet. For one thing, nobody would show up for the last papers anyway because by that time everyone was sick to death of Hemingway, including Hemingway himself, who had slipped out the door after the first-night cocktail party. Also, I really couldn't bear to see anybody. I decided I would wait until the next conference to learn if Marianna had crawled safely back out of Africa (I imagined her on a bed as big as a continent), and if Claire Stewart and Buck Buchanan, the post- and pre-historic, had finally done the beast with two backs.

Instead I ate an early and cheap lunch at Chartier, up on rue Montmartre, and after wandering hopelessly around the neighborhood for half the afternoon, eventually found myself in a movie theater a few blocks from the Place de l'Opéra.

A French film was showing I had read a review of in the *International Herald Tribune* and I was thoroughly enjoying it for the first ten or fifteen minutes until I realized there were no subtitles and I didn't understand a word anybody was saying. That's when it really hit me, with a shock of recognition, that I was *in Paris*, or at least the *theater* was in Paris.

The film's setting, until things turned for the worse, was your typically French countryside, one vast, rolling, sun-drenched, cookbook-cover garden, Eden encore, dotted with red-roofed farm houses, lined with narrow, winding roads. The characters included a film director, a cameo role played by the egotist who actually directed the film, and, at first, several women and a young boy and girl, each meticulously groomed, made-up, dressed, as the French would have us believe, by God. The women, light and dark, each breathtakingly beautiful in her own way, wandered aimlessly in and out of camera about the director's great house and gravel terrace and lawn, often held in zoom or slow motion, while alone upstairs, the boy and girl, who looked suspiciously like brother and sister, let their clothes float to the floor, and giggled and cooed under the white sheet. Inevitably, the film being French, everyone started talking and talking, and one by one each of the women talked herself into bed with the director. Of course the small matter of motivation, on the women's part, and the absence of good looks, intelligence, and charm on his, were of little consequence, since this was in fact his film. In any case, I the viewer, the voyeur, once—or is it twice—removed, fully appreciated the abundance of gratuitous nudity and love-making. Everything, indeed, was huffing along just fine until other men showed up. That was when the actual *story* began, with the various motivations, plot, and subplots. Laughter, ridiculous action, tears. From what I could gather, one of the women, in her early twenties, had stolen something of great value and either had it in her possession, hidden away close by, or, *a Dieu ne plaise*, had lost it. The other women were angry or envious. There was an increasing amount of shrill emotion and shouting. One of the older women slapped the trouble-maker, and three of the men, who had arrived in a black Citroën, got pretty violent themselves, threatening the women until each turned on the other, and everyone turned on the young woman. Only minutes after the three men threw her into the car and drove off, a plainclothes policeman, or possibly a high-level government official, showed up, asked questions which, *Dieu merci*, everyone refused to answer, and, after an angry warning, stomped out. When at that point the film itself flickered, the sound slowed, groaned, then sped up again, it suddenly occurred to me that the review I had read, which played an essential role in my understanding of what was going on plot-wise, may have been of another film altogether. After all, I had not actually seen a valuable possession of any sort, and the fellow in plain clothes could very well have been the poor young woman's father. What motivated the characters, the whole pack of them, suddenly went up in smoke. Increasingly frustrated by my failure to grasp the principal action, not to mention the life-illuminating themes that hung upon it, I found myself turning in desperation to the various sub-plots and peripheral actions, which involved, I *think*, a woman who spent the first half of the film searching for her small child, another woman who told stories to large rocks, a house guest who could not find her room, a nymphet— the girl romping earlier with the boy—who maneuvered the director himself into an indefensible position, and, *Dieu merci* again, all those sweating bodies. Of course it was impossible to tell if this film was pastoral romance, comedy, farce, *drame psychologique,* or adventure story. Whatever it was, I was trying to sit back and enjoy it, this fantastic light show—and at a certain point, in fact, I found myself absent-mindedly unzipping my pants as a small boy might—when suddenly the whole garden scene switched to Paris: the black and white of a cobble-stone street at night, three evil-hatted men giving chase, behind them a whirling blue siren and the face of The Father, and far up ahead, barely visible at the horizon, a woman racing—*falling*, I should say—into the wedge of dark.

Then lightning struck. The screen flared up, sputtered, and the whole theater went black as pitch.

I was hastily zipping up when the lights went on. A timid voice came over the speakers. "*Regret*" was all I caught.

The theater was almost empty. Those few of us, scattered into our own worlds, sat still and waited. I glanced across the aisle, down a row, at a woman I quickly realized was Edwidge. *Edwidge the moviegoer.* I froze in fright, I don't know why, and slumped in my seat. For two or three minutes, stretched to eternity, I felt a burning loneliness. Then the lights went down again and, mercifully, the screen filled.

I eased out of my seat and, head bowed, marched up the aisle and straight out to the street.

Hurrying down boulevard des Italiens, I got as much distance between myself and the theater as possible. At Place de l'Opéra, I stopped to catch my breath and gawk at the monstrous old Opéra Garnier. A gang of American tourists lounged on the steps. They looked exhausted. Myself, also. No doubt they had spent the day shopping at Galleries Lafayette or waiting in line for their mail at American Express. That was it, all right. People would keep coming to Paris forever.

A woman I suspected was Swedish—tall, blue-eyed, so ghostly fair in the bright May sun I doubted she was real— looked me over at the crosswalk, and I wondered what she saw: a middle-aged, unattached male of the species, obviously not French, a secret in every pocket, eyes forlorn and hungry, passing through Paris. When the light changed, she stepped out ahead of me and, pacing her, I watched her cross. At the curb I caught up with her and we turned together along the tables of Café de la Paix.

"*Jack?*"

A man shot up from his chair. I stopped.

"Yes?"

"It's Homer here," he said, grinning. "Homer Corn?"

"Yes, of course," I said, though I had never actually seen Homer Corn, not even a photo. He was exactly what I should have expected: tall, mustached, extraordinarily handsome in a rural sort of way, his eyes bright, curious, ready to please. I had not come to Paris to find him. Still, I had found him.

"Please, will you sit down? I don't drink. It will sure help me with this waiter."

I gave one last look after the Swedish woman, who vanished into the crowd, and reluctantly I sat down. When the waiter came, I ordered a double Jameson's on the rocks, a small dish of salted peanuts, and another Coca-Cola for "mon ami du Nebraska."

"Boy, I do envy anybody who understands a foreign language," Homer said. "Every one of them is a mystery to me, like women."

"Myself, I have no ear for any language but my own," I said.

"Honestly?"

"Honestly."

"I never thought I'd see you in Paris, Jack," he said. "But I'm glad you're here. I was pretty angry with you, mostly when Carol was ill."

"You can be as angry as you like,' I said. "In the end, I was a lousy husband."

"I was angry because you'd had the time with her I didn't.

Because you got to know her like I couldn't. You'd been with her when she became the extraordinary woman she was, right here, in Paris. I believe this is where her soul was found."

"Was it lost?"

"The Bible says every soul is lost until it's found," Homer said. "Thanks to Carol, my own soul was found twice."

"Is that right," I said. "So, she told you all about Paris?"

The waiter brought our drinks. Homer insisted on touching glasses, then gazed out across the street at the opera house. Though I assumed there was nothing remotely like it in Nebraska, his attention did not seem arrested by it.

"There were some photos. You were in quite a few of them. Early on, she gave them to me to look at, then hid them away. Truth is, Carol seldom talked about Paris. And she never talked about you, Jack. We were together just two years—it feels like my whole life, in fact—and your name hardly ever came up. That's how I knew it was you and Paris she was always thinking about. She'd locked you and Paris up inside her, like in one of those diaries girls have. That's where all her writing went too. I never actually saw a word she wrote, at least not until she started dying. Can you believe that?"

"Let's face it, Homer. With you she had another kind of life altogether."

He took no offense. In fact, his eyes searched for what kind of life that might have been. I myself could not begin to imagine it.

"She couldn't receive love," he said finally.

"What?"

"It's what she said about herself. We were up in Minnesota, just before we were married. I took her to mean she couldn't conceive for some reason. We weren't going to have any children. And of course we didn't."

"That's nobody's fault."

"She had the two paintings by Mr. Walker. I'd be very glad if you took one."

The sidewalk was bustling now. Everyone hurrying, everyone with packages. Beautiful, long-legged women walking quickly.

"You keep them," I said. "So, now you're in beautiful Paris."

"I've come here to look, like a kid hanging over a big wall into a garden. I thought I might get a glimpse of her, Jack. Get to know who she was here in Paris, in this beautiful place, like you say, before she started to die. Can you help me?"

"Look," I said. I searched around for the waiter. "I can't even help myself."

"Because if you can't, I will have missed her."

His eyes welled up. I had a vision of Carol passing right through his life like a ghost.

"She wasn't in any pain, didn't you say? The Walkers showed me your letter."

"It was a tumor, you know, in her brain."

"No," I said. "In fact, I didn't know. Was there nothing anyone could do?"

"It was inoperable. Radiation might have slowed it, but she didn't want that. She cried about it, of course. She was angry. Who wouldn't be?"

"I can imagine how difficult it must have been for you."

"Me? The worst of it was watching her lose her speech. It had started with that anyway. It's how she knew something was happening. She had been talking to someone, the twins next door, I think, and she couldn't get the words in the right places. It was funny, she said, because her whole life as a writer, that's what she'd struggled to do. But now she couldn't get them right. After a while, I found myself helping out, especially when there were other people around. She would say something. Then I would repeat it, you know, the way she intended it. She introduced me to everyone as her translator. I mean, when you think about it, I was just about the last person in the world to explain what she was saying. But it was something I could do. You see? When things got worse, and the words hurt to listen to, she stopped talking and wrote everything down on a pad of yellow paper. She'd push it at me, and of course everything was all garbled, like before, but at least the horrible noises were gone, she said, and usually I could straighten the words out, fill in, make some sense of it. She didn't want to go outdoors anymore, even to the hospital. A few people visited. Neighbors. My mother and her husband. Three of her cousins came down from Minnesota. Near the end she couldn't write anything that made any sense at all. I would be there right beside her, of course, trying to tell everybody what she wanted to say. Heck, you were the one who should have been there, Jack. You're the writer. You knew her. You would have known what she meant. Of course I did my best. She would shake her head when I got it wrong, or didn't say it the way she wanted it, and nod when I got it right, which always made me happy, the way her eyes would light up. Still, it was pretty hard work. I can tell you my respect for the writing profession went up a good amount. By then she couldn't move around much. I carried her downstairs in the late morning and helped her eat something. She had to eat. Then carried her back up in the afternoon. I gave her the morphine myself, you know. They taught me so I could do it. Finally, she didn't want to come down. She didn't want to see anybody. She only wanted me to stay up there with her, if I would, when she was awake. I suppose I talked a lot in those hours. You know how it is. You just keep talking. I know what I was trying to say. I was trying to put my words into her mouth so she could speak. I told her I loved her. I tried. I told her I loved her with all my heart and soul. And she reached her hand up to my mouth and looked at me. Her eyes were suddenly so open and clear, like still waters. It scared me a little. But I swear to God I went down into them that night, before they closed. I know I did."

Now his tears flowed, and they were still flowing when the waiter, a man with nothing but business on his own face, came over to the table.

"*L'addition, s'il vous plait.*"

"You can just tell him I'm from Nebraska," Homer said, wiping his eyes.

I rested my hand on his. "He knows," I said. "You'd be surprised how many Nebraskans come to this café."

Homer smiled.

"Do you believe in the afterlife, Jack?"

"This *is* the afterlife," I said.

He looked out at the Opéra and tourists and around the busy plaza and at the metro station everyone was hurrying down into and at the small round table the waiter had just cleared.

"Boy, the whole thing is another country," he said.

"Have you been up to Montmartre yet?"

"That's where they've put all the artists. Is that right?"

"I'm afraid the real ones are dead. But there's a great view up there of the city. You can see it from one end to the other."

"Then let's go up," he said.

Orders

Pleasure Boat Studio fulfills orders placed by telephone,
fax, e-mail, or mail. Response time is immediate.
Free shipping on pre-paid orders.
Send check or money order to:

Pleasure Boat Studio
8630 Wardwell Road
Bainbridge Island • WA 98110-1589 USA
Tel-Fax: (888) 810-5308
E-mail: pleasboat@aol.com
URL: http://www.pbstudio.com
Terms and conditions: standard to the trade and available upon request. SAN: 299-0075

Pleasure Boat Studio Books & Chapbooks are also distributed by:

Small Press Distribution:Tel 800-869-7553•Fax 510-524-0852
Baker & Taylor: Tel 800-775-1100 • Fax 800-775-7480
Koen Pacific: Tel 206-575-7544 • Fax 206-575-7444
Partners/West: Tel 425-227-8486 • Fax 425-204-2448
Brodart: Tel 800-233-8467 • Fax 800-999-6799
Ingram: Tel 800-937-8000 • Fax 800-876-0186

from **Pleasure Boat Studio**
an essay written by Ouyang Xiu,
Song Dynasty poet, essayist, and scholar,
on the twelfth day of the twelfth month
in the *renwu* year (January 25, 1043)

I have heard of men of antiquity who fled from the world to
distant rivers and lakes and refused to their dying day to
return. They must have found some source of pleasure there. If
one is not anxious for profit, even at the risk of danger, or is
not convicted of a crime and forced to embark; rather, if one
has a favorable breeze and gentle seas and is able to rest
comfortably on a pillow and mat, sailing several hundred
miles in a single day, then is boat travel not enjoyable? Of
course, I have no time for such diversions. But since 'pleasure
boat' is the designation of boats used for such pastimes, I have
now adopted it as the name of my studio. Is there anything
wrong with that?

Translated by Ronald Egan
THE LITERARY WORKS OF OU-YANG HSIU
Cambridge University Press

Edwin Weihe teaches modern
literature and directs the Creative Writing Program at
Seattle University. A graduate of Brown University and the
Iowa Writers' Workshop, where he studied with Richard
Yates and Kurt Vonnegut, he has been a Senior Fulbright
Lecturer in American Literature and Culture in Aachen,
Germany, and Antwerp and Leuven, Belgium, and has lec-
tured widely in Europe on interdisciplinary topics in litera-
ture, philosophy, and art. He teaches a summer abroad course
in Paris on the Rise of Modernism, as well as Seattle
University's Writers Workshop in Ireland. *Another Life &
Other Stories* is his first book.

BALLOON ANIMALS

Jonathan Dunne's Books

Balloon Animals 2012

Living Dead Lovers coming autumn 2013

BALLOON ANIMALS

A Novel

Jonathan Dunne

It takes a wise man to know when to let go a rising balloon but a brave man to hold on... Anonymous

DEDICATION

Dedicated to my wife Ruth for believing in me and giving me time to hide in the attic. You are my North Star.

Love to my two little girls, Maia and Chloe. If I could only keep your giggles in jars...

ACKNOWLEDGMENTS

Big thanks to Detective Fink at Iowa City Police Department for his friendship and expertise.

Huge thanks to literary scout Betty Schwartz who first told me all those years ago that I had "something" and all I needed was some "tweaking". Thanks Betty, still "tweaking".

Thanks to Kevin Panacchia for artwork.

PROLOGUE
Egg 'n Spoon

I hear the cheers and applause as I bullet towards the finish-line, running away from the end of the world. I pick out Vera's ecstatic face in the crowd of parents in the school-yard with my noble grandfather, 45, standing lop-sided in the gap where Clinical Dad should've been. Vera gets so excited at my uncanny stealth and balance that her wig comes loose at the forehead. Horror: she doesn't know. *Christ, she doesn't know! Somebody, please, tell her!* But nobody wants to tell her, not out of malice but out of respectful pity. It looks as if this mother's life has been nothing but a lead up to my participation in this egg 'n spoon race. I guess she's proud but it doesn't say a lot for everything else that has gone before me. Not knowing whether to laugh or cry, my nine year-old reason runs directly towards Vera with bug-eyed terror and sick fascination. I cross the line of several classmates and trip them up in the process, sending a flurry of eggs and spoons into the air. Parents bellow with laughter but I've never seen my mother bald in broad daylight and desperately want to protect her from the rain and the world. 45 is standing next to my mother. I wonder why he is the only calm face in the crowd even though he has already noticed the two-foot flapping gap between Vera's egg-head (the day that's in it) and the flying squirrel. I know now because he had swopped eggs before the race and supplied me with a hard-boiled super-glued egg and cryogenically frozen spoon. At least, that's what he had me believe. I'm having the dream again…

1.
Crisis in the Mirror

Two hours before my little world does a back-flip, I feel the uneasiness in my waters. I may have a bladder full of stale Scrumpy Jack but that doesn't cloud my gut. My gut says that today is going to be a make or break kind of day. Maybe it's the bitter-sweet fact that I am turning thirty today or maybe it's that I'm waking up from my recurring memory-turn-nightmare where I gatecrash the egg-'n-spoon race. I could've won. Really, I know why I've woken with this nervy feeling. I'm planning to tell Charley everything today; it's about time I told him the truth. It's always surprised me how he hasn't found out because everybody else in town seems to know about it and laugh behind the backs of what's left of us Rowes. Chinese whispers are born here in Old Castle. They go 'round the world, then end back up here on a scrap-heap of rumours and lies. Believe me; I know what's left of us Rowe's because I have a degree in genealogy from Trinity College Dublin. Then again, Charley lives the nocturnal life of a tree sloth and moves like one when he's smoking his obscenities from Holland so maybe it doesn't surprise me that he's oblivious.

A knock comes on my bedroom door while I'm staring up at my inspiration notes that I've lodged in the springs of the overhead bunk-bed where Tommy once slept. Nuggets of encouragement that I'd left as morning greeting-cards: *C'mon, Jonny! ... You're a Winner, Jonny! ... Up 'n at 'em, Jonny! ... Ya' make yer own luck, Jonny! You're the king, Jonny!*

By the way, I still live with my mother. These strategically placed notes had been the Reiki Mistress's idea, not mine. They're starting to depress me.

'Yeah?' I cringe as a thumping wallop pounds the inside of my head. No answer comes but I can hear some

slipper-shufflin' around the hallway. '45, I know you're
out there.' I lever myself up from the pillow but little
shapes whizz before my eyes. The sudden surge of
queasiness flattens me back down on my orthopaedic
pillow and I wait for it to pass. I stare at my ceiling, trying
to stop the spinning by focusing on my *Return of the Jedi*
lampshade. I had planned to change it for something more
adult (subtle shade of lilac) but such memorabilia has
become cool again. I catch a glimpse of myself in the
mirror as I fall out of bed. I can't help but notice how I'm
there but not there. This has been happening with alarming
frequency recently. This morning, I'm just a shadow of my
former self. I'm disappearing. Maybe I should take this as
an omen regarding the state of my nerves this morning. It's
not as if I smoked much of Charley's Mexican Black or
Brown last night.

Grabbing one of my glossy genealogy magazines from
the stack, I quickly open my bedroom door. 45's standing
there with a guilty expression on his old, old face. I love
him like a father, literally. He'd been staring at my door for
some time judging by his body language. He's done up in
his finest '70's brown suit, silver hair greased back from
the forehead and worthy of a Hammer Horror film. Camera
pan down: the tartan slippers take from the effect. Brillo,
45's home-help, had helped him into his fancy-dress; that's
all it is nowadays. The old man lost his sense of time and
place a long time ago.

'Happy birthday, Jonny,' he says with that wistful
smile, 'Here, I got you a little somethin'.'

In shock, I turn around to see if anybody has heard him
speak. 45 has always had brief moments of clarity and half
remember things but I'm still bowled over every time he
comes out with something coherent, right out of the blue.
Fair enough, he's handing me a cold sausage for my
birthday but he *has* remembered my birthday. 'Oh, um,
thanks,' I falter, taking my birthday present from the old
man. 'You, uh, shouldn't have…'

'I know,' he responds with a bashful schoolboy smile. He comes over all vague and gawps down at the cold cooked sausage in his hand as if he'd just realized that it was there. 'I shouldn't have...' he repeats to himself absently. He stays fixed on that sausage for some time and I know he cannot bring his eyes up to meet mine. Sometimes, I wish the mind thief, Mr. Dementia, would just take 45's rational thinking away forever because it brings a tear to my eye to see the old man get embarrassed like this. Who am I to judge a war hero? Sometimes, I think my noble grandfather knows me best, despite the fact that he sits on our back doorstep most mornings waiting for a one-way bus back to his childhood in Iowa. He's obsessed with our back door-step. Never wants to leave the place, just like an old sheepdog. It never dawns on him that the local bus company doesn't offer a direct route from 128 Hydrangea Drive, Old Castle, Ireland, to Iowa, North America. In the fairy-tale world of senility, 45 runs free and it's a beautiful heart-breaking thing. Either way, Mr Dementia has given 45 a one-way ticket and he's taking the whole bus-load with him.

'Thanks but I've already got one.' I joke, holding up the cold sausage. I give him a quick one-sided hug. 'Maybe I'll have it with a cuppa later.' I manage a smile and almost gag. 45 gazes through me, nodding. Something's different about the old man today, as if he wants to say something but not sure how to vocalize it or has forgotten what it is he wants to say. Normally at this time of morning, 45 would be sat on the doorstep with a battered old suitcase he had brought with him from his homeland of Iowa sometime during the 50's.

Like the doorstep, he never left Europe after his term on the front line in the Second World War, although 45 seems to range from World War II to 'Nam and back again these days so I'm not really sure which war he fought but he's missing one knee to prove it. A double-whammy: a ball of lead had removed his knee-cap and the inner workings of

4

his knee, leaving him walking the Earth at a 45° angle, like a listing ship. The year happened to be 1945. He proposed to Nan around that year. Got down on the only knee he had. It was that noble gesture that had won her over, apparently.

I never knew Nan; she had left this world before I was old enough to have accumulated memories. All I know is that she died before her time in small-town controversy right here in Old Castle. Maybe God had seen fit to end Nan's affair through the medium of the buzz-saw. She had been having an affair, see, with one of the timber mill workers. She used to work in a sandwich bar here in town and would insist on hand-delivery to the boys down at the mill. She fell onto her lover's buzz-saw during an 'encounter' in one of the back-rooms of the mill. All this information is second-hand. I cannot vouch for any of this but Vera backs up the story ... so does 45 but I take everything he says with a pinch of salt.

45 never went back to North America after that. Some days, I can almost see those rolling fields of Iowan corn in his rheumy eyes. Other days, I spot the fear in them as the bombs and bullets rip the air around his addled head. He's a man who seems to be constantly on-the-run from something.

'Jon, I'd like to invite you and your family to my place for a birthday lunch of sauerkraut and a dollop of something on the side that I've prepared for you.' The old man slaps my cheek which leaves a sting. I don't appreciate being slapped during a hangover but decide to keep that to myself.

'It was meant to be a surprise,' he says, 'but I had to tell you cos I'd probably forget.' He smiles apologetically and I just melt. Maybe it's the liquor still dribbling in my system but I could just bawl right now; cry for an age. Sob for what's left of 45 the knee-capped war hero ... weep and blubber with ecstatic happiness and wonderment for having made it this far.

'So, you comin' or what, son?' 45 probes again, eyes

5

hopeful wide. He slaps my face for good measure and I bite my tongue.

'Sure, let me get cleaned up and we'll see you at your place.' His place is our place. Sometimes, I get the feeling that he wants us to play along.

'Happy birthday, Jonny!'

As 45 trails off, mumbling something about spreading his home-help for dessert, the rest of my family: Vera, Tommy, and Susan (aka Alba) jump out from behind the fake Pothos ivy and smother me in birthday wishes and kisses.

'45 was the decoy,' my brother Tommy rejoices, 'but he's good at that because he fought in a war.'

I hold the genealogy magazine to my crotch area, striving to hide my semi hard-on that's accentuated by my psychedelic paisley pyjamas. It pokes several legs and hips in the birthday mêlée.

I break free and scramble to the bathroom with my head reeling. The unsavoury experience prompts my solar plexus to do a backward flip and I just make it to the bowl before I regurgitate everything from last night. Apparently, I *had* gone for that kebab after all. That was quickly followed up with the inevitable diarrhoea, or souping, as Charley and I have lovingly come to call the process. I make a fast mental note, between crouching and sitting positions, of never ending up at The Old Quart again … again … again because we always end up at that shit-hole.

I call Charley on my iPhone once I'm finally sure that I'm empty.

'Uh?'

'Cha, the egg-'n-spoon dream again.'

At the time of the actual egg 'n spoon event, Vera had been after a three-month bout of chemo and she looked like she had been living in a dark cave. I have fond memories of taking the toupee to bed with me at night, just to have the comforting smell of Mother by my side. It helped fill Clinical Dad's void when I called out his name in my sleep.

Not even my glow-in-the-dark rosary beads helped and that's saying something. Vera didn't mind lending me her rug because Vera is not your average mom. I used to pretend to be that James Bond baddie fondling his fluffy purring Persian and Vera used to get a great kick out of that. "You have to laugh because you'd cry if you didn't" was Vera's motto – still is.

'Get over it,' Charley answers groggily. 'I haven't gone to bed yet. I've been on *Gears of War* since we left the Old Quart; playing some crazy fuck from Venezuela. All I get all night is "you sonna-beeetch" in my ear-piece. "I know where you leeeve, sonna-beeetch, I know your mamma too, huh. You think she like to feeel the tip of the devil's forked tail, huh, sonna-beeetch?" I kept telling him that it's only a game in his own Spanglish but I don't think he understood.'

Charley Monsell works at PC City by day and moonlights as an amateur IT guy by night when he's not playing against some anonymous cyber opponent.

'I think you should give up video games; they're playing with your sense of reality again. Speaking of reality: turning thirty has given me some insight into my life at present, Cha.' I think about this but it doesn't make much sense. I think about it again and realize that it makes nothing but sense. 'What I'm trying to say is that, ever since the egg-'n-spoon incident, I feel as if

I've gradually been fading away: twenty-one years of disappearing in the mirror as I wash my teeth; all that's left of me are my fillings. My whole life up until now has been nothing but one big egg-'n-spoon fest. Where have I been for the last twenty-one years? I've got a degree in genealogy, can track my roots all the way back to the coffin ships, and I've got an *identity* crisis. That's called irony.'

'That's called fucked up.' Charley snorts, hawks, and practically vomits down my end of the line. 'Hey, why do you think they call white-sound white? Since when do sounds have colours? White-sound sounds more like grey to me, kind of like grey matter.'

'Uh-huh.' I can hear Charley puffing on the other end so decide not to take much notice of his ramblings. He tends to question the unquestionable when he's smoking for medicinal purposes.

'You're Jonny Rowe,' Charley speaks into my ear as he takes another hit and holds it in, 'you're thirty today and you've done *nothing* with your life, sweet fuck all. You've got your degree, sure, but what have you done with it? Who takes a degree in gynaecology seriously anyway? Your mind's on overload, kid. I wouldn't worry 'bout it.'

I decide not to correct Charley; life's too short. 'I woke with this odd feeling in the pit of my stomach this morning, Cha, and it's not going away.'

'Aw, don't worry. They probably watered down our drinks at The Old Quart.'

'No, this is different; I don't have the acute pain in my appendix this time.'

'Who says appendix have no function? What *is* their function? We shouldn't just throw it out. We should recycle and donate appendixes to Africa.'

'I'm talking about the sort of vibe you get before something happens, y'know, like ominous and foreboding are the words you'd probably find in
Collins pocket thesaurus.'

'That's a make of dinosaur; *dictionary* you mean.'

'Whatever, Cha. If we're talking expressions and idioms then the calm before the storm would be apt. I feel it in my waters, man. I've got it in my waters, real bad. Maybe it's just that I finally don't recognize myself in the mirror anymore.'

'Like tellin' the future shit?' Charley yawns dramatically into my ear.

'What? No, not really. I've just got this sneaking suspicion that today is going to be more than my birthday. Don't ask me why, it's just a feeling. Maybe the world's going to end. Anyway, see you at two in the bong-house.

Cha? *Charley?'*

He's snoring. I can hear him from wherever he's dropped his mobile. I desperately want to tell my best friend about my past, right there over the phone, once and for all. If I'm being honest with myself, I know the reason for my identity crisis.

2.
Birthday Party Horror

'Welcome to Tommy's karaoke, yea-yea, Tommyoke, the Best in the West, yea-yea.'

My older brother Tommy has taken the karaoke machine out to our back-garden for my birthday get-together. M.C. Tommy is putting on that smooth amber Benidorm-dance-hall-for-the-retired voice. He bought the machine on e-bay last year and is serious about the craft of karaoke, still toying with the idea of taking it up full-time. I tried to talk him out of it because of the sheer competitive nature of the game and the seedy world he would inhabit. Tommy's going to become a karaoke-master some day and I envy him because he's got a goal in life. He once told me about a venture which he planned to launch in either Vegas or Thailand. He would call the concept *Marryoke* where young drugged and drunken couples would marry each other through the noble form of karaoke verse.

Tommy goes on to introduce members of the family with the same cheesy smile that matches his oily voice, swinging the mike every now and then, passing it from one hand to another with real panache. He skips the invitees who he isn't familiar with (mostly Vera's work colleagues from the cleaning company at the airport). 'Now, yea-yea, who's up for a number with Tommy?'

45 is sitting on a fold-up deck chair in the patio by the clothesline with the rest of the family and strangers. I can see him from my vantage point through the cob-webbed window of the six-by-six bong-house – green-house – where Vera keeps her orchids and kentia palms and I keep my ailing marijuana plant which doubles as either a passion flower or a Japanese maple, depends on who I'm talking to and their level of botanical knowledge. 45 looks dapper in his seventies brown suit. For the occasion he is wearing his tattered Bank of Ireland green, white, and gold peak-cap

plus tartan slippers. A killer combination.

'C'mon, who wants to do a number with the Tommy?'

45 has his hand held in the air like a kid at school wanting to answer the question. My wet bed sheets that Vera hung out to dry this morning are flapping in his face but nobody seems to care. Half an hour ago, during my birthday lunch, he held up his fork and asked Vera what its purpose was. Vera uttered a little chuckle to the others and passed it off but everyone cringed and felt the tragedy.

Tommy deliberately overlooks 45's outstretched arm because he has to do his routine. 'You're all a little shy, yea-yea, so Tommy will offer up one of the golden-oldies: *Angels* sung by drop-out Robin Williams.'

Somebody in the crowd corrects him but Tommy's on his number now and nothing will get in its way.

Tommy's girlfriend, Lucy, loves her boyfriend's alter-ego. It turns her on and she told me that with her own filthy mouth while she was sober one night. Tommy says she drinks to stay sober so bully for him. Besides, he doesn't like the other Lucy all that much just like Lucy doesn't care for the real Tommy all that much: perfect harmony in symbiosis. Looks like I'm not the only one suffering from identity crisis. Lucy says that, sometimes, she doesn't know if she's talking to Tommy Rowe or the Karaoke Master. I can see her now, sitting at the back of the get-together with a pint of cider in her left hand and, correct if I'm wrong, but the whorish little maid is fingering herself discreetly as Tommy executes amateur dramatics with his microphone.

'Tommy's got an infectious karaoke voice, literally.'

I can just about see Charley beyond the blanket of dense smog we've worked up between us. His camouflage khakis blend nicely with the sub-tropical foliage. 'Say what you want about Tommy,' picking up on Charley's sarcasm, 'but he's done well for himself there. Lucy's a beautiful girl with a cracking personality and not afraid to hold back in public.' I peer through the window again.

'You feeling any older today? Just psyching myself up for when it happens to me.'

Charley's two months younger than me but looks ten years older because of his unhealthy habits.

I think about his question. 'Maybe, yeah, I'm not sure. Shit we did in our twenties suddenly seems dumb. I mean, jumping into the Christmas tree in Galway with crash helmets on our heads just seems retarded now.' I sigh. 'I think I need to find a place of my own and stop using my studies as an excuse to sponge off Vera. My genealogy degree finished years ago, y'know. I only moved back in to complete my PhD thesis on my family tree but here I am, five years later, and all I've got are a trunk, some bare branches, and the dole. I don't even have a driver's license!'

'You should include a tree-house as a metaphorical point of interest in your family tree.'

Charley has something valid with that concept but I'm still raw from the previous night and can't think too much. 'At least Tommy's got the excuse of getting married next year so there's light at the end of his tunnel.'

'I bet there is,' Charley quipped, 'guess where she wants to put that microphone.'

I sneak another peek through the bong-house window. Lucy's hand is down the front of her jeans, up to the wrist now. 'What about my tunnel? Where's the light for me, Cha? Huh? Where's the light for me?'

I look at the smouldering end of my doobie and wonder whether it's making me paranoid about my immediate status but decide that, if anything, it is numbing reality. 'Once I finish my thesis, I'm outta here. Get my genealogy PhD under my belt and fly the coup.' I flap my hands for effect.

'What's your thesis on?'

'Dunno.'

'What will you do when you finally get it?'

I take a deep breath and blurt out, 'Private investigation.' I'd said it without even thinking about it because if I had thought about it I would've kept it to myself for another year. It's an idea that I've been harbouring for a decade and seriously thinking about it for more than a year. 'Anybody who hears that I've got a PhD in genealogy will want me as a P.I. I will use my genealogical skills and my natural sense of curiosity to track my prey.'

Charley throws his head back, bawls and splutters amongst the foliage. 'I suggest you figure out your own shit before solving other people's shit. Look at you, Jon, you're a disgrace.' His nostrils have flared a little.

'Charley, remember, anger management.'

'Girlfriendless … houseless … practically penniless … and every other something-less. Plus, you don't even know if you exist which begs me to question my own existence.' He pronounces these words slowly and clearly for caustic effect and that's what first attracted me to Charley. 'Y'know what your problem is? You don't know yourself but you know everybody else. Give your chakra some TLC my friend and it will return the love by giving you a glimpse into the real you.' Charley curls his fists and makes some mystic signs in the air. 'Go have a session with the Reiki Mistress. Blow off some steam.' Charley winks and clicks his tongue then takes a puff on his road-cone and tucks his ratty Rasta-locks behind his ears. I hadn't realized how much his skin had cleared up.

'What's with the hostility? Give me that spliff, it's not helping you. You're no better off than I am.' I take a long draught of Scrumpy.

I reach out to take his drug when he says, 'That's not the point. I *enjoy* who I am. You're not at one with yourself.'

Charley's on the verge of adding something else but trails off into oblivion as is his tendency and asks some question about chameleons. I consider my best friend sitting on the dusty sky-blue Cortina seat on the floor of the bong-house. His simple yet sophisticated insight shocks me at times. 'Charley, if we ever get separated along the way, I'll remember you for those words.'

After Tommy winds up *Angels*, 45 gets to his feet and pulls on his slippers. He approaches Tommy in slow motion and whispers the track in my brother's ear before literally breaking into *'I Did It My Way'*. Tommy fast-forwards the backing-track to catch up, 'Yea-yea.' Mid-way through the first line 45 thanks everybody for coming and to help themselves to sauerkraut.

'I can't ever remember a day when he didn't have Alzheimer's or some forgetfulness. He's been hazy about his life in general. Nobody seems to know anything about his American days. He never expressed a wish to go back there or talk about the place so we just kind of forgot about his previous life and adopted him as our own. He must've seen terrible things to make him forsake the country that had sent him to destroy the Germans.'

'Huh?' asks Charley.

'Nothing.'

45 sings his heart out, inventing half of the words and mumbling through verses but succeeds in
delivering the song in a much more noble way than any
of the previous cover versions. I really feel a surge of pride for the old man as he flaps his hands about and sings into faces with his bristled jittering chin; faces he no longer recognizes.

'He *has* done it his way. Those people out there are treating him like an ape in a zoo – throw him another peanut and see what he does. It's disgusting.'

Charley can't see 45 from his vantage point but can hear his Iowan twang on the crackling microphone. 'Yep, so much for animal rights. He's better off where he is.' Charlie points to his temples and puffs smoke rings into the humid heavy air to emphasize his point.

I sum up by saying, 'Noble.' I swallow a gulp of Mexican Brown or Black or whatever it was that had come from up Charley's ass (it hadn't come from there originally; he had smuggled it in from Amsterdam – his ass was more of a stop-over in Schiphol airport).

Bloated after my birthday lunch, I slide from the bong-house table and levitate towards my marijuana plant. I unzip, then baptize it with a warm gush of amber piss. 'I'm not sure that pissing on the plant's going to revive it, Cha. It looks deader since I started offering it more nitrogen.'

'You've surely got some idea to base your thesis on?'

'Hmm?' Charley had been suffering a time-lapse and had kicked back into our previous conversation.

'Maybe I should delve further into my family tree.' I imagine my family sitting on various branches of my marijuana plant and piss on the branches of the relatives I don't care for. I think about where Clinical Dad sits and decide that he will provide compost for the shit that he is. I'm not sure if that is a good or bad thing.

Outside, 45 bobs, weaves, and works the room/patio as if he'd been entertaining all his life. He can't remember who he is nor remember the lyrics but he's got great stage presence. He circles the patio, slapping women's asses whenever he gets the chance and fists men's chins, even making obscene gestures behind Brillo's large back with his microphone. That gets big laughs which makes me wonder what kind of party this is turning out to be and more to the point: do these people not know that the old man's not in his right mind.

'Where did this car seat come from? I've been looking at it every day for I don't know how long but know nothing about its history.'

Charley studies the leatherette of the old Cortina seat he's sitting on.

'Funny you should ask me that today,' I prompt, growing fidgety. I sup a little Dutch courage from the 5-litre gallon of Scrumpy Jack we keep topped up at the bong-house. 'Vera had it scrapped some time after Clinical Dad had left the, um, the parking ticket.'

'The suicide note, you mean.'

I nod reluctantly. 'She likes to come in here and sit in the Cortina seat and think about what could've been.' I close my eyes and step out over the edge of the canyon. 'Cha, I've given this a lot of thought during the last week and I've made the conscious decision to tell you the story of the scrapped Cortina seat you are sitting on. I think it may be directly related to my identity crisis: my reason for not being at thirty.' I check 45 through the dirty window pane for good measure. He has ended his song to a standing ovation of flying peanuts. Now my sister Susan is out there with her Alba chorus, singing a Lady GaGa number with all the robotic moves. By the way, my younger sister Susan is mysterious. She's the one who turned Goth on its head in my town. She became albino with some superficial plastic surgery to her epidermis that lasts six months a time. She pays for it by holding illegal fun-runs and collecting for non-existing charities. She is wild, enterprising, and has a growing number of followers. They call themselves Alba. I don't know if that's the collective or each cult member is called Alba. It's not easy to miss them in town. Ever been to a milk-bottling plant?

I sit on the ground next to Charley. 'You're right: the air *is* cleaner down here.'

'What's with the seat, man?'

'I'm not sure whether I remember the sky-blue Cortina or maybe it had always been just the photograph,' I begin. 'Clinical Dad is sitting on the bonnet in the snap-shot, sporting a monumental beard, hair down over his ears, and a red lumberjack shirt. Just hair in general and I had come to the conclusion, even at that young age of fourteen, that Clinical Dad had been hiding or hatching something in his beard. It was just a cover. If you want to know what he looked like then you may recall the dwarf Gimli in *Lord of the Rings*.' I reflect, 'They looked happy in the photograph. Clinical Dad went missing soon after that. Family and police targeted the sky-blue Cortina because there weren't many sky-blue Cortinas around Ireland or Europe. The car

16

was found on the pier by the river in town with a weather-beaten message lodged under one of the windshield wipers.'

'Weather-beaten?'

'Several passers-by … joggers… dock-workers … known prostitutes … had taken the message for an illegal-parking fine and walked right passed Clinical Dad's suicide note.' Fishing in my inside jacket pocket, I produce the battered note. 'Christ, you sick pap!' Charley's disgusted. 'Jon, man, you've got to be *mental* to keep a suicide note in your … I mean, how long have you been going around with that in your … I

mean, it'll bring you seven years bad luck. Get rid, my son, get rid.'

'"Vera & Co,"' I read on, *"Sorry, I must leave you now. My work here is done. I'm going on to a better place. Clinical Dad."*

After processing the note, Charley summarises by commenting, 'Christ, he makes himself out to be a super-hero saint.'

I nod in agreement. 'Father Teresa was my first impression. The Clinical Dad bit was added in later,' I clarify. 'I could read by the time I was nine years old. Vera never wanted me to know Clinical Dad's name. I vaguely recall taking trips down to the river with Vera, Tommy, and Susan. We would stand on the bridge and gaze down into the swirling freezing murky waters of the Arra. I never knew why we went on excursions to the bridge; just stop and stare down into the river and then walk home. Sometimes Vera would cry symbolic tears into the river. I suppose that she was half expecting to see his corpse float by but I didn't know it at the time. All this happened before his funeral – they never found his body, see.' I hint but Charley's in a far-away place. 'I mean, how could anybody drown in the Arra? It's only six inches deep in places and full of rock. It's impossible to be swept down-river. How could they not have found his body, Cha? Where would it go? There's not even enough water for the swans and ducks.'

'The Polish *ate* the swans.'

'That's an urban myth. They would go for the ducks first – duck-liver pâté. Let's get back to the point: they *never* found his body.'

Charley frowns after a delayed period. 'No closure?'

'It was the words Clinical Dad had used: *"must" "on"* and *"better place"* that held a certain sense of ambiguous mystique and urgency.'

'Nice vocab.'

'Thanks. Over the following months, Vera explained to us that Clinical Dad had gone to a very far-away mystical land where he had to serve the queen of Fantasia – little did we know then that he was serving a queen of a different sort.'

'Drag queen? Sorry.'

I'd just dropped the first heavy-duty clue but Charley's mind is clogged again on Mexican Brown or Black and I don't have the balls to spell it out so I beat around the bush. 'That led to us asking difficult questions about mystical Greek beasts such as the Minotaur and goblins, shit like that.'

'Goblins.' He shakes his head incredulously. 'It's in the least likely of places where we find solace.'

I get up to have a look through the window at the proceedings. 'Brillo's standing like a statue in the back yard, delivering an old Eastern European folk song with the same expression as if telling the guests that they have a terminal illness.'

'I'm almost embarrassed to say this, Jon, but I've always found something erotic about Brillo, maybe it's her maternal plainness, aprons 'n shit like that. She's got a husband back in Eastern Europe so maybe she's forbidden fruit.'

I choke on a ball of exotic smoke. 'Yeah, a stale water-melon.'

Charley looks a little worried, 'I've *fantasized* about her, Jonny, but as I'm about to wind up proceedings,' he executes a vague pulling sequence, 'I realize how big her back is. Domestic farm animal comes to mind and I've wilted like a tomato plant in full sun.'

I roll around in the sub-tropical foliage, laughing like a rare jungle species. I gain control of myself and take a deep breath, working out an angle to come at the more fragile points of Clinical Dad's story.

'Remember those times when you didn't believe what I was telling you and you asked me to swear on
my father's grave?'

Charley shakes his head. He's gazing at something amongst the foliage.

'Well, I've been swearing on his grave for the last two fucking decades, Cha, so you probably can recall a *single* instance.'

That catches Charley's attention. It's all bubbling to the surface now. My face grows hot. He looks up at me with his bulging red eyes and I could swear on my father's grave that a giant tropical toad is looking up at
me from amongst the flora ... only I can't swear on his grave – not any more.

'That's a terrible thing to say,' Charley opines. 'Actually, there's a special word for what you've just said. It begins with S...' and Charley's gone again.

'I lied any time I swore on his grave – two times over in fact. Lied about swearing on his grave and lied about lying to cover-up for a lie.'

Charley looks more confused than usual. He takes another hit on his spliff to clear his head and asks me to repeat what I've just said.

'Look, let me simplify it for you: he didn't commit suicide, Charley.' I inhale a deep heady gulp of bong-house air and 3D shapes heave like sea waves across my line of vision.

Charley snorts and sits up in the Cortina seat, trying to

come to terms with the revelation I had just revealed to him through the medium of Scrumpy Jack and Mexican Brown or Black. 'What the fuck…?' He ponders the possibilities and wipes his eyes with the heels of his palms. 'He was killed? How did he …?'

'Charley … Cha!'

'Car accident? Train? Not murdered surely? Wait,' something horrid dawns on Charley's foggy mind, 'he didn't commit suicide at all, did he? Just got a regular heart attack or brain hemorrhage…'

'I *lied* every time you asked me to swear on my father's grave. All those times that I had made outrageous claims: speaking with the dead … knowing the recipe for Coca-Cola … doing the Reiki Mistress up in the pine wood – well, I was telling the truth in that instance,' I admit. 'You think I'd swear on my father's grave if I could speak with the dead? Not noble.'

Charley's flabbergasted and displays this by taking an extra long drag on his spliff and holding it into until he turns grey. 'The Reiki Mistress?'

'Huh?'

'The *Mistress?*'

'What can I say? She opened up one too many chakras.' The Reiki Mistress, A.K.A eco-warrior, A.K.A Guinevere Hannigan, lives in a draughty caravan in the public park. Reiki's just a side-line. Her principal work consists of taking care of the coursing hares with loving care before they're ripped to pieces by two dumb greyhounds. A Rottweiler couple protect Guinevere from possible straying gypsies.

'She's got a beautiful figure beneath all those layers of hippie hemp and a pair of owl eyes to gaze into your soul, brother. If she just kept her mouth closed then she would be close to perfection but…'

'The voice, yeah, like a grown woman putting on a little girl's voice. It's disturbing,' concedes Charley.

'She's got a degree in Business and Finance but aims to

use it to "irrigate the world of corruption." Speaking of beneath all that hemp, y'know she asked me to go cut my nails halfway through foreplay. She told me that if she wanted a Caesarean she would've ordered one – not that she's too posh to push.' I'm stalling again and Charley knows it. I take a long swig from the drum of home-made apple juice and chew down on apple bits. 'What I'm trying to say, Cha, is that Fantasia turned out to be La Manga and the queen turned out to be that slut who used to work at the post-office.'

Charley says with a waning sense of hope, 'The Minotaur and goblins?'

'Grotesquery.'

'Aw, pity.' A distant memory illuminates Charley's face. He flicks a lever and the Cortina seat brings him up to sitting position. 'Wait! You're not talking about the cracker with the mane of long black hair?'

'The very same,' I concur, impressed with Charley's sense of recollection.

Charley's excited now, wildly tucking dreads behind his ears but he only has two. 'I used to go to the P.O. just to watch her lick stamps!'

'*All* the lads came in with their empty self-addressed envelopes ...'

Charley nods. 'I know it's wrong to say, Jon, but your shit of an old man went out in style. She was my queen of Fantasia too.' He takes a swig of apple-juice. 'I lost my virtual virginity to her.'

I feel the darkening frown crease my face as I do my sums on my gold Casio calculator watch. 'We can do her for child molestation, Cha. You must've been fourteen, fifteen max.'

'No, my first,' he gestures the same loose pulling sequence I had displayed just before; 'wank was dedicated to her – my *virtual* virginity.'

'A friend of the family spotted them together on a beach in La Manga.'

'Smooth. La Manga? Isn't that a Japanese comic?'

'It's on the coast of Spain. It sickens me, imagining them there on that tropical sand, two beached beluga whales, sand wedged between their cracks where the sun don't shine...'

'Continue,' Charley eggs me on.

'...while he knew that he had left three kids and a loving wife behind – a loving wife who had enough problems of her own...'

I don't need to tell Charley that I'm talking about the cancer. He remembers the toupee with mixed feelings – like me, deep down, if I'm not kidding myself. 'He didn't even have the balls to say that he was leaving us but pretended that he was dead. What an evil prick. Is it any wonder that Vera doesn't want me to know his name?'

'And the worst thing is that you've been swearing on his grave for the last two decades.' Charley's going off on his own tangent. 'The wise mountain-people of China say to be careful for what you wish for because it just might happen. Maybe you've already wished him to his real death and the previous one was just a trial run. He could be dead for all you know.' Charley stuffs his joint between his lips and holds up his hands. 'I'm not saying that you've killed daddy but the possibility is there.'

'He's *not* dead: he's been lodging money into an interest-bearing account for me. I've got about ten grand.'

All this is new for my friend. 'Is that all?'

'Huh?'

'Just work it out on your calculator watch. He left 128 when you were nine. He must've been lodging fifty cent a week over twenty-one years.'

'He only opened the account five years ago.'

Charley's thinking. 'Why are you always sponging off me, then?' He looks as if he's going to add something to that but loses the thread of the conversation. 'I mean...'

'It's an interest-bearing account, Charley, with a fixed term of five years. There's nothing I can do. My hands are tied. It's up next week. I take it out today and I lose three grand. And I'll pay you back, y'know I'm good for it.'

That seems good enough for Charley. 'What will you do with the cash?'

'Probably open a private investigation office in Dublin or London, maybe even Brooklyn.'

'But you've got to hand it to the bastard: he worded the suicide note perfectly and strategically placed the car without ever mentioning his death; just waited for people to draw their own conclusions. *"Going on to a better place"* normally means Heaven or Valhalla but not El Mango. The thing is this: technically he didn't lie to your mother.'

'True,' I concede. I had thought about this before. I'd thought about Clinical Dad from every angle.

'Don't you want to know his name?'

'Don't want to know it, Cha,' I lie. Knowing my father's name would've somehow given me closure on that sorry episode of our lives. 'He can grease my palm with forty shillings of silver but –'

'Ten thousand euro isn't forty shillings of silver, Jon.'

'In today's exchange rate, yes.'

'Now I can understand why you went into genealogy. Your family tree is a yet-to-be-discovered species lost in some jungle: you receive money from the living-dead. You don't know the living-dead benefactor's name but you take the money anyway. Your grandfather has no idea who he is anymore. Susan is, well, white … Tommy's Tommy … and you don't know who *you* are?' Charley announces sarcastically. 'Of course you don't, Jon, my son, why would you? You're a lost lamb bleating on the side of a mountain. God *looove* you, private investigation and a PhD in genealogy are the perfect couple. It makes complete sense. Well played, my son.' Charley pauses. 'And does 45 even have a name? It's always been just 45, hasn't it?'

'Denny Rowe. That's the first time I've ever mentioned his name.'

'Naw, he looks more like a 45.'

Outside, Vera calls my name. 'Jonny, c'mon! We're all waiting.'

I pop my head outside the door of the bong-house. 45 is standing in front of the crowd, microphone in one hand and gesturing me to join him with the other. I freeze but put on a brave face. I turn to Charley before I leave. 'I'm glad we've had this little chat, therapy, y'know. I think I should start seeing myself in the bathroom mirror again. I don't feel as insignificant.'

I levitate towards the crowd, the fresh air hitting me hard and sending me into another pleasant spiral. 'I'd just like to say a few words.' Vera's half-shot on alcopops and her slurred sentence sounds more like she wants to *save a few birds*. 'Jonny's a man today,' she mumbles into the mike.

I sense her subliminal messaging coming my way immediately: *Get out of my house, get a job, and start paying for your bedroom or I'll rent it out from under your ass or how 'bout I rent your ass...*

She smiles and toasts in my direction. 'Our 20's are for dreamin' and our thirties are for what-we-could've-been. Happy birthday, Jonny!'

'Happy Birthday!' yell the guests.

'Yea-yea,' goes Tommy.

Vera's last statement doesn't have a subliminal message but I have read between the lines and I will never give up the idea of opening my own private investigation agency.

Tommy passes a second microphone into my hand, speaking in broken language, 'Yea-yea, best in the west … make or break, Jon, yea-yea.'

Suddenly, 45 turns my back to the crowd. 'Jonny, kid, do an old man a favour?'

I'm gearing up to sing a duet with 45 and he hijacks me in front of all these people. 45's never asked for a favour in his life and I'm thunderstruck. Everybody's waiting and watching and my mouth's dropped open into a comical O expression on my face, I just know it.

'Take me back home when all this is done, huh? I'd do it

myself only I'm afraid they,' flicking a thumb over his shoulder, 'might turn me in: what ya' see isn't always what ya' get. You do that for 45 and he'll come back as a blonde bombshell with a chassis you could eat your dinner off, hmm. How 'bout that, son?' Then, with a sense of resignation, he tells me, 'I never belonged here. My heart's somewhere else.'

To the rest of the guests, it must seem that I've got stage-fright. I've known 45 most of my memorable life and I've never heard him speak so lucid. Why now? In front of all these guests who are Vera's work-mates, basically. I'm taken aback by 45's candid words. I'm wondering if what *I* see is what I get. I want to tell him that his *head* is somewhere else. The old man is fretting so I place my hand on his shoulder to steady him and forget that we ever had this conversation. 'What do you want to sing?'

'I won't be safe until I'm outta here for good,' he whispers, 'the whole goddamn show, hoop-la.'

I cast a glance over my shoulder. 'Which song? *Pleeease.*' I see a distant acceptance in 45's eyes that I don't care for all that much. I slap him on the back and flash a bewildered smile to my family and strangers. Brillo's looking at me with a stony expression; her eyes eating into the core of my soul. I can see her mentally undressing me and carrying-out a set of fetish procedures which border on torture. She makes me feel as if I'm hiding something. Am I? More to the point, is 45 hiding something? He knows I'm not going to ask more questions with our audience awaiting our duet.

45 leads off with *I Did It My Way* again but I'm not sure I have a song in me now nor am I sure that I've just heard a lucky streak of random words that happen to fall in together to make sense. I make the effort to wail into the mike, joining in on the chorus and looking into his eyes that are, I sense, trying to suggest something but my mind is cloudy on drink and drugs. Vera is on her feet clapping. Next to her is a stranger taking photos of us. That

worries me a little. Across the yard, beyond the guests' heads, Charley is bopping at the door of the bong-house. He ducks away and comes up at the window, his bare arse to the cob-webbed glass. I mention this between lyrics and everybody turns around to get a glimpse of Charley's doughy buttocks but he's too quick for them.

When we finish our number and do our bows, Vera announces that Brillo would like to say a few words. A silence looms in the crowd.

'As custom in my land, when you have thirty years old, a mountain witch must give you the rite of passage.'

I am expecting a little more clarification on that but Brillo lays down the microphone with an echo and takes me by my hand. She leads me back inside the house to a roar of raucous laughter behind me and Tommy's sweet amber goading tones, 'How 'bout a round of applause for Brillo and the birthday boy about to become a man, yea-yea.'

'I became a man when I was eighteen!' I cry but nobody wants to know.

Brillo takes me to her bedroom, closes the door and pulls the curtains. Her dark beefy outline sits on the bed to a creaky chorus of rusty springs. I immediately suspect foul play. Now, I understand her ambiguous words to be taken literally and wonder which passage in particular she's speaking of because I'm not willing to travel down any of them. Not without a guide. How could Vera have agreed to this sick game? I blush in the darkness of Brillo's hired bedroom. She grabs me by my hand.

'I don't *need* the rite of passage, believe me.' Expecting to feel a sagging tit, I feel the silicon of her latex pillow instead. In the dim light, she gestures me to sit next to her on the bed while mumbling some highland gibberish. Next thing, I've got a piercing light shining in my right eye. I go to pull away but Brillo's got me by the wrists like a hand-cuff.

'Relax, Pampaquino, I'm going only to look into

26

your eye-hole.' Thankful that she doesn't want to look
into any of my other holes, I gladly agree to her tractor
beam. I'm so close to her now that I can smell garlic on her
breath even though garlic hadn't been on the birthday lunch
menu. The sudden image of Brillo's face so close to mine
is really off-putting. Brillo gives a little gasp as my right
pupil expands and my iris contracts.

'What is it?' I'm slightly alarmed now. 'Have you
found something?'

'You are going on a journey...'

'What time? Where?'

'It's time to say your goodbyes.' 'Huh?' Before I have
time to assimilate what has just occurred, the beam of light
is gone and the bedroom is in brightness again. I'm led
once more from her bedroom like a child and she locks the
door behind us as if I'd want to go in there again.

'Where am I going, Brillo? I can't drive ... I've got
Scrumpy-Jack and Mexican Brown or Black in my
bloodstream.'

'I cannot tell you anymore other than ... *pack your
bags.*'

'There you go again with the sound-bytes! Jesus!
What're you talking *about??*'

'You must leave, Jonny. There are forces at work behind
our control. *Run, Pampaquino!*' Brillo looks possessed.

'Would you please stop with the movie clichés and
break this down for me. You mean *beyond* our control,
don't you? *Who* am I saying goodbye to? *Where* am I
going? *When* am I going? Is it me that's going somewhere
or am I saying goodbye to somebody else going
somewhere?' Then I remember my sinking feeling this
morning – an ominous and foreboding instinct.

'All I know,' Brillo added, 'is that ... *your time is
near.*'

We cross the threshold and back outside to the patio
to another cheer and applause but I am confused by Brillo's
words. I don't have time to reflect on the mountain witch's

speech as 45 comes ducking and bobbing towards me. For a moment, I think that he wants to engage in a friendly boxing match for the benefit of the crowd and I hold up my fists to his face...

'I want to give you your birthday present, Jon.'

'Oh.' I put hands in my pockets.

45 digs in his inside suit pocket and pulls out a red balloon. The guests cheer in response to his motor neurons. He stretches the balloon between his gnarled fingers. 'They didn't have any blow-up dolls in Tesco...' His chin jitters.

I know by the robotic way he says it that he had been coached, probably by Tommy, judging by the way he was ready with the punch-line. The crowd falls around the patio laughing like idiots but laughing like they would at a young child who had just uttered something rude without knowing it. In the background I hear, 'yea, yea, yea.'

45 puts the balloon to his lips and puffs into it. With each blow the liquored-up guests cheer and applaud, '*Oi!*' ... '*Oi!*' ... '*Oi!*' By now, anything that moves deserves an encore. To my surprise I begin to make out: *Happy Birthday ...nny!* along the face of my balloon in black marker. I cannot make out the last word yet. Vera looks as surprised and perplexed as me.

It's as if 45 has never suffered from the forgetting disease. This is remarkable and anybody who knows our situation is also beginning to see the importance of this moment and soften off into a quiet respect. Vera's anonymous workmate is up on her toes and taking snaps again. Should I know this woman?

As 45 huffs and puffs, I grow a little disappointed to read: *Happy Birthday Fanny!* People begin to laugh all over again and point at the bold marker script on the big red balloon inflating in 45's shaking hands.

Tommy's rolling around on the lawn in fits, obviously having orchestrated the whole thing. It's his hand-writing, I'm sure of it. But just to see 45 blow up that red balloon is a breath of fresh air.

45 briefly breaks from his blowing and gazes at the
words. I know by his reaction that he has no idea why the
strangers are laughing – the young child again – and

it breaks my heart. He takes a deep gulp to a rapturous
applause and blows again. He does this several times to an
'Oi!' from the onlookers...

And things are about to get weird...

45's face begins to turn the same colour as the balloon
but he insists on blowing up my birthday present. Angry
veins begin to pop in his temples inside his cute party-hat.
He had replaced his Bank of Ireland hat and I'd hardly
noticed.

'It's big enough, 45, um, thanks!'

But he insists on blowing until the balloon is stretched to
capacity. He puts a knot in the base of the balloon and, with
surprising agility, ties it with a red party streamer. He
hands it to me. I take it but he won't let go. He hangs his
head low and for a moment I think that he's fallen asleep.
'45?'

When he looks up at me again his terrified eyes are
bulging and his swollen face has turned a garish purple,
and the most tragic of all, his party hat is gone lop-sided.
For a brief hallucinatory moment, the balloon
and 45 look like Siamese twins.

Somebody screams...

Vera shoves people out of the way and drunkenly
runs to 45 as he gasps for air before dropping to the tiles.
Everybody else crowds around him. I get pushed out of the
way in the stampede, leaving me holding my balloon and
feeling like a lost child in a big super-market. To disperse
the crowd, Tommy tries using a squeal of wailing feedback
between his mike and speaker but it only adds to the chaos
while some people thank Christ the ambulance has arrived
in record time. People drop to the ground and do nothing
but panic and cry in drunken stupors.

'Somebody do something!!' I hear my voice in the
distance but nobody knows what to do. I try dialling 911

twice on my iPhone, my fingers shaking so badly that I can barely punch in the numbers. I get through to a moron who obviously has spent a life-time being on the receiving end of an emergency call. As I give our address, I gaze at my birthday guests slapping and poking 45. Tommy props him up like a ghastly life-size marionette and tries a dodgy Heimlich maneuver. In the struggle, 45's party hat rolls down onto his face like a puppet beak in a surreal theatre play. 45 slumps to the ground and Tommy screams as he puts his lower back out. Lucy screams after that, taking her hand out of her crotch, and runs to her fiancée's aide.

I stand back and watch my birthday bash landslide and backslide into a morbid nightmare. I pick 45's party hat off the patio tiles and strap it to my head and hug my balloon – all that is left of 45 who was here just a moment ago.

With growing unease, I realize that 45 is living in my red birthday balloon.

3.
45's Essence

'Do you understand what I'm trying to say?'

The following day is Wednesday and we've got more strangers in our house but this time it's for 45's Irish wake. Vera has decided that being a man from Iowa, her father would've appreciated the ancient Irish tradition. There's a fine line between drowning one's sorrows and celebrating as far as I'm concerned and Vera seems to have jumped into 45's farewell with more gusto than I care for. So surreal, 45's everywhere and nowhere at 128 Hydrangea Drive. He sits in an open coffin on the kitchen table in the middle of the living-room. Yes, sitting. Vera figured that he would like one last look around 128 before retiring to the ground so she's propped him up with Brillo's orthopedic pillow. Strangers mingle and shuffle around his casket to have a morbid gawp at his pallid shell. The old man is dressed in his Sunday best and looks as if he's going somewhere as usual. I can't get to terms with the fact that he is three feet away from me but also on the other side of the Milky Way by now, up there in the night skies, a million light years off. As a mark of respect, I have refused to remove 45's birthday cone-hat from my head since yesterday. The elastic band is beginning to chaff into my ears but I suffer for my sins: the sin of being 45's death catalyst. In his honour, I've stopped all clocks at 45's time of death: 3.20 in the pm. My cheap Casio gold calculator-watch that Charley had given me for my 29th birthday says 10.55am. I couldn't stall time on this digital watch without taking out the battery which I couldn't do, managing to snap three knives in quick succession. Time stops for no man. At this time, on any other day, 45 would've been sitting on our back doorstep, waiting for his bus to Iowa. He didn't even sit at the front doorstep to make matters worse. Not only was there a Greyhound bus coming for him but it was coming down the hallway and out the back door. Maybe his ghost is sitting out there now. I decide to have a look but all that's out there is the cat, Molly, curled in a ball. I sigh and go back inside to the Reiki Mistress and stand vigil by 45's cold side.

We continue our conversation.

'But do you *really* understand what I'm trying to say?'

I ask the Reiki Mistress who paces my living room pensively with a tuna canapé held constantly to her lips as if she's whispering to it. She lays it down half-eaten and takes hold of my hand.

'I *emphatically* understand without you even having to say it, Jonny. He's everywhere and nowhere,' eyes gawping around the room while sprinkling something like fairy dust with her wiggling fingers. Every time the Mistress opens her mouth I'm reminded of a Disney cartoon character and more so while chomping on canapés and mini-muffins. She could be perfect with her swarthy Mediterranean looks and hemp. Still, we're all diamonds in the rough, according to Charley, only achieving true perfection at the time of our deaths. She grabs hold of my hands again but I pull away. It's in bad taste to show signs of affection in the presence of 45's noble corpse. I doubt he would agree with me. In fact, he most likely would have a crack at the Reiki Mistress if he were around.

'At the moment,' I tell her while looking at 45 taking in the scenery, 'I don't even know how to react to a slice of bread.'

'But that's just it, Jonny. That's you all over. You don't *have* to react to a slice of bread, just pick it up and toast it or perhaps smother a light blanket of butter across it … or maybe a dollop of chutney. You think too much.'

The whole house smells of 45, literally, I've just sprinkled his last bottle of Old Spice on the advice of the Reiki Mistress. I think it's clashing with the finger food. She recommended that I baptize the house in his holy water to exorcise any evil spirits that might try to wedge their way in. Personally, I think she has invited herself for the free finger food. She's going ape-shit on guacamole.

'He's here. I know it.'

'Jonny, your grandfather's spirit has travelled with the speed of a hotmail attachment to where it is to reside and take care of business.'

I genuinely want to know where 45 would consider his real home. 'And where would that be?' To think that he's not here with us would really hurt, I think.

'Je ne se quoi, Jonny. I'm not a clairvoyant, just sensitive.'

I didn't study French but I'm sure this expression is out of place here but I don't have the heart to tell her and not really interested anyway in my melancholic state.

'Who are all these people?!' I fight to keep my voice to a whisper so I stuff a kitchen towel into my cheeks and pull it out again. I'm a mess, I know it.

'Pull yourself together, Jon.'

'I want to slam that coffin shut and tell these strangers to go home. It's not a *bloody* side-show.'

'They're paying their respects, Jonny.'

'I never saw any of these people 'round here when 45 was alive. Why should they give a shit now? Why didn't they come and pay their respects when he was alive? Leeches! I knew the finger food was a bad idea!' I realize that I'm calling my on-off girlfriend a leech but she lives in a special drawer in my box-shaped heart.

It dawns on me that nobody here really knew 45. He's an unknown quantity propped up in a wooden box. They know what I know: how he fought in World War II or some war where he lost his knee; how he came to settle down in Ireland after seeing terrible things in Germany or was it Austria? How he had married Nan and how she two-timed him once she got the whiff of senility.

'45 lived half of his life in and around Iowa and nobody knows anything about that. There's nobody here that provides a connection to his previous life.' There's something starting to really bug me about that but I'm not sure yet what it is.

'A ghost ship lost at sea...' The Mistress stares into space while nibbling on pistachios.

The Scrumpy Jack is kicking in now and I feel my hobbled speech pattern. 'I don't want ... I don't want to give his farewell too much thought because if I do I could run screaming from here any moment now. The magnitude of never ever seeing him again is like falling down into a black bottomless pit of pining.'

'Mini-muffin?'

'Thanks.' I wash it down with another gulp of Scrumpy straight from the five-gallon drum which I keep by my side.

'Doesn't he look so peaceful,' says a stranger who's just wandered in. It's the same woman who had been taking snaps of my duet with 45.

Of course he looks peaceful, you fucking idiot – he's dead!! Do you think he looks noble and peaceful by choice?!

I want to scream but the Mistress, who knows me by now, shoves in to protect me. 'Deep breaths,' she advises with a cautious smile. 'Remember my relaxing pointers.' We had done some transcendental meditation in her caravan during our strictly plutonic sessions. But it always ended up with me taking advantage of her when her eyes were closed. The erotic effect wore off when I noticed that she had started to open an eyelid slightly in anticipation of my advance ... and put her lips.

'I uploaded the photographs of the birthday party onto my Facebook page, by the way. Oh, they're hilarious, you should see them. You there singing *I Did it My Way* with 45. So symbolic: sort of onimous really when you think about the song he chose.'

I respond, 'Ominous, yes.'

'His farewell tune: he was telling us that he was to be remembered by the words of this majestic song. Do you know that?'

'Um, well…'

'Your birthday snaps and videos have since been viewed by 254 people on Facebook – mostly friends of friends which make them strangers in my book – *Face*book.' She chuckles at her inane self and prods my sternum which I don't love. '*You* are famous. You (prod) … are (prod) … famous (prod). We have become best friends on Facebook.'

'Sorry, you are?'

'Mary. I'm V's boss.'

'V?'

'Your mother – Vera. I'm the one who's responsible for high turnover of staff at the airport but I say scheisser – that's German – keep those foreign nationals on their toes and don't let 'em get too comfy or they'll slip right in under our noses.'

'Uh-huh, just like evil spirits.' Am I nude? I feel a longing wish to lie down beside him, 45, in his coffin. I probably wouldn't fit so I would have to lie on him and that's called necrophilia. 'It looks so claustrophobic in there. The coffin's too small.'

'He didn't have a problem getting into small spaces from what I've heard.'

'Huh?'

'A bit of a lady's man, if rumours are to be believed.'

'Oh, will you excuse me,' I flash Vera's boss a courteous smile, 'I think I'm deaf 'n dumb.'

Mary puts her arm around my bony shoulders. 'Don't worry, the pine'll hold him in.' She clicks and winks and all sorts of facial gestures that I think may be tics.

From a safe distance, Mary looks adoringly at 45's waxy glued complexion. 'They did a great job, don't you think?'

'Whatever.'

'He looks really dapper.' She takes a tipple of the mulled wine, peeks over her shoulder and mutters out the side of her mouth, 'He looked deader when he was alive.' Before I've time to react she's winking and contorting again.

'Y'know, he slapped my bottom once when nobody was

looking.' She looks proud. 'Not the same thing as when everybody's looking.' She blinks another grotesque wink. 'Tut, tut.' She slaps her wrist.

'I wouldn't get my hopes up,' I warn Mary, 'he used to slap my bottom too.' I grab the Mistress's hand and leave for my bedroom. I can feel Vera's boss's eyes on my buttocks as I recede down the hallway.

When I get to my bedroom, Charley's lying in my bed next to 45's Siamese twin. My big red balloon is resting on my pillow by Charley's head while its string is laced onto the headboard. They look cute, the two of them lying in my bunk-bed.

Charley flicks a thumb at the balloon. 'Just keeping the old man company.'

I had placed a photograph of the old man on my bedside locker. I had taken the snap while he had been waiting for the Iowa bus one morning. I light a candle and place it next to his photo but quench it when I see that the balloon reacts to the heat thrown from the flame. 'Killing him once was enough.'

'Jonny, you had nothing to do with 45's death!' The Mistress isn't taking any of my self pity. 'If it hadn't been the balloon it would've been something else: faulty socket … slip in the bath … choke on some cheese … swallow his tongue. Take solace in the fact that he died while doing something for you.'

'I put him in that coffin,' I announce in my best condemning voice. Charley asks. 'But isn't that against the law or something? Something about placing unwitting elderly in places where … or …'

'No, Cha, I mean, in a roundabout way. If he hadn't been blowing up my balloon his heart wouldn't have blown up.'

'If, if,' Charley's taking no prisoners either. 'If I wasn't Charley then I wouldn't be here.'

'Here, here,' offers the Mistress. 'You have a conscience after all, Charley.'

Charley sits up and lovingly tucks the balloon beneath

his arm. 'What are you going to do with 45?'

'I was thinking of climbing to the top of the water reservoir in the park and setting him free.'

'Naw, you definitely don't want to do that.' The Reiki Mistress had obviously thought about this option. 'He'd just come down on the football pitch and have seven colours of shit hammered out of him.'

I flinch at that thought while Charley skits. We ponder the dilemma of 45's last dying breaths suspended in my birthday balloon.

'You could ingest your grandfather,' suggests Charley, out of the blue.

'Hmm?'

'You could swallow your granddad.'

The Mistress and I look into his glassy eyes and decide not to pay too much attention to anything he would say during the next hour. But the more I think about that image, the more I like the idea. 'I suppose it would be the ultimate mark of respect. We would become one in noble gesture.'

'In some Asian countries, the young picnic on their dead elders, babe.'

The Mistress is playing along with the idea which begs me to think that maybe I *should* inhale 45. I think about it a little more and decide that it's riddled with flaws. 'We wouldn't have 45's best interests at heart. He was a free spirit and a tour of my lungs isn't freedom. Can you imagine what would happen to him when I smoke one of Charley's exotic cigarettes?' I manage a weak smile imagining 45 traversing my twin bronchioles.

Vera pops her head in the door. She's flustered and her hair's all straggled and wild. She's got dirt stains on her face and her hands are filthy along with her knees. 'Has anybody got the right time? All the bloody clocks are stopped...'

'Where were you or should I ask?' I ask.

'Digging.' She answers as if I should know where she's been. Maybe I should; obviously she's been digging.

'Okay. Do you have to dig today?'

'Problem with the sewerage system.' Vera nods to the window so Charley and I take a look out onto the back lawn. The lawn looks as if moles have been to visit only moles don't exist in Ireland. She'd attacked the lawn in a haphazard way, digging great random chunks of dirt and turf.

Charley, the Mistress, and I exchange glances.

'I flushed a few minutes ago,' Charley admits, 'and there was no problem.'

The Reiki Mistress inflects her helium voice, 'the sewerage system did you say? Were you looking for pipes or treasure?'

'It's fixed now.' Vera snaps and disappears from the door, telling us that she must get dressed "for the funeral". How *cold*.

'I think her father's death hasn't hit her yet,' Charley observes, loosening his tie.

The Reiki Mistress nods, 'How *peculiar*.'

I agree with them.

Five minutes later, Vera comes back in dressed in sombre black. The last time she had used this outfit was at Clinical Dad's phony funeral.

'Did you manage to notify his family in Iowa?' Charley asks Vera. 'Just reverse the charges.'

'His family's here.' Vera counters, quite out of character, 'He doesn't have family in Iowa.'

I can't let this slide. 'Of course he does,' I protest. 'He was from Iowa, so in theory, he has family there.'

'Jonny should know, Vera,' says the Mistress, 'he's the one with the degree in gynaecology.'

'That's right, Guin. I deal with vaginas on a regular basis.'

'Amen,' praises Charley.

'I've cleaned up dad's bedroom,' says Vera to Charley, 'if you want to stay tonight. I expect it'll be a late one.' She addresses me. 'Maybe you'd like the old fountain pen he never used? It's a Sheaffer mottle-brown fountain pen with 45 engraved on its gold-band top. He always said that he'd never use that pen until he found the right moment to use it. I guess he never got around to it.'

I can't believe what I'm hearing. 'Am I the only one here who thinks it's wrong to stay in 45's room tonight?'

Charley doesn't think anything of Vera's obscene suggestion of staying the night in his bedroom. He thanks her but turns down her offer, citing 'creepiness' as the main reason not to sleep in the same bedroom as 45. 'Guinevere might like to stay.' I can feel Charley's mocking eyes searing into me.

'No thanks,' answers the Mistress readily. 'The room needs time to settle.'

I take what Charley and the Mistress say with a pinch of salt, but *Vera?* 'Why do you want to wipe 128 clean of any evidence that 45 ever lived here with
us? What's wrong with all of you? He's lying out there
in the living-room and you just can't wait to get him in
the ground.'

'Call it tying up loose ends, Jonny.'

How can Vera be so flippant? There's a heavy silence in my bedroom. Vera gazes longingly at the big red balloon lying on the bunk-bed. 'Poor bastard...' She smiles a benign smile.

'How could you be so heartless to him?' I'm enraged. 'That man sitting in that box out there was my foster-dad and you *know* that! Not that creep-fuck who left a false suicide note for his family. Fucking *loser!*' I want to take back what I've just said even though it's what I think of Clinical Dad. I can't control my feelings. Get a grip, Jon. Get a fucking, *grip!*

'Oh, dear Jesus, Jonny! Since when? *What?!*'

I'd forgotten that I hadn't told the Reiki Mistress and now Vera's expression too has gone Technicolor Disney to match the Mistress's face.

'Don't worry,' calming Vera, 'Charley knows

39

everything … and now Guinevere knows.' I offer a brief apology to the Mistress. 'Charley knows everything because he happens to be a great therapist. I'm suffering from identity crisis, see.'

'That's rich,' quips Vera. I can't help thinking that there's a double-meaning in there somewhere.

'Babe, I thought I was your therapist?' The Mistress's body language becomes one tight defensive slip-knot. 'And the Reiki? Hmm? Transcendental medi-tation ring any bells?'

Vera's begun to make whining sounds and Charley's expression becomes concerned but I continue my line of attack. 'It wouldn't make any difference to me if Clinical Dad re-wrote that note and really did fling himself into the river because I'm shot of that whoremeister.' *Whoremeister?* I wouldn't have been able to get away with that adjective under normal
circumstances.

Vera's whines are turning into long pining cries
now. She hides her face in her hands and begins to sob. 'Jonny, look at it from my point of view: I've been
caring for a stranger for most of my life.'

'Stranger?!' What's she talking about?!

'Nobody here knows about his life before meeting my mother. He never spoke about his war-time days because of the horrors he saw. Later in life he went senile so the chances of ever finding out more about him became remote. Lost cause.'

The Mistress takes on a mystical aura. 'An island.'

'45 swept your Nan off her feet with his one knee, tomfoolery and shenanigans but if I had had a time-machine, maybe I would've tried to talk mother out of marrying him…'

'Have you seen *Back to the Future*, Vera? I think you could identify with it.'

Vera thanks Charley through a mist of tears and sniffles.

'It's like adopting a dog from the pound cos you don't

know what you're bringing into your home; especially a man-dog that tends to wander.' She shakes her head to drive home the point.

'Nan's the one who *wandered*.' I feel the awkward silence even before I finish my line. We had never spoken of Nan's infidelities at 128 or her death at the teeth of her lover's buzz saw. I'd spoken about it with Charley a dozen times and ole' Buzz had become something of a running joke. I feel Charley squirming next to me. I can feel his nerves. He's gonna jump and say something and I almost hear him do the *Bzzzzz* and I shoot him a look which begs him not to say it. I'm increasingly finding it difficult to separate reality from more-or-less-reality.

'But that'd be calling her a bitch.' Charley's untimed quip trails off.

'Bang, there, it's out. Feel better now, Cha?'

Vera's in her own world. 'I was the one who invited him to our place when mother passed on. I was the one who cleaned up his shit and piss from the acorn flower-pot because it wasn't the toilet.'

Thankfully, I hadn't seen that but I take Vera's word for it.

'I'm the one who turned the other cheek when I saw him slapping Brillo's backside going up the stairs … *and* coming down it. How do you think that made me feel?'

Charley shakes his head in disapproval but I know what he's thinking. Brillo, the domestic farm animal. By the way, Brillo isn't our home-help's original name – that's unpronounceable. Tommy and I came with that one: comparing Brillo's coarse mat of hair and head to one of those Brillo pads that are used to scour dirty plates etc. We used the name behind her back for three years before she walked in on our conversation. On the spur of the moment, I explained that Brillo is the short for Brilliant and she seemed happy with that.

'Nobody from 45's American side has ever tried to contact him since I've been his daughter and that's forty-nine years so, in my book, we were the only family that dad ever had.'

I happen to agree with everything Vera says. There's logic in what she's saying. It's all truth but I've never seen Vera try to track down anybody. She never came to me, being a student of genealogy. It would've been a pleasure to discover 45's American family tree.

Vera continues her rant. 'Who forked out for personal home-help for him, hmm? Don't think for a minute that your waster of a father ever helped me financially.' Vera looks at me for support but I stare out the window. 'Besides, he fought in a war and that deserves some respect despite losing his poxy knee-cap in 'Nam to a pair of dwarf Ewok cooks...'

'Gooks,' I interject. 'It's a racial slur.'

'... who used his knee as a pogo-stick,' vents Vera. 'All I'm saying is that it hasn't been easy for me these last few years. I'm the one who battled cancer and it seems that I've been battling against something all my bloody life...'

Christ, I'd put the cancer away in a file marked UNFORGETTABLE.

Vera begins to cry. Her whole body convulses as she lets go and bawls for time that has passed. On the Mistress's cue, we sit down on my bunk-bed beside her and hold her until the wave of sadness passes over. I guess all this had affected her more than she had been letting on. '45 *was* my dad despite what you may think, Jon. Don't forget.'

I *had* forgotten. In my own little disowned world I had overlooked Vera. I've never seen her look as forlorn as she does now, sitting on the edge of my bed; ageing fifteen years in minutes like a cheap film special-effect. Her hair is scraggly and the lines in her face and the dark bags under her eyes are bloated and cracked on turmoil and pent-up feelings that I guess I will *never* understand.

'Sorry.' Now, my pleasant Scrumpy buzz is starting to wear off. This whole thing feels like I'm after waking up from a horror nightmare only to realize that I've woken into a worse one.

The high-pitch beep of a car-horn breaks us from our trance.

'The hearse,' announces Charley, taking a peep through the curtains.

'C'mon guys, time to get the show on the road,' says Vera.'

'Don't worry, Vera,' The Mistress consoles my mother by putting her arm around her waist, 'life's all about opening and closing chakras. Sometimes you have to close one chakra before you can open another, especially if there's a draught. Believe me; I've opened enough chakras to know.'

The Mistress looks up at me and all I can manage is a stiff smile and a wink? It just happened. I'll blame it on a tic if questioned later. Although, I think it's the best line she could've possibly offered at such a sad juncture in our lives and I feel I should call her Guinevere out of pure respect. I hope she picks up on my wink as an approval but not a sexually-charged one. I lost my virginity to the Mistress some years ago when she let her guard down during Reiki. On hindsight, it's probably what she's really talking about now; her sexual peccadilloes.

The hearse beeps its horn again. The driver keeps his finger on the horn a little longer this time, allowing it to sing its full melodic beeps. It's a tune that you might hear in the middle of New Delhi traffic which I think is in poor taste considering that we're grieving.

We straighten ourselves up and lay 45 down to rest in peace. Charley, me, Tommy and three other strangers lift 45's coffin. I've never understood the saying "dead weight" until this morning. The pine coffin chews down into my clavicles and, according to my genealogical Studies, the Rowes have always had bony clavicles – all the way from the famine. We negotiate 45's wooden box from the living room, knocking off a chunk of plaster by the door, and walk soberly down the hallway. I cry for the loss of 45 but cry more for the fact that nobody else seems to be crying because nobody else gives a shit because nobody else knows 45 like I do – did. Maybe I cry the most because it was my birthday balloon that had given him the heart attack. And now, carrying his carcass to the ground, I wonder if I ever *really* knew him. Why would I think that now? Vera seems to be as much in the dark as me when it comes to the island we call 45.

I refuse to remove my party-hat.

4.
Stain-Glass Secrets

The mass service is fast and efficient which suits everybody. Nobody here is a church-goer because serious illness has caused everybody to lose their faith and trust in fate instead. As I sit through the service and listen to the droning priest, I know there's still something bugging me. Something 45 had said before he passed. The guilty notion that I'd put him in that pine box still niggles at me. One thing's for sure: there's more of him in the big red balloon tied to our church pew than in that pine box on stilts.

Happy Birthday Fanny! is garnering a few sideward glances, especially from Father Moran but I refuse to hide the balloon on moral principles and likewise say no to removing 45's birthday cone-hat.

'I'm not sure whether it's within the church rules to allow a balloon into the house of God,' he says before the service, 'never mind the fact that it openly advertises women's vaginas. Vera, you of all people should know that.' He whispers these words into my mother's volatile ear while offering his condolences to others.

'Excuse me? What the *hell* does that mean!?' Vera snaps. I've never seen her so irate with red blotches erupting on her face.

Father Moran decides to play down his previous comment so offers a messy smile. 'C'mon Vera, it's not a party.'

'Were you born under a head of cabbage, Father?' Vera counteracts, in no mood to entertain this hypocrite, 'Why don't you ring Rome and ask them how they feel about women's,' raising her voice, '*vaginas?* The big V, hmm.' Her nostrils flare like a dragon's. I can feel her static electricity sitting next to her and my birthday balloon gravitates towards her.

'I think you'll find they share the same opinion,'

answers Father Moran, smiling his flabby turkey-jowl grin that doesn't reach his eyes. The sour stench of stale liquor wafts in on his breath and I guess that he's half shot.

'Whether you like it or not, *you* were once inside a vagina.' Vera's livid. 'Ask the Virgin Mary how she feels about vaginas or maybe she doesn't have one?'

I make a point of fixing a sailor's knot onto the balloon string in her defence which throws Father Moran's demeanour. He quickly completes protocol by briefly offering his hand to the rest of my family like a pop star slapping the out-held hands of his fans. He turns in silent anger and blows out the alter candles and orders the alter-boys to light them correctly this time. I tell Vera that he wouldn't have said such things if he had been sober. I make a mental note to write a letter of complaint to the pope.

Halfway during the mass service, I briefly flirt with the idea of making public what 45 had meant to me as a father-figure and how he had moulded me into the man that I am today but I don't think a church is a place to do it for various personal reasons nor do I think it will do any justice to 45 considering the man he had moulded me into, if that makes sense. I look at the big red balloon dangling from the pew in front of me and feel a certain sense of comfort that 45's still floating around inside there, but a little anxious too because he has to be set free. It isn't in his nature to be cooped up like this in a balloon.

Then it happens…

Jesus of Nazareth…

If ever I witness divine intervention then it has to be now. The sun comes through the stain-glass window above us to the right and casts a multi-colour hue onto my birthday balloon held firmly between my knees,

revealing (and at this point I let out an audible *'Huh?!'*

which turns several heads in my direction*)* something sitting inside the lip of my balloon. I remind myself of symbiologist Robert Langdon in *The Da Vinci Code*.

At the altar, Father Moran makes a point of breaking

from his vague mumblings and cranes his neck to get a better look down at the sparse congregation. He clears his throat and continues muttering an *Our Father* while I study my balloon without trying to draw attention, turning it over in my hands a few times and see, to my amazement, that there's a note in there!

I cannot believe it! 45 had slipped a note into my birthday balloon!

My brain becomes scrambled. I have to tell somebody so I turn to Charley who is sitting in the pew across the aisle to my left with the Mistress and a few other strangers. We, the family, are on this side of the aisle. Vera's sitting on my left so I have to signal to Charley across her stern face and further across the middle aisle. Bear in mind that we're sitting up at the front pews, so close that I can pluck one of Moran's nasal hairs if I wish, not that I'm inclined to do so. I lip-synch M-E-S-S-A-G-E but Charley just frowns and lips back at me, *huh...?* I mime every possible clue and combination but quickly get so frustrated that I resemble my red birthday balloon. As a final desperate gesture, I start jiggling my balloon in front of Vera's face until Moran begins to throw me dirty looks. After a few more minutes of sweating, I get the Reiki Mistress's attention and mime to her what I've just found but she cannot read my lips nor hand gestures which surprises me considering she regularly engages in astral projections. I try Tommy on my right but he just shrugs his shoulders and holds Lucy's hands, far too close to his crotch region for my liking. Jesus, I need to get a life. Then I try to make contact with Susan or Alba (not sure if that's just her or her and her followers). She's brought two of her Alba sect members with her, flanking her on either side like demented angels. They wear their angelic white Goth outfits and, for the first time in their lives, actually fit in with the occasion. She sends me back a lip-synch reading: *Yeah, it's a balloon, Jon...* followed by a long exasperated sigh. *Get over it!*

I have no choice but to sit tight.

Father Moran closes the service and leaves the stage prematurely after gulping an extra goblet of wine for the good of the Old Testament. Maybe he's right, I reflect, it shouldn't be all about the New Testament.

Once again, we carry 45's coffin down the main aisle. Alba carries my balloon in the procession. Tommy ducks out early from beneath the coffin as we come to the principal door. I hear the other pall-bearer's grunts and heaves as their legs shuffle under the extra weight. Charley's on that side and I know he's got weak ankles and some would say he has a tendency for having weak wrists but I refuse to accept that. The casket veers off course to the left of the door and leads us into the candle stall as Charley's ankles pop, spilling hot red wax onto our suits and the bald red carpet. I curse Tommy under my breath but he assures me that he has a surprise in store which is why he drives off ahead of the hearse at high velocity in his Opel Kadett.

It's raining when we get outside the church. We slide 45 into the back of the hearse and Alba collectively and reverently hand me back 45's balloon essence as part of the ceremony. We make a bee-line for the cemetery at the top of the hill. Vera, Alba, Charley, the Mistress, and I travel behind the hearse with Mary – Vera's boss. Nobody can stomach her idle comments, even Alba who normally doesn't show signs of emotion, stick their fingers down their collective throat. Stuff like, "Wonderful service" and "Moran really knows how to put on a good show *despite* being a drinker." She speaks into her rear-view mirror but nobody wants to meet her eyes. There's some consolation in thinking that she's talking to a mirror. I want to shove my fist down her throat but she's Vera's boss. I feel like I'm going to my own funeral.

When we get to the cemetery, Tommy and Lucy are standing in the centre of the graveyard under a Paddy Power bookie's umbrella. Then I see the karaoke machine amongst the headstones and Celtic crosses – a futuristic machine with lights and buttons in an old and sombre world of limestone. The patio umbrella from 128 is shielding it from the mist. I beckon Tommy to give us a hand carrying the coffin but apparently he isn't on pall-bearing duty, he's karaoke MC, yea-yea.

Vera swears at consecrated ground, 'Has he lost his fucking mind?'

'Tacky,' responds the Mistress in her hideous voice though she is fetching today in her alternative black dress that reveals far too much curve and hemline to seem respectful. It always amazes me where we seek comfort in times of loss and sadness. I seek comfort in those curves. 45 won't condemn me for that, I'm sure.

The driver of the hearse orchestrates 45's extraction from the belly of the hearse. We each get under the pine box and heave upwards. Somebody, I think he might be a tinker or a travelling gypsy, bellows *'1 ... 2 ... 3...'* and I hear Charley's ankles pop free again. I feel a desperate need to turn back the clock as we cross into unknown territory of the bone-yard. I try to stall but the momentum of the coffin carries me across the threshold.

We walk solemnly up the path.

Tommy, barely audible over the chugging generator powering the karaoke machine, announces: 'Yea-yea, 45, we never knew who you really were but we accepted you as one of our own because everybody's
got secrets, my friend, yea-yea, and I guess you're taking yours to the grave...'

I'm not sure what I think of the karaoke-master's words of wisdom but I decide that they're quite noble
and truthful in a way.

'To a man who did it his own way, yea-yea...'

A shiver skitters up my spine for the second time as
45's voice booms high above the din of the generator and floods the grey cemetery. For a horrible moment, I think he had had second thughts about where he was about to go but then I hear my own voice and realize that MC

Tommy had recorded our final number together on my birthday. I fight the impulse to run screaming. Hearing the old man's voice again makes the hairs stand on the back of my neck. Salty warm tears flush my eyes.

We lay the coffin on its stilt table.

Ghostly Alba passes me my balloon and I grasp it with white knuckles. Having a balloon full of helium would make my life so much easier. That way, it wouldn't get caught up in my legs like now. In this grey light, I notice that Alba's skin has begun to lose its bleach. She'll probably raise another fake fun-run before the month of February is up.

Father Moran jumps up from behind a gravestone looking every bit the demented Jack-in-the-box. He's eager to get things moving but can't begin until our duet from beyond the grave finishes. The longer our recording goes on, the redder Father Moran becomes. The grave-diggers had laid a large sheet of cardboard which we're standing on because the ground has turned to muddy slush. But then I realize that it had been for Moran, not the grieving family. Moran begins to speak but nobody can hear him over the generator nor do we really care. He roars and we watch his flapping hands bless the coffin and rid the ground of evil spirits. He looks like Mussolini from where I'm standing.

By the time Father Moran finishes, caked mud has reached up his black trousers towards his undercarriage while we stand safely on our cardboard island. He gives a disgruntled sign to lower the coffin and with a sinking heart, I pass my big red balloon to Vera. I grab the ropes with Charley, Tommy, and a stranger. We lower45 down into the wet ground from where he had come, not literally, although it had always seemed as if 45 had dug a tunnel from God-knows-where and just happened to come up like a gopher in my town. I experience a desperate yearning to pull him back up. There's no going back after this. Vera throws flowers onto his casket and she gives me his tatty Bank of Ireland green white and gold peak cap that he had worn every day while he waited for his one-way bus back to Iowa. I drop it down into the black hole and the peak thuds on the pine. The red-faced grave-diggers take their cue to begin back-filling 45's grave. They work in tandem, fast steady strokes, filling in the hole as if there's a chance that 45 might try to make a last desperate run for it. Knowing that he wouldn't make one last ditch effort puts a hole in my chakra like a polo mint. I need some TLC at the hands of the Mistress.

One by one, people drop away until it's just Charley and me. Charley doesn't say anything, just slaps me on the back, pops his ankles back into their sockets, and leaves me to be with my graveside thoughts. The Reiki Mistress indicates to call me with a make-believe phone before walking off into the rain with the others. While Tommy's putting away his equipment he accidentally presses the play button again and I hear 45's nasal tones for a brief moment; marring the overall final goodbye effect. When Tommy finally switches off the generator the silence that follows is as intense as a cardiac flat-line…

And then there's just me and my red balloon, my balloon and I. I remember what had been bugging me earlier during the funeral mass. It was what 45 had said to me before he gave me the balloon: *Take me home when all this is done.* He had also mentioned something about a blonde with a chassis but that seems immaterial now. *I'd do it myself only I'm afraid they might turn me in. I won't be safe until I'm outta here for good, the whole goddamn show, hoop-la.* His words intrigue me. Who might have turned him in? Should I have even listened to his addled words?

And then it comes to me as I stand by the graveside: my purpose in life. My whole erratic existence seems to fit into this moment like completing a five-thousand piece jigsaw for the blind. 45 has whispered my epiphany to me from beyond the grave.

I hold up my balloon to the muddy pile next to his open

grave like Arthur had raised Excalibur. I pull 45's party hat
from my suit pocket while briefly looking over my
shoulder to see if anybody's watching. I strap it to my head
with a definitive sense of purpose, by Christ. 'Let's
continue with the party that we never finished,' I declare.
'No,' I sing in rhyme that briefly passes off as hip-hop
melody, *'Let's get this party started...'* I clear my throat.
I'm nervous, I'm *actually* nervous. 'Firstly, my PhD thesis
will be on you, my noble friend. It's been staring at me all
this time. Yours truly will record your life to complete my
PhD in genealogy.' I make a mental note to purchase a
diary – the same one you are reading from now. 'Secondly,
I will return you to your homeland of Iowa and release
you among the ears of corn. "Take me home" – your
words, not mine. This is what you had meant, isn't it? But
you weren't to know that you were about to die. Maybe this
is just fate; let's go with that for now. The best things in
life – and death – happen with fate. Like the Knights
Templar did before me, I will provide a safe passage to
your promised land. Thirdly and finally, this quest will also
act as my first private investigation case – getting to know
45, we'll call it. You, 45, will be my first client. I will
throttle three birds for you with this one stone,' raising my
balloon, 'and hand-deliver them to you, plucked, trussed,
and packaged.' I pause as a *fourth* bird flutters into my
telescopic rifle sight. 'This quest – discovering my
grandfather's past identity – will help me cure my own lack
of identity, by Christ. Four birds, one stone!'

A gust of wind blows up and snaps my birthday
balloon from my grasp, whipping it across the cemetery.
Now, very much caring who's watching, I run, thanking
Christ that 45 hadn't inflated my balloon with helium. I
curse like a docker while trotting across several people's
graves and committing terrible sins in the process. I see
those dead people drinking Bloody Marys at a bar named
The Three Coffins. Suddenly they shudder; a Mexican
wave shivering along the counter. They tell their pale dead

buddies that somebody has just walked over their grave which gets big laughs. I verbally apologize and run on, holding my breath, never losing sight of my red balloon and expecting it to burst any minute as it dances amongst the headstones. If it's going to burst anywhere then it better be here and I derive some consolation in that knowledge.

One of the grave-diggers manages to corner my balloon at the other side of the bone-yard. 'Bit of a risky place bringin' a balloon, don't ya' think?'

I hadn't thought about it.

He mumbles something as he passes me 45's vessel. He lugs a spit into his hands, greases the handle of his shovel, and continues digging a hole.

Sweating, I cross the bone-yard and stop off one last time at 45's grave. I realize that 45 has just transmitted a worthy sign. The very moment I had mentioned our journey, he was off like a kid. God bless him. I smile to myself at his ingenuity, and then bawl
hilariously at the old man's graveside. Brillo's B movie clichés spring to mind: *Time to say your goodbye ... pack your bags ... Forces at work beyond our control ... the time is near.* She had predicted my passage to Iowa as opposed to my back passage which I was sure she was going to interfere with in some demented way. In another way, Brillo had also predicted 45's departure. Fate has brought us together and has somehow melted us into one –

'Wait,' I say aloud.

I'd forgotten all about the secret note. How was it possible to forget the note? I guess I'd just gotten wrapped up in the melancholia and attempted escape of my balloon. I hold the balloon up to the sky and squint. In relief against the grey clouds, I see the darker outline of the folded piece of paper. But with a sinking feeling, I realize that I'm in a classic catch-22 situation...

If I open the balloon, I get the message, literally. However, 45's carbon dioxide is gone to the four winds. If I want to keep his essence then I'll never know what the message says! I curse 45 under my breath but the old man hadn't known that he was going to pop his clogs. This is an important factor and prompts me into thinking that the message might contain some *odd* information, presuming that there are words on the piece of paper. After all, why would 45 conceal a note in the balloon if he could've just spoken its contents to me? Maybe the words written on that note were never *meant* to be spoken aloud. Thinking like a detective now, I come to the conclusion that something stinks and it's real fishy. It doesn't add up, then again, the old man was senile so nothing much ever added up. The doctors told us that he would have moments of clarity, but even then, those moments could get confused.

I fish for half a doobie that I had left in my suit pocket from this morning. I spark it up and inhale deeply, apologizing once again to the corpses for the toxic fumes. Holding in a ball of Mexican Black or Brown, I suddenly freeze...

Can it be possible? Minute wrinkles have begun to appear on the face of my balloon. The red balloon's a little less taut around the edges, by Christ. An element of floppiness has set in since 45 handed me the balloon just yesterday.

All I manage to say is, *'Oh Fuck...'*

By default, I regurgitate the same words that our biology teacher had once shoved down our throats: *'Osmosis: transportation of water molecules over a semi-permeable membrane.'*

I quake as the notion hits me: 45's been seeping out since yesterday. He's a left a minute trace of himself wherever I've taken him.

Suddenly, it's a race against time before 45's molecules transport themselves across a semi-permeable membrane.

5.
My Dirty Protest

'For the last time Cha, where's everybody *gone?*'

I'm standing beneath the old twisted cedar pine at the cemetery gates on top of the hill, you know the one. It's cold and the rain's bucketing down. All I've got is a crumbling birthday cone-hat for wet-weather gear. I make a point of sheltering my red balloon under my suit jacket. In the pouring rain, it's some consolation to think that 45 is warm and cosy inside his bubble – he deserves nothing less. An old man at a bar had once told Charley and me that balloons, in general, tend to deflate faster in colder conditions – funny how every subject always finally comes around if you live long enough. I give 45's Siamese twin a slippery Eskimo kiss. Something sick flutters inside me when the tip of my nose caresses 45's wrinkled face – only it isn't his face, it's my birthday balloon. Its premature ageing worries me. Like a midget, it's a beautiful little thing dying before its time. I silently curse Vera for buying the balloons at the Chinese market. Had nobody ever told her that the balloon quality in shops designated for special occasions is superior to the Chinese light-weight? They may have invented the Chinese lantern but, please, don't mess around with the high-end balloon market.

A drink would be nice now, maybe that bottle of ouzo that's been sitting in the living-room back at 128 since the beginning of time when we had that family holiday in Greece. A few weeks later we had no family.

I had decided to call Charley on my iPhone 4S. I'm having a crisis of a different type now – I *must* be if I'm calling Charley for advice.

'Cha? I *can't* hear you!'

Then I hear my brother Tommy's amber tones emanating from the karaoke machine in the background. I just miss the first part of his song introduction: '...singing

55

that revolutionary number Chumbawamba's *I Get Knocked Up... But I Go Down Again...*' The singer sounds like Lucy judging by the tom-cat whines. I listen more carefully this time as rain-drops create a soggy film between my ear and my iPhone, realizing to my horror... 'Please tell me that's not Vera *singing?!*'

'That's Vera singing.'

I feel faint. 'Couldn't wait to get back to celebrate, huh? How could she? He's only been in the ground minutes and don't forget that his noble soul lives on in my birthday balloon.' I look at my big red balloon, quickly tracing the words: Happy Birthday Fanny! 'Noble.' Salty tears come to my eyes and cocktail with acid rain.

There's a brief pause on the end of the line. 'Jon, try and see it from her point of view. For her it's like trying desperately to lose ballast on her sinking balloon to get above her shit of a life.'

Normally, with Charley, I make a statement and he comes back with a variation of my statement, like casting out my line but the same miserable little worm keeps coming back on the end of my hook. I had learned a strategy in my twelve years knowing Charley: I say something and I prepare my next thought or statement while he throws me back the Frisbee. I rarely listen to Charley in other words. On the other hand, Charley comes out with some gems when he takes the initiative – like now, for instance.

Vera's wailing and whining in the background, and for a moment, I can see her in her hot-air balloon, rising above her shit of a life and arcing high over the cemetery here in town, waving me fond goodbyes as she floats majestically up into the bubbling grey cloud forever. 'Hasta Luego, Lucas!'

Clinical Dad's words echo in my addled mind: *My work here is done ... done ... done... done...*

'Your mother's going nuts, Jon.'

Charley's words are lost to my mother's wondrous hair-

56

raising cries of relief. I'm happy not to see it for myself; that would be just too disturbing. Over and over again, I hear her sing the chorus with wild viciousness in my ear-hole. I feel alone and shuffle up to 45 for comfort and the obligatory breeze blows up. 'What do you mean "nuts"?' I know exactly what he means: she had cast off those sand-bags that had been chaffing into her ankles. She's happy to be rid of the weak links to her old life but 45 had watched my back from a distance for twenty-one confusing and wonderful years.

'She's pulling out her hair but she's perky as a snowman's cock, Jon.'

There was a day when she used to wear a hair-piece, I think solemnly. Her character, just like her cancer, had gone into submission. So who is this woman screaming on my iPhone?

'She's happier than I've ever seen her – maybe *too* happy. Christ, you don't think she's finally gone over the edge, do you? She *has* been on that edge recently, Jonny. Jon?'

'Uh-huh?'

Pause down the line. 'Gotta go. I'm just going to help myself to another pint from the keg in the kitchen. Then...'

'Hey, I was saving that keg to celebrate my PhD in genealogy.'

'Exactly.'

I want to tell Charley about my revelation and that I'd chosen 45 as the subject of my PhD thesis but he doesn't give me a chance.

'I'm off to the bong-house to do a number. After that, Brillo's going to speak gibberish about that famous serial killer who she used to date when she was still a human. *Bleak*. Where are you, by the way?'

'Christ, Cha, where do you think I am? I'm still at the *cemetery*... You lot drove off without me.' I shudder as a flurry of rain-drops slip down inside my shirt collar from the pine needles overhead. 'Did anybody notice that I wasn't around?'

'I'm not sure, um; we thought you wanted to be alone. Where's 45 now?'

'*Now?* He's here where I am. What do you mean? He's in his bubble where he should be. Where else would he be?'

'Like Michael Jackson – that didn't work.'

'Can somebody come and get me? I'm soaked and I need to pack. Charley, there has been an epiphany. I have had my epiphany.'

'Father Moran gave me nothing.'

It takes a second for me to understand. 'No, I mean, I finally know what to do.'

'About what?'

'Well, everything. Look, I've just realized that I'm talking to you in the cold rain when I could be talking to you face-to face which I think is better considering the news I have. See you at the bong-house in ten. We don't have much time. By the way, I've got big news, major sound-bytes...' I'm beginning to sound like Brillo. Charley hangs up without further delay so I call in a taxi to collect me.

When I hang up, I notice that I have a missing call but I don't have time to delve into it further because a wild lady with a wayward glint in her eye comes my way and asks me, of all things, 'Do you want to be contacted by the dead for a meager sum?'

I pick up a trace of a foreign accent though she seems to be Irish for intents and purposes. My first reaction is to look around for a hidden camera. I think I see something above my head in the old twisted cedar but it's just a pigeon. No, wait, I check it again. It seems to be too still, not even a coo. I clap my hands and the pigeon shits itself and me as a result. 'Jesus of Nazareth!' This has to be the most surreal thing that has ever happened to me. 'What a bizarre question,' I declare, wiping pigeon shit from my breast pocket.

'Well, I just happened to be passing and I saw you hanging around the graveyard. I'm a medium who can put the dead in contact with their living friends and relatives.'

'Then why are you asking me? A pigeon just shit on me.'

'I just thought you might offer yourself to be contacted. If there's anybody in there who might have any interest in contacting you, well, your approval might make the passage easier.'

This is just too weird. 'Sorry, but I've got all I need right here.' I hold up my balloon for the woman and that seems to satisfy her peddling. 'I know we're in an economic crisis at the moment but that doesn't mean you can take advantage of vulnerable people. Just because I'm wearing a funeral suit outside a cemetery doesn't make me needy.'

The woman nods, flashes a smile and crosses back over the road to a chauffeur-driven Mercedes. Before her dog's body closes her door, she calls back to me, 'I wasn't going to charge you. I'm doing this for my sins.'

* * *

'Sorry about the wait.'

Fuming, I sit into the taxi an hour late and bursting to take a piss. Out of respect, I hadn't wanted to piss on consecrated ground or civilian ground in close proximity. I had also debated four times over whether to walk home or not but kept hanging on for one minute more that never came. I would've been home long ago.

My boxer shorts have grown soggy in the rain and the warm icky feeling of rain encapsulates my scrotum. The sensation isn't too bad after a while, almost comforting in a world gone cold and stale.

When I was younger, I had an issue with peeing: like an incontinent old man, I could never go on cue. Vera used to run the tap to coax me into urination every night before bed. The sound of running water has the same effect on me to this day so I'll blame the rain if anybody asks. I look through the taxi driver's rear-view eyes in defiance as I open fire upon myself in some desperate cry for help. I'm so angry with the world by now that I willfully open my bladder and let a warm gush swallow my crotch in a dirty protest. I squirm in ecstasy. My already wet boxers and trousers (and regrettably some Skoda upholstery) soak up my urine and the naughty feeling of just letting go is unadulterated shameful bliss. What is wrong with me? Not sure, but I must recommend this technique to the Reiki Mistress.

On the way home, I ponder whether to include this minor character flaw in my PhD thesis/slash/quest diary and decide that *everything* should go in: genealogy is the study of people, their flaws and triumphs.

'Dennis is going through a rough separation from the wife.'

'Who's Dennis?' I probe.

'Me.'

'Oh.' I wonder why the taxi-driver refers to himself in the third person; maybe to escape his depressing life. The driver had been eyeing us in his rear-view since the moment I had sat in and pissed myself.

'Wanna keep the balloon in the boot, um, Fanny? Or maybe you're going to Fanny's birthday party. You don't look like a Fanny.'

I'm in no form for this puppet. I want this man to shut his mouth and drive, please. 'Thank you for the compliment but, please, forget Fanny.'

'Not easy,' the driver quips.

'Jonny's my handle and asking me to keep my birthday balloon in the boot is nothing short of an insult.'

I have decided that people are going to start treating my birthday balloon with the respect it deserves. I'm running on a higher plain now. 'Besides, you'll only charge me for boot usage.'

'Keep it as an airbag then.'

The CB radio squawks on the dash. Dennis answers.

'One-nine to the copy, Dennis here.'

'You fucking *cunt*, Denny! You changed those fucking locks again but Mike's got a pile-driver, *pile*-driver! One-nine to the mother*fucking* copy.'

The driver Dennis clears his throat and switches off the radio. 'Crank call. Probably travellers.'

I nod, feeling a little insecure in the backseat of a stranger's car. I'm a little boy all over again, looking for my daddy, but all I have is a sinking balloon with the word Fanny on it. I seem to lose focus on what my big red balloon is all about but I put my insecurity down to my thought-process as a nine year-old boy.

'So it's not your birthday then?'

'No, why would it be? I don't look like Fanny, do I?'

'You tell me.' The driver gestures me to have a look in his rear-view by angling it towards me.

'Huh?' I sit up to look in the rear-view and see, to my utter embarrassment, that I'd forgotten to take off 45's birthday hat. It had turned into papier-mâché on my head. I redden up and ease it off then lay it on the seat beside me.

'Hey, watch the upholstery,' warns Dennis but he doesn't know the half of it.

I will dry it later and resurrect into some other form; an egg carton, perhaps.

'So it's not your birthday then?'

'No, it was my birthday the day before yesterday.'

'So, where's Fanny?'

'She's living at 128 Hydrangea Drive which is where I need to be.'

During the short journey, the driver called Dennis manages to recount his entire marriage to me. He tells me all about his messy separation and how his wife had falsely accused him of "tampering" with his children just to get custody of them. I'm not paying much attention until he says, '"Dennis knows you."'

'Great,' I offer. 'Would Dennis mind introducing me to me? I don't recognize myself since I turned thirty years old.

61

I have belated identity crisis you see.' I ask Dennis to put his foot on the pedal. I flash him a glance of my ailing balloon in the rear-view which I think is reason enough but he looks even vaguer.

'You're on Facebook singing with the old man: *I Did It My Way.*'

'Is Dennis one of my friends?' I ask.

'Dennis didn't get a chance: the wife cut his internet connection and chopped up his credit cards.'

When we get to my front yard, Vera's boss's Fiat Punto is almost parked in our front porch. I pay Dennis the taxi-driver and give him a tip because I pity the fool and I'm starting to feel guilty about relieving myself in his upholstery. That was just wrong but it felt right at the time.

Charley glides across from the bong-house, looking light as a feather. 'Man, Jonny, Brillo's stoned in the bong-house. She's,' he searches the wet tarmac for the word, 'mental.'

6.
Message in a Balloon

The bong-house looks like any other garden shed from where I'm standing but I shiver at what lays inside. I pass my birthday balloon to Charley and ask him to look after 45 while I have a shower and a quick change into something dry but decide that that's a bad idea because Brillo is an unknown quantity and I don't trust her with my noble grandfather. She would eat him alive and that's my privilege.

I duck inside home, snapping 45's Siamese twin from Charley's wandering grasp. Passing by the open living room door, I throw my entire family and Vera's boss a dirty look but nobody notices. '*Happy* now?!' I call out but nobody notices. 'Happy 45's finally *gone?*' Nobody notices. 'Don't worry, he won't be back.' Vera's down to her bra and quite drunk, raving into the karaoke machine like Johnny Rotten, occasionally using the microphone. In general, just feedback. She's having some kind of catharsis but I can't understand why. All I know is that what I see repulses me despite my cemetery revelation. The degrading scene before me only urges me on to complete my quest. Mary's up and taking snaps of Vera (should I be worried?) while Tommy and Lucy are fingering each other behind the red leather sofa, plastered against the family portrait wall with a wild gap and vague outline in the middle of where Clinical Dad used to be; kind of like how I imagine my chakra must look. Vera had had any
pictures of him removed and his image professionally erased from family photos. Susan – Alba – is playing chess at the table with another (let's face it) freak –   Alba – whose superficial skin-whitening chemicals have caused an unsightly allergic reaction. She was used in a recently aired documentary, '*Sometimes It Can Go Wrong...*'

Maybe my whole family should be on it. Vera's fancy

plush pillows had been flung around the house as if I'd just missed the pillow-fight. I don't understand. Tommy's and Susan's reaction is more of a non-reaction and Alba (not sure if that's just Susan or her collective group of cronies) seems to function on a different plain to the rest of us. A sheet of bullet-proof glass exits between us. I can see her and she can see me but that's it. Fair enough, my brother's and sister's relationship with 45 was an estranged one because senility had gotten between them but Vera...? And Mary's a Nobody. So who am I left with? 45 probably made the most sense if I really think about it and he's not here anymore. The only solace I will find here today is at the bong-house. I wail over the noise, 'You've all committed a murder here today!' Nobody notices. 'Murdered the memory of my grandfather! Have you rocks got no *feelings?!*' I look around the trail of destruction for something else to say. 'All these live wires and open bulb sockets sticking out around the house must've played with your brains over the *years!*' 128 has been a mine-trap since Clinical Dad threw himself into the river. I grew up with fizzling high voltage wires sticking from walls. Vera had never bothered to fix them. I think she had left all those open sockets and wires in the hope that Clinical Dad might come back to make the house more user-friendly and perhaps have a conscience. I don't want to think about it too much because where is my conscience? I've been sponging off Vera and the least I could've done was some light electrician work.

Nobody notices. I storm off to my bedroom in a melodramatic huff. I lay my big red birthday balloon down on my bottom bunk by 45's shrine, and then light my candle by the photograph of 45 sitting on the back doorstep. I strip out of my soaking funereal get-up and jump in the shower. I don't feel like singing today. As I catch a glimpse of my weak reflection, I see that 45's birthday cone-hat is nothing but a giant bird-shit of papier-mâché on my head. Please tell that I didn't put it back on?

Yes, I did. Charley had thrown me with his theatrics.

With regret, I remove the ruins from my head, plop it into the toilet bowl, and flush. Turning my sadness into fighting spirit, I assure myself that my plans won't also go down the tubes.

I get back to the bong-house. Charley's sitting on the old Cortina seat, puffing on an exotic number. He quickly relays the fact that the shit he's smoking is so illegal that he has to call it by a different name. He has decided to nickname it Rolled Gold.

Meanwhile, Brillo has her fat red butcher's head stuck in the vice on the worktop and laughing sideways like Old Mother Hubbard. Her prediction *had* come true. She really is a witch.

I try to lip-synch this succinct fact to Charley while playing charades: gesturing a long nose and high hat but he thinks that I'm blowing him a kiss and sends me one back. He tells me to put it in my pocket for later. It's funny but I'd never noticed that vice before, neither had I noticed any of Clinical Dad's other tools. I had grown up with them around me – like the live wires and open sockets – and had become accustomed to their ominous presence. Charley floats across to Brillo and begins to tighten the vice.

'Cha?' The concern in my voice betrays how I had seen Brillo: a piece of furniture always in the way.

The home-help guffaws some more.

'I've never seen Brillo stoned,' I say with sick fascination as Charley squeezes up on the vice.

Charley can't take anything seriously. 'Me neither! This shit's a head-buster!' He hides inside his dreadlocks and laughs heinously, smoke wafting up around him as he turns the vice a little more. The smile suddenly drops from Brillo's side-turned face and she half yells before screaming something in Eastern European with sheer horror etched in her twisted ugly face.

'Christ! You'll kill her!'

Charley releases her, chuckling as he unwinds the

handle, 'Naw, her hair would've acted as a sponging effect.'

128 has become a mad house in 45's absence. They say absence makes the heart grow fonder.

Brillo sighs and physically lifts her head from the vice in her big hands and continues to converse with Charley in stoned gibberish. To my astonishment, he answers her back in the same high-end inaccessible banter that only the truly stoned can understand.

Charley rolls me an exotic road-cone and freshens up his and Brillo's with a sprinkle of something here and a roll of something there. At first, I decline Charley's DIY rolly, citing that a life of crime and drugs only leads to negative identity. On retrospect, I have *no* identity and this carry-on is all I've ever known with Charley so I ask him to roll me two, please, lodging the second spliff behind my ear. 'In times of crisis, we cling onto what we know.'

'What's on your mind?' Charley asks. I gesture them to sit down and check the foliage for any hidden people. The Reiki Mistress had fallen asleep once in the bong-house. We didn't find her till the following day. Apparently she'd enjoyed her stay, being a new-age hippie, she knew what plants to eat and what plants to admire from a distance.

'Okay, I've categorized this into themes: Number one: Release 45 amongst corn – got to get back to corn.' I speak as if I'm reading this from an internal memo. 'I'm taking his remains back to Iowa where he belongs.'

'Poppycock!' screams Charley. 'You're focking nuts...!'

'Cha, his soul won't rest until he is amongst the corn.' The same wild excitement rises in me again that I'd felt on the hill. 'I'm going to go, Cha! I'm going to find out who 45 was before he came to us and I'm going to use this knowledge to complete my PhD, by Christ. 45 will be the subject of my thesis and he will also be my first private investigation case!' 45 knew about my aspirations of becoming a P.I. He was the only one I had told because 45 was the odds-on favourite for forgetting first. 'Wait, there's one stone but four birds...'

'Huh?'

'Yes, four birds, one stone!'

'Huh?'

'I will also solve my identity crisis by *discovering* the true identity of –'

'Of 45, yeah, okay, we get it.'

'I'm taking him back to his corn fields, Cha.' An insane impulse to celebrate suddenly grabs me. 'I'm going to Iowa, Charley! *Iowa!* I can't believe it but I know it's what I have to do if I want to find myself.'

Brillo is clapping and cackling now.

Charley laughs from the comfort of the Cortina seat and wolfs down some apple juice. 'Christ, this *is* a revelation!' His eyes roll in his head and come up three liberty bells. 'But it doesn't have to be *real* corn, does it,' Charley suggests, 'like we don't go to the Red Sea to be baptised when we're babies. We go to the local church font because babies are oblivious like 45. A frozen bag of Jolly Green Giant will do.' He mumbles something to Brillo who laughs hysterically and openly grabs her crotch with excitement like a four year-old that just needs to pee, now, please. I turn away in disgust. I can smell her sweat or, Jesus of Nazareth, sour sexual tension...

'Since when can you talk Eastern European, anyway?' I ask Charley.

'Since an hour ago.'

'Jesus, you should be on *Lassie*, no, you should *be* Lassie. And no, the JGG doesn't make the cut – somebody's going to see a twenty-meter giant standing in the middle of a corn field. Besides, a man from Iowa knows the processed stuff when he smells it. 45 would turn in his balloon if he knew what you were suggesting, Cha. Ironically, my second point I want to talk about is that 45's shrinking big-time.'

Charley splutters his cider on Brillo's face. 'I told you that *months* ago,' Charley insists. 'Or else I was getting taller.'

'No, I mean, in the after-life. The balloon's beginning to deflate.' I ask for a sip from the five-gallon he has camouflaged amongst the lawnmower petrol cans.

'Jesus, Jonny, 45's gonna seep big-time. He'll end up like Mike TeeVee if you don't keep an eye on him.'

Brillo's pudgy face flushes and giggles. 'Mike TeeVee! Mike TeeVee!' She makes a couple of flying pistols out of her hammer-fists and leave off a few rounds that are more intimidating than the real thing. Willy Wonka seems to have struck a chord with her.

'I should've known that my birthday balloon would start to lose its figure as it got older. How many post-Christmas balloons have I found behind the sofa, shrivelled up into old lady tits.' I swipe an involuntary peek at Brillo. She had opened an extra button to reveal some cleavage. Charley and I could take one low-swinging mammary each and use it as a hammock. She's like a teenager being let out for the first time.

Focus, Jonny.

'I have to go to the bank first – my interest-bearing scheme is up today. I also need to see the Reiki Mistress to prepare me for my journey, open some
chakras, astral projection, etc.' I pick up my iPhone. 'She's by appointment only.' I've got another missed call from the same number as earlier so I dial the number. It burrs down the line twice before somebody picks up.

'Hello,' I answer. 'I've had a few missed calls from this number. Hello?' I hear breathing in my ear. 'You can say what you want,' I tell my anonymous caller, 'but, please, don't breathe because that shit's spooky, especially if you've got asthma,' I quip, masking my fear of anonymous callers and the seedy underworld they inhabit – not that I get many: this is my first. 'Hello? Who's there?'

'Is it a woman?' asks Charley excitedly. 'Here, pass it to me. A heavy-breathing woman is a turn-on. Give it here…'

Humpty Dumpty in a curtain dress, Brillo pants like a

dog and spoils the good image Charley has created.

'It's a man, I'm sure of it.'

Charley swipes my iPhone. 'Look, if heavy breathing is your sales pitch then I recommend you call a hotline. Good *day*, sir.'

The caller hangs up. 'It's a chicken,' I tell them.

'Hey,' Charley suddenly remembering, 'you said you've got real sound-bytes. What's happening?'

'Yes,' I glint, 'I've been keeping the best for last, Cha. I didn't want to tell you because it would only cloud the rest of today's agenda. Now that we've got it clear that I'm taking the old man back to Iowa, I'd like to share some shocking news…'

Charley sits back down on the Cortina seat but raises the back to sitting position. Brillo's come back to us after her hit of Rolled Gold. Her beady eyes look more demented than ever, the same ones she had used to peer into my soul on my birthday.

I leave them on that cliff-hanger and hurry back to my bedroom to protests from Charley.

In the living-room, Tommy's dedicating Michael Jackson's *Black or White* to Alba (Susan and her walking-dead friend) playing chess at the table, yea-yea. Vera's smoking a cigarette. The first time I've seen her smoke since a long-lost cousin's wedding. This means that she's in her element and I have to admit that I'm happy for her because, after all, she has fought her share of life's battles and come out the other end, tainted but alive. If she wants to smoke a goddamn Silk Cut Blue down to the butt then who am I to stop her? But again, I witness a fine line between celebrating and mourning the burial of a loved one. I understand Tommy's reaction because he's a well-meaning moron and if Vera's happy then Tommy's happy and Lucy's extra happy, all aboard the clit train! God I envy Tommy.

When I get to my bedroom I suffer a delirious moment when I see 45 lying in my bed, by his shrine. His frail body wasting away beneath the covers and only his balloon of a noble head showing. It's just a matter of time before Tommy draws a smiley face on it or start calling it Wilson. It's endearing and I'd be lying if I said that I didn't feel myself clam up but the image is off-putting by the same token. I put it down to Charley's Rolled Gold and move on with my birthday balloon.

Brillo and Charley had worked up another marvellous blanket of sweet exotic perfume in my absence. Amongst Vera's foliage, Charley has become a sloth – three-toed; not the five-toed variety – and Brillo has taken on the magical essence of a rarely seen creature.

'C'mon, out with it. What's the big deal?'

'45 left a message in my balloon.'

Seeing that I'm not kidding, the goofy expression slowly drops from Charley's face. 'Huh?' He stares at the balloon in my hand. 'What...? How...?'

'I saw it during mass. *That's* what I was trying to tell you.'

'Interesting developments but how can you read it if it's in the balloon? Chicken or the egg syndrome. You risk putting the old man's afterlife in danger.'

'Um, yes, at a stretch. This is my predicament, see. Any ideas?'

'Plenty.'

'About 45's cryptic message?'

'Um?'

I pass Charley my red balloon with care and he accepts with equal respect. 'You're an occasional hacker,' I tell him, 'this shit should come second nature to you.'

Charley holds up 45's bubble close to his face and stares at it with misty eyes for a long, *long* time. I almost feel guilty as every pained expression passes across his stoned boggled-eyed face as he ponders the mystery of the message in the balloon. He gets up from the cursed Cortina seat and gravitates towards the cob-webbed look-out window and hold's 45's spirit up to the light. The balloon

70

looks like a womb from where I'm sitting on the potting table; the note – foetus – clearly visible.

Born again, I think to myself.

Charley seems to wake from his stupor; intrigue and mystery etched in his face. 'Firstly, to crack a code, symbiologist Robert Langdon says that we have to actually *see* the written text or symbols. You mentioned that the note is cryptic but Langdon also says that we don't know if a message is cryptic until we actually see it.'

'Brilliant, I hadn't thought of that.' 'There's an ancient Chinese theory that,' Charley trails away while I wait with bated breath and, again, concerned that I have resorted to Charley for advice, 'if you stick scotch tape onto a balloon, then you can stick a needle through the tape and through the balloon without injuring the balloon *or its contents.*'

I'm intrigued. 'Hoop la!' I punch the air while quoting one of 45's favourite expressions. I give my red balloon a walloping hug but release it when I see how much it crumples away beneath my embrace. 'Yes … and?' There's a definite sense of hope in my voice now.

'No, it's just a *theory*. I mean, I don't know if we can ever incorporate this into our little ship-in-a-bottle pickle.'

My heart sinks. Thunder rumbles in the distance. Heavy raindrops begin to fall on the roof of the bong-house until it becomes a solid sheet of noise.

I raise my voice to be heard over the rain. 'Cha, I'm under pressure.' 'I need solutions to my plight. Please don't speak if it's a general observation. I need specifics. Right now, 45 is in danger of being converted from CO_2 into O_2. I need to see what that note says and follow his instructions.'

Something rustles amongst the undergrowth. I'm reaching for the pitch-fork when Brillo appears amongst the leaves. I'd forgotten all about her in my excitement. She heaves and grunts herself to her feet and moves towards the door while pulling her curtain dress way too high above her knees. She makes a run for the house through the monsoon rain, muttering lost words as she splashes.

'Jesus of Nazareth,' is the only reaction that I can muster as I get a flash of blue varicose veins set against the background of my patio. Suddenly, I feel anxious and can hear my digital calculator watch ticking down

45's final breaths after a life-time of watching over me following Clinical Dad's null-and-void suicide, even though he regularly climbed into my bedroom wardrobe. What a kick in the balls it would be now not to solve the puzzle. The old man knew that I would get a kick out of solving this mystery and I'm not prepared to let him down. His words whisper in my conscience:

Take me home when all this is done, huh?

I hug my balloon, keeping the bad thoughts away, just how 45 had told me to do when Clinical Dad wasn't there at night to save me from my nightmares.

"Yes, your wardrobe is full of dribbling monsters and that tapping on the window isn't a branch in the wind and that red light that you see across the room isn't the stand-by light on the television. But you, you Jonny, are the biggest bastard monster there is and one of these sons a bitches tries to scare you from your perch on the doorstep and they will pay the price. You, Jonny, are the dominant male monster in this house, hoop-la! You're a sleeping dragon, Jon, ready to singe monster ass. Night, night, my boy, sweet dreams."

I feel his kiss on my forehead and I whisper sweet-nothings in his celestial ear and put my balloon hard to my own ear and listen to the vacuum inside. It would've been easier to just tell me, I think again, or leave the note on my bedside locker where I could find it and read it at my own leisure. He wanted *me* to find the note, not anybody else.

'Here.' Charley breaks me from my stream-of-consciousness by sloshing the half gallon of cider in front of my face.

Brillo appears at the door, soaking wet. Her sopping wet

curtain dress hugs her curves in a Mister Michelin kind of way and I look at my Converse trainers in pity. Grotesque, God loves her. Charley's eyes are all over her but not in a good way, more horrified than anything. He has already admitted to having had carnal thoughts featuring Brillo. They say you should never meet your heroes...

Brillo holds out a flashlight to me; the same one she had read my future with. She flicks it on and holds it up to my balloon and I instantly know what she's proposing.

'*Brilliant!* Brillo stands for *brilliant!*' I pat her on the head to show my appreciation. I take the flashlight and point it into the soul of my birthday balloon. 'Why didn't we think of this?' 'Because it's too simple, that's why. Only simple-minded people come up with the best ideas – the every-day shit that we've all come to love – Velcro; the coin system for shopping trolleys; the common clothes peg, etc.' Charley gets up and close and personal with 45's soul-bubble. 'It's like we're looking at 45 in a bell-jar of formaldehyde in an old dusty museum. I hope he's not offended. We're practically exhuming him.' Charley says the same to Brillo in Eastern European, and again, I marvel at Charley's resourcefulness. They'd only been in here an hour before my soggy arrival. And bang, even before I've got time to stop it, I have the image of taxi-driver Dennis trying to bleach out the sour smell of piss from the backseat of his Skoda. I sincerely regret that and vouch to call him whenever I need a taxi. 'I understand,' I concede, 'but we need to see into his noble soul if we are to help him.' I lift the balloon above our heads and pass the flashlight to Charley. 'Now, I want you to point directly onto the base of the balloon and crack the code.'

Charley, sweating now, fixes the beam of light on the note but the shake in his hand quickly consumes him and I notice that his eye-tic has returned with vengeance. He keeps tucking dread-locks behind his ears until there are no dread-locks or ears left. I have started to sweat too,

Realizing that I'm on the brink of something that we'll all remember for the rest of our lives. I feel like one of the Goonies. 'Brillo, take the flashlight and repeat the process. Charley's a mess.' I do my utmost to hide the nervous quiver in my voice.

Charley hands the flashlight to Brillo and he may as well be handing over the Olympic flame. Brillo jams her spliff into the side of her mouth like a rookie and holds the beam on the note with the precision of a James Bond laser. We have come full circle; now the mountain witch is looking into 45's Pandora's Box of secrets and I feel giddy with excitement. The heady smoke rising from their spliffs makes me dizzy and I sway back and forth above them like a possessed shaman.

'There!' screams Charley. *'There!!'*

'Whagh! Fuck!' I drop the balloon with fright, just catching it in mid-air before plummeting into the ground.

The whole thing must've taken half an hour tops. Brillo yells something back in gibberish and slaps Charley across the back of his head, following it up with a knuckle-duster to the ribs. Everybody's suddenly screaming at each other in the bong-house. I'm queasy, claustrophobic, and want to run screaming from my garden shed. 'Everybody, calm the fuck down!! Just calm the *fuck* down, thank you, please.'

I've gotten into a habit of saying *please* and *thank you* in places where I normally don't show my manners. This is a sign of my underlying distress, having to constantly thank people for nothing. 'Now, Cha, you were saying?'

Charley gulps. 'I … know … what the … note… says.' He peers about him with a gormless expression as if realizing where he is for the first time.

'Close your mouth, Charley. What does it say?'

'It says…'

'Shit, no, I've changed my mind! I don't want to know what it says!' I suck up a deep breath through my nostrils, quailing in my Converse trainers. 'Okay, go on, I'm ready.' I close my eyes.

'Happy birthday, that's what it says.'

I register that information and process it. 'No, that's what the outside of the balloon says. We're talking about the note inside 45's Siamese twin. *Inside*, Cha, please, thank you.'

Charley nods gravely. 'It says happy birthday and three X's that probably mean kisses.'

Brillo leans in and reads the vague scrawl inside the balloon's transparent red skin. I can smell the garlic again, more potent than ever. It's seeping from her pores. '*Happy birthday, Jon,*' she says in her Eastern European accent. She pouts her lips and smacks them three times in an act she thinks sexy but a mustard gas victim must've had a similar look. I roar at the aluminium roof and slam it with the heel of my fist.

'What does *that* mean, 45?!' I'm beginning to regret not taking up that weird lady's offer back at the graveyard.

'It means that –'

I stop Charley from embarrassing himself. 'I *know* what it means, Cha, but what good is that to me?!' I shake my big red balloon violently before apologizing. 'No, that can't be right. That's incorrect information.' I read the message for myself:

Happy Birthday, Jon, X X X

There it is, plain as day, in 45's scrawl, I'd know it anywhere. That eliminates Tommy's involvement. 'Wow, great thank you, 45. That's the best you can offer?' I demand from my red balloon which is beginning to look embarrassed, I think. 'I'm taking you all the way back to your homeland of Iowa where you can do all the R.I.P'ing you want and this is the best you can do?' The bong-house begins to spin. I think I'm going to pass-out.

'You could be up to your tits in corn by now,' Charley rants to my birthday balloon. 'Who said it was a secret message in the first place?'

'Steady on, Cha.' But with a sinking feeling, I realize that Charley's right. Maybe I had been hoping for something else...

I notice that Brillo has been frowning at my balloon for some time now. 'Do you mind not staring, please? We don't stare in this country, thank you.'

Her wiry vulpine eyebrows suddenly meet in the middle. Her shoulders hunch and she grunts, she *actually* grunts. 'Hold balloon still, Pampaquino. Hold him still I say for time is running out.'

I freeze. Brillo flips her lit doobie back into her mouth and pouts her cheeks like a demented hamster. I'm beginning to feel that I don't know her very well. She tosses the balloon while keeping the flashlight on it.

'Look, Pampaquino!'

I'm too nervous to look at anything so Charley sidles up alongside her sodden carcass and reads the words that become the beginning of the end of the beginning.

7.
Message in a Balloon (Cont)

Jonny, tell Candy I'm alive. I've never stopped loving her and still got her face tattooed to my scrawny white ass to prove it just as she's got my ugly puss on her smooth behind which is a comforting thought during these dark times. I had always planned to go back for her. Tell her to come and get me. Jonny, I didn't say these words so we will never speak of this. DO NOT TELL VERA.

Dismissed. 45.

FAO: Candy 1010, Anamosa, Jones County, Iowa

SLAP!

I'm gobsmacked as my gob is smacked by a deathly cold palm from beyond the grave. It's 45's scrawl, all right, barely legible. He had written the note with the fountain pen that Vera said that he would never use until the right moment came. The handwriting is messy and blotted. The *Iowa* is more of a paint-ball smear and I have to use my imagination to decipher other words but we all get the picture. I guess the Sheaffer's moment had come after all. Vera told me that I could have it as my inheritance. I make a mental note to collect it later. Charley's reaction to the note is to swallow a ball of Rolled Gold and volleys it down with a gulp of Scrumpy. I do the same but grab the lawnmower's two-stroke mix instead. The unexpected burning sensation that rips open my gullet and esophagus causes me to spray two-stroke in all directions, quickly diverting from 45 at the last second. Most of my regurgitation thankfully covers Brillo. She smiles graciously and accepts it. She gets the situation and I'm getting to like Brillo, but as a person now. The shock of drinking petrol is so great that it actually gives me a fresh perspective. It jolts me out of my paralysis.

'I'm dumbfounded,' managing to string a sentence

together, 'literally find myself dumb at the idea that 45 had known a woman called *Candy*. And he still loves – loved – her? What's that all about? What about Nan?'

'Nan was doing some four by four down at the mill, Jon.'

I love Charley's black-'n-whiteness.

'She got tired of him playing strip poker with Molly.' Charley looks at the Mistress. By the way, the Mistress had strayed in some time during our discovery. She had to go back to the caravan to feed her bitches, apparently. 'Molly's the cat.'

'I *know* who Molly is, Charley.' The Mistress flares her nostrils in disdain. 'You seem to forget that I've known Jonny since kindergarten.'

'Did you know Molly at kindergarten too?'

The Mistress slips Charley's spliff from his fingers and takes a suck on it. 'Though on and off, admittedly.'

'And literally,' quips Charley, looking for his smoke.

I'm not paying attention to this petty squabble. My mind is on higher plains. 'We all know that Nan didn't go down to the mill to fool around with the buzz saw. She had a reason to go behind his back. According to my research with various family members, i.e. Vera, Nan was a much-loved figure in town.'

'Especially down at the timber mill,' jokes Charley. 'Sorry.'

'Something's missing, Cha. I feel it in my waters.'

'*45's* missing.' Charley clears his throat and takes a steady draught of Mr. Scrumpy Jack. 'Candy is something that the Americans call chocolate, right?'

Brillo, the Reiki Mistress, and I look at each other for an answer.

'Well? Yes or no?'

'Yes,' I answer.

'Candy could be a metaphorical black woman or a woman of half-cast descent, i.e. a black mother and white father. The opposite also works. In this case, tanned half-cast dairy-milk chocolate. However, if Candy was a *black* beauty then she would've been dark cooking chocolate. That much is clear. We can look into it further and say that Candy wasn't black at all but as white as 45's doughy ass and now we can throw *white* chocolate into the recipe.'

'Yummy!' Brillo kneads her pot-belly.

Charley's on a roll. 'Really, we don't know anything about this sweet Candy character.'

'Have some respect, Cha.'

'Nothing I've said here is racist. I'm talking about chocolate or *candy*.'

'I'm talking about 45's posterior,' correcting Charley.

'Posterior tattoo, Pampaquino.'

'Yes, thank you, Brillo. Having Candy branded onto his rear-end doesn't sound like 45. And what's with this dismissed business? That sounds like military jargon.'

Brillo grabs Molly from her favourite blanket in the corner, flops her onto her own head, and then marches up and down the bong-house. Charley rolls into a Kentia palm bawling with laughter, probably because Brillo doesn't know Molly very well and he knows what's about to happen. I laugh because it's quite a good imitation of the Buckingham guard but she's got her facts all wrong, geographically and every other way. We're all laughing hard now, real rib-rippin' gut-busters. Molly sinks her claws into Brillo's scalp and there's nothing Brillo's scouring pad hair can do. It's the fastest changing of the guard in history. We roar with high mirth, crotch-wrecking hoops and howls of laughter that leave my six-pack in shreds. It's my first time hearing Charley laugh so hard and it's a beautiful thing to witness here in the comfort of our little bong-house jungle, a day before I set off on my wild goose-chase. It reminds me of the day us Rowes visited Dublin Zoo. That had been the last day that we had spent together before we began to grow up and go our separate ways; a last supper of chips and nuggets amongst the golden tamarinds. It was also the day that 45 had made the

9 o'clock news by wandering into Bongo, the albino gorilla's enclosure. We still don't know how he happened to 'wander' into Bongo seen as the rare albino gorilla was surrounded by bullet-proof glass and roof-netting. 45 sat with Bongo and ate shoots for twenty minutes before anybody realized. More curious was the fact that Bongo had treated 45 as one of his own. Even the baboons respected him and that's saying something. Funny, how just a year later, Susan would do a Michael Jackson and bleach her skin and call herself Alba – I'm not sure if that's just her or her collective group. The Bongo incident had a profound effect on her and I know that she still secretly takes a train to Dublin Zoo and gazes into Bongo's sad red eyes through the bullet-proof glass.

Brillo's screaming and running, crashing into everything in the sweet-perfume haze, toppling pot-plants to the ground. Molly won't let go now. Once her claws find purchase she rarely lets go. Brillo wears Molly like a crown of thorns. Charley, meanwhile, has laughed himself into a stupor and is rocking steadily

back and forth on the Cortina seat. I feel a strange wave of lonesomeness and see this funny historic episode as if I'm watching it on a home-video. I know that I've already mentally begun to distance myself from my life as I know it. I have an overwhelming itch, literally and metaphorically, to understand the meaning of my surrogate father's cryptic message (not that there's anything cryptic about it), and I know that I will have to go to Iowa to see for myself because 45 *wants* me to go to take care of some unfinished business. Of course, when he wrote this note he wouldn't have known that his death was just around the corner. He also wouldn't have figured out that I had already committed to taking him back home to Iowa. Great minds think alike. Will I meet this Candy character there? Who knows? The sooner the better because I see more wrinkles surfacing on 45's soul-bubble. I take a neat swig of the Briggs and Stratton's petrol, breathing smoke and fire.

'Climb between my scaly wings and we shall fly to the state of Iowa for I am the Sleeping Dragon. Guin, how 'bout that SMS? Hmm? Some chakra-work for my journey?'

The Reiki Mistress just throws her eyes heavenwards. 'Of course, dear.'

'I need to prepare myself mentally.'

Charley interrupts by saying, 'Couldn't have put it better myself.'

'I'll meet you later. Charley, let's go to the bank. My saving scheme is up today.' I marvel at how my plan is coming together. It's as if everything has been leading up to this. 'I need to prepare my pocket financially.'

My iPhone buzzes in my pocket. 'Hello? Yes? I'd appreciate if you didn't stop wasting my battery... You obviously have no idea of the battery-life on an iPhone 4S?' I'd already clocked the same prank-call number as before.

'Sorry, I don't. Jonny Rowe, correct?'

'Huh?' I wasn't expecting to hear a voice and suddenly forget what to do when somebody else speaks on the other end.

'Hello?'

'Yes?' I think the show-bizz voice belongs to Tommy having a laugh but the sincerity throws me.

'Great. Jonny, I'm calling you from the public relations department of McDonald's Restaurants Ireland.'

I look at my iPhone as if this might clear up matters. 'As in Ronald McDonald?'

'That's me.'

'Uh-huh. I never knew Ronald McDonald was a prank caller.'

The speaker laughs off my vague allegation. 'Jonny, you are our one thousandth customer this month and we'd like to offer you a range of McDonald's products to choose from.'

'Um, okay.' It feels much longer since I've been to

McDonald's but I instantly go along for the fast-food ride.

'If you could pass by this evening between 7 and 7.30pm to your local McDonald's outlet and Ronald can meet you personally to give you your mind-blowing prize…'

'Ronald?' I recall that I have a session with the Mistress at the same time. 'Could it be at 5.30?'

A white-noise pause comes down the line and I'm sure that I hear a sigh. 'Okay, 5.30pm then. Look forward to meeting you again.'

Again? I think I would've remembered meeting Ronald McDonald the first time. 'Excuse me, when…'

Ronald hangs up and honks his red nose down the line at me.

8.
Candy in a Haystack

Just after 3pm, Charley, 45, and I float to the Bank of Ireland here in town. We had left Brillo in the bong-house with Molly attached to her head. We were calling her Crockett for a finish. They would've made a beautiful couple at Derby Ladies Day. The Reiki Mistress had gone back to her caravan in the park to prepare herself for our healing session later.

My head's a swirling 2-stroke mix of feelings and thoughts. 'There'll be no funny business while our eyes are closed tonight,' I tell Charley, 'just pure unadulterated laser surgery on my chakras for my Iowan quest. Now that I'm on the subject, do you think I should be concerned that the Mistress only engages in sex through the medium of transcendental meditation?'

'Maybe she's insecure?'

'It's a continuous accident as far as she's concerned. In turn, this makes *me* feel like a continuous accident which isn't good for moral, Cha. This doesn't tally with meditation's goal. I'm just taking constant advantage of her when she has her eyes shut. But by pouting her lips, the way she does sometimes, she's just taking away the element of spontaneity. Tonight, I will insist on P.P.T.M: purely plutonic transcendental meditation and possibly on a permanent basis, henceforth.'

Charley's not really paying attention. 'Do you know where you're going in Iowa?'

'The address is on the note, Cha.'

'Is it?'

'Well, yes, you were there. Candy 1010, Anamosa, etc... What's wrong?' Charley's trying to get at something. 'Just get to the point, Cha.' I'm acutely aware of time and 45's gradual osmosis through the balloon's semi-permeable membrane. There could be a trail of 45 tailing off behind us like a disgruntled Disney skunk for all I know.

'I did some research,' says Charley, 'and Anamosa's got a population of five and a half thousand.' He holds up five and a half fingers.

'And?' I'm getting that slippery-dip feeling again. 'We've got the postal code: 1010. That'll narrow it down. There's surely somebody there who knows a Candy; there can't be many.'

'1010 is not a postal code, Jon. Anamosa's zip code is 55205.'

'Then what's 1010?'

'1010, over and out.' Charley shrugs his shoulders. 'You didn't notice anything, did you?'

I'm intrigued but not in a good way. 'Notice what?'

'I can confirm that some of the address is missing. You always told me that I'm good at breaking codes, right?'

'Well, I always said that there's a touch of Langdon about you but I wouldn't go so far as to say that, um.' Jesus of Nazareth, I've got no time for this time-wasting. 'Get to the point...'

'Part of the address is an ink-blot. In theory, if you follow this address, it should lead you to a giant ink-blot town somewhere in Iowa. It won't even be called Ink-Blot because that's what the address would say. No, it would be a...'

'Cha, c'mon, please, stick with it.' I ask Charley to simplify it for me. By the way, I don't recommend a walk around his mind, especially after dark.

'The address is hidden underneath a blot or else the ink ran and the address became a blot. Either way, the address is a careless scribble or he shouldn't have used cheap recycled paper that has a blotting effect, much like a kitchen towel or common snot-rag.'

This is news to me. But it's true for Charley; the note does look like a blue Dalmatian from a distance.

'There's a series of italics that have expanded into a blot, Jon. Directly after *Candy 1010*. It looks like four italics that have merged into one blob.'

I look at my balloon with, I have to admit, a feeling of contempt. How could 45 have shown something to Charley and not me?

'When do you plan to go to Iowa?'

I look at my watch. 'Friday.'

Charley comes to a stop. 'But today's Thursday!'

'Yes and Friday comes after that – tomorrow. The sooner I put this to bed the quicker we can all get on with our lives. The faster I'll make sense of my own existence. Why wait? There's a flight from Shannon at 9am.'

'Yeah, well when you get there you'll look like a tool, wandering from house to house looking for Candy in a haystack. Eventually you'll turn into a bum with a sour smell and a beard. Nobody will want to give you the time of day. You won't find this Candy character so desperation will urge you to cut your losses and release the old man in and around the first corn-on-the-cob you see. But,' Charley points his accusing finger in my face, '*you* won't rest thinking that you never found this Candy character.' Then pointing at my balloon, '45's soul will roll in corn-hell till you deliver his undying love for Candy in his dying message. Decipher the full address and...'

A pretty woman passing by gives us some strange looks and why wouldn't she?

'... voila, Lassie, come home.'

'He wasn't dying when he wrote those words.'

'Oh, do I hear tones of weakness?'

'No, it's just that he didn't write that note on his death-bed. He wanted me to track down this Candy character. He was ready to meet her.'

'You sure about that?'

I don't know where Charley's taking me with this.

'Okay, so Candy's his bucket list, then. Who cares? You can't go to Iowa on this flimsy information.' He sums up the situation: 'Candy in a haystack, my friend.'

Charley's right. I need more information. I've only got

one crack at this before my return flight home. This is turning out to be one hell of a PhD thesis plus my first unpaid private detective case!

Charley stalls and pulls on my arm. 'We need to see that tattoo, Jon.'

'Huh?'

'The tattoo on 45's,' Charley makes some air-commas, 'scrawny white ass.'

'It's a little late for that.' I don't like the way Charley's looking at me right now. 'We might have had a chance back at the house with the open coffin but now it's not an option.' I horrify myself that I'm even entertaining Charley's nonsense.

'Do cemeteries have opening hours? They shouldn't. The dead should be allowed to come and go whenever they please. It's a bit of a waste of time if you ask me. If I'm a ghost, do you think a closed gate is going to stop me?'

'I think it might be to keep the living out.'

'Not us. We go in tonight.'

What's worrying me now is that Charley hasn't grown tired of his tomfoolery and even seems to be serious about this. Jesus of Nazareth! 'No, Cha! Are you *insane!?* Lay off the Rolled Gold. You're smoking too much.'

'He's taken her down with him, Jon! All we need to do is take a photo of his rear-end then blow it up and we've got our Candy character. It cuts our odds by ten to one.'

'We're *not* blowing up 45's arse! What's *wrong* with you? Is it not enough that his spirit is trapped in a balloon besides you digging up his private parts? No, this is a delicate subject, Cha. I don't think we should be so, what's the word, flippant.'

'Once you've got her image, it's going to cut your work in half. We've got half an address. We need Candy's face and we need 45's ass to find it. She's got him on her ass but that's not an option right now.'

'Just quit while you're ahead.'

Charley quietens and I wonder what his burnt-out mind

is going to come out with next. 'Do you know what's the most mystifying of all this?'

'I can't imagine anything more mystifying than exhuming 45.'

'That note that 45 wrote with his trusty Sheaffer pen.'

I turn to Charley.

'The note seems to be written by somebody else. The writer of the note doesn't suffer from senility or memory loss … the opposite if anything. The old man speaks about a period in his past life with this Candy character as if it were just yesterday. He's speaking about a time long before we existed, Jon. Robert Langdon would say the same thing if he were here with us.' I turn from Charley and frown at my balloon questioningly. Charley's right again. I've been so taken with everything else that I've overlooked the finer points of this mystery. The note is completely out of character for 45 who willingly wore his underpants outside his pants like Superman. The hidden note seems to have been written by a man sitting at the steering-wheel of his life with a dashboard of controls at his finger-tips, capable of reversing into the past without difficulty, displaying love for this Candy character in the back-seat of this metaphorical vehicle, and the acuteness of avoiding possible road-kill by swearing me to secrecy. Yet, it's 45's handwriting.

'Jonny, I've got one question in all of this.'

'Yeah?'

'We have more info about this Candy character than 45. Where are you going to release him if you don't know where he comes from exactly? I mean, Iowa's a big place, right? *Bigger* than Anamosa and look at the problems we've got there.'

'Look, the man's an enigma. I think he'll be happy to know that he's back in Iowa.'

'Maybe Candy will tell you.'

I hadn't thought about that. It gives me the shivers just thinking about it.

Jonathan Dunne *Balloon Animals*

18 hours to departure…

9.
Revolving Doors and Nose Bleeds

We arrive to the revolving doors of the Bank of Ireland. Charley says he'll wait outside because banks make him nervous so I duck into the revolving doors behind a svelte woman much too important for me. The way she just effortlessly slips into those revolving doors; I know that I'll be safe travelling with her to the other side.

Suddenly there are complications. Of course there are.

Severe interest in what the woman's got tucked inside her business suit causes me to temporarily overlook 45's whereabouts. The oncoming swinging door closes in too fast behind me, leaving 45 straggling along behind me in the next set of revolving doors, nothing connecting us but a length of red streamer. Jesus of Nazareth! I can see him through the glass, always behind me, being gently nudged on by the door's rotation and, at the same time, being dragged in towards its grinding mechanics.

I panic and tug.

Before I know what's happening, 45 has become caught up in the intrinsic mechanics of the circling doors. I let go of the shiny red streamer, remembering one of 45's nuggets of knowledge:

What do you do when the toilet roll gets out've your hands? Let go, Jonny, just let the damn thing go an' cut your losses.

I do the same now and thank 45 for his insight from beyond the grave. I scream to the security guard on the other side of the door. *'Stop the doors!'* as we go around in ever-decreasing circles but he just smiles in at me like one of us is an idiot. This bastard's enjoying the Big Event; he has been sitting ring-side all for day, waiting for my arrival.

The confused woman, who has been travelling in my capsule, tries to help me but she doesn't know what to grab, me or the balloon, so she just stands there bent at the knee with open hands as if she's waiting for a rabbit to appear from its burrow. We go around again, another ride on the merry-go-round. The security guard's smiling face passes by … and out of view. My vertigo and blind fear are playing games with my sense of space and time and I insist on smashing my face against the glass walls.

The woman's screaming to be let off the ride now.

I cry, *'Don't burst! Please, don't burst!'* Suddenly inspired, I bawl: *'Help!! My child is caught in the door!'* I scream again, *'My child! My dear orphan child!!'*

One of the bank tellers appears and shoves the security goon to the side.

I see their gawping faces three times over by the time the door comes to a final stop. Exhausted, I apologize sincerely and attempt to explain to the traumatised lady and the chubby redhead bank-teller why my child looks more like a red balloon. I can see from their stony reactions that I will *never* be able to convince them so I flash my interest-bearing account booklet in the red-head's face. She sniffs at it and follows my booklet to the counter once I unwind 45.

She asks me to wait in the queue and that's when Charley catches up with me, roaring his head off with evil laughter despite his fear of banks.

Five minutes down the line and it's my turn. I know that I'm already off to a bad start. 'I'd like to close this account, please. It's up today. I'm going to Iowa.' I speak to the same red-head through the hole in the glass. Charley is still laughing from my revolving-door trauma.

'Uh-huh.' The teller types my details into her computer. I take that brief window to check over my big red balloon for damage. I hold it up to the fluorescent lights. I presume 45 has survived but my balloon's weary and grease-smudged. I make a mental note to purchase some anti-wrinkle cream in Tesco; probably not a good idea to ask Vera if she has any. Not today, at least.

'Jonny Rowe?' the teller asks with raised eyebrows.

'Why?' asks Charley. 'What have you heard?'

The teller nods at Charley and smiles politely and looks at me questioningly.

'Pay no attention to Charley. He gets paranoid in banks and not without reason owing to the current recession.' I chuckle nervously at my own wise-crack but the teller fails to the see the humour.

'Your bank book says Jonny Rowe. Is that your name? Bank protocol, sorry. We don't hand out ten thousand euro to any Tom, Dick, or Harry.'

'Well I'm not any of those three lads; I'm Jonny, ha, ha.'

The woman behind the counter has been a rock for millions of years and today's no different. I try to get a grip on the situation but 45's near second-death experience has rattled me. I need a drink. I clear my throat and apologize without saying as much. 'Yes, I'm Jonny Rowe. Thank you.' I feel like an idiot and my face grows redder than my balloon while she checks her screen. She taps her flower-patterned manicured nails on her corrected incisors. 'It's up at 4.30pm, today,' she informs me.

I check my gold calculator watch: 3.55pm. I don't need to use its subtraction facility to work out the remaining time. 'But that's forty-five minutes.'

'Thirty-five minutes, yes, that's correct,' she says coolly, 'so you'll have to wait thirty-five minutes.'

'But I'm going to Iowa with my grandfather's, uh, ashes. I need that money for my flight and lodgings and whatever else pops in-between.'

Charley interjects for good measure, 'Time is of the essence, Miss,' checking her name-tag, 'Keane.'

'I'm sorry but you and your grandfather should've thought of that before you opened the account.'

'I'm *sorry* but this account was opened years ago by Clinical Dad and the time of day wasn't something he was especially interested in seen as he was technically dead.'

Charley's in flying form: 'Time stands still for no man in bed with the queen of Fantasia, surrounded by hobgoblin hand-maidens.' He vaguely repeats the same pulling sequence he had gestured in the bong-house, 'Milk and honey, Miss Keane.'

'When are you travelling, Mister Rowe?'

'Friday.'

Charley's annoyed. 'Would you stop saying Friday and just admit that it's tomorrow. Just say it like it is. Friday doesn't make it any further away.' Maybe subconsciously, I am trying to distance my departure. Charley's profound but he's got no idea. I look at the teller's bored face behind the glass. It's useless trying to argue with this woman so I argue for the sake of arguing. 'Look, I've had a Russian Mountain kind of a day. SO, if you could just pass me over my money, I'll be on my way.' A painful rictus grin setting in by now.

Miss Keane comes over all duck-like. 'Take your grandfather's ashes to the Cliffs of Moher,' she quacks back at me, 'the highest cliffs in Europe. Everybody goes there. Big business but...' looking over her shoulder, 'night-time. The Americans lap it up cos of their roots 'an all that. They're coming over by the busload to release their loved ones over the cliffs. It's turning a little messy over there, cops etc, so people come at night to say bon voyage to their loved ones. If you can't wish bon voyage to him there then you may as well take him into outer space and that will cost you.' She whips a page from a note-block on her desk and jots a number across it. Am I hearing things? My expression says this to Charley while Charley just frowns and shrugs. 'Ring this number. He's fast, efficient, and cheaper than the rest. He only works at night.' She looks around surreptitiously. 'He took care of Uncle Joe. But watch it because there's a strong up-draught from the ocean below.' She draws a quick squiggle of a diagram to illustrate the up-draught on the same note and slips it under the glass towards me. Am I having a nightmare? 'You'll just end up getting ashes up your nose and in your ears, every open orifice.' She turns her back a little from the teller to her left and speaks from the corner of her duck bill. 'It's a balls to wash out and tends to stick,' scrunching her nose. 'Happened to us: everybody's got a little piece of Uncle Joe in 'em.'

I have no idea what the teller's talking about but strangely intrigued nonetheless. I'm about to tell her that I have 45's last ever living breaths floating in my balloon but she has already asked me to step aside. 'We'll talk in half an hour.'

'What are we going to do for half an hour?' Charley asks as if it's a year.

'I could do with a swift one. We've got half an hour to kill. My treat.'

Charley looks at me as if I'm joking but I'm not. I think he's been a little off since I revealed the truth about Clinical Dad's false suicide note. Charley leads us from the Bank of Ireland. I've been traumatised by the bank's revolving doors and Charley needs to push me into the revolving doors while I hug 45 close to my chest.

We cross Bridge Street to The Hound. Charley, I, and my big red balloon, take a high-stool each at the counter in the dark interior of The Hound. The shady interior of the Hound suffocates under a sticky layer of cigarette tar from the days before the smoking ban. The smell of cigarette smoke still lingers after some five or six years.

We order a creamy pint of Guinness each and a couple of Cyril's 'bombs' – a house-special comprising of bread-crumbed mash surrounding a hot core of mince-meat. A local sea-hag is sitting down at the other end of the bar with bleach blond hair and more gum than enamel. She's nursing a bottle of Satzenbrau when nobody else drinks the stuff; a relic of the '80's. She cackles to herself and occasionally dips into her peeling leather-imitation handbag for a peep into her make-up mirror, as if expecting her date to peer back at her. She's a woman who'd been stood up all her life and I'm sorry to say that I identify with her though on a far-off level. Inside the bar, Cyril's sitting on a beer keg in the shadows, listening in on our conversation which hasn't happened yet because we're enjoying our Guinness and bombs too much. I hadn't realized how hungry I was. Cyril looks the same as he did ten years ago; a handsome old bryl-creemed devil in over-all dungarees, like something out of *The Waltons*. He peeps across at Charley and up at his dreads. 'From down here, it looks like you've brought in an old mop.' No wonder the smell of cigarette smoke still lingers in the Hound – Cyril's smoking. 'Exactly – he cleans up the mess I make.'

'Wow, Jon, witty!'

'Thanks, Cha.' I turn back to Cyril. 'You're like a little state of your own.' I hint at the lit cigarette between his fingers but my sarcasm goes amiss. 'You're like the Vatican.'

Nothing.

'Smoking is prohibited.'

'This is my establishment,' answers Cyril and takes a drag. 'You won't mind if I light up then.'

'Yes, I do, Mop. I don't mind payin' my own fine but I won't pay for yours.' Cyril smoothes down his silver hair with his paws and emits a hearty guffaw.

Then he does that thing that Charley and I find amusing (it is the reason we come in here). Cyril sucks in air through both sides of his tongue and teeth like a little slavering animal trying to defend itself. 'What are you up to these days, Jonny?' *Suck ... siphon.* 'I've had an eventful week, Cyril. In case you haven't heard the bad news –' The telephone rings and Cyril turns away to answer. Up at the other end of the bar, the old hag cackles at me.

'Cyril don't give two flyin' shits what you do, son. He's just bein' polite.' She cackles some more phlegm and suckles from her bottle of Satzenbrau.

I'm wasting time. I've just a few hours with Charley before we say our goodbyes and I want to explain to him why I had kept Clinical Dad's true version of events to myself. To cut a long story short, I tell him that it was easier for me to let on he was dead rather than alive because nobody questions a corpse.

Halfway through our beverages, Cyril stands up from his beer keg to stretch his legs and catches sight of my red balloon sitting on the stool to my right. The winning salesman's smile he had greeted us with melts from his face. 'You'll have to remove the balloon if somebody needs a seat. Who's Fanny?'

I cast a glance around the Hound and kindly point out to Cyril that there's nobody in his bar besides Gagool up the other end. As I say this, I notice a trickle of urine coming from her stool, dripping quietly onto the stone floor of the Hound. I nudge Charley's ribs with my elbow and nod in that direction. Charley spots the piss and mimes F-O-C-K, saying it would be faster. I'm on the verge of telling Charley about my own dirty protest in Dennis's taxi but I'm ashamed of my impromptu leakage though I felt liberated at the time.

'If needs be,' I say to Cyril, 'I'll buy my balloon a drink. Let me assure you that there's more than meets the eye here. This isn't your average party-pooper.' I wink at Charley and keep 45's celestial noble presence to myself for now. A warm feeling moves through me knowing that 45's with me, right here in the Hound. We'd never been here together as mortals. It's like a whole new phase of our relationship is beginning to happen.

'Knowledge is power,' mumbles Charley.

'What's with the hostility, Cyril? Where's Manny? He normally runs the afternoon shift.'

'Depression 'n anxiety.' *Suck 'n siphon.* Cyril mouths it off like he's talking about a couple of unwelcome drinkers who come around every now and again to cause trouble. I can feel Charley's eyes on me and we both gaze about the bar. We understand Manny's plight. What had I ever seen in this dump? It's worse than the Old Quart if that's possible. Am I beginning to see my old haunts for what they really are? I feel the need to sprint again.

'Found him lyin' on the floor here last Friday in a pool

of Guinness, gawkin' up at the ceilin' like an owl with smoky-eyed, Miss D. Barrel, givin' him a lover's bite – slippin' him the tongue, she was.'

Charley's confused. 'The owl was slipping who the tongue?'

'He had the double-barrel shotgun I keep under the counter cocked in his mouth with his toe on the trigger.'

'Is that even possible?' asks Charley.

I try to work out the logistics of this. 'Excuse me?' Cyril has never struck me as an L.A. noir kind of guy. It worries me to think that there's a double-barrel shotgun just behind the counter, probably pointing directly at the fork of my legs. 'I told him to go home an' clean himself up.' Cyril gestures vaguely to his face. 'Bloody *disgrace*.' He sighs wearily and sits back down and begins to whistle a jolly tune which is decidedly out of context with this sudden lull in the Hound. I giggle into my pint, spraying froth, while

Charley pisses himself but he's wearing his khakis so the darker green patches camouflages his stain. Charley suffers from a weak bladder since his older brother (Morgan had been three years old at the time while Charley had just turned a year) had confused Charley's penis for his slinky and got it wrapped up in the netting of their play-pen, causing a build-up and resulting perforation. Charley's been wearing camouflage khakis ever since. And, shoot me down if I'm wrong, the Medusa dreads covering his face are actually covering his childhood embarrassment.

'Still goin' 'round with your head up yer arse, Jonny?' asks Cyril. 'I'm not slaggin' you off or anythin', just askin'.'

Instinct tells me to lay my right hand on my birthday balloon. It gives way a little too much beneath my fingers which makes me want to hurl. To think that 45 might seep and spend eternity in the Hound gives me the shivers. He'd end up like Manny only looking down from the ceiling.

'Still scratchin' yer sack? Hmm? Don't take it literally.' *Suck 'n siphon.*

'Pervert,' Charley interjects. 'Why are you so obsessed with Jonny's sexual organs?' Charley's knuckles have turned white around his pint glass. I pat him on the shoulder in a manly way to quieten him. We both know that this stems from the slinky incident.

'Just thought Jonny might've gotten his finger out besides playin' tag with his own balls.' He takes a luxurious pull on his cigarette.

'There he goes again, Jon.' Charley's going to flip. 'In the space of thirty seconds he's verbally raped you with your own finger.'

'Though that Jonny might've gotten a job besides spongin' off his poor mother and the same goes for that no-good limp cuckoo yank.'

Charley coughs into his pint and shouts, 'Racist!' at the same time.

I thank Cyril for his unwanted opinion and quaff half my pint straight down.

Charley, sensing danger, follows suit.

Siphon 'n suck. 'I think there's somethin' that American snake's not tellin' us.' He wiggles his finger about the air again. 'If you really want to know what I think…'

'No thanks,' I answer. '45 was my grandfather. He stepped into the void and brought me up as his own after my father jumped into the river.'

'Reminiscent of the Jungle Book,' Charley clarifies.

'Thank you, Cha. I am Mowgli and 45 is Sheer Brilliance. I won't tolerate the likes of you bad-mouthing him, Cyril.'

Cyril's openly cupping his testicles while sitting on the beer keg. 'All I'm sayin' is that he slipped in under the radar. Surprisin' seen as he has more tin in his knee than the Tin Man. Don't take it personally, Jon, it's just an observation. I've got your mother's best interest at heart.'

I'm not sure I like the sound of that. 'Can you keep your observations to yourself, please?' I knock back the last angry dregs of Guinness and stare hard at Cyril inside the time-warped counter. 'I wouldn't talk ill of the dead, Cyril, if I were you.' I reach for the lip of my balloon and revolve it between my fingers. '45 died yesterday in case you haven't heard – while blowing up my birthday balloon. He's in here and he's heard it all.'

Cyril gawps at my big red birthday balloon, 'Huh?' as if the date and time of his premature death was printed on it instead of Happy Birthday, Fanny! 'Jesus, Mary and Joseph, get that thing *outta here!*' He flashes the sign of the cross three times.

'Yeah,' Charley pipes up, adding his tuppence
worth, 'he's been here all along, like a hidden camera. C'mon, Jon, let's take our custom to the Old Quart where we're not wanted.'

'Why should I take out the balloon?' I ask, looking for a fight now. I've had it with the narrow-minded hicks in this town.

'Health and safety for one! Go on, get yer coats and go on about yer business. I won't have any loiterin' on these premises.'

We get up to leave but not before finishing our Guinness, which is the creamiest in town, to give Cyril his due.

'I should give Vera a call.' Cyril smirks. 'Give her a friendly shoulder to cry on.' Cyril winks behind the rising smoke.

'How dare you!' I hiss.

'She's got some extra room in the house now. She needs a man about the place. Kick you lot into line for starters.'

I stop at the door and almost pop 45 on the hinge. 'What did you just say?'

'Who fed 45 and kept him in nappies?' Cyril sneers. 'Have you seen the price of nappies recently? With wings … without wings … you'd want to be literally *shittin'* money.' Cyril pours himself a double shot of Jameson from one of his own optics. 'I know that you've got your hands down your pants for the last half decade and…'

Charley intervenes, 'There he goes *again*.'

'... never gave your mother a single cent of that money your daddy sends you.' By instinct, I gaze through the half open door towards the bank. 'How do you know about that?' 'The town told me. You'd be surprised what reaches my ears here on any night of the week. I'd kindly oblige your mother a few bob if she ever needs it and you can carry that message to her ... a fine woman who needs some ballast in her life.'

He leans over the counter and licks his lips. 'Some lending institutions offer a cooler-bag or coffee-maker but I offer cash on the hip. I'd gladly let Vera go search for it if she really wants it.' *Suck 'n siphon.* 'Nobody ever reads the small print...' Wink, wink.

I quickly decide my course of action: *nobody* rubbish's Vera. She's been through too much. Cyril isn't a man who understands the power of words so I calmly pass my balloon to Charley, 'Get ready to run.' I turn back, lift the hatch, and jump in behind the counter. Charley tries to stop me but is too late as I allow Cyril the honour of understanding the power of my four knuckles that smashes squarely into his drink-puffed nose, producing a magnificent double-barrel red gush. *'Bluagh!'* I hear Cyril gurgle behind me as I sprint from The Hound. I turn back just in time to see Miss D-Barrel looking down her snout at me and Cyril cocked behind her.

Charley roars *'Fooock!'* in slow-mo as he follows up the rear, passing me 45 in a relay race.

There is a Chinese theory that a crazy man can outrun a train so I *must* be crazy as I sprint across the square with 45 comfortably riding my slipstream. All I can hear is the slap of my shoes on concrete and Cyril's mean words concerning Vera's integrity. I don't stop running until I get to the mocking revolving-doors of the Bank of Ireland. I watch them for a moment, going around in circles, which kind of sums up this afternoon. I know I shouldn't have run and I can hear 45 whispering sweet-nothings in my ear. *Sleeping Dragons never run away, only Slopes and Gooks and every other yellow-bellied newt run for cover.* His blatant racism is almost endearing.

The revolving doors swallow us up as we go back inside and join the queue, the worst for wear and the object of some disgusted stares. It's obvious that we've been up to skulduggery.

'Seven thousand euro?' I ask the same red-head teller. 'But you said ten thousand half an hour ago and

that's about right going by my calculations.' I work my monthly lodgements out again on my gold calculator watch while Charley's busy keeping an eye over his shoulder for Cyril.

'Yes, that's a seven followed by three zeros. That might be tricky for you because of the quantity of zeros which could represent a confusing total of *zero* but I really can't simplify it any further, Mr Rowe.' She spots my calculator watch and I stop her before she opens her mouth.

'But I can't travel to Iowa to set my grandfather free on that kind of money plus open a private investigation business. A lot of interest accumulates over five years.'

'Exactly, Mister Rowe, this is an interest-bearing account which means that the bank charges you interest on the interest that you earn.'

'Don't try to confuse me with your fancy jargon, Miss Keane.' My previously numb fist is starting to pierce and I notice that my knuckles are grazed from the high impact on Cyril's nose. In fact, he'd left some of his nose on my knuckles. 'And to think that 45 wore your cap; it makes me want to puke in the face of Bank of Ireland. Obviously 45 didn't know his arse from his elbow towards the end – or the beginning – but he took part in free publicity on your bank's behalf. Doesn't that mean anything to you? Have you no dignity?' A wave of red heat gathers at my shirt collar and migrates northwards across the plain of my face but her blankness speaks volumes.

'Just as well that the hat's dead and buried then,'

Charley concludes and I happen to agree with his acute observation. I think of the green, white, and gold cap lying on the cold pine, suffocated in cold black mud. I'm sorry now that I hadn't sent something with stars and stripes down with him, anything, a tea-towel, just as a goodwill gesture. And that leads me to thinking that, seen as he did fight in WWII or 'Nam, he should've gotten a twenty-one gun salute with the star-spangled banner draped across his pine besides having an unknown gypsy help us lower him into the ground.

'How would you like it?'

'As fast as possible,' I say in a resigned voice. '*Cash.*'

The teller slavers her thumb and forefinger in response and begins passing out wads of fifties and hundreds with her saliva on each bill, something that I find disgusting. Maybe if she had been a fitter teller then things might be different. I might've actually enjoyed watching. Jesus of Nazareth, I'm starting to fall into the same trap Clinical Dad fell into. 'Isn't there a machine to count that?' She quickly counts up seven thousand but it doesn't look like much on the counter.

I'm excited though because these very notes will take me to Middle-America where I will see, with my own eyes, 45's home.

The idea that this journey to discover the real 45 will provide me with my PhD thesis is almost too great to contain. Then I realize that I need *dollars* not Euros and I relay this to the teller.

The teller does her arithmetic. 'That's six thousand dollars.'

'*What?* But that's even less!' I protest. 'The Euro's *stronger* than the dollar.'

She raises her weary eyes at me. 'Not today it isn't. I would go into current economics at the European Central Bank but you two don't seem the type.' She quacks at me and clucks with her self-complacent bill.

Charley tells her that she's not his type either.

I clench my hurting fist, inadvertently squeezing in
on 45's dying breaths. A terrible image assaults my
senses: 45's crimson face … eyes popping out on stalks
just like those joke-shop slinky-specs. I guess ole' 45 just
had a déjà vu. 'I am sorry. That's the last thing you need.'

'No need to apologize, sir.'

'That wasn't for your benefit; that was for my balloon.'

The teller makes a piggy face and stands and strains to
get a glimpse of my balloon below her line of vision.
'Who's Fanny?'

'Just gimme the goddamn money, please, and I'll be on
my way. Thank you.' I pass my big red balloon to Charley
with care and stuff the face of Benjamin Franklin into as
many pockets as I can find and leave through the same
revolving doors and watchful of their pitfalls. As I stuff the
last of the dollars into my pockets, the red-head teller tells
me to cut my losses and set 45 free at the Cliffs of Moher.
They've never looked back as far as Uncle Joe's
concerned.

We take to the alleyways to avoid Cyril's detection. He
probably can't leave the Hound unattended and wouldn't
let the sea-hag to help herself to his Satzenbrau but he can
watch the street from his beer-keg.

I experience mixed emotions about Clinical Dad: my
bright side wants to thank him but my dark side wants to
kick his stupid ass over the moon. I know what the love of
a stamp-lickin' woman can do to a man. That's just the way
us men are built: weak. But that's no excuse for what he
did to Vera and the rest of us. That phony suicide note was
the work of a fully-feathered chicken-shit that seriously
needs its neck wrung. Still, I've got some money now.

'Yoo-hoo, Jon. Come back to me, bud.'

'Twenty-one years, Cha, and this is all I have.' I smack
my pockets. 'At least, I've got some TLC waiting for
me back the Mistress's place.' Suddenly, I remember.
'Ronald McDonald!'

'Where?!'

16 hours to departure…

10.
Bring Out the Clowns

'What time is it?' checking my calculator watch. '5.30pm on the nose. Ronald McDonald wants to see me.'

Charley looks deep into my eyes. 'Jonny, you might be waiting for me to tell you that this is a dream but it isn't. So whatever you say and do from here on in will have repercussions.' He pinches my arm and I tell him to go fuck himself but in a nice way. Being so wrapped up in this Iowa thing, I had completely forgotten to tell Charley about my telephone conversation with Ronald McDonald. I explain the whole thing to him so he comes along purely because he'd never met Ronald McDonald in person.

When we get to McDonalds ten minutes away on the other side of Old Castle, I go to the counter and tell a fragile boy that Ronald McDonald is expecting me, just for laughs. Momentarily looking up from his napkins and straws, he manages a smirk for my benefit. He asks me for my order and, again, I tell him that I'm indeed here to meet, perhaps not the clown himself, but certainly one of his reps. 'I was the thousandth customer this month.'

What am I doing here? I should be planning my quest; taking care of things; taking care of 45 who's still seeping. There's no getting away from the tiny sagging creases that have appeared in my red balloon.

'I didn't realize we were running a promo. So, who did you say rang you?' He looks up at me for a split second, clocking my balloon. 'Who's Fanny?' He fills never-ending trays with Happy Meals with weak wrists and spindly fingers. Obviously he's here to make money for his medicine or law degree. 'I don't think we're running a promo at the moment… No, I don't recall any memo.'

'Well,' I tell him again, 'he said he was Ronald McDonald.' I look at Charley. 'It couldn't have been Tommy? He's good but not that good.'

Charley rules it out immediately. 'It's too original for your brother.'

Turning back to the brittle teenager, 'The speaker on the phone told me that one of your people would meet me here at 5.30pm to show me what mind-blowing prize I've won or something to that effect.'

'Dunno. Go ask him yourself.' The boy nods to a point somewhere behind us...

Fuck...

I am *dreaming*...

A blast of shocking reds and yellows hit me. Sitting in a booth, all on his own beneath a bunch of bright helium balloons is Ronald McDonald, idly picking at what appears to be a Big-Mac meal and a large coke. He rifles inside his yellow dungarees and whips out a mobile phone and dials a number.

As he does, my iPhone vibrates in my pocket. I deliberate whether to pick it up.

'Maybe it's not him,' Charley surmises. 'This happens all over the world twenty-four hours a day. How many times have you seen someone dial a number and your phone rings?'

I sift for my iPhone amongst my dollars and hit the receive button. I say nothing ... my eyes are on Ronald's scarlet lip-stick lips.

'Jonny?'

I lip-read as the fast-food clown says my name in my ear-hole. It's him all right. 'Yeah?' I answer with hesitation.

'You have an appointment with – '

'I'm standing in front of you.' I give a little wave of acknowledgment.

Ronald looks up from his cucumber slice which he had removed from his Big Mac. Our eyes lock and for a moment I still have a chance to run screaming from McDonalds.

'Hi. I'm Ronald McDonald.'

'I'm Jonny.'

I'm playing along with two charades. Firstly, I'm
playing along with Ronald McDonald who introduces
himself with such honesty -and integrity that I'm supposed
to believe that he's Ronald McDonald. I don't think that I'd
ever come here to actually see Ronald McDonald calling
me on my phone. Secondly, I'm playing along with the
man posing as the famous clown.

'That's Charley…' thumbing in Charley's direction.

Charley nods in Ronald's direction and Ronald waves
back enthusiastically like Charley's a kid. At the same
time, he's talking in my ear, more hushed this time.

'I'd like to talk to you in private.'

And now I have no doubts. My waters are right,
incredible as this may sound. "Again" he had said on the
phone. I recognize the face under the face paint, despite the
twenty-one years that have passed. I turn to Charley in a
daze. 'Let's talk tomorrow, Cha. That man isn't Ronald
McDonald; that man is Clinical Dad.'

Charley's jaw drops. He gulps and a dribble of saliva
slips from the corner of his lips onto his army-surplus parka
jacket. He looks retarded but I know I look the same; just
an average couple of morons standing in McDonald's. I
vaguely nod to tell Charley that everything's going to be
okay. Charley returns the nod back at me and reverses out
the door, literally.

I turn to meet the longing gaze of Clinical Dad or Ronald
McDonald; I'm not sure whose make-up I prefer right now.
I've got to say that I feel a closer bond to Ronald
McDonald at the moment. I've certainly seen more of him
around and can readily identify with an actual working
clown rather than my father the clown. Let's stick with
Ronald for now. I've yet to find out whose face beneath the
face beneath the face belongs to.

Ronald beckons me over to his booth while wiping the
corners of his scarlet and white lips. I approach warily and
sit down. He offers me a French fry but I blankly refuse.

'Happy birthday.'

'It was until you showed up.' Not really; 45's in my balloon now. I'm amazed that Clinical Dad's using his own orange hair to pass for Ronald McDonald's 'fro. The likeness is uncanny. Kind've like a method actor. Clinical Dad has simply grown his hair for the part.

'You know who I am, then?'

'McDonald.' I say with conviction. 'Ronald McDonald.' I wish I had my own face-paint to hide my feelings. 'So let's keep it that way.'

'No, I'm not *the* Ronald McDonald. I'm – '

'I'm more comfortable with McDonald's mascot for now.' I answer back coldly. 'I prefer that than speaking with a drowned ghost in McDonalds. Still hiding your face, I see. You just can't help it can you. You even had a beard in that old photograph of us sitting on the bonnet of the Cortina. Obviously up to something even then.' 'The face-paint is part of my day job but it also, y'know, allows me to hide from the locals who probably want to throw me in the river again – for good this time.' And then, with a bite of humble pie: 'I'm not proud of what I did, Jon.' Ronald looks himself up and down and fixes to make himself more respectable than he already is in his clown costume. 'No, don't misunderstand me. I don't normally dress like this. I don't live in McDonaldland … I'm not in cahoots with the Hamburglar despite what the Press claims. But do I know Mayor McCheese? Yes, personally, so if have any neighbours that need removing…'

He's trying to make me smile and I almost do.

'I work here.' He holds out his yellowed gloved-hands to the interior of McDonalds as if it's a five-star eating emporium. 'Wages are shit but I get to dress up as Ronald McDonald.'

'Uh-huh,' clocking his red-and-white striped top inside his yellow dungarees and clobbering red shoes.

'And I get three square meals a day – including McWraps – and coffee whenever I need one.'

My silence speaks volumes.

'Um,' Ronald fidgets with his 'fro, 'I'm here to get the numbers up. Stand at the door ... wave do-daaa ... that kinda thing.' Ronald attempts a meek wave and emits a half-hearted chuckle that lapses into nothing. 'It's just not the same when y'know who I really am and I know the customer.'

'You don't know me but go on.'

'I've tried to ring you a few times, Jon, but I always chickened out when I heard your voice. I wanted to wish you happy birthday. You've turned thirty, right? You had an eventful party, I hear.'

'That's one way of putting it.'

My heart suddenly skips a beat when I realize that 45's streamer isn't in my hand... It had slipped through my sweaty palm while talking with the clown. I drop to the floor and crawl on all fours without dignity, searching between peoples legs while apologizing for the disruption. '45? Where are you?' I actually call out his name like a child that has wandered off. I'm looking for my dead grandfather in a birthday balloon at McDonalds while having a late lunch with a real clown claiming to be Ronald McDonald: yes, I'm struggling to find myself.

'Jon! Here...'

Ronald McDonald calls me. I turn back to see my birthday balloon in his yellow glove.

I return to my booth and snap it back.

'Careful,' he smiles, 'I think it wants to start somethin' with one of my balloons.' Ronald goes about to honk his nose but fiddles with it instead.

'Your balloons float cos they've got a lotta hot air.'

'Helium, actually.'

'My balloon doesn't float because it *doesn't* have hot air. Actually it does have, in a way.' I can see the confusion wrinkle beneath his paint. '45's in here. Best clear that up now before this gets any more confusing than it needs to be.'

Ronald McDonald takes a sup of coke. 'Yeah, I've heard all about that.'

'You've heard a lot. Have you been spying on us?'

'Vera told me. She gave me your number. Figuring that the old man passed away, she thought you might've needed somebody to fill the void. She thought that maybe we could, y'know, patch things up. Your mother and I, well, things are more complicated but I thought that you and me, maybe we could...'

'45 filled your void for most of my life. You will never fill his void because you're not big enough a man.' I'm aware that I'm talking in innuendos and sarcastic metaphors. It's a defence mechanism that I can't shake. 'And why was Vera talking to you anyway?'

'Well, I'm in town and I thought it would be weird if I didn't call 'round, y'know.' He says this in a matter of fact kind of way while daubing ketchup onto his fries. 'Now that 45's not around anymore.'

'Oh,' I exclaim, 'you thought that not calling 'round for a cuppa would be weird after you wrote your own suicide note over two decades ago only to be discovered with a prostitute. Yes, of course, you're right. Not *calling 'round* would probably be in bad taste.'

'Jonny, you don't know the circumstances and Philomena wasn't a hooker; she worked in the post office so have a little respect.'

'She licked stamps like a whore.' I don't know what's come over me nor do I know how a whore licks a stamp but I can imagine. 'My friend Charley used to fantasize about her! He was nine years old and losing his baby teeth at the time!'

Ronald weighs that concept up. 'Still, though, have a little respect.'

Respect? What would you know about respect? I think about saying this but decide that my caustic one-liners will only get me so far. I could keep flipping everything back on Clinical Dad all day but that's not very intelligent. I

109

need closure now or maybe an opening first and *then* a closure. All the time, my trip to Iowa is in the back of my mind and my race against time before 45 melts. There, another example: we were never in McDonald's when he was alive but here we are and I guess that a trace of him will linger with the grease fumes for eternity as well as mingling with sour dregs back at The Hound. 'Look, Ronald,' *Ronald?* 'I don't *need* to know the circumstances. No matter what has happened, you shouldn't have left Vera and us out to dry. Just be a man and *leave* like a man, shit happens, I know that now. Pretending that you're dead is the lowest of the low because now I've gotten used to the idea of you being dead so what I see before me is,' and I'm digging a well for myself, 'a drowned ghost who has, um, been reincarnated as Ronald … McDonald.'

At this point, something grabs my attention right outside our booth window. A giant spider has just crawled from the litter bin but the pock-marked body and hairy legs metamorphose into Charley's face and dreadlocks. I shake my head and grit my teeth as if to say: *not now, Cha.* 'Do you know how much Vera's suffered since you jumped into the river?'

Ronald has spotted the spider too. 'Is he okay? He doesn't look okay.'

'That's just his face.'

'Oh. Look, Philomena and I are not together anymore, Jonny. Anyway, I've been keeping an eye on your mother from a distance.'

'Oh, how thoughtful.'

'You didn't see me at 45's funeral but I was there … in the background.'

This surprises me. I should've seen that hair a mile off. It would've stood out in a cemetery.

'I was wearing a big parka to keep the rain off my paint. I'd just nipped out for the funeral.'

A-ha!

'I've been keepin' an eye on you too.'

'What's that supposed to mean?'

'Y'know…'

He's hinting at something but I shake my head. 'Nope…'

'My son … my legacy.'

'I'm not your legacy.' Here we go again: tennis tit-for-tat.

'I'm talking about our little nest-egg.'

A sour taste is coming to my mouth. 'My little nest-egg? The saving's scheme? What about it? Didn't come to much after taxes and interest on interest was deducted … but thanks.' I mean it. 'But that doesn't change the fact that you are nothing to me but a hazy memory.'

Ronald McDonald speaks after a pensive silence. 'I'm broke, Jon. I live here.'

'In McDonald's?'

'McDonaldland, baby, 24-hour service. I've got a sleeping bag out back in the pantry between the ice-cream powder and cups. My colleagues are keeping it under their hats for now. The manager sees me come 'n go but I return after he finishes his shift – only a matter of time before he catches me.' He pauses for effect. 'I can't deny that my life here is peaceful but I need to disconnect from work, y'know.'

'That's an understatement.'

Jesus of Nazareth! Of course! Now I know where this strange episode of my life is going. I'd failed to read the goddamn small print of this little fiasco. 'You got in touch with me cos you know that the savings scheme is up today. You're not here to wish me a happy birthday at all! You're here – *I'm* here – for the money!'

'Relax! Here, have a chip.'

'The same money that you'd put away for yourself just in case…' What a day this is turning out to be. I clinch my already damaged fist. Could it be that, after a life-time of never having an altercation, I would use my right fist twice in the same day? But there's something about knuckle-

sandwiching a man in face-paint. I have no beef with
Ronald McDonald who is sitting ten feet tall in front of me.
I just can't summon the anger to mash his fat red nose.
Ironic that Cyril also has a fat red nose but that's burst
capillaries from a life-time of dipping into his after-hour
whiskey optics.

Charley's up on his toes outside our window, seeing my
new shocked reaction.

'Aw, c'mon,' pleads Ronald, 'I've had a rotten time.'
Tears build up in his eyes and begin to trickle down his
cheeks, ruining his make-up. He's acting, I'm sure of it. He
sniffles inside his plastic nose. 'I was in the mirror of the
public jacks for half an hour this morning putting on make-
up as you do when a group of little boy-scouts came in to
use the facilities, just walked right in on me. They'd come
to Old Castle just to see *me!* Their captain or whatever he
or she's called heard that I was in town on a radio spot. I
think I must've traumatised most of them,' he reflects.
'They came into McDonalds as boy-scouts but left as men
with broken dreams which is kind of beautiful really
because it's what I've become. What about giving your dad
a few bob, just to get him on his feet? I'll pay you back
with interest.' In perfect timing he winces, grabbing his
stomach. 'Prostate stones, nothing serious but can be lethal
if left untreated,' he reams off, obviously having read it in
an online symptom checker.

'My dads will never get to their feet cos they're *dead*:
one drowned in the Arra twenty-one years ago and one died
yesterday. And I don't need that kind of interest that you're
offering.' I'm shaking. I snap the pack of Benson &
Hedges on the table, presumably Ronald's, and spark one
up, right there. I inhale deeply and my head goes woozy.
Ronald's looking at the lit cigarette and the blue tendril of
smoke rising from it. His eyes dart to the counter and the
customers and he's growing nervous.

'Put you in an awkward position, have I?' And then I
utter a line that I would feel proud of later. 'Not nice, is it?'

'You'll get me fired. I can't afford that right now.'

'Y'know, I used to sit on the bridge when I was a kid, expecting you to float by below me doing the back-stroke. On my own for hours, just sitting there and waiting for you to come home in your wet clothes. Today, I even missed you a little bit while I was stuffing your dollars into my pockets. In my mind, you had redeemed yourself a little.'

Ronald blinks profusely.

I think he's about to cry or look for forgiveness.

'Y-You mean you've got the money on you?'

I should've known.

The clown nonchalantly flicks a chip into his mouth but I can see surprise beneath his paint. I'd rattled him.

'Why, uh, would you change it to dollars, Jonny?'

Oops...

'None of your business.' My misfired line immediately smacks of conspiracy. I avoid eye contact and I know he's found a fissure as he sits back and takes all of me in.

'Where are you goin', Jon? Strange time of the year for a holiday.'

'I just fancied a long weekend in New York. I'd love to meet Woody Allen.'

'Horse shit, you're goin' to Iowa. Am I right? I know you better than you think I know you, Jon. 45 was from Iowa, isn't that right.'

I redden up and the guilt is everywhere. I'm trying to sneak 45 behind my back now but Ronald glimpses my balloon. I can see his eyes narrowing (pronounced by the surrounding face paint) as he puts two and two together. 'Jesus in a bucket, I *am* right! You *are* taking him back to his own place; hence, the dollars.'

'So what if I am?' That's my confession right there.

'Does Vera know about your impending trip?'

'She doesn't need to know.'

'Oh, but she does, Jon. She *needs* to know about you going to Iowa.'

'Why?'

Ronald allows my question to roll around inside his outrageous natural 'fro. 'There are things that you don't know, Jonny. Let me put it in terms that you can understand: ghosts should be kept in the closet; not gays.'

'Uh-huh.'

'And you think that *I'm* the black sheep of the family. I'm your fairy godmother, Jon, and I'm granting you an introductory free wish: stay clear of Iowa. Don't go digging up the past. It's gone to the ground with the old man. Leave it there.'

'I've got a degree in genealogy. I dig; that's what I do.' I can't deny the pride in my voice. I've always wanted to use that impressive line.

'And I was the proudest father when Vera told me that.'

Jesus of Nazareth, I'm so overwhelmed and confused right now. Clinical Dad's ghost sits before me in McDonald's as a reincarnation of Ronald McDonald who is in fact my fairy fucking godmother but he/she thinks that I think that he/she is a black sheep. 'Fair enough, you may as well be my fairy godmother, but why's it not a good idea to go to Iowa?' He can pick up on the desperation in my voice, my waters know it.

'I'm just saying that it's not a good idea to go without Vera's consent.'

'That's rich. But 45 told me not to tell Vera.'

I see the astonishment through the clown's tragic make-up.

'Those were his express wishes in his will.' His *will?* Yes, maybe the note was his last will and testament. And why am I even telling this clown what 45 had said? '*Please*, don't tell her.' Why do I feel like I'm arguing with my dad?

'I'm sure we can cut some sort of deal here.'

Ah-ha, here it comes... A longing part of me wants to cry or punch the clown. It's the part of me that secretly wishes that maybe this was the beginning of a new chapter in my life. Christ, I shouldn't feel so let down; I've only

Jonathan Dunne *Balloon Animals*

known him five minutes. 'The penny drops for a second time and it's a dirty one that keeps coming back.' There we go with the metaphors but I've got my back against the wall of promises that I'd made to 45 and myself.

'A slice of the cake should keep Vera out of this. Let's say: three grand.'

'What?'

'I truly regret this, Jon. You can't imagine the embarrassment I'm feeling right now.'

'You don't look too embarrassed.'

'That's just the paint masking my pain.'

'Three thousand euro? But, wait...' Subtracting three thousand euro from six thousand dollars on my gold calculator watch leaves me with the bones of three grand and I point this out to the clown. 'Half of that will go on my flights cos it's short notice and what 'bout my...' *private detective agency* I almost blurt.

'I'd hate if Vera were to find out. Believe me: I'm doin' you a justice.'

'You just want the money.'

'I can't deny that that's also a factor. I want to get up in the morning and not have an egg Mc-Muffin for breakfast and a shower would be nice. I'm not knocking McDonald's facilities but just a shower...'

By now, my olfactory system has become accustomed to the smell of McDonald's grease and in its place comes the musty aromas of stale sweat. 'How long have you been working here?'

'Since your grandfather passed on.'

'Yesterday!' I can't believe it. 'You've only been working here since yesterday!'

'But I still have all the hardships that I mentioned. They've all happened just once – twice including this morning – but it still qualifies. Like I said, I thought that you and I could pick up where we left off.'

I want to believe but my waters tell me that he's toying with my emotions. I want to say exactly this but it sounds maybe more for lovers. I get up to leave, grabbing 45 tight in my fist. 'Like I said, you just want the money so let's keep family out of this. You can tell Vera whatever you like. I'm still going to Iowa on research purposes for my PhD thesis. 45 will be my subject. So,' thinking myself quite clever, 'I'm going on official business.' I would've rounded that off by adding that tracking down 45's people would also be my first case as an unlicensed private detective. 'By the way, Ronald ... fairy godmother ... black sheep, whoever you are, don't try to contact me again, thank you. Oh, don't get me wrong: I'm happy that you got in touch because now I can see how pathetic you really are.' I'm smiling now but my mouth is doing that involuntary quivering thing again. 'I had doubts, you see. Every now and again I would give you the benefit of the doubt because we're all human and born with imperfections – hairline cracks as the Reiki Mistress would say – but asking me for the money that you had put away for my well-being confirms that you're one slimy individual who has no morals after having twenty-one years to stew in what you've done to your family. I can now rest knowing that I've missed *zilch*.' I mean and stamp every word. I stub my B&H out in Ronald's cucumber slice and beat a hasty retreat. Behind me, I hear Ronald McDonald call out: 'Okay, so I made a mistake. I'm sorry, keep the money. But you're still my son and I advise you not to go to Iowa. Can o' worms, Jon! Can o' worms!'

Charley's at the door to meet me. 'What? How? When? Where?'

I catch a glimpse of Ronald sitting alone amongst his balloons as I shut the door behind me. I've never seen such a sad forlornly clown; a product of the times we live in. It's true for Smokey Robinson and the Miracles: there's nothing more tragic than the tears of a clown when he's sitting alone in McDonald's.

Jesus of Nazareth. I turn back inside to Charley's protests and fish out two thousand dollars out of my pockets and leave it by his gloved hand. 'It's not three but I think you're doing well with two.'

Ronald doesn't say anything but just looks up at me with big eyes. His gloved hands come for the money but grab my hand instead. 'I lost my son once and I don't want to lose him a second time. Don't go to Iowa!'

I admit that his ultimatum does shock me but I know he's trying to frighten me out of making a man of myself. 'I'll call you when I need advice.' I won't get another opportunity to ask the question that's been bugging me for two decades. 'Why did you leave?'

'You wouldn't understand.'

'Try me.'

'I fell in love with a stamp lickin' whore.'

I snort in reaction to the clown's honesty.

'She two-timed me. I lost it all.'

He's about to say something else but I don't give him a chance. Trembling, I leave Ronald McDonald to stew in his own greasy juices. I doubt I'll ever see him or my money again and it doesn't bother me; some things are meant to be tasted just once.

As I leave, it hits me. Wait! That's *it?!* Have I just met Clinical Dad after twenty-one years? Talk about an anti-climax.

'Who's Fanny?' comes to my ears before I slam McDonald's door behind me.

15 hours to departure…

11.
Small Town Rumours

My expertise is my past – Rowe's past – but on our
sobering walk home from the bank I glance into the near
future and this is how it's going to be:

I will take 45 to the cliffs of Moher just as the crazy red-
head bank-teller had advised and leave him to the mercy of
the shrieking gulls. I won't complete my PhD in genealogy
because I won't have a subject for my thesis, now that 45 is
being regurgitated as rubber pellets to fluffy chicks on the
side of a cliff. I forget my aspirations of opening a private
investigation agency and I won't be a private investigator
because I'll spend the rest of my sorry life investigating my
own life and trying to uncover where it had gone wrong.
Charley's ravings and musings keep me entertained on the
sobering walk home yet I'm assaulted by a barrage of
confusion and negativity, I also see how my funds are
depleting without ever setting foot in Iowa. I'm plagued by
omens yet Benjamin Franklin's keeping my testicles from
shrink-wrapping on this cold and dark February evening. I
can't bring myself to look at my red balloon with nothing
but bad vibrations coming down the line of my streamer as
we saunter back to 128 Hydrangea Drive.

I'm so angry that I strike myself in a masochistic wave
of insecurity as we pass a Tesco Express. Again, there are
forces beyond my control and I liken my impromptu self-
flagellation to my dirty protest in Dennis's taxi that seems a
century ago. Let's call it the caveman-searching-for-his-
place inside me.

'Fock!' Charley backs away instead of saving me from
me. 'What's with the *hostility?*'

Customers and foreign-national shop-assistants gawp out
at me through the window as I nonchalantly knuckle my
left temple in a deadly repeated move I had once learned on
a Bruce Lee film with dubbed threats. I curse in original

version this evening though, scream for justice: my plan to release 45 in his homeland of Iowa is sliding into a series of ominous signs and farcical portents. If I was a superstitious man, I would probably hide under my bed or in my wardrobe, whichever I get to first. Since when does the Sleeping Dragon hide in his wardrobe?

'Enough's enough. Wait here.' I duck into the Tesco Express and purchase a small bottle of alcohol from the cosmetic section, a cloth, and a permanent marker. I also purchase a moleskin diary which is what you are reading from now.

Outside, I sit on the footpath and ever so carefully, remove Tommy's Happy Birthday Fanny! from 45's defaced balloon and write RIP with a cross beneath it. I intentionally leave out a name. 'My birthday balloon will remain an unmarked grave until 45 decides to reveal himself to me. My goal will be to add his numbers only when the real 45 chooses to reveal himself.'

'And to help us do that, 45 needs to reveal his arse to us.' Charley lays his hand on my shoulder and gives it an encouraging squeeze. 'Candy in a haystack, man.'

This time I opt not to give him the satisfaction of answering. I watch our shadows appear, merge, and disappear as we traipse beneath the sodium orange of the streetlights. That's me, right there, on the pavement. I must exist if I'm casting a shadow. 'And there was me thinking that it would've helped my identity crisis by meeting Clinical Dad. He's a clown in all aspects – just a sad clown living in a made-up world. What does that make me?'

'A half-cast clown...'

'Hundreds of years of Rowe history and it's all been leading up to little Jonny who's too afraid to come out and play. My birth; a billion-to-one chance and this is the best I can do with the opportunity I've been given? I must be a major let-down to my fore-fathers who built Brooklyn Bridge. Sometimes, I regret taking that degree in genealogy; I feel the pressure of my past building up behind me like the Hoover dam, y'know that kinda pressure, Cha?'

Charley nods but how would he know.

'It's getting to me, Cha. I need to fix the future to fix the past.'

'Well, that's what you're doing, isn't it. Take 45 back home and you will redeem yourself and make things right with your forefathers.'

I turn to Charley as he sparks up an old Rolled Gold doobie-butt. As dusk falls I see the glow in his devilish face and hear the burning hiss of his spliff. We smoke the Rolled Gold between us in a last gesture of friendship. It's as close to blood-brothers as we will ever get because, though I love Charley, I don't know where he's been.

'It's hard to think that I'll be in Iowa this time tomorrow.'

'Strange how these revelations happen the day before you travel. Somebody's trying to tell you something, Jonny, but I'm not sure if they're urging you to stay or go.' Charley hums The Clash's *Should I Stay*...

I agree. 'This week has probably been the most eventful in my life, especially today.' I list off everything that's happened in the past forty-eight hours in one breath. 'And my waters are telling me that today isn't over yet. At least I've got my encounter with the Mistress to look forward to.'

'True. How do you feel about meeting your father after all these years?'

I give Charley's question serious thought. 'Nothing-bordering-on-pity. The disturbing image of seeing him in the guise of Ronald McDonald will stay with me forever. I don't regret giving him the money because now I've done my bit...'

'Bought your freedom...' Then, right out of the blue, Charley comes out with, 'Cyril may be a lop-sided pillar of the community but I think that there are worse in town.'

Then I remember that Charley had tried to *stop* me from

hitting Cyril. 'Why are you so in favour of Cyril, anyway? You tried to stop me from smashing his face. He deserved it, making wild assumptions about Vera. Just because a woman is available doesn't mean that she can be spoken about in such a way. Available doesn't mean free. I'm available for Christ's sake but I'm not free!'

'The Mistress?'

'Aw, that's just something to tide us over. We love each other in our own way but in *that* way.' Charley's avoiding my eyes. My waters are telling me that he's keeping something from me. 'Cha?'

'Y'know sometimes when you put off saying something until the right moment arrives?'

I nod. 'Uh-huh.'

'The moment has arrived.' Charley's looking at me now but with Basset hound eyes. For the first time in my life, I see that the clouds have lifted from Charley's dilated pupils. 'Jon, Vera's getting a bit of a name for herself 'round town.'

I play dumb. 'What kind of name? Mother Teresa? I've told her umpteen times to stop being so bloody charitable. I mean, the Red Cross charges for their charity work, no? Donations, etc? She's constantly helping … helping … helping.' The sound of my own voice is helping to block out what's coming next.

'No, more of a *Debbie Does Dallas* kind of vibe.'

'Uh-huh.' I haven't seen the film but I've heard of it, unfortunately.

'Sorry to come at it with such aggression but I think the situation warrants it. She's become a loose woman, Jon. She's come unhinged. She was spotted in a compromising after-hours position on Dom's pool table last Saturday night. Dom had a lock-in for his only customer, Vera. What's the likelihood of that? Filled her up with drink. The police raided the place as Dom was, um, about to pot the black. Sorry, I tried to tell you when you rang me from the cemetery but it wasn't the moment.' He tries a smile but it looks painful. I think that Charley's maybe enjoying this deep down. He's thrilled to bits that it's him that has been chosen to tell me.

'Did he?' A perverse side of me wants to know if this game of pool was consummated.

'What?'

'Pot the black?' I'm asking this question for a reason. 'Did he pot the black? A game isn't won till the black is in the pocket.'

Charley gawps at me in a subdued manner. 'Let's just say he broke the pack and leave it at that.'

'Exactly! Dom wasn't seen potting the black. I'm surprised at you, Cha, getting sucked into small town rumours.'

'Oh, it's not a rumour, Jon. She *was* on the pool table.'

'What *about* it?' Jesus of Nazareth. 'They exchanged a kiss, so?' I'm putting up a brave front. I don't mind who Vera sees but when it gets back to me like this, well... My mind's racing, tracing back along the months to see where Vera had come unhinged or had she always been undone, only now it's coming to light? And why wouldn't it? The day I've been having... Certainly, the pressure of taking care of 45 has been a burden for her but surely not enough to put out about town. Brillo does most of the plough work but leaves the mental strife to Vera. Vera's been going out at the weekends ever since she got the all-clear from the oncology department and more power to her... but that was years ago. I realize that I've fallen into some kind of twilight zone, spurred on by my pitiful dole money ... spurious PhD talk that never happens ... finding that job that never appears (not that I look very hard) ... get a pad of my own, hilarious. 'Vera's only human; a man in her life now and again isn't a sin, Cha.' If I don't back Vera up nobody will. Tommy and Alba are in worlds of their own. Maybe I shouldn't care so much?

'Now and again...' Charley peters off.

'So, I'm to understand by your ambiguous comment that

122

it's not now and again?'

'Jon, look, I'm not ready to judge anybody…'

'True.'

'But in a town like Old Castle, people get tagged easily. She's become sort of a running joke in town: nobody knows which barman will be snatched next. Cyril wasn't making wild accusations.'

'The black wasn't potted.' I'm unwilling to let go that concept, yet, I'm suspended in disbelief. My own mother has been moonlighting as a woman with loose morals and I'm the last to know about it.

Charley takes a left at the top of Hydrangea Drive for his own place. 'Let me know what's happening.' That's Charley's way of saying goodbye. I'm not sure if I'll see him again before my quest. We don't like goodbyes but prefer to go on hiatus. 'If you're serious about tracking down this Candy character then you need more evidence, Jon!'

I walk on with the seedy image of my mother with her hands down dirty Cyril's over-all dungarees in my voyeur's eye. Cyril with his old-world brace-straps and that makes it all the more obscene somehow, like an explicit duty my mother Vera has to carry-out on a routine basis; the business of undoing the straps. I need to relax so I close my eyes momentarily and take a deep breath … as my forehead crashes into a lamp-post. I regain my composure, having a quick look around to see if I had been seen, then resort to the Mistress's technique of mentally tracing my family backwards through history to the high-kings and their druid advisors on the Rock of Cashel. Where's a druid when I need one?

When I get back to 128, I open the side-gate and sit myself on the back doorstep. Why had 45 been so obsessed with this perch? I hold my birthday balloon up in front of me, look 45 in the face, and ask him out straight like a man, 'How am I going to do this?' I'm nervous and embarrassed to talk about sex with Vera. Maybe if I had had more of it offered to me during my lifetime then it wouldn't have been so bad, built up a tolerance kind of thing.

A breeze picks up and siphons through the privet hedge, showering me in more rain-drops. I shiver and wait for an answer from 45's noble spirit but all I get is the sound of the 'burbs...

And then it comes to me in an electric-blue flash of undiluted inspiration: 45's sending subtle messages which I have to de-code. And that's just it – there's *nothing* to decode because the answer is in the concept. He wants me to drop subtle hints to Vera rather than storming into the subject of the bottomless pockets in Cyril's dungarees and Dom's pool pockets. I will speak in metaphorical tongues.

When I get inside, I discover that there's something burning or had been burning, judging by the acrid stench. Tommy and Lucy have left a message on the living-room table: *Gone to the Dogs*. I agree completely, looking at the devastation of the post-wake-slash-celebration. On second thoughts, they've probably gone to the dog- track in Limerick city. Lucy likes an occasional gamble: she's going out with Tommy, after all. Next to that note is another written in Alba's (I'm not sure if Alba is just Susan or the collective) handwriting: *Gone to Hobbits*. Hobbits bar advertises itself in the local media as 'Halloween, every night of the Week!' which quickly loses its novelty if you ask me. That's where Old Castle's freaks and outcasts congregate and mate nevertheless. I have always suspected that 45 had never made much of an impression on Tommy or Susan and this is the proof of the pudding. They're just kids. The karaoke machine is on a loop, playing out Jefferson Airplane's *Somebody to Love* to a comatose audience: Vera. She's the main attraction here and is sprawled out on the sofa, microphone still in her hand. I count at least three empty Rioja wine bottles in close vicinity and a half bottle of ouzo left over from the good old days. I can't keep my eyes from straying to Vera's chest. She's clearly braless. Somebody had lain her bottle-green Jameson whiskey polo t-shirt over her. I can't resist from questioning which bar in town she had gotten that freebie. Why haven't I noticed it before? Because, Jonny, you're living on cloud cuckoo-land.

Deciding to put my detective skills into motion, I sniff out the source of the smoke. It might be the naked electric cables that fizz and spark every now and again, in homage of a man who had left his family to the elements, literally. I follow the caustic tendrils from the living room, crossing the hallway to the kitchen … to the kitchen sink where a half-burnt pearl-white bra lays curled up and smoking inside the basin. Jesus of Nazareth, Vera's burnt her bra in some shambolic and symbolic suffragette gesture. Fearing the worst, I take 45's spirit-bubble to my bedroom and tie him up to the head-rest of the bottom-bunk. I light the night-light on my bedside locker and whisper 45 to hang in there. I lock the door behind me and almost swallow the key. On the way back to the living room, I plan out my metaphorical conversation with Vera.

'Vera?' I nudge her. Her eyes half open but she's looking through me so I shove her a little harder. Again, lights are on but nobody's at home. Taking the microphone, I hold it to the karaoke's speaker. A scream of feedback screeches out and for a horrible moment, I'm back at my birthday party and 45's suddenly not a noble human being anymore but busy *being* a writhing thing on my B&Q patio tiles.

Vera sits up, stuttering *'Fire! Fire!'* As she flounders, her Jameson's t-shirt slips to reveal her naked chest. Jesus of Nazareth, I'm not ready for a nudist colony just yet.

'There's no fire, Vera,' calming her down, 'at least, not yet. We need to talk about, um, stuff.' I hand her back her freebie t- shirt and look into the empty fireplace filled with chewing gum wrappers while she pulls it on. I turn back to see her with her legs pulled in tight to her rib-cage in a manoeuvre that *should* spell shame and embarrassment. 'Yeah, Jon?' But nothing seems to be the matter in her defiant overtones. 'Did those gypsies threaten you again? Sorry, I must've nodded off.'

I quickly clock the state of emergency in my living-room. 'Uh-huh.' Unperturbed by this minor hiccup in my investigation, I continue with my metaphorical line of questioning. The polo t-shirt gives me the ideal kick-off. 'Nice t-shirt – now that it's back on you, ha, ha, ahem. It looks like a pub-freebie. There are *free* things in life after all: things that we receive but don't give anything in return.'

Vera gawps at me cockeyed. 'Codswallop, there's nothing free in this life, Jon. I'm testament to that.'

I can't argue with that. 'The air is free. How much do we pay for that?'

'We borrow the air. Pay-back is inevitable. Look at your damn balloon.' Vera hurts me with her candid views. 'Yeah but money isn't everything.' I can't hear myself think metaphorically so I press pause on Jefferson.

'Almost.'

'Don't be fooled; it's not as if the banks give you a free *cooler-bag* or *coffee-maker* if you take out a loan. I think banks should give away free puppies when –'

'Huh?'

'A puppy, y'know, baby *hound*. Find a good home and treat it with *respect…*' I'm going off on a tangent, about as smooth as riding a bare-back cactus but despite having slid into a quicksand of innuendos, I feel that I'm on fire. Maybe this method will come in handy when – and if – I get my private detective license. Lull them into a false sense of security. 'Have you tried your hand at billiards? You should try it. It's more sophisticated than pool.'

There's silence save for the karaoke machine humming ominously in the background. 'I'm going to let you think about what I've said to you. When I get back we can delve further into this.'

I go to the kitchen and prepare Vera a strong mug of tea and gaze at the half-burnt bra and its implications. I don't like it. When I get back to the living room, Vera is half way up the chimney in what can only be described as some sick Christmas fantasy. I'm happy Charley's not here to see this. 'What are you doing?'

'Looking for something.'

'What would be hidden up the chimney?' I'm intrigued.

'People used to hide things up chimneys years ago.'

'Things? Random and vague.' I lead Vera from the chimney like a confused patient and sit her back in the sofa. She curls up, her sooty hands clasped around her knees so that her nipples aren't on display inside her sooty polo-shirt. She looks calm, too calm for my liking. 'Please tell me you picked up on my earlier metaphorical points of interest?'

Nonplussed, Vera shakes her head.

I lean over and pick up the bottle of ouzo from the stone slabs in front of the empty fireplace, uncork, and down a third of Dutch courage, thank you. As the liquorice heat bubbles in my chest, I open my mouth and dribble out the words that have been sloshing around in there. 'Charley and I called into the Hound this evening for a...' almost blurting out *farewell* 'beverage 'n bomb.' I pause, giving Vera ample opportunity to squirm but she doesn't. 'And, um, we got talking to Cyril and, uh,' another slurp of ouzo and still no trace of nothing in Vera's deadpan tired expression, 'is there something going on between you and the barmen of this town?' I gauge Vera's reaction intently but she doesn't react. Her eyelids just droop lazily. I don't know if she's going to explode or fall back to sleep.

'What's your point, Jonny?'

'My *point? That's* my point, Vera. I can't make it any clearer than that. Cyril seems to think that you two could be close, as in dungarees close. And being raided on Dom's pool *table?'*

'Listen to yourself tuning into small-town rumours.'

'And are they?'

'What?'

'Rumours, Vera?' Calm down, Jon, she's not your teenage daughter.

'Well, no, but they could be rumours. Dom and I weren't raided because we were having sex on his pool table; we were raided because Dom was selling alcopops to under-age drinkers.'

'Yes, I *know* that. And don't think by using the word *sex* that it makes you look any more adult and responsible.' I pause. 'Wait, Cha said that the black wasn't potted?'

'Oh, so now we're getting to the bottom of it. Little Charley with the perforated bladder is spreading rumours.'

'This is worse than I thought and Vera's not too fazed. I can't believe that you did it with that fucking moron. How can I eat another sausage in this house again, now that I know where you're hands have been? Sorry, I've forgotten that we're no longer speaking in metaphorical tongues. Cyril says that if he had cash on the hip he would gladly let you go fetch, doggy.'

'Well, you don't have to worry about that. I've got things covered. Between my wage and your father's meagre donations I make ends meet. Look Jon, how can I say this without sounding *off*: don't poke your nose in where it's not wanted, 'kay, darlin'? I might've had a few encounters but what about it? I'm a single woman in her early fifties and I deserve to take a little lovin' when I get it and give it back.' Her bemused expression sails away to distant lands before floating back again. 'When the Big C grants you pardon,' she searches for words, 'you've been given a second chance, y'know. Don't worry, Jonny, I'm just making up for lost time. I've been through the washing machine, y'know that.' She sits back and hugs herself. 'I've shrunk but I haven't lost my colour.'

I like the metaphor.

'Look, Jon. Cyril's been one of my admirers ever since your father decided that his "*work here is done.*"' She puts on a deep idiot bastard voice which doesn't sound anywhere near Clinical Dad.

'Not even close…'

'Huh?'

'That doesn't sound like him.'

Vera's mouth opens but nothing comes out. She tries to speak again but can't find the right words.

'Why did you give him my number?'

'So,' Vera heaves a deep sigh, 'you've met him.'

'It would've been nice to be consulted first. He caught me off-guard by posing as Ronald McDonald.'

This information is obviously new to Vera. 'The clown? I knew he was in the vicinity but I'd no idea that he's dressing up as a clown which is quite apt. Did the chicken-shit wish you a happy thirtieth?'

'Yep, at the beginning. Why did you give him my number?'

'He hasn't been my husband since the days of standing on the bridge waiting for his corpse to float by but he's still your dad and I shouldn't get in the way of that.' Vera snorts. 'Ducks was all that floated by.'

'How could you.'

'He's trying to make an honest man of himself, Jonny.'

'By dressing up as Ronald McDonald?' I still haven't told her about the money or the fact that his stamp whore had licked one too many stamps.

'The country is in crisis.'

'He called to meet under false pretences, Vera.'

Vera raises her plucked eyebrows and lets her head lob loosely forward onto her neck. 'Excuse me? This wasn't part of the deal. He told me that he just wanted to wish you a happy birthday and leave it at that. Where did this happen?'

'Burger King. Where else would Ronald McDonald be, Vera? How long has he been sniffing 'round 128?' I'm struggling to contain my anger now. 'How can you let that whoremeister weasel his way back into our family?'

'Wait, you said "at the beginning"?'

'He didn't want to wish me a happy birthday. This is the problem. He wanted to *verify* that it was my birthday because, guess what, my saving's scheme is up today.'

'Yes, I know. Spend it wisely.'

'Wisely? Um, yeah.'

Vera's sits bolt upright. 'Jonny?'

'He asked me for a loan.'

'Bless my arse in parsley sauce.' Vera's face melts from curiosity to shock to red anger. *'That prick! That fucking loser fuck!'* Vera bawls. 'I knew I shouldn't have trusted him. I *knew* it! I'm sorry, Jon. I only wanted to make things better.'

'I know, I know.' I sit next to her and take her hands in mine. 'Look, he's gone now.'

'No, he's not! He's down at McDonald's right now, twisting fucking dog balloons! Oh, JESUS!!' Vera screams at the ceiling before floundering to the floor in a delirious haze. 'I'm going *dooown* there!' She's so angry she's almost singing now. 'Where are my *shoooes*?! Get my fucking *sneeeeakers*! I'm gonna dunk his poxy ginger-nut into the hot fat!'

Grabbing Vera, I swing her back onto the sofa. 'I've sorted it out. Relax. Let it go. He's a pathetic creature and needs all the help he can get. I'm glad I've met him because I know now that I haven't missed anything.' I blurt this out with no hesitation or doubt.

'You didn't give him money?! Please tell me that you didn't pay that ginger prick a single penny?!'

'No.' I lie for Vera's benefit and I also keep the fact that the stamp whore had two-timed Clinical Dad. Both Ronald and I know that that two grand is the price to pay to make him disappear and to buy our freedom, Charley's right again. 'Look, let's forget about that now. We won't be hearing from him again.' I think about a lot of things while I hold my mother in my arms: *Singing with 45 ... 45 dying at my birthday party ... my shrinking red balloon ...revolving doors ... leaking relics of the '80's in the*

*Hound ... Crunch of nose cartilage ... secret messages ...
Brillo's piggy head lodged in a vice ... Iowa ... Ronald
McDonald's warning ... Clinical Dad ... 45 ... 45 ...45...*

Vera withers in my embrace. 'I'll be next ... or
Susan or Tommy. I won't rest knowing that Ronald
McDonald's in town. I know why he's back. Believe me,
it's nothing to do with wishing you a happy birthday. I
know that now but he's got a way with words and he had
me convinced. What a low thing to do.'

'Why is he back?'

Vera comes over all strange. 'I'll tell you about it some
time.'

'Okay.' I don't want to push her. Sounds like something
private; sounds like something that children
don't need to know about their parents. I sit back on the
floor and absorb the ouzo dregs and the very dregs of
Greece itself. I begin taking dollars from my pockets and
throw them on the floor at Vera's feet. This is my letter of
resignation. 'I want you to have this. There's five thousand
dollars there or maybe a little less.'

'What's this?' Vera's eyes growing wide.

'This is what's left of my interest-bearing account. I
want you to have it.'

'Dollars?'

Jesus of Nazareth.

'Um, yes, they recommended dollars because I'll gain
from the exchange at a later date when I go to open my
detective agency.'

'Uh-huh.' Vera nods in a vague way. I'm not sure that
she believes me. 'Put your money away, Jon. I may have
my problems but money isn't one of them for now.' My
chin decides to jitter all on its own again. Sadness and
excitement are beginning to swirl inside me. Despite the
delicate knowledge that Vera is braless, I swallow her in an
all-encompassing hug.

'I've got a date with the Reiki Mistress,' I tell her
proudly. 'She's going to clear my chakras before my...'

I'm on the verge of blurting out *bon voyage*...Now is the time to tell her of my impending journey to Iowa.

I desperately want to know who this Candy character is and why Clinical Dad aka Ronald McDonald advised me not to make the trip. And 45's lucidity in his message is also puzzling. But I've made a promise to my surrogate father not to say anything to Vera.

On the spot, I invent an excuse that should cover my ass and quest. 'I'm going to, um, London for a few days.'

'Oh? Is Charley going with you?' Vera likes the idea.

'No, um, just myself. I want to get away from this place after, y'know, the last few days, they've have been a bit crazy...' There's an understatement. 'Just throw bread-crumbs to the pigeons in Trafalgar Square, that kind of thing. I'm going tomorrow – tomorrow morning.'

'You're not wasting much time.' She peters out into deep lost thought. 'People have been appearing and disappearing these last few days.'

'He left a note in my balloon.'

I have it said before I come to my senses. The intensity of the moment mixed with the ouzo has produced a chemical reaction which has weakened me.

Vera's blood pressure visibly drops. 'What do you mean?' The sincerity on her face is utterly frightening.

'Vera?'

'Jonny?' She masks her shock by attempting to smile but her lips tighten to wax-work proportions. 'I'm curious, that's all, 45's dementia hadn't allowed for much free-thinking.'

I've never seen Vera putting up an act. She's always been a say-what-you-think-and-be-damned kind of woman but now she's clearly acting and not very good at it. I regret saying anything. 'Y'know...' prompting Vera to come to her own happy conclusions. 'What do you think the message says?'

'Happy birthday?' she asks with hope in her voice.

'Yes!' I rejoice at my brilliance but tone it down.

'That's it. Clever, huh? Who would've thought that he'd be capable of such an innovative idea?' I'm thinking about myself when I say these words. I have successfully lured Vera into her own comfort zone. By using reverse psychology, I've given her the option of drawing her own conclusions. It is a method I will use when I start up my private investigation agency.

The weight of 45's hidden message-in-a-balloon suddenly hits me. Its implications are almost overpowering, Candy in a haystack. Maybe Charley's right. Perhaps I do need to get more information before my quest begins tomorrow. I prefer not to think about that.

Vera lies back on the sofa and releases a long drawn-out sigh. 'Enjoy having your chakra opened,' Vera murmurs. 'Switch off the light when you go.'

I do as she asks. 'G'night.' I look back into the darkness of the living room and see her vague outline on the sofa. It is official: Vera's hiding something.

Vera asks the walls and the darkness: 'Why are men so good at leaving messages?' she mumbles into the darkness and snores.

14 hours to departure…

12.
Sky Spirits

My big red balloon skips and rides the cool evening air as we cross town towards the park where Guinevere, the Reiki Mistress, is waiting with warm hands. I've gotten used to the idea of having a balloon follow me by now but it still occasionally gets caught between my ankles and trips me up. On Bridge Street, a Japanese import Nissan Micra sitting on its axle, passes by with a cargo of wannabe gangsta punk-ass rural biatches. They hurl abuse plus a smouldering butt at me and my birthday balloon. I try to shield 45 from the barrage of insults but there are just too many but I do manage to keep 45's soul-bubble from coming in contact with the twirling molten ash. I don't care – *we* don't care – what anybody says now. We have a purpose.

'Fuck you!' I call back after them but quickly shut my mouth when the brake lights glow red in my face. The Nissan whines into reverse. Shit. Considering the circumstances, I decide that the best course of action is to play retard – my health depends on it. It's a concept based on the opossum's playing-dead defence mechanism. It's amazing what we can learn from nature. I buckle at the knee, lob my head at a forty-five degree angle, and twist back my right wrist holding my balloon. One of the rural biatches gets out and walks back towards me like one bad mo-fo with acne. I moan and gurgle. *'Aagh... Moaaa...'* The homie turns on his heels and calls me a spastic but I can see that he's out of his depth. They drive off into the night, parping their horn, and possibly feeling sorry for the retard out on his own after dark. I feel guilty for imitating a retarded person but it's the first thing that comes to mind.

A silver Opel Kadett bombs passed, overtaking the SUV Nissan Micra going one-way on Bridge Street, bouncing on its axle through the roundabout in front of the church.

I'm about to yell *Fucking Lunatic!* when I see that *Vera* is behind the wheel, on her way to McDonald's, no doubt. I'm not surprised. She's carried a fiery temperament since her fight with cancer. We pass like ships on this crazy night. The town is unravelling. I won't follow Vera because I've my own destiny to take care of. The faster I get to Iowa the better. It's a showdown between Vera and the clown now. I washed my hands with two thousand dollars.

When I arrive for my appointment with the Reiki Mistress, a couple of Rottweilers are sitting outside her coffee-and-beige caravan door like a pair of sentry gargoyles so I give her a missing call to let me in.

She greets me at the door. 'Good evening, Jonny,' flicking her long combed hair back from her face, 'I hope my bitches didn't threaten you?' I look about for some bitches but all I can see is a couple of guard-dogs. 'A couple of biatches came at me on Bridge Street... with a knife but I fooled them with my cunning.' Before I step inside, the Mistress whispers words of a mysterious language and flashes some symbolic symbols around the creaky door hinges and the Welcome mat. As I step into the caravan, I'm ashamed to say that there's a brief mili-second when I want to leave 45 outside with the bitches. Maybe the Mistress and I are going to explore our chakras on a bestial level and I don't want 45 watching. If it was any other balloon I wouldn't really mind. I've heard that it is fun to watch but knowingly leaving my big red balloon in a strategic position at the end of Guinevere's consultation bed is just warped.

The Reiki Mistress looks like Cleopatra tonight, exuberant in the background of a jungle sounds CD. The warm candle glow coming from inside the caravan accentuates her exotic Mediterranean beauty.

'Ooh,' she coos in her insanely high-pitch bird voice, 'is that for me, babe?' spotting my birthday balloon. 'Trying to make up for being late, are we? I love balloons, especially red ones. They're so romantic.'

Jonathan Dunne *Balloon Animals*

'No!' I answer defensively, almost thumping her. 'Sorry, like I said, a car-load of gypsies made fun of me on the way over here. I pretended I was retarded to look normal.'

'That mustn't have been difficult.' The Mistress is busy oiling up her hands. She reminds me of a vet lubricating her glove before going up the vulva of a cow. That prompts me into thinking that she's planned some serious chakra business this evening, considering that Reiki is a strictly hands-off affair. She had worked as a masseuse in a spa at the Hilton hotel in Limerick city after completing her master's degree in business and finance.

Without seeking written permission, the Reiki Mistress catches me unawares by swiping up my birthday balloon. She trails it across the room behind her with a complete disregard for health and safety, passing three inches above the bed of nails she had purchased on E-bay. I feel every nail. She shakes her head and tut-tuts as she skips across the caravan. Lithe on her feet, she quickly wrestles 45's soul onto her consultation bed. She inhales deeply and flashes some symbolic symbols. 'Your surrogate father's essence floats within this balloon. I will prepare his soul for departure by a laying-on of the hands.'

I feel faint. She speaks some mumbo-jumbo and proceeds to oil up my big red birthday balloon. 'These essential oils which I harvested myself will help keep the good in and the bad out on your journey to the New World.'

I can't help but notice a Tesco jumbo1-litre bottle of Coconut and Orchid Oil extract by the sink.

'Mischievous spirits are constantly lurking for new places to inhabitate...'

Inhabitate?

'...and balloons, by nature, are porous creatures. Add both and what do we get?'

I shrug my shoulders.

'Wrong attitude, Jonny. We get an exorcism.' As an after-thought, she adds: 'The secondary effects of my home

136

remedy extract will function as an anti-wrinkle cream and weather-proof your grandfather in general.'

'Great!' I manage to answer but I'm frightened. The room is growing excessively hot. I wonder if it's me or the thousands of spluttering candles that throw the Reiki Mistress's devilish pulsing shadows onto the warped plywood walls.

She turns to me when she has finished with my big red balloon. 'Why have you come to me tonight?'

'You know why. I want you to prepare me for my outbound journey.'

She pouts her lips and suddenly whirls about the caravan kitchen cum dining room, making mad witch-doctor symbols and muttering under her breath. Taking that as my cue, I squeeze my eyelids shut and fight the crazed giggle that bubbles in my chest. 'So, how have you been doing spiritually? Got much Qi energy or astral projection going on?' She has her hands over my crotch now and the heat emanating from her palms is giving me a real stiff one, talk about astral projection. Opting for my tight Levis hadn't been a clever move. I glance across at 45, freshly lubricated and glistening in the candlelight. Is my birthday balloon looking redder than normal? One of us is ashamed on a sub-conscious level, I'm sure of that. This is a special night for both of us, I feel. Again, I understand that I've been more places with 45 in his current state of decomposition than we ever had been before my 30th birthday. It's a nice thought to think that our relationship is being taken to the next level.

I turn my attention to the Reiki Mistress who is taking me in with her amber saucer-eyes. 'Between you and me and the recesses of my mind, Guin, I'm struggling to find meaning for my existence of late. I need to explore myself,' then adding as a quip, 'unless you want to explore me.'

'It might be worth paying five euro extra to get in front of the queue if you're flying with Ryanair tomorrow.'

'Huh?'

'I had a race once with a Chinese woman across the tarmac to find a seat on a Ryanair flight. I took her wide on the outside and she just bolted when she saw me pass her. The Chinese, you couldn't be up to them.'

'Um, yes, I hadn't thought about that. I haven't even booked my ticket yet.'

'You're leaving it a bit late.'

I agree. 'I'll do it when I get back to 128. It won't be Ryanair, they just do European flights. As I was saying, I'm having an identity crisis. I think my past is catching up with me. But, yes, you would think that I would know how to deal with that, but I don't. I'm a genealogical student with identity crisis.'

'Is that physically possible?'

'What?'

'Catching up with your past.' She's concentrating her energies on my head now. 'Remove your shirt, please.'

'I'm not sure if it's physically possible.' I'm determined to open one of Guinevere's chakras tonight and I will agree to *anything*, even quantum physics. Let's face it: there are more ways of opening energy channels than ancient Chinese traditions.

'Jonny, did you ever think that your father's shenanigans somehow give you meaning? Maybe even validity? Rather than being a hole in your life
without direction?'

I haven't told the Mistress that I met Clinical Dad today who is a professional clown now. 'Meaning? No, I don't think he gives me much meaning.' I'm sure she's trying to wind me up. I open an eye and all I see is another unblinking eye looking back at me...

Hang on; it's her left cherry-pink nipple...

Surely there are boundaries when it comes to Reiki but she always insists that there should be nothing blocking our energies. Here, here!

'I mean, you've got an *excuse* to be angry, babe: that

makes you feel the pulse, right. Do you understand what I'm saying?' She's undoing my jeans now.

'I feel the pulse all right.'

'Ok, but let's say your old man really did throw himself in the river.' I peek again to see the Mistress throwing something imaginary away like a banana skin to represent Clinical Dad's plunge to the waters of the Arra. Now she's got her top completely off. 'There: he's gone. Adios.' She wipes her hands clean. 'There's sweet Fanny Adams you can do about that but just accept it.' She nods as if the voice she's just heard isn't her own. 'And that's my point, right there – acceptance: that's something that you've never been able to do because your sick fuck of a father is alive.'

I try a test. 'Ronald McDonald.'

'Yes, Ronald McDonald,' she repeats in her high-pitch voice without giving it any further thought. This girl doesn't listen. 'So your head is in a dilemma: he's dead but he's not dead. It's a two-headed snake. Deep down, you know that he's still out there and that's what's got your knickers in a twist. He's a loose end.'

'No he's not. I paid him off today.'

She's still not listening. 'Are you ready?' she asks.

'I've never been more ready in my life.' I reach for her sweet behind nestled inside her draping see-through hemp but realize that she's just asking me if I'm ready spiritually. 'I'm re-building myself. This trip to Iowa will help me find the real me. I'm sure of it. It will fill in the blanks in my life. It'll give me a better sense of who I am and cure my identity crisis. Bridge...'

The Reiki Mistress interrupts, 'I mean...'

I continue. '... the gap across the crevasses that have opened my chakras. Spending some quality time with me is just what the doctor ordered. But this trip's about 45, not me.'

'No,' interrupts the Reiki Mistress, 'I mean, are you ready? Shouldn't you be packing or something?'

'Oh. I'm travelling light. I'll buy clothes along the way

like the Hulk.'

'Oh, how romantic! I think you're deficient in vitamin C. Place yourself on the bed of nails, please.'

'Yes, it is romantic.' I mistakenly take that as my cue to place, *grab*, Guinevere's love-heart buttocks.

The Reiki Mistress spins on one heel with the stealth of a cobra … clasps my right hand in a martial arts move which I can't identify, maybe a tiger-claw. She snaps back my wrist until I hear a vague grinding of cartilage. I scream like a little girl. The bitches start barking outside.

'How dare you!' She's hissing, *actually* hissing. 'Never, *ever*, touch me when I'm in the zone, Jonny! We've spoken about this, remember?' She slips into her junior-infants teacher voice, meanwhile the jungle mood-sounds (toucans, howler monkeys, macaws) continue to come at me from a couple of cleverly concealed speakers. 'What's the golden rule with a sleepwalker? Hmm? What's the golden rule with antibiotics? Hmm? I'll tell you, Wandering Jonny: let them take their course!' She fans herself up and down, 'Same principal, Jon, same *principal!*' rolling her eyes for effect. Now her voice has gone an octave higher and I can't distinguish of it's the capuchins or the Mistress.

'I never *know* with you, Guin?! You've got your tits – *beautiful* tits – in my face and what am I s'posed to think? Christ! There's a fine line between prick-teasing and holistic healing if you want my opinion. You've dislocated my wrist!'

'We've discussed this, Jon. We need no cross-wire interference if we want our Qi energies to fuse.'

Her rant is just grey-noise. 'Did you hear what I've said?! You've *dislocated* my *WRIST!*' The pain's excruciating and I'm becoming nauseous. 'How can I go to Iowa with this wrist?'

The Reiki Mistress suddenly comes to her senses. Realizing what she's done and begins running around the caravan looking for her home-remedy coconut and orchid extract. 'Oh, sorry, sorry, Jonny. Please forgive me. I don't know my own strength sometimes. Here! Rub this on!'

'I need a *doctor*, not your buy-one-get-one-free Tesco offer!' I regret saying that but the red-hot searing pain's swallowing me up now. I'm going to be sick. 'Get me a bucket!' The energy suddenly drains from my body. I fall to the floor and my extremities become a writhing swarm of ants and pins and needles.

The lukewarm salt-water of the Arra river rushes over my face, floods my nostrils and washes out the inside of my cranium. Fetid smell of dog-breath rises from the boggy waters. My wrist is trapped beneath a rock and I'm drowning. I can feel the current bubbling in my nostrils and drowning my brain. Vera's washy face is peering down at me from South Quay Bridge overhead and three other little heads; Tommy, Susan (not yet Alba; I'm not sure if that's the collective group or just Susan), and me gawping down on me. Vera's warm tears have turned fresh-water into salt-water, hallelujah. Now, I'm looking down into the river with my family and Ronald McDonald's blurry outline is looking up at me through the dark water looking a lot like Stephen King's It. His giant orange 'fro is waving back and forth in the river current.

I come to the surface of my nightmare in the A & E car-park of Limerick Regional hospital. I'm sitting in the back seat of the Mistress's Volkswagen Beetle – the original Beetle – with a Rottweiler on either side of me. The bitches are licking and slobbering across my face and I know now that their warm salty slobber has been the dreamlike delirious waters of the Arra, complete with fetid dog breath.

'Jonny! Oh, thank Christ in Heaven, you're back with us. C'mon.'

The Reiki Mistress drags me out of the Beetle and hauls me across the wet tarmac towards the doors of the A & E. I swoon again, realizing that I don't have 45. I indicate to the

Mistress that I need my goddamn balloon, please. 'Will you forget about the fucking balloon!' swearing under her breath but doubles back to retrieve it from the boot of the Beetle. I virtually die and come back to life again when I see her unlatching the bonnet ... but remembering that the Beetle's boot is its bonnet.

She drops me at the doors and runs away, worthy of any gangster or orphan movie.

The rest is history.

I float into A&E with a limp wrist and a red balloon. I'm ready for my gay-pride parade. A nurse comes from nowhere and flashes a snapshot while I'm doubled over in agony in the waiting room. I presume it's for a case study, my medical records or some shit, but I won't be surprised when I debut on Facebook.

* * *

I get a taxi back to the caravan some time after midnight. Pile-Driver Dennis happens to be on-call tonight. Are there no other taxi-drivers in Old Castle? He complains about the deal that life has thrown him but I don't want to listen. I've had enough for one day. After getting some curious looks in the rear-view as we drive through the public park at midnight with a weak wrist, Dennis drops me off at the Mistress's two-tone caravan in the park.

'Where's Fanny?'

I completely blank him.

'Who died then?'

'You tell me.'

Despite the dull pain still pulsing in my wrist, I manage to slide the Mistress's number onto my iPhone screen and press her. 'Call off your bitches, bitch.'

I'm ready to strangle her but the Mistress appears at her door with a glass of green liqueur and invites me into the wonderful world of dolphin verse. She carefully places 45 on a fold-up chair as if she's a nurse working at an old folks home, 'Upsy-daisy, there we go Mr. 45, nice 'n easy now, uh-huh…' then takes my wrist in her hands and performs some unadulterated Reiki right there on the threshold. 'Sorry,' she whispers in my ear … then takes a bite of my ear and I guess now I cross the treacherous void between holistic medicines into foreplay. This time I get it right. As we fall to the bed of nails I slam-dunk a tea-towel over 45's big red face. As the Mistress undoes my Levis, I can't help but think that I'm Tom Hanks and that balloon over there is Wilson.

Two minutes later, we're making love on the bed of nails. The Mistress insists on going on top to open some chakras that have never been opened before. All I open is my back. She squeals that it's easier to find her g-spots (she has more than one) on the bed of nails but I'm convinced it's the nails that are finding the sacred g-spots – they can't miss.

Thirty seconds of frantic, pained though cocksure penetration later, we celebrate our act of lovemaking by waltzing around the caravan to *Love Will Tear Us Apart (Again)*. I couldn't have put it better myself. We then free-style to *The Killing Moon* and come together again for the poignant *Play With Fire*. We finish the evening held in a tight embrace, circling the caravan to *Psycho Killer*.

'Are you trying to tell me something with all this love song violence?'

We twirl each other into the night then we somehow haul our asses aboard the roof of the caravan and set free a pair of Chinese sky lanterns. I ask her to release one more so that the spirit of 45 can also take to the skies, not that he isn't in a balloon already. We write our names on the balloons in big black marker. I suggest we write three nicknames and the Mistress finds that hilarious so we write: LARRY, HARRY, MOE. I fight back the tears as I watch our spirits climb despite the drizzle. Maybe it is to be an omen of things to come; a harbinger of something unimaginable just around the corner … or maybe not. I've got the quirky feeling in my waters again. My gut's clouding over.

To finalize our evening together, we smoke a marijuana joint between us and launch some illegal fire-rockets into the night-sky. My waters are telling me that this is the last night that I will be with the Mistress on a sexual level. If it means foreplay without the bed of nails then I'm sorry, Guin. I love you but not that much.

I call Dennis for a taxi-ride home.

'Dennis thinks that that was quite a fantastic light show. By the way, let her know that one of her suspensions is shot.' He flashes a sly smirk at me in his rear-view as we drive homewards through the park –

'Buaagh!' Dennis lets out a sound I can only describe as that of a forlorn puck-goat. At the same

time, something rolls across the bonnet of his ruby Skoda taxi…

9 hours to departure…

13.
How the Buck-Stag Rolls

'Stag!'

Dennis sticks on the brakes and goes mental on the Skoda's horn in front of me, finding every other lever on the way. 'A fucking buck-*stag!* It came from the *bushes!*'

He seems sure that a male deer's just rolled across his bonnet but deer don't roll across bonnets and if they do it wouldn't be here in the public park at one in the morning; that's not how deer roll. I point this out in the brief-lived chaos. 'Where is it?' Dennis is afraid to look out his window and I have to admit that I'm in no hurry either, half expecting to see a form run across the beam of the our headlights.

We sit there in the darkness while the Skoda's engine idles, wipers thumping back and forth while indicating left and right when there *is* no rain, on a path that has one beginning and one end...

Now it's my turn to scream when something appears at my window. My first impression is the same enormous hairy spider that had crept out of McDonald's dustbin that keeps Charley in its underbelly. Charley's dreads, when caught in Dennis's headlights, had taken on a life of their own.

'Cha?! What the ...?'

Charley slaps against my window pane with all the panache of a zombie. He tries to open my door but Dennis tells me that he has the child-lock on. Momentarily, I wonder if Dennis had flicked on the child-lock just for me or whether it's just a safety feature.

Dennis climbs out, cursing and swearing at Charley, and opens my door – asking me first if I want it opened.

Charley's frantic. 'Jon, can I have a word?' He scrutinizes Dennis closely. 'In private.'

145

'What the fuck are you doing here, Cha? I'm always glad to see you but…'

Charley leads me away from demented Dennis and the idling Skoda. 'We can talk in this thicket.'

'Thicket?'

'Jon, you're making a big mistake going to Iowa without more facts. Have you forgotten that all this shit happened thirty or forty years ago?!'

I haven't forgotten; I just never thought about it in the first place.

'Man, you need all the evidence you can get if you're to carry out 45's dying wish.' As he says this, he reaches into the undergrowth and pulls out a pair of shovels then pulls a Fuji camera from his army-surplus camouflage jacket which explains why Dennis or I hadn't spotted him amongst the rhododendron bush. 'Built-in flash. I'll print the photo and pass it to you.'

'Charley, you need to go into a room for a few days and swallow the key. Get that monkey off your back.'

'There's only one monkey here and he couldn't be on my shoulders cos I'm looking at him. This is when friends pull together, Jon.' His crazed look is only heightened by the shadow of the branches cast by Dennis's headlights. 'Let's do it tonight while the earth is still fresh. What am I saying? It *has* to be tonight. You leave in a few hours. I just can't let you go, Jon. I'll have it on my conscience. This means as much to you as it does to me.'

And for a moment, I think tears come to Charley's eyes.

Dennis gets back into his taxi, still swearing, and reverses to pour his full beams onto us hidden in the rhododendron.

Charley nudges me back. 'Go back further into the thicket.'

'Thicket?'

'All I'm asking you to do is help with the digging. I'll do the dirty work. We need to see the old man's posterior, Jonny. Candy in a haystack. There's no getting 'round it.

146

You just sit tight and keep an eye out for vigilantes. Don't worry, 45 won't have begun to decompose yet.'

Jesus of Nazareth. 'Charley! That's my surrogate father you're talking about!' I briefly wonder why I'm whispering.

'Gravity will have taken his blood to the lower parts of his corpse and congealed but that's gravity for you; get over it. The fleshy internal organs will be the first to go but we've got time on our side.' He takes a spliff from his khakis and sparks up. He sucks, holds, and then offers it to me. 'Probably the last we will share before our Iowan showdown.'

I take a deep gulp on it because I need it right now and pass it back with a shake in my hand. I don't know what Charley has given me nor do I want to know. All I know is that I feel like I can climb trees after midnight like a sexy vampire. Am I insane? Have I lost all direction? For some bizarre reason, the thought of exhuming 45 for the good of his restless soul seems quite plausible and burgeoning on saintly.

Against all odds, I find myself taking on Charley's insane proposal. 'Give me a minute with the balloon.'

Charley nods. 'You're doing the right thing.' He slaps me on the shoulder and shuffles off to leave me with my thoughts.

I lift the balloon to my lips and whisper, 'I love you, 45. Help me find this Candy character. Are you okay with this, old friend? I have your best interests at heart. We don't have much time and my waters tell me that you're squirming down there, six feet under. Let me help you to take you back to where you come
from. Do you agree?' Talking face to face with an ailing red balloon in a mid-night thicket doesn't bother me. I listen to the sounds around me and wait to pick anything which could be seen as a possible sign of divine intervention...

Dennis blows on his horn. I take that as a yes.

Charley's pissing up against a sycamore when I find him. 'Nobody is ever to find out about this, *especially* Vera.'

Charley taps me twice on the cheek. 'Our secret, promise. Will we tell the Mistress?'

'I just said *nobody!* I may as well open a porthole to hell if the Mistress finds out about this.' I get into the back of Dennis's taxi. 'Change of route. Take us to the cemetery.'

Dennis frowns back at me. 'Gonna bury something?'

I turn cold. 'Ha, ha.' *No, actually, we're going to dig something up.* 'We need to use the boot.'

Dennis goes to get out but I insist that he relaxes after his stag-shock. 'Let Charley do it.'

At the same time I hear the clang of shovels behind me before Charley sits in with a wide grin.

Dennis eyes us both suspiciously in his rear-view before changing up into first. He tells us about his soon-to-be ex-wife as we wind our way through the public park.

'By the way,' turning to Charley, 'how did you know that I'd be here?'

'I followed you.' Charley finds this perfectly normal judging by his answer.

'What? Where? When?'

'When we parted sweet company after McDonald's. I doubled back after collecting the sh– '

Cutting in, 'Luggage, yes, continue.'

'Um, yes, after collecting the luggage from the garden-shed.'

8 hours to departure…

14.
High-Ho! High-Ho!

We pull up outside the cemetery gates at half one in the morning to a dark background overture. It doesn't feel right being here. The dead sleep sounder than ever and a light frost has begun to creep across the landscape. We tell Dennis to pull up at nothing a little beyond the graveyard to throw him off our scent. Speaking of scent, Charley reckons the conditions are perfect to exhume a corpse.

'The cold ground will have kept the body in a fresh state and –'

'The corpse has a name.'

'… the north-bound breeze will carry any foul smells northwards, opposite to town.'

'What are you lads up to?' asks Dennis, switching the overhead light on for extra light on the matter. He gets a good look at the two of us sitting in the back seat.

'We're going to stay here for the night,' says Charley without a pause while Dennis casts a glance over his shoulder at the cemetery wall.

Charley skips to the Skoda's rear. 'Open the boot and we can get our overnight luggage.'

I chime in and pay Dennis in dollars and convince him with a healthy tip to stay put in the taxi while we retrieve our overnight camping luggage from the boot. As I say these words, mad clanging comes from the rear of the Skoda so I just speak louder. 'Go an' get locked drunk. That's what Dennis would do. Visit the kids but let your ex down the arse-end of the alphabet where she belongs.' Dennis laps it up, cannot get enough of this tough talk but I'm falling into the taxi-driver's crazy schizoid trance. It's true; 45 always believed that the freakiest shit happens down country lanes. I need another smoke of whatever Charley had given me to get me through the next hour.

Dennis bids us goodnight with heavy suspicion.

149

In silence, we backtrack once the Skoda turns a corner and jump the cemetery wall. Mid-air, I get this flutter in my solar-plexus, watching my almost gravity-free balloon shoot upwards passed my face while gravity drops me downwards. It's the same gut-feeling that I'd gotten when we'd come through these same gates with 45's coffin biting into my clavicles. In a strange way, it's almost as if I'm the one going down underground while 45 stays above-ground for now. It's surreal. How have I allowed Charley to talk me into this *extreme* course of action? 'Cha, another puff of Dutch courage, please.'

We sit on the freezing cemetery wall and share a joint between us.

'Remember, this *is* a love crime,' says Charley, pulling a balaclava over his dreads.

'Huh?' is my reaction.

He hands me a second balaclava. 'But still a crime…'

'Balaclavas are sinister and they make me claustrophobic, Cha.' It's the first time that I've ever worn a balaclava. 'He might not recognize me. He'll think that I'm a vandal robbing his grave.'

'No time to be clockstrophobic now, Jonny. How do you think 45 feels? And this is 45 we're talking 'bout here. Of *course* he'll recognize you. What's to take from his grave? A Bank of Ireland freebie cap?'

Reluctantly, I take the head-hood from Charley and pull it down over my features and place my doobie back in my mouth. I'll probably exclude this from my PhD thesis but probably leave it into my diary account version.

The graveyard is vaguely luminous beyond the orange sodium streetlights. There's enough light to guide us through the myriad of tombstones to the mound of fresh earth where 45 lies. As I tread carefully, a notion dawns on me: even though I'm about to do undertake the horrendous act of exhuming the body of my grandfather, I feel that I am actually living for the first time in my life. I'm filling every waking moment with something that will count when I look back on my youthful days. The irony is that it has taken my grandfather's death to give me life.

Somebody had fashioned a makeshift cross from an old broken hurley and stuck it at the head of the grave. I live an odd three-prong shamrock moment as I wrap the streamer of my balloon around the ash wood of the hurley: I can't decipher whether 45 is still wandering aimlessly around 128 or in my birthday balloon or here under my feet. I have no doubt that the living part of 45 is suspended in my red birthday balloon. I give it a peck on the cheek.

'Hate to break up the love-affair but let's dig.'

'Hang on; you said that you'd do the dirty work? And look at my wrist. How can I shovel dirt with a wrist like this?'

'I was speaking metaphorically, Jonny. I *will* do the dirty work but this isn't the dirty work. C'mon, why do you think I brought two shovels? We're digging up *your* grandfather, not mine. C'mon, he's over there somewhere...' Charley relights his smoke and offers me a toke but I refuse, wanting a clear head when this happens. I've already got a buzz going with the previous roll-up.

I'm ready as I'll ever be but Charley's rolled magic is fooling nobody. I heave a sigh, trying to get air into my constricted chest. 'What if we're caught?'

'Who's going to catch us? Ghosts?'

'That doesn't help, Cha. I'm outta here when the first shovel hits wood.'

'Deal,' agrees Charley. 'Now dig. I don't care if it's with one hand. Do as they do in India: wipe ass with one hand and eat with the other.'

I'm too nervous to speak, on this dawn of resurrection. My nerves are shot to pieces and I find that I'm soon digging with a numb wrist. We quickly break into our stride, working alternately: cut ... dig ... throw. The night becomes more surreal as we dig lower into the cold ground. The notion dawns on me that I'm digging into the past.

Will I include this in my PhD genealogical thesis? Probably

not. How many students have been dedicated enough to their genealogical studies to dig up a relative to find the truth about their past? I'd probably get a distinction on my PhD certificate but exhuming bodies is illegal in this country without a license. A flush of emotions run through me like diarrhoea. As I dig, I become obsessed. Faster and faster, I dig down, *cut ... dig ... throw ... cut ... dig ... throw* into the deepening blackness as if it has all been one horrible mistake. '45 shouldn't be down here! He's alone in this fucking hole with the worms and grubs! How could I have left this happen?'

'Jonny...'

'How did this happen?? He should be at home sitting on the back doorstep. So what if he's waiting for the Greyhound back to Iowa?! He never did any harm to anybody and it isn't as if he consummated his desires with Brillo. What *happened??* He slipped through *my fingers!?* He...'

'Jonny! Go periscope!' orders Charley in clipped tones.

I realize that Charley's calling me. 'Huh?' I come out of my hallucinogenic reverie with tears in my eyes.

'Peri-scope!' Charley stops digging. 'You're jabberin' like a possessed man, Jon! Man, you're so not

ready for this. 45's dead, Jon, but his spirit lives on in that balloon so pull yourself together for the balloon's sake.' He flicks a thumb over his shoulder, 'Periscope,'

and begins to shovel more frantically, huffing and puffing on this freezing night.

I climb up top and keep an eye for vigilantes. I'm lightheaded. I realize that I've been holding my breath down there, waiting for something to come out of the mud and grab my shovel. What am I doing? A sudden moment of clarity consumes me and all I want to do is RUN. I'm digging up my grandfather. Please, please don't let him feel the degradation that I feel.

'What's this?'

I panic. 'What? What?'

Charley holds up a flap of mud and shakes it. I recognize the vague green, white, and gold of 45's tattered Bank of Ireland hat. Something topples over inside my rib-cage. *This is a wake-up call, Jonny,* my conscience says to me. *Charley's going to strike wood any moment now. Do you want to be here when he does? You've still got time to fill that hole back in and go home if your waters are telling you that you're doing something that you shouldn't.*

Thud...

Too late...

I begin to hyperventilate. 'Oh Jesus ... Jesus ... Are we doing the right thing, Cha?' The thought of coming face to face with 45's corpse is something unfathomable. 'I don't think I'm up to it, Cha. I can't do it.'

Charley fishes in his pocket for something and throws it up at me. 'Stop your ramblings and gimme some light.'

I catch a tiny torch and flick it on, throwing some light on this desperate situation as Charley scrapes earth away from the top of the coffin. Jesus of Nazareth.

'Where are the damn *keyholes?*' Charley feels around in the mud in the dark, passing the blade of the shovel over the lid of the coffin. Panic starts to bubble in Charley's voice and that's the last thing I need now, believe me. 'More light, *c'mon*, Jonny. Are you with me, Jonny? I should've brought a packed lunch. I'm starving.'

I'm so nervous I can't even flick the goddamn switch on the torch without missing ... plus my hands are freezing.

Pang!

The blade of Charley's shovel strikes the first brass knob, sending up a spark and frightening the living shit out of me. For a hallucinatory moment, I believe that we'd dug down too far and hellfire had come looking for us and our sins of the deceased flesh.

'Yes!' Charley triumphs. Quickly, he finds the second brass keyhole. He produces a key and a box of matches from his bottomless khaki army-surplus pockets. He takes a match from the box and strikes it, throwing temporary light

153

onto this hideous scene unfolding below me. *What* have I done? The truth of what we are doing suddenly comes alive and a cold fear sends me into a tight knot of goose-flesh.

'Smoke!' I blurt. 'Gimme a goddamn smoke of something!' I'm losing it. I'm using the word goddamn when I never use it. The whole thing seems cheap somehow. The last thing I want to do is cheapen 45's image. That sinking feeling that there's somebody standing behind me is constant now and I don't know whether to run or stay...

'I'M OUTTA HERE!' I spring from my haunches and sprint through the headstones towards the streetlights and the wall we had climbed over. As I do, I see 45's soul-bubble blowing gently on the temporary cross in the light breeze. I stall. I know that we must finish what we came here to do tonight. I owe it to the old man. He reminds me of a beautiful exotic bird that I've managed to capture in my own back yard. I try to feed the bird but the bird refuses to eat and is dying slowly. It needs to be amongst its own kind.

I double back and stand sentry. Charley wasn't even aware that I had suffered a momentary lapse.

'What are you doing?'

Charley's after cracking a match and passes it over the coffin lid in one smooth swoop.

'Checking for methane,' answers Charley. 'Decomposing bodies.'

'*What?!* Shouldn't we have brought a canary or something?!' I'm not whispering anymore. 'How will we know if there's methane, Charley? When we *explode?*' Jesus of Nazareth.

'Joke, Jonny, lighten up. I need to see the keyholes a little closer.' Charley sparks another match and quickly localizes the keyholes. When the match quenches he fashions a spike out of its tip and proceeds to...

'More light!'

...clean out the keyholes. Then he produces a brass key.

'Hey, why does Charley Monsell have the key to my grandfather's coffin? Just wondering.'

Before I can stop him, Charley has inserted his key and twists. Then he locates the second and unlocks that. 'Relax, Jonny. These keys are generic, like the ones you open your water-meter. My hysterical aunt's got a funeral business. She's got these keys lying 'round at home so I just took one.'

I hear a definite click from up here.

'There! It's open. Lights, camera, action.'

'Hurry on before I regret it!' I look out over the headstones to the streetlights off in the distance. A freezing fog had set in while we had been digging.   Charley's words have stopped coming up at me.

'What?' I lower my voice and ask again. 'What's wrong?'

'How am I s'posed to get to the body if I'm standing on the lid of the coffin? There's no room to move. This doesn't happen in the movies.'

None of us had considered this logistical complication. The thought of 45 lying on the other side of the lid that Charley's standing on terrifies me, all waxy pale and glued eyelids.

'You're going to have to lower me down into the hole by my ankles. I'll work from over the coffin.'

Desperation is sweeping in fast. I know this because my face is a mat of cold sweat inside this balaclava. I panic and pull the balaclava over my face to breathe short harsh breaths. Charley jumps and scrambles to the surface, pulls my mask back down, and allows his body to fall over the lip of my grandfather's grave. I have no choice but to grab his ankles before the hole swallows him head-first.

'Hold me, Jonny, for fuck sake! Here Candy!' Charley whistles a dog, 'C'mon, Candy! Smile for the camera!'

My feet begin to slide in the loose earth... 'Charley, hurry...!' Below me, I hear the lid of the coffin being prized open. Jesus of Nazareth, what have I done?

The cold night becomes strange and washy and I'm going to faint or throw up. My grip on Charley's ankles weakens and he drops six inches downwards before I save his khakis but, unfortunately, Charley keeps falling while his khakis stay in my grasp. I grimace as my best friend unintentionally moons me under the light of the full moon. Charley's arse is a recurring mutual feature in our friendship and turns up at the least likely of times.

Charley lets out a muffled scream.

'Sorry!' I apologize for my lack of concentration. 'I think I'm going to be sick.' The ungodly sight of Charley's crack isn't helping.

'Fock you!' Charley bellows from the depths, 'I just gave 45 an Eskimo kiss! Almost slipped him the tongue. Thank Christ he's been glued shut! FOCK!! I'm the one who should be getting sick!'

'This was your idea! I'll pull you up. C'mon, get your pants back on. I'll lower you down again.'

'I started so I'll fuaaagh...' Charley begins to heave and wretch and a crazed giggle flutters in me somewhere. I know if I start laughing now I'll drop him into the coffin. I focus like I've never focused before on all sad things, grabbing his ankles in a vice-like grip and keep him there, suspended over my dead grandfather's open sarcophagus.

'Don't move!' Charley sways below me as he takes his mini-Fuji camera from his pocket. 'Hold it … Hold it steady...'

'Hurry on! I can't hold you!' I'm screaming now. Anybody happening to be going for a late-night walk will *run* past the cemetery tonight if they're not wearing headphones. Charley wriggles in my hands as he manhandles 45's corpse into – I'm afraid to look – a position where he can see the old man's posterior end.

I'm presuming all this but I can hear the buckle of 45's belt being undone. God forgive me... Strange thoughts come at me: why wear a belt? Why even bother closing it? Charley's underpants and trousers are in my fists and my dead grandfather's suit pants are down around his ankles. Does the cemetery have night security? Will he or she understand the word necrophilia?

'I've found her!' Charley rejoices. 'Candy in a haystack no more!'

I almost drop Charley with relief.

'Say cheese, Candy.'

I just happen to peer down into the darkness as Charley's mini-Fuji lights up the hole in brilliant flash-white. This flash image of 45 will only go away when I'm in my own grave. I know it. It's been engrained
into my being.

Charley slams the coffin lid shut and I haul him up in a dead-hour haze. Charley pulls up his khakis and we quickly fill in the hole in silence before beating a hasty retreat from the cemetery at the top of the hill.

It's after three a.m. and Charley and I walk down the hill towards the lights of town with my birthday balloon riding our slipstream, thinking about what we'd just done. We both know that we've witnessed something here tonight but we probably won't know what, exactly, until we're old men with the gift of hindsight. I can't shake that skewering sense of violation that's niggling into my conscience.

Halfway down the hill, Charley stops and looks at me. 'I forgot to put a memory card in the camera. The internal memory's full.'

Just as I'm beginning to take on the features of a werewolf under the full moon, Charley tells me to relax and that he's only joking.

I'm too tired and strewn-out to react.

Ten minutes later, Charley stops again. 'I forgot to pull up his trousers.' He's not joking this time.

Words fail me so I keep walking down the hill towards town.

In time, the itch to go back and pull up his trousers will fade and I'll accept that it doesn't really matter anymore.

Before Charley and I turn off for our respective homes,

he tells me that he'll print the photo tonight. 'But when will I give it to you? You're going in a few hours.'

'Um, yeah, I need a favour.'

I tell Charley how Vera thinks that we're travelling together to London so I ask him if he would mind meeting at 128 in the morning, just to keep up appearances. Charley doesn't hesitate. He's a true friend despite his idiosyncrasies.

'Now all you've got to do is find a woman in
Anamosa who fits the snap-shot – and it is a good snap – only because the tattoo is almost better than a photo. That will be fifty percent of your work done right there.'

'And the other fifty?'

'You'll have to talk her into dropping her knickers to see if she's got 45 kissin' her ass. Ying-yang, yo.'

He's right but there's one problem. 'Cha, I'm not a gynaecologist despite what you think. I'm a genealogist. Talking women out of their knickers isn't what I do. It's a highly sophisticated practice. Sex with the Mistress is an ongoing accident. We're fooling nobody but ourselves.'

Charley sums up. 'You've found the woman on the man's ass now you've got to find the man on the woman's ass.' Then he beats a retreat. I watch him appear and disappear under the streetlights with his shovels over his shoulder. You've got to love him.

'Cha?' I call after him.

He stops and looks back…

I point to my head.

He doesn't understand at first but then removes his balaclava.

I ring Dennis who answers on the first tone. He tells
me to go fuck myself for ringing him at this ungodly hour but then realizes that I'm not his ex and gladly agrees to pick me up at 6.15 am.

This photograph better be worth it.

There will be no sleep tonight.

6 hours to departure…

15.
Departure

I do manage to sleep after all. I guess that my body and mind needed over-exposure shut-down. It's been a traumatic twenty-four hours. I wake on Friday morning for my departure to Iowa with fluttering wings in my belly – not quite butter yet not exactly fire. I look out my bedroom window to an early morning that is still night – the same night that I dug up my grandfather's body for the purposes of evidence. Speaking of which, all that seems like nothing now but a blurry nightmare. My bandaged wrist feels much better despite the pain of the digging process. Funny how nerves had numbed the pain while we dug. Still, my meeting with the Reiki Mistress had been a bitter-sweet encounter but I feel that she actually opened some energy channels and dislodged most of my pre-flight jitters. I feel wiser today for having dislocated my wrist, thank you. Incredibly, 45's soul-bubble also looks as if it has benefitted from the overnight soak in the Reiki Mistress's orchid and coconut extract. It's endearing to see it all shining and rearing to go home.

Barely able to contain my excitement, I swing open my wardrobe and choose my best clothes for my excursion – casual but smart. I opt for my Jack & Jones black turtle-neck and the same skin-tight Levis that had been responsible for my ill-timed attack on the Reiki Mistress last night. While I shower and sing *I Did It My Way*, I ponder where I will be having my next shower.

Having showered and towelled off, I stroll down the hallway where I'm suddenly met by an acute sense of déjà vu, unable to put my finger on my sixth sense. All I know is that something has triggered something. Nevertheless, with my mind on releasing 45, I skip down the stairs with my big red balloon, gay as Shirley Temple with my weakened wrist. I don't know why but 128 seems foreign to me in this early-morning silence. The old place has got the same buzz as a hotel, as if I've just stayed here a few days and now I'm heading home. In a way, I think I am.

I meet Vera in the kitchen. She has her back to me but I've already spotted the tears in her eyes (a technique I've been honing for my work as a private detective by being more receptive to my surroundings).

'Morning,' I greet her, being as nonchalant as possible despite the impending circumstances.

'Morning, Jon.'

Is she avoiding my gaze? Perhaps she feels a little embarrassed about last night. No, she has been crying, that's why. For some reason, she's looking rougher than usual this morning, more tousled.

Busying herself with sliced pan and Tupperware, 'You got in late.'

I try pretending that it's a morning like any other, but Vera keeps sniffling and my conscience gets the better of me. I sidle up next to her and give her a big hug. 'Don't be sad,' I whisper, 'it's just London. This is going to give me some time to think. Look at it as my sabbatical. Some time away will be good for me – give me a better sense of who I am and my predecessors who have gone before me.' I attempt to smile. 'This trip will, uh, cure my identity crisis.' I tend to waffle when I'm nervous and now Vera's going to get suspicious.

'And where will this catharsis happen? On the Big Eye? Correct me if I'm wrong but you are going to London for a long-weekend?' As Vera speaks these words, I notice that she's preparing her beef and spring onion sandwiches for work at the airport. 'Onions,' she sniffs, 'lethal this time of year.' She wipes her eyes with the sleeve of her dressing-gown and blows into a kitchen towel.

'S'pose.' There was me thinking that she might actually miss me. I have to remind myself that Vera doesn't know about my quest. Of course she's not crying;

I'm going to London for the weekend with Charley. Anyway, I don't like goodbyes. But what I'm more interested in now is the dirt engrained under her nails. She's been digging again, sometime during the night like a feral animal. For some unknown reason, she's been digging since we spotted the uprooted lawn during 45's wake. Or is it my imagination? Still, I can't complain – I was also digging last night. I also dig on a metaphorical level when I'm tracing ancestors. We're diggers, what can I say.

I butter a croissant, clocking the cemetery dirt beneath my own nails. I run to the bathroom and grind the nail-brush across the tips of my fingers a few times. I feel like a certain Roman emperor and, in a way, I am. I return to the kitchen and drink a black coffee while I listen to the radio news. The news-reader speaks about a hay-barn in Old Castle, County Limerick that burnt down last night.

'The remnants of what is thought to be a Chinese sky lantern has been found at the scene this morning.'

I choke on my toasted croissant.

'The authorities are seeking anyone who may have information to come forward. The police are also looking for assistance in the whereabouts of an individual known locally as Moe in relation to the inquiry.'

I splutter into my coffee as a member of the police tells the reporter that Chinese sky lanterns are becoming "fashion" in Irish households, both indoors and outdoors.

45's spirit incarnation has burnt down a hay-barn. He's taking on a life of his own. A harbinger of doom? Of course not; 45's simply living a fuller life in death, that's all, having visited half of town with me and now torching a hay barn. Dare I say that this is becoming *fun*?

I write a curt note and leave it on the table for Tommy and Alba, just telling them that I love them in my own way like they love me in their way. We tend to leave messages at 128: something that's rubbed off on us since the proto-type suicide note.

Vera spots my bon voyage message and frowns. 'What, you expect to be pecked alive by the pigeons in Trafalgar square?'

I'd completely forgotten about seeing Vera last night breaking the speed-limit on Bridge Street; perfect excuse to change the subject. 'Hey, I saw you joyriding 'round town last night. Where were you going?' I know where she went.

'Um,' busying around again with more sandwiches, 'I went for a pint of milk. The fridge was empty.'

Her excuse is implausible. 'You went down to McDonald's, didn't you?'

Vera sniffs the air in defiance. 'What if I did? I was peckish so I went to the drive-thru for a Happy Meal.'

She's up to something. I knew that last night before I left for the Mistress's caravan. 'The speed you passed me at on Bridge Street suggests that you would've probably driven *through* McDonald's. You went down to see the prodigal son…' I leave the accusation hanging.

'It's a long story.' Vera's avoiding the issue. 'It started before you were born.'

'Yes, I know. By the way, you know how to make me feel insignificant.' Shit, what if Clinical Dad took out his promise and told Vera about my trip to Iowa?

Something zany clicks somewhere inside my brain.

No, it can't be possible…

I turn and climb the stairs and tip-toe down the hallway, passed Vera's bedroom. I don't look in because I can't bring myself to do it but I can see it at the corner of my left eye as I had subconsciously seen it on my way down for breakfast ten minutes ago. I backtrack and peer at the enormous red shoes cocked at the bottom of Vera's double bed. I'd recognize those shoes in any shoe line-up. Red flapping shoes with yellow laces and filling those shoes is Ronald McDonald snoring in Vera's bed. Maybe I haven't woken up yet. Talk about taking your work home with you. To add to the confusion, Ronald's costume is dirtied and his giant red shoes are caked in fresh mud.

What is happening? Were we all digging last night…?

There's a bum clown in my mother's bed. I'm not sure whether I should jump into the bed alongside him and ask him to tell me a story while lying in the crook of his arm or snap that same arm while he sleeps.

I need to run more than ever but I contain myself as I go back downstairs in the same daze that I'd felt coming back from the cemetery last night.

When I get to the kitchen, Vera is propped against the counter trying to hide behind a mug of tea. She's looking at me with a tentative expression that I can't quite fathom. Tears are in her eyes and I'm starting to doubt the strength of those spring onions.

'Jon, some things just cannot be explained.'

'UFO abductions can't be explained, Vera; how a living-dead

Ronald McDonald wannabe ended up in your bed *can* be explained.' 'Nothing happened. I felt sorry for him. He sleeps in the goddamn pantry and he stinks to high Heaven of barbeque sauce.' She adds for my benefit, 'Time heals all wounds and in time you will understand. Keyword: *time*, Jon. You should know about that; you're the one with the degree in genealogy. Oh, here,' she hands me a wad of cash. 'He had no right to take that from you.'

Vera hands me back the money I'd given to the

clown. 'Don't want it. It's blood money.' I leave it on the counter next to the bread-bin. Emotion flutters inside me: I'm angry with her for having given in so easily when I think about all the suffering that that man upstairs put us through. 'You keep it. Pay an electrician to fix the light sockets.'

'Oh, don't be so bloody proud, Jon,' snaps Vera. 'That's your money now *take* it.'

With reluctance, I take the money and distribute it amongst my needy pockets. I tell Vera that I've forgotten something and go back upstairs, directly in to Vera's room. Lost in thought, I watch Clinical Dad's sleeping face for some time. From his nose upwards his face paint is immaculate but the lower part of his face is a smear of make-up where he probably –

No, don't think about that.

45 had always taught me to act first and think later so I employ his teachings now by swinging back my elbow and go to sock him right there across the right cheekbone ... but I can't. As I said, there's something about hitting a man in face paint and costume. Instead, I empty my pockets and throw the blood money back at him and leave the bedroom.

I'd checked flights before I went to bed last night and saw that one American Air flight leaves around 9am. Just as I'm beginning to worry about the time a car-horn blares, waking up half of Hydrangea Drive. I pull back the kitchen curtain and recognize Charley sitting in the back seat of the Skoda taxi parked in our driveway. I also recognize Dennis the taxi-driver whose estranged wife's lover's got a pile-driver.

'All ready?' Vera asks.

'Ready as I'll ever be, Vera.' I turn to give her one last hug goodbye and she catches me off-guard by presenting me with a bum-bag to store my dollars and a garish turquoise and purple Technicolor weather-beater. I put it on. 'How do I look?' Should I be embarrassed to wear this or is it just different?

She nods approvingly. 'Keep it on you at all times. You won't get lost.' There are fresh tears in her eyes now and she's nowhere near an onion. 'I made those sandwiches last night, by the way.'

Did Clinical Dad tell her?

I squeeze Vera. She holds me long and hard and I'm beginning to suspect that she knows more than she's letting on. 'Beheading doesn't happen anymore at Tower Bridge, Vera.' I ease myself from her desperate grasp and give her a business-like peck on the cheek. Nobody wants to drag this out. I nod curtly, grab my small rucksack I had previously packed, and close the front-door and the

164

metaphorical front-door that leads to the old me. As I close the door, I tell her, 'You got it right!'

Her confusion answers back.

'You said genealogy!'

My balloon and I sit into the back seat next to Charley. I wave out the back window at Vera who's standing on the front doorstep. Her draping dressing gown is revealing far too much skin, far too early in the morning. The quicker I leave the front yard the better for everyone. I was hoping she would take the closing of the front door as a hint. Like in a spy movie, Charley looks around before passing me over the photographic evidence of 45's posterior.

Wow!

Immediately, I know that it wasn't a complete waste of time or desecration of 45's tomb. The tattoo artist was obviously talented and probably made a living out of his skin art, maybe still does. The tattoo hasn't grown fuzzy down through the years; its lines are sharp and clear as the day they were forged into 45's ass. Where and when did it take place? I don't know but I will find out. The bleach blond looking back at me is almost a photograph in itself, from her waist up. She's got big blue elfin eyes that haven't run with 45's saggy butt-cheek. In the middle of her face she's got a cute nose. It's a dinky nose that the disillusioned would pay for nowadays but never get it just perfect like God did, the king of plastic surgeons. She' got high cheek-bones on either side of her button nose but the bleach in her hair coupled with black roots and shadow-lines under her eyes suggest something else. The artist captured certain weariness in the face of this Candy character. What's more striking about the tattoo is
that there are vertical lines between her and me. She's got her hands resting through them and the fat wedding ring on her finger is a focal point. The plot thickens. She's smiling at me through the black lines, as if to say *Catch Candy if ya' can*...

165

Oh, I'll catch you all right; it's what I do. I will combine my genealogical and P.I. skills to hunt down your ass, literally. I'm coming for you...

Dennis switches the ignition while sizing up my semi-stripped mother but all that happens is a distinct click. I keep waving at Vera whose dressing gown has slipped down another few inches, the smile on my face beginning to ache now. I had envisaged a crisp military send-off but this is just messy. 'Do we have to suffer? I'll miss my flight to Iowa.'

'That fucking bitch with a capital *F!*' Dennis curses under his breath, frightening the rictus smile off my face. He swings off the steering-wheel, slams his door open, and ducks down out of sight. Charley and I exchange glances and I shrug at my balloon tucked safely between my knees. 'Thunderin' whores!' We follow Dennis's muffled tones to the lower half of Dennis jammed beneath the taxi. The cursing and swearing that comes down the Skoda's exhaust pipe is unadulterated pollution; colourful language in which Dennis experiments with various tones and hues. He hauls himself out from beneath the taxi, dragging himself along our wet tarmac drive, his red face smeared in oil – war paint. He's holding a greasy pipe in his hands. 'Fucking bitch cut the fuel line. I wouldn't be surprised if she got her pile-drivin' goon to cut the brakes while he was at it.' As an afterthought: 'He's a qualified mechanic. That crosses the fucking line: you can accuse Dennis of tampering with his kids, even cocking young drunken lady passengers on their way home from the disco, but never, *ever*, mess with a man's fuel line.' I'm beginning to panic. Even my red balloon has notched up another set of old-lady wrinkles since getting into the taxi. 'I've got to be at Shannon airport in thirty minutes, please, thank you. Call another taxi to take us the rest of the way, *please*.' I'd have been faster taking 45's poxy bus to Iowa. 'I don't even have my ticket yet.'

Charley looks at me with incredulity in his face.

Meanwhile, Vera's still standing on the front door-step, waving and smiling robotically. Her ruby dressing-gown's billowing in the morning breeze now, intermittently exposing her pubic mound inside her frillies like a Parisian high-street peep-show. Jesus of Nazareth.

'Uh,' mortified, I open my mouth and say whatever. 'After a person's been through what she's been through, I guess one treats their body as a temple and proud to show it off whenever and wherever.' This is true if Charley's rumours are to be believed. Well, they are; Vera confirmed them.

'I didn't think our weekend in London would have
such an effect on her,' comments Charley who is also looking at Vera in a new way.

I'm getting a tad agitated now. 'Dennis, how about that other taxi?' I prompt him with an anguished smile.

Dennis, with his war-paint, looks me up and down as if I'd just come from the clouds. 'Dennis works for himself. There *is* nobody else.' He pauses.

Intervention, here we come... 'But Dennis's gonna do you a favour cos you did pass Dennis a nice tip yesterday and Dennis always remembers a kind gesture. If only his bitch of a wife would do the same.'

* * *

A tow-truck pulls up outside the sliding doors of Shannon airport Departures just after 7am. Charley and I pull up in the same tow-truck with aching ribs. The driver, Rory, (a grease-monkey friend of Dennis who owes him some unknown favour) has a speech defect: couldn't pronounce his r's. I'm normally not a morning person but, oh Lordee, did Charley and I have some fun with Wowee. I'm debating whether including this in my thesis because it exposes me in an unfavourable light but my diary version takes the good with the bad and students of genealogy will understand that. It's that killer combination of macho mechanic coupled with sensitive speech defect. I'm sure Wowee's parents hadn't known about his speech impediment when they christened him. Wowee told us how he got into the "tow-twuckin' business by accident" when his "Subawoo bwoke down on the M1." I couldn't look at Charley for the entire trip but I could feel the jitter of his giggling ribs next to mine. Then, of course, Charley had to ask him if he had a Rolls Royce.

I'll miss Charley.

I dismount and Charley carefully removes 45 from the cramped space inside the cab of the truck. In my drive-way, the tow-truck driver had suggested that I tie my birthday balloon to the winch of the truck but I caught Dennis making a loony sign.

I give Charley a manly clap on the back and he engulfs me in a hug, even kneads my buttocks, which I try to appreciate but maybe it's crossing the line. I peel him off me when there's no sign of him letting me go.

'Miss me?' It's my way of telling Charley that I'll miss him.

'Probably not but I'm still going to come 'round to your garden shed.'

I nod and smile. It's comforting to think of Charley there all alone in the bong-house. That's called loyalty.

'I'll keep the Cortina seat warm and keep Brillo drugged up to the eyeballs. She's hilarious when she's high,' he admits with a loving expression. His eyes become watery but there aren't any onions near Shannon airport. The only explanation is that Charley's actually displaying an emotion: an acute sense of loss. I've never seen it before and hope to never see it again: it's grim but beautiful. 'I could still come with you.'

I tell Charley that this is something I have to do alone and he understands.

'Promise you'll stick to the programme: let 45 off in Iowa and find this Candy character and tell her about 45's dying wish. That's all you need to do. Don't go digging.'

Charley clears his throat. 'We've done enough of that already.'

'Yeah,' cutting him off. 'It wasn't his dying wish. He had written it before he –'

'Jonny, I'm not splittin' hairs here. It was a wish he expressed before he died.'

'I prefer not to think of it like that because that puts more pressure on me.'

'You've got one chance to put this right, Jon. Start with Candy and work your way back. It's the only way of finding 45's roots.'

He's right. I searched every drawer, nook, and cranny of 128 without finding a single address. As matter of fact, there's no evidence that 45 ever lived with us. I did, however, retrieve 45's Sheaffer fountain pen.

'When you come back, I want to see 45's name on your balloon. Do good by 45, Jonny, and God'll do good by you.' Charley climbs back into the tow-truck like some kind of evangelist with a tow-truck who offers stricken strangers the free aid of his tow-truck on lost highways.

And that's that. Now, I'm all alone.

16.
Close Call

A pretty girl with a soft Scottish brogue and a wave of highlights greets me at the American Air check-in desk in Departures. She doesn't judge me or my balloon which is a breath of fresh air and a nice pun considering our immediate circumstances.

'Good morning,' I smile, stiff with nerves. 'I want to go to Iowa today.' That sounds borderline retarded. She knows it and I know it. She waits for more information but looks at her computer screen when none comes.

'Okey-dokey, sir. We've got three flights leaving for Iowa, um, today, as it happens. Which airport are you flying to, sir?'

'Um, I don't know.'

'Uh-huh, well, we fly to three destinations: Des Moines which would be our main hub, then there's Dubuque and finally Cedar Rapids.' 'Which airport is nearest Anamosa?' Then I chuckle to myself. 'Yes, I know I should've researched this before now but I, uh, was digging up my grandfather's corpse to find a tattoo on his ass.' I spit it out as a one-liner. I laugh some more to show that I've got a wonderful sense of humour. I've been aching to tell a stranger about last night. The young woman smiles back at me but in a pitying kind of way. She's beginning to look a little impatient and considers the infinite queue growing tireless behind me. 'Sir, this line is only for people with tickets. What I suggest is that you put a euro in one of those internet points scattered around the airport and Google it. Do a wiki-search on the three airports and see which is closer because my geography teacher only knew the location of the bar across the road.' She jots down the three airports for me. 'Sorry, I can't be more help. I suggest you hurry because the gate closes in twenty minutes.' She shoos me away like I'm a stray sniffing around her calf muscle.

'Very kind.' I've always wanted to say that. I take myself and my balloon to the nearest internet point. Instead of doing what the pretty girl suggested, I use my iPhone. I quickly discover that Iowa's slap-bang in the middle of the U.S.A. Then I research Cedar Rapids and see that it is just twenty-seven miles from Anamosa. 'Bingo!' Just as I'm congratulating myself, my battery flashes and my iPhone 4S dies in front of me. Shit, I haven't brought my adaptor. Nevertheless, unperturbed by this minor hiccup, I double back to the Scottish girl at the American Air check-in desk and inform her that I wanted a ticket to Cedar Rapids, please. She informs me that I will have to go to the American Air ticket desk. She gives me directions which I follow. I also ask her if she's got an adaptor for an iPhone 4S but she asks me to move along.

At the American Air ticket desk, I'm met by a gentleman close to retiring with an angry shiny bald head. I give him my details and he asks me if it's a single or return ticket and I make the mistake of asking my balloon. I try explaining my relationship with my birthday balloon but apparently I fall into a higher-plain category that unnerves him, neither being a terrorist or idiot. I end up insulting his lack of hair and Baldy calls security and has me man-handled to the sliding-doors of Departures which I think isn't called for. I protest and let everybody in Departures know about my noble intentions until a kind American couple wearing flowery clothing accompanies me back to the American Air ticket desk. They complain to Baldy about his mishandling of my delicate situation. They demand that he show a little compassion for my noble cause and leave me looking at my startled reflection in his bowling-ball head.

'One-way or return?' He asks again, visibly trying to keep it together. He mumbles something about déjà vu and waits for a response.

'You think shaving your head makes you a tough guy?' I'm eye-balling a tributary vein that has risen on his forehead. He's about to answer but I shush him and make a point of asking my balloon out of spite this time. 'What do you think, 45? Hmm?' I know that I have to set a time-limit. My funds will quickly run low after paying for transportation, lodging, and food expenses. I execute some fine mathematics on my gold calculator watch. I will give myself two days and on the third day 45 will rise again. 'Return three days from today. I'll gain with the time difference.'

Baldy checks his little calendar. 'Flying back on Monday, 21st'

'If that's what it says, tough guy.'

Baldy looks at me with contempt. I hold my head high and stare that old fucker down, right the fuck down … until he tells me the price of my return ticket.

'That's fifteen hundred dollars.'

'Huh?'

'One-five-zero-zero … dollars or add a little if you want to pay in euro.'

For some reason, I can't get the price into my head, the way he's trying to bedazzle me with his sarcastic zeros. I punch out the numerals on my gold timepiece and stare hard at them. 'But that's eating up what I've got left from my interest-bearing scheme. Please, isn't there some kind of deal we can cut here? I've already told you that I'm taking back my granddaddy's a–'

He's playing an air-fiddle before I've finished. Prick. He smiles and I'm going to deck him any minute now. 'You realize that you're playing with people's lives here?' I can feel my body tense up. I've begun to generate surplus electricity and my balloon has begun to gravitate towards my ankles and climb up my calves like a randy poodle. I reach down inside the front of my Levis, pull out my money-belt, and throw hard cash at him in return for my ticket. I'm regretting throwing my blood money at Clinical Dad aka Ronald McDonald as he slept.

'Gate 4.'

I don't bother to thank the bald man, why should I. I need to hurry; not only is it a race against time to get home but my cash flow is in serious peril of turning viscous if I keep forking out this kind of money.

A man about my business, I make my way to passport control. I'm travelling light so I can by-pass the check-in desk. I join the queue for ten minutes while whispering sweet-nothings to my red balloon. 'Don't worry old friend, you'll soon be with your own kind.' I keep an eye on my calculator watch and my balloon's rate of wrinkling which seems to have gotten worse with stress. I flash my ticket to the airport security guard who looks at it, scans it, and sends me towards the scanners before he calls me back. 'Where are you going with that?'

I look around. 'What?'

'There, look, there's a balloon there in your hand,' the security man points out. 'That's a potential time-bomb, sir. Who died?'

'This is ridiculous,' I protest. 'Aren't there special laws that allow the transportation of human remains?'

Somebody in the queue gasps, repeating, *"Human remains"* and other comments, *"What flight's he on? Maybe we can make a connecting flight in Charles de Gaulle…"* Before the day's out, these anonymous travellers will be telling their families and loved ones around the world about the story of the brave boy with noble intentions. The mention of human remains prompts the security guard into tuning in his walkie-talkie and discreetly tells the person on the other end that they have a "situation."

'Ok, so maybe I should re-phrase that,' I concede.

'But, you see, this balloon contains…' I'm becoming self-conscious. By now, the queue is more interested in me and my big red birthday balloon than in removing their belts and shoes for the security scanners. 'Okay so he's more of a gas than remains.' It's no use. 'Show some compassion, please, thank you.'

Over the loudspeaker, I hear that gate 4 is ready for boarding. I grow fidgety and suffer an overwhelming impulse to either run or river-dance my out of here.

A foxy woman comes up to meet me at security. 'What's the problem, sir?' She looks Russian with her beautifully cold, sharp features and dreamy blue eyes. Impeccable English.

I turn my back to the queue of onlookers. 'Actually, it's of a sensitive nature.'

The woman shrugs, pouts, and purrs in a bring-it-on kind of way.

'My grandfather's ashes are in this balloon – not his ashes, per say – but his last breaths while he was a part of this mortal coil. He died while blowing up my birthday present.' I rattle my birthday balloon to emphasise my birthday present.

'Coil? Sorry, sir, your birthday? Uh-huh,' clocking my balloon, 'who died? Could you accompany me to check-in and we can solve the problem without holding up the rest of these passengers.'

'My flight leaves in fifteen minutes. They've already started boarding.'

'You will have to come with me if you want to board any flight.' She suddenly takes on the presence of a loaded KGB spy. Reluctantly, I agree. I have no choice. As I follow the woman, I watch her svelte ass swish back and forth inside her tight skirt and wonder how Brillo and this fox could come from the same corner of the world. I caress my birthday balloon and tell 45 that everything is going to be okay.

At check-in, I'm introduced to a customer-service representative. The Russian lady explains the situation to a young tanned man with bleach-blond hair and teeth behind the check-in desk in a conspiratorial mumble. He listens intently, blinks profusely, and insists on studying both sides of my ticket even though one side is blank while eying my balloon intensely. 'Who died?' chuckling to himself. Oh, yeah, this guy is hilarious. He steals a glance in my direction, registers my bandaged wrist and my rainbow weather-beater. After what seems a life-time, the anti-terrorist pin-up leaves without acknowledgment. The Bondi Beach bum twiddles his Bic between his fingers and studies my ticket some more for good measure. He produces an enormous blue file and sifts through it, going 'hmm, uh-huh,' while passengers board my plane. 'We appreciate that this is a delicate situation, Mister Garfunkle.'

'Rowe.'

'But we cannot allow your balloon on this flight or any flight without making some pre-flight preps. Birthday or otherwise.'

'Preps?'

'Yes, preparations. You could be a terrorist and that balloon you're holding could be laced with anthrax.'

'That's my grandfather you're talking about. How about showing a little respect?' The black cemetery hole in my conscience creeps back. My traumatized mind is taking cautious steps around that hole as Charley snaps his Fuji flash. A wave of insecurity washes down over me. I start to panic again, checking my watch and feeling helpless as my plane gears up to go. Meanwhile, on a microscopic scale, 45's essence is escaping through my balloon's porous skin, and speaking of porous skin, I've begun to break a sweat beneath my weather-beater. How long will it take before 45 becomes part of the air-conditioning system at Shannon Airport?

'We here at American Air aim to satisfy *all* our customer's needs. I'm sure we can come to some arrangement. I notice that you're not taking luggage with you, Mister Garfunkle?'

'Huh? Yeah, you noticed right. I'm doing a Hulk.'

'Ah! Nice.' He smiles a gleaming row of pearls, clearly, having no idea who the Hulk is. '*That's* clever but I think you mean Dr David Banner – the Hulk just burst the stitching on his clothes.'

I'm dealing with a smart-ass, a clued-in one, worse again. 'Look, can we cut to the chase? My flight's going to leave without me and 45 is undergoing osmosis.'

'Okay, so that implies that you haven't paid baggage fees or availed of our wonderful array of travel insurances. Surely, a man like you would've taken some insurance for your balloon's well-being.'

'What? I don't understand.'

I suddenly become famous at Shannon Airport as my name is called out over the speaker system. Apparently, I should run to gate 4.

'That's me, please! They're calling me! Please, I think I'm going to puke.'

'We, at American Air, encourage you to puke, Mister Rowe.' He flicks open his fists in front of his face in an explosive gesture. 'Our air-hostesses are not mere trolley-dollies that flash their cleavage, lottery tickets, and gourmet lunches for your convenience; they work wonders with, how can I put it, *fluids* left in the toilets of all our long-haul flights. Do you see what I'm getting at?' He winks at me like he's had a lot of practice. 'Do you see the trouble we go to for your comfort, sir?'

'Just, get to the point, please, thank you.' Jesus of Nazareth.

'We have introduced a new surcharge on balloons, sir.'

'What?! It says that in your paperwork there?' I can't believe what I'm hearing.

'Just checking that the extra fee doesn't exist yet. Of course, we will have to introduce dimensions etc but I won't impose this on you seen as you're our first balloon-customer. Lucky. However, we will have to draw the line at helium, I'm afraid. Helium rises. That's just asking for trouble, destabilizing the aircraft etc.' This guy is just winging it but he's as smooth as Tommy on the karaoke machine. He leans over his check-in desk and peers down at my trailing red balloon. 'Clearly not the case.' He flashes an android smile.

'This is preposterous.' I begin to search for a hidden camera. 'A balloon doesn't weigh anything.'

'Either does anthrax, sir. It's not the weight but the air-space said balloon occupies inside said aircraft cabin.'

'You're going to have to do some major negotiating when you arrive at the pearly gates, bud.' I clinch my fists and ask him the price of the goddamn surcharge. 'Profiting from the dead, that's what you're doing.'

He rifles through a bunch of papers and muses some more. 'One hundred euro also payable in dollars or pounds for your convenience.'

'Oh, for my convenience? I'm so lucky. Just pulled that figure out of thin air, did we? This is horse-shit! It isn't my custom to make a scene but this is outrageous.'

'I feel your pain but won't you do it for your poor grandfather?'

'Emotional blackmail is an American Air policy also?' Enough is enough. I decide to call his bluff. I hold my balloon up in front of travellers and workers alike, my fingers at the lip of the balloon like in a Sergio Leone film. 'I'll open my birthday balloon and release my grandfather right here, right now. Put that in your pipe and choke on it.'

When we have a quiet moment between ourselves, I will apologize to 45 for using him as a bargaining tool and also that this customer-service rep would choke on his essence.

The man scrunches up his nose as if a bad smell has just wafted his way. 'Of course, you *could* be a terrorist,' he hints. 'I'm just taking your word for it that you're not. If I was to hand this over to the police, I'm sure you would miss this flight and probably be black-listed from any flights leaving the country.'

Think fast Jonny. 'You're right. You're absolutely correct. What was I thinking?' I snap my ticket from his hands and leave the check-in desk. I walk coolly towards the closest toilet. Behind me, I can hear him telling me that I won't get through security in his overtly gay overtones.

I get into a relatively clean cubicle and latch the door behind me and dry-gag on seeing the surprise that had been left by a previous traveller who had been obviously thinking about being held thousands of feet above-ground by mechanics that sometimes fail. I do the right thing and take a piss while I'm in there. Then I do something that I have never tried inside a public cubicle. I stuff 45 down inside my turquoise light-weight weather-beater, mumbling angrily to myself about the state of the world and how nothing is sacrosanct any more. 45 slips down my front comfortably without being conspicuous thanks to the puffy nature of Vera's weather-beater.

I heave a deep breath and vacate the cubicle, then power-walk to passport control, sweating profusely now, but it feels comfortable to know that 45 is so close to my heart, we almost merge into the same person: half Jonny; half 45: Jonny 45, we sound like a member of the native tribes that once roamed Iowa. We fuse during these panicky strides to get out of this country.

The queue moves rapidly. I hand my ticket to the same security guard and he waves me through. I almost kiss him but that would only draw attention to my undercover work. But there's still one hurdle to go: the scanners. I pray that Shannon airport hasn't installed those new pervert scanners that can see into your very soul. Thankfully, they look like the traditional type from where I'm standing. I whip off my belt and drop my jewellery (gold calculator Casio watch) and wallet into a tray. The lady at the scanner gestures me forwards and these tentative steps have been the longest and most awkward since I was fifteen months old. I try to look normal as I approach the scanner. My birthday balloon's nestled nicely inside my weather-beater but now I realize that it's causing me to hold out my arms further on either side of me like a fat man. I almost revert back into my play-retard trick that I had performed to lull the Micra gypsies away from me and my balloon back in Old Castle. I'm an utter disgrace as I pass through the scanner in a ball

178

of sweat...

Just as I see the alcohol section at the duty-free, the scanner beeps. Jesus of Nazareth. Thank Christ that the chastity nature of my snug-fit stone-wash Levis saves me from soiling myself.

The security woman approaches me and waves her hand-held scanner up and down the fork of my legs and right over 45 hiding inside my weather-beater. He can probably sense the wild thumping of my heart from wherever he is and surely this will earn me a gold star and forgive me for exhuming him last night.

'Remove the jacket, sir.'

'Huh?' I begin to wobble. 'Uh, uh, it's a weather-beater.' As my knees buckle beneath me, the individual who is on screen-duty tells the woman that a jacket zip doesn't "constitute a sharp implement."

Thank you! At least there's somebody in this godforsaken place that doesn't suspect the worst of people, which has caused me to hide my birthday balloon in shame.

From a distance, the security who had waved me through tells me, while staring at his screen of anonymous people's intimate belongings, 'lose the jacket in future if you don't want to be taken aside; it attracts attention.'

And that's the beauty of it. All the attention had been on the gaudy turquoise and purple weather-beater. The weather-beater leads people into a false sense of security. This new concept brings the term undercover to a whole new concept and I make a mental note to thank Vera when I see her. "You won't get lost." That's what she had said. Now I see the double-meaning in that.

I make a final dash for gate 4 with excitement tingling in all my nerve-endings. I quickly work up a steady rhythm in my legs and attain tremendous speed as doors, lights, people and luggage whizz by me. Alas, when I got there, two American Air workers are closing the doors.

Jesus of Nazareth.

'Wait! We need to get on!'

The ground-staff look at me coming towards them and beyond me for a second person.

'Relax,' one of them advises.

The second man tells me that there's an hour delay due to "technical difficulties."

I'm elated but ready to punch one of them after all I've been through. I'm starting to get the impression that I'm not meant to get this flight.

Without being rude, I stop them from spinning any more of their bureaucracy bullshit. I turn and tremble my way back to departures where I retire to Sheridan's Bar. And guess what? The dude behind the counter has an adaptor for an iPhone.

* * *

An hour later and halfway through my fifth pint of Guinness and second Irish coffee (I'd decided that a little celebration was in need because I'd smuggled my balloon through security), a cleaner's mop practically knocks me off my chair. I had nodded off: a cocktail of late-night grave-digging and Sheridan's Guinness. I come to myself and dribble, noticing that a French family sitting across from me had been studying my balloon and its strange symbols.

'Sorry, love,' apologises the operator of the mop and moves on, weaving in and out of Sheridan's furniture. To my horror, I recognize Vera. Half-pissed, my gut tells me to call her back. 'Vera…?'

She has her ear-phones in so Mary Coughlan's probably drowning out my drunken call with her smoky tones. My gut kicks in, asking me what the fuck I'm doing? I've already said my goodbyes back at 128 and besides, Vera thinks you're going to London with Charley. *Idiot.*

As I watch my mother work her mop into the horizon, I wonder if she's thinking about why she's ended up sleeping with a clown. Why had she let Clinical Dad back into her life and ultimately ours? Isn't she questioning why that loser-creep borrowed – in inverted commas – two thousand dollars from his son's savings account that he opened? I feel a wave of intense love and admiration for her but I can't deny my suspicion. Clinical Dad back at 128, who would've thought it after all this time? It's nonsense but the more I ponder this point the more it seems that all this has happened too easily after so much time. I don't know if it's my doctored coffees or a mixture of exhaustion and raw excitement but I'm suddenly useless against the stream of tears that openly flow onto my table. I mean, *what* a woman, Jesus of Nazareth. She's been through the belly of the dragon and come out the other side, waving her mop. That takes a lot of effort, hauling mop-ass through the intestines and anal sphincter of a dragon. She never complained, never asked for help with 45 while I presumed that fresh air was taking care of him while I pulled fluff from my belly-button. Vera deserves all the good fortune in the world but I'm not sitting comfortable with a strange clown sharing my mother's bed.

My flight comes out over the loudspeaker as Vera disappears amongst the wood and chrome. Needing a boost, I retire to another public toilet and text the Reiki-Mistress with my newly charged iPhone. I request some pre-flight remote Reiki and astral projection if she's got the time. Then, I pop 45 inside my weather-beater, apologizing once again. The more I hide him, the guiltier I feel about it but I'm sure 45's spirit knows that it's for the best. Security will be tight. f this PhD thesis diary were a thriller, then I'd probably end this chapter by transmitting the following: we are walking into a shit-storm with nothing but a weather-beater to protect us by.

'Flight 2204 to Cedar Falls, Iowa is ready for departure. Please go to gate 4.'

17.
Smile Me a Lullaby

Somewhere over the Atlantic, a dangerously cute tanned air-hostess starts slamming over-head lockers above my head and then raises my window-blind, shoving it down again. I had seen her pass by three or four times through my hangover slumber, curiously looking down at me. Sometimes she had passed by with the trolley outside official feeding times; rattling cutlery on the biscuit tin she uses for change and sometimes the change itself.

'Listen,' I'm real grizzly like a bear, 'Why is it *policy* never to let passengers just get a simple kip?' I'm queasy and not in much humour to entertain or to be entertained. I'd drunk two pints more than was good for me back at Sheridan's. It had seemed like a good idea at the time because of the elation of my successful smuggling of 45 through customs.

Our plane banks sharp to the right and my stomach goes with it.

'Just a twenty-minute siesta, but no, if you're not banging those overhead lockers or asking for change in your little plastic cup then you're asking if I want a lottery ticket or some damned roasted gourmet coffee, which is, let's face it, watery black coffee. Can't you see that I'm asleep? How can I drink coffee when I'm asleep? I'm on *edge* all the time.'

With a wow-factor sexy Spanish accent, the airhostess asks me if I'm feeling okay but not in a breezy air-hostess kind of way, no, she actually cares.

I fall in love right there even though I have no idea what she's talking about. The Spanish lady discreetly points towards my belly region. 'I didn't mean to disturb you but you seem to be, eh, how do you say, swelling? Sir.'

'Huh?' I look out my window at the clouds to try and clear my fuzzy head. 'Can you say that again?'

'Have you eaten something that doesn't, eh, agree with you?'

I hear *fuck!* inside my head before my body reacts. I peer down inside my multi-coloured weather-beater. *'Wha...? Shit!'* Passenger faces peer back at me like a family of meerkats to search for the source of the mid-air profanities.

'We were no sooner above a cloud – clouds in general – when you began to swell out like a *globo* ... balloon I mean.'

I play it cool but can feel the glisten of sweat beneath my designer goatee. But she's right; I am swelling like a balloon and why wouldn't I with a balloon under my weather-beater? The fluttery feeling of panic begins to creep in again. I could explode any moment. That would be a colossal waste of money and time. 'And,' nonchalantly, 'what would happen if I happened to have a balloon hidden inside my weather-beater?'

'Do you?'

Surely she's not playing along? 'Do I what?'

'Have a balloon hidden inside your fancy jacket?' she chirps.

'My weather-beater?' I falter at this gorgeous girl's beauty. I redden like my balloon within. 'No ... *Yes*, yes, please. Balloon, yes, red.' Jesus of Nazareth, I must seem mentally-challenged to this Latina. I speak like an automated voice calling out a telephone number with a robotic rise and fall on each number.

'May I, eh, sit down?'

'It's your plane.'

She sits into the free seat next to me and I tell her the short version of the long version as 45 steadily expands inside my weather-beater. Without going into details, I tell her that my life has been up and down like a whore's knickers recently. I don't lie. She gets a good kick out of that one. What a sense of humour. What a little dynamo, she is. 'Please don't tell. You never saw my swelling stomach. Okay? Deal?'

She obviously finds the whole thing quite amusing, judging by the cute dimple in her chin if that's anything to go by. Thankfully, she agrees to keep my swelling to ourselves, even cracking a joke, asking me if I'm happy to see her or if that's that just a balloon in my fancy jacket? Is she flirting with me? I try hitting another double-entendre back at her, 'pop goes my weasel,' but I just sound needy. 'So,' turning to business 'why's my balloon expanding? I need to solve this fiasco, like, now.'

'Maybe your grandfather has decided that he's had enough. He's giving you a sign from beyond the grave that he wants out.'

Christ, last night was his chance if that's the case.

'Maybe he's not happy with you dragging him across the world? Maybe he doesn't, eh, want you to know the real 45?'

I hold her in my gaze. Is this girl for real? Her insight astounds me and I tell her so. Here's a female on my gut level, both figuratively and literally. I feel like balling her up and keeping her inside my weather-beater but two is a crowd. I give some serious thought to what she had said but feel that she's, maybe, having a laugh with one of the locals. 'Please, don't play games with this. I've come too far now to simply explode.' I had overlooked the possibility of spontaneous combustion. 'I need to get to the toilet to sort this out.'

'No, please,' a tinge of panic had slipped into the air-hostess's voice, 'that's the last place you should go. You might not be able to, eh, get back out.' The air-hostess gets up. 'Wait here.'

I follow her cute little tush right up the aisle until it goes directly through a door and … into the cockpit. I get to my feet and yell up along the aisle. 'Please, no!' Meerkats pop up and look back, some even taking ear-phones out of their ears. I gesture an apology and sit back down and speak into my weather-beater. *'"Take me home when all this is done"* that's what you asked me to do and

184

that's what I'm doing but please, I beg of you, if you can hear me in there, *relax*.' It's useless. My big red balloon starts to show below my chin. I look like one of those coastal birds (name escapes me) with a scarlet pouch-sac beneath its bill. I ease down my zip to release pressure on my sac, careful not to get its skin caught in any teeth. I pull 45's makeshift urn from my innards.

All the old lady across the way has to do now is simply look in my direction to sink the plane with the screams that will linger on after death switches out the lights.

I try hiding the balloon beneath the seat in front of me but I barely have room for my knees, plus the Levis factor doesn't give me much room to manoeuvre with. To coin Charley, I'm bricking it now. The balloon has grown so wide that it begins to lose its red vividness and the RIP is pulsing, screaming out at me.

Rest in Peace ... Rest in Peace ... Rest in Peace... If ever I thought that 45 might be sour about last night's debauchery then it's now.

I resort to my natural sense of cunning, checking my immediate surroundings. I'm seated at the back of the plane, good, so that eliminates passengers accusing me of being a terrorist.

Yes, maybe I can get away with it. I sit into the aisle seat and give 45's soul twin the window seat. Just sit him down, like a curious child wanting to see the Atlantic below. The air-hostess comes swishing back down the aisle all business-like, swopping sandwiches and teas with a winning smile on her face.

Jesus of Nazareth but this girl's something special.

What is she doing on this plane? Taking her life in her hands every single long-haul day? She's one of those people who see the best in everybody and I need someone like that in my life to bounce off. Since Clinical Dad deserted us I tend to see the worst in everybody. They say opposites attract.

She hands me a chicken and stuffing sandwich and tells

me that it's on the house. I thank her for the kind gesture and lay into the stuffing.

'I asked Capitan the reason for your balloon's, eh, sudden inflation.'

'Excuse me?' Am I hearing things? 'You didn't tell him that I was on the plane, did you?' I say this as if the captain has already heard of us and to be vigilant. 45's infamous soul brother and his burly minder with the rainbow weather-beater had left a trail of deceit and destruction across the South West of Ireland and now moving west to the U.S. to find Soul Brother's lost twin. We aren't bad by nature but society has twisted our sense of good.

'No,' answers the fetching air-hostess, breaking me from my stream of consciousness. 'I told him that my, eh, cousin's friend once smuggled a balloon onto an aircraft exactly the same as this one but with a serial number that differs by one digit. I told Capitan that, eh, my cousin's friend wanted to know why her, sorry, his balloon reacted in such a peculiar way.'

'Brilliant!' I spray stuffing all over her uniform. I blush bright and apologize. I'm ashamed to admit that the radiance coming from this girl has blinded me to 45's plight. He could've burst by now for all I know, drunk and blinded on this sky-angel's beauty.

'You look like the terrible twins, eh! Eh!'

'Yes...'

'Sitting there with massive red faces! *Ay, por dios!*'

She grimaces and ogles as if imitating my own face. I find it off-putting to be frank. She giggles and says something to herself in Spanish which she doesn't translate, little bit of a let-down to be quite honest. She grows serious as fast as she had begun to laugh at me – us. Her dark eyes flit back and forth from my face to my balloon and back again. 'Yes, I can see the likeness.'

This trip is becoming far too surreal for my liking. 'Uh-huh, so what answer did the captain give you?'

'Capitan says –'

'Capitan? Wait, that's Spanish.'

'He prefers we call him Capitan.' She leaves it at that. 'He says that the drop in air pressure inside the cabin caused the air inside my cousin's friend's balloon to expand. Apparently balloons are very temperamental when it comes to flying. They sense troughs and spikes of air pressure more than humans.'

I marvel at this new knowledge and laugh with admiration and wonderment. I repeat, 'Troughs and peaks, eh.' I wonder to myself why that old bum Charley and I had once met in the Old Quart had failed to mention this succinct fact about balloons when he seemed to know everything else about their upkeep. 'So what's gonna happen now?'

'Yes, Capitan says that we will begin our descent in five minutes and that should've returned my friend's cousin's, sorry,' with cute little clenched fists, she forces the last part of her sentence as she tries to recall what Capitan had told her, 'my cousin's friend's, balloon to its original state but to be aware of stretch-marks.' She smiles proudly and heaves a sigh.

'*Stretch marks?* Capitan said all that?'

'He's really brainy.'

Why should I feel a spike of jealousy? I barely know this girl.

'The Reiki Mistress gave my birthday balloon a massage only last night with her, um, coconut and orchid extract home-remedy.'

'Oh,' she clicks her fingers, 'the one from Tesco? The two-for-one?'

I nod. 'So, I think that may help with the stretch marks. Yes, it's all making perfect sense now. My birthday balloon is 45's born-again womb, carrying her offspring to the reeds of corn in Iowa – if I ever get there – where she will give birth amongst the reeds. That will explain the stretch marks. Perfect. Everything has a reason.'

187

The air-hostess sort of wanders off mid-sentence, leaving me with my pregnant thoughts. She returns with a small pill and a glass of water. 'I think you need to, eh, relax. We carry these if patients, sorry, passengers have panic attacks. It's Xanax. Take it and I will watch over you and your grandfather's remains. We have another hour to Iowa so I suggest you rest.'

'An hour!' I can't believe it. I was in Shannon only an hour ago. 'I thought it takes six or seven hours to fly to Iowa?'

She giggles again. 'You were asleep, seely-beely.'

'Excellent.'

'We won't be flying any higher so your balloon won't be under any extra stress. As Capitan said, we'll begin our descent now; I'll wake you up when we're almost there.'

'Thank you, Flo.'

She smiles but frowns a little. Obviously my Florence Nightingale simile has gone amiss on her. I'm a tad dubious but decide in the end to follow her advice. The last three or four days have been intense and I lack sleep. My nerves are shot to pieces. I take the little pill and down it with a glass of tepid water. 'Please, keep an eye on my grandfather.'

She produces a light blanket from an overhead locker which she still manages to slam, and lays it over my birthday balloon. Is this girl for real?

I grow very dopey and the world has become smoother and warmer. 'What's your name?' I hear my voice from far away.

'Ruthy.' She smiles me a lullaby.

I slur, 'Oh, that's wonderful.' Only I say 'wunderbar' instead of 'wonderful' but I don't know any German. I see her electric smile as my eyelids droop. 'I dig: that's what I do.'

'That's nice. Shush now.'

'I dig for roots...' Am I still speaking or is it in my head?

'Yes, that must be, eh, fun. Please, relax now, Jonny, and let yourself sleep.' The air-hostess's voice is silken on the sensitive hairs of my inner ear. This must be love. I'm comatose but still feel a reaction in my loins nestled in my Levis at how she pronounces my name.

* * *

I'm nudged awake. Ruthy is looking down at me just like before I fell asleep. 'We've begun our descent into Cedar Rapids. Put on your belt.'

45's balloon is still sitting beneath the blanket in the window seat. I give it a discreet peck and gaze out the window to see an expanse of flat plains. The surge of electricity that lights my nerve-endings tells me that I'm here: Iowa! My quest is about to become real.

'Almost there, buddy,' I whisper to my balloon. It looks just like E.T. peering out from under Elliot's blanket and being up in the air makes it so much more real.

45's soul-bubble slowly but visibly deflates back to its normal self as we drop from the sky. I'm ecstatic but it's showing signs of wear and tear and it breaks my heart to see it like this. The Capitan was right; he does have stretch marks. Maybe I can text the Mistress and ask her advice. I discreetly apologize to my birthday balloon beneath the blanket and lift it just enough to give 45 a glimpse out the window at the rolling plains of home. I cannot see any corn though: all I see is acres of earth-brown fields where corn grows in summer. What had I been thinking? It's the winter here like it is at home, only colder. Capitan's voice tells his cabin crew to take their seats for landing in his generic captain's voice. Ruthy is sitting up at the very front of the plane next to another crew member only half as pretty. She winks back at me. 'Saucy mare…' I lip-synch at her but immediately regret it because she regretfully tells me that they're not serving any more food.

189

Before I know it, our wheels have touched down on Iowan tarmac and the roar of the engines and air-brakes is exhilarating.

I've made it! I'm in Iowa!

I stuff 45 inside my weather-beater and wait for the plane to open the back door next to me which means, in theory, that I will be the first to leave but my little air-hostess friend is up the other end.

I tell 45, 'I must get her number!'

I fight against the tide of oncoming passengers. There are a few moments when 45 threatens to pop as I bump and crash into angry passengers but matters of the heart are reckless. Here is a girl on my level and I have the sudden gut urge to tell her so.

'You're a little forest pixie,' I proclaim when I finally reach her. 45 had always taught me to speak my mind but the minute I say it I regret it, it sounded better inside my head where it should've stayed. I clarify, 'We – my balloon and I – want to thank you for all your help and your understanding. I was wondering if I could have your number?' I can't lose.

Ruthy grabs a pen, a paper coaster, and jots something down. At the same time, one of her colleagues down the other end of the plane asks for assistance, apparently a fat man has gotten jammed in the cubicle with his pants down. 'Gotta go...' Ruthy hands me the coaster and disappears into the crowd like a firework; a long-haul Mother Theresa.

Gripping the coaster in my fist and tucking 45 into my weather-beater, we leave the plane and step onto Iowan soil just after mid-day. It is absolutely freezing. The time difference has been kind to me. I uncurl the ball of paper while skipping across the tarmac at Cedar Rapids Arrivals:

Call me: 66-44-

She hadn't finished writing her number but just petered off to scrawl. Now that I think back, it was around about the same time that the fat man had screamed, something about his damn piles and suction in the pressurized toilet.

190

Jonathan Dunne *Balloon Animals*

I glance back at the re-fuelling plane but my quest eclipses my heart: life's a series of troughs and peaks and I'm on the clock here.

18.
The Party Bus

I breeze through passport control at Cedar Rapids some
time after mid-day, floating just like my brother-in-arms. I
can relax until I have to go through customs again from
Cedar Rapids. What am I talking about? I'll be coming
back alone. This is a one-way journey for one of us. A pang
of sadness almost moves me to tears as we cross the
squeaky-clean main hall with 45 at my bosom, seeing
through my eyes.

Once inside Arrivals, I release 45 from the trappings of
my weather-beater. My birthday balloon has sunken lower
than ever and worse still, the Capitan was right; it has
saggy stretch-marks. Already the journey is proving too
much for this old soul. I'm reminded again that this
excursion isn't leisure but business. To any passer-by, I
might give the impression that I'm ashamed of my big red
balloon the way I pull it out of my weather-beater like
something dirty but it couldn't be further from the truth:
I'm here – *we* are here – to tell Iowa that 45's back and
ready to reclaim his hidden past. I feel a great sense of
pride as we walk through the airport building ... until a
member of airport security with a turban approaches me.

'Sorry, sir. We've had some complaints about your
balloon from various passengers and I have to ask you to
take it outside the building. They feel it's in poor taste.'

'Excuse me?'

'They feel it's in poor taste. They've got nothing
personal against the actual balloon but some people find
your balloon offensive in what it says – the RIP part mainly
and the cross doesn't help. People feel terribly sad and it's
pissing on their parade.'

This sounds great in the user's Indian or Pakistani
accent. I'm ready for this wise-guy. 'What would you
say if I was to tell you that this balloon is an unmarked

grave until I find out the real identity of its occupant?'

'I'd say that either you or the balloon will still have to leave the building – preferably both, sir. This is a family building, sir.

We like to keep Cedar Rapids clean.'

'This is outrageous! Haven't you ever seen *Lassie Come Home*?' I'm not sure where I'm going with this but probably something to do with the spirit of Lassie.

'I never had a modicum of interest in the television sir; rots your eyes and leaves the mind impotent.'

The turban on the gentleman's head tells me that he's probably of Pakistani extraction. 'Do you mind if I ask you your name?'

'Policy says…'

'Just try to forget about your policy,' shocking myself with my rudeness, 'and I say that with all due respect.'

The security guard nods, rolling that concept around in his head while I take a few steps backwards, grasping 45's string tight, and ready to leg it if I have to.

'I say balls to the system on a daily basis, sir, but in here.' He points to his turban. 'If truth be known, I don't give a modicum for policy but whoever pays my wages has got my loyalty.'

'Noble,' I comment and hold out my hand. He takes it and tells me that his name's "Hitesh, sir. Hitesh Sharma."

'Hitesh, how do you think your family in Pakistan would feel about you terrorizing a young man for carrying a balloon?' I'm not sure what he is disagreeing with. 'What?'

'I come from a family of Indian smugglers, sir, not a modicum of similarity with our Pakistani friends.' He seems to come alive, weaving his head in a mesmerizing cobra-like fashion. I think that he's trying to hypnotise me. I look at my balloon, careful not to fall under his snake-spell. 'In India we have parties and celebrations every night of the week and why wouldn't we for the love of Ganesh? With over a thousand Gods and the sweet scent of the white jasmine flower to make love to at night.' His happy pearly smile fades, just like the jasmine, and his head grows still.

'However, I'm from Albuquerque, sir, and we do things very different in Albuquerque. Personally, I don't have a modicum of interest in your balloon, it seems quite harmless, but I work for the airport and the airport says go or you'll find yourself outside sharpish.'

'I've got this balloon for medicinal purposes, Hitesh; my grandfather's dying breaths are suspended inside this balloon, and I am taking him home to release him amongst his own kind.'

I'm a fool for thinking that my love story might melt Sharma's hard exterior.

'That is quite admirable, sir, but as I've said before, I'm from Albuquerque, and I don't give a...'

'Modicum, yes.'

'...modicum about your adopted grandfather's posthumous writings... I work for the highest bidder which happens to be Cedar Rapids Airport Authority.' He's getting thick now.

'Posthumous, yes, nice choice of word, Hitesh, I must remember that one but I won't comply with airport policy. I've come too far to be degraded.' The black cemetery hole in my chakra threatens to raise its weary head. 'Nobody's going to silence my grandfather. I feel more love for the old man now than ever before.' I strut away, leaving Hitesh standing there, rolling his turquoise ring on his pinkie finger.

A minute further into the belly of Cedar Rapids airport, I check over my right shoulder and, as forecast, Hitesh is tailing me, perhaps five meters back, ducking
down behind inconspicuous rubbish bins and luggage. 'Just doing my job, sir,' a pillar says with an Indian lilt.
Then, as if reaming off a line he has once been grilled on: 'I must be seen to be doing my job, sir.'

Starving, I decide to kill two birds with one stone by brightening up the security guard's day. I side-step into an eating establishment going by the handle of Sam Adams pub. I ask for the menu from the bespectacled individual behind the counter and take a quick gander through it. Through a series of unlikely reflexions and optical effects, I clock the security guard standing outside to the left of the door with a face of anger. 'Can I speak to the boss?'

'Sir, you're talking to him.'

'Hi, I want to know if you have any problem with me carrying a balloon into your fine eating emporium?' I hold up my balloon next to my face. I smile stupidly, as if trying to convince the man that my birthday balloon and I are related which is what I don't want him to know. Again, I struggle with the fact that people only see a mere balloon and not a reincarnation which the balloon is becoming, I fear. Maybe he would react as Cyril did in the Hound when he threatened me with Health & Safety before I mashed his face. I'd forgotten about that but I don't regret it. Nobody cheapens Vera's name but I won't be mentioning that there was a clown in her bed this morning ... yesterday morning, whenever it was. I'm living in a jet-lag time-warp right now. The Reiki Mistress warned me that this excursion would play with my sense of reality.

'As long as there are no hidden cameras buried in the balloon, I don't care,' the man quips but I'm not sure if he's serious. I hold 45 up to the light. 'Nothing but a posthumous note. I'll take a seat.' I reach into my back pocket to pay with some loose cash instead of digging into my money-belt (it's a mental thing) and almost hand a carrot-sized doobie to the manager. I redden up like my birthday balloon and choke a limp rictus smile. Where the hell has that come from?!

The manager fixes on me with an unimpressed stare. 'We only accept cash or credit card.' And then as an afterthought, 'though I can't say that I'm not tempted.'

'Uh-huh.' No wonder Charley had been so interested in fondling my arse-cheeks back at Shannon airport. The bastard had slipped me a joint. In a bluster, I pay the man plus a generous bribe-tip and sit down quietly to enjoy the finest 'shake and Frisbee-size hamburger I've ever laid my eyes on. The three pork sausages had been just plain greed on my part. I chew my food slowly while mentally cursing Charley. I'll laugh about it later but I'm breaking out in a cold sweat now just thinking about what had been in my back-pocket as I walked through Shannon airport security. There was me fretting over a balloon. I chew meticulously, savouring my meal while the security guard from Albuquerque of Indian extract paces back and forth outside the restaurant. I have found a neutral place of solace in a time of war. I'm enjoying the chase because I'm defending 45's noble honour. I am a knight templar and this is my quest. I jest by waving my giant hamburger out at the security guard but he insists that he isn't hungry. I wiggle a sausage at him and I see the momentary doubt in his face but not even the sausage can lure him into the eating house.

I leave Sam Adams. The security guard follows me again. I do a few needless laps of the main hall, birthday balloon in tow. I look for a Greyhound ticket office to get to Anamosa. I ask an airport worker but he tells me that the Greyhound just runs long- haul. Again, why hadn't I researched all this before I left? I think of 45 sitting on the back doorstep at 128 awaiting his long-ass haul from Limerick to Iowa. This memory prompts me into kissing my birthday balloon. The security guard has noticed that I'm starting to veer and wander, growing sentimental with my balloon. He approaches me as I leave the building.

It is freezing outside. It has been snowing judging by the slush on the ground. I notice a happy-go-lucky group about my age hanging outside the main exit. They've got rucksacks and backpacks and are in high spirits. It's obviously some kind of tour waiting for a bus out of here. Hitesh the security man approaches me.

'Where are you going, sir?'

I guess now that we're outside the building I'm no longer offensive. 'Anamosa in Jones County.' Saying the location aloud makes it more real now. I'm no longer talking in the darkness of the bong-house with Charley.

'Yes, about twenty-five miles from here. Fall in with this group then, sir. It's a tourist bus and a tour-guide that will take you through the more *interesting* sights of the area.'

'I'm not here for tourism purposes; I'm on a quest.' I point to my balloon for clarification.

The man nods but points to the group of young people nonetheless who seem much too ecstatic to be going on a sight-seeing excursion if you ask me. 'If you have time to waste, sir, then that's okay dokey. You'll wait another,' checks his watch, 'hour before the next regular bus gets back in. There are hold-ups on 54. If you care a modicum for your deceased in-law you should heed my advice. Do you believe in reincarnation, sir?'

I take this subtle loaded question two ways: either he's telling me that 45 won't reincarnate or will and when he does, he'll hunt down my ass for time-wasting. I'm not in a position to second-guess. I'm on my own in a foreign country with an ailing balloon. The lows and the highs of the flight hadn't been kind to 45's soul-bubble. Jesus of Nazareth, it's starting to look a lot like an old woman's tit. The old man would turn in his grave if he thought for a second that he'd become an old tit.

I nod a thank-you in Hitesh Sharma's direction and sidle up next to a couple of jolly girls: a hippy and a conservative. 'Sorry, um, are you waiting for the bus also? I need to get to Anamosa.'

The wired hippy girl looks me up and down … my bandaged wrist … my multi-colour weather-beater but my balloon gets most of their loopy-eyed attention.

'I love your persona.' The butty girl sizes me up with raised eyebrows and prods my balloon with her stubby finger. 'It's the balloon. It's like your side-kick – an extension of your self.'

'Well spotted. But please don't, um, don't do that.' I want to explain why it's rude to prod my balloon but I hold off for now. 'We're sensitive, that's all.'

'Cool,' they say in unison.

'Yes, I suppose we are.'

The girls flash each other glances and burst out in hearty guffaws. The bean-pole girl who resembles a jewellery shop with so many facial piercings tells me that I'm absolutely hilarious. She's laughing so much that she gets the sniffles and I'm disgusted at how she blows her nose with all those metals loops getting in the way of her nostrils. Surely she needs to bleach them on a weekly basis.

'I don't think it's the balloon at all,' says the chubby conservative who seems relatively intelligent with her spectacles. 'I think it's the seriousness that you give your persona that does it. But, okay, the balloon gives you the validity you need.'

I thank her for her psychoanalysis but tell her that I don't have much cash to spare because I was robbed by a has-been wannabe clown. It's the truth.

Big laughs...

'Sure, Anamosa's on the route, right?' The lanky girl checks that with her frumpy bespectacled friend who tells us both that it's on the route to Dubuque which is their destination. 'Who invited you anyway? It was Tom, right?'

'I invited myself.'

Apparently, I'm a riot. Another round of unadulterated laughter only now I'm starting to think that the twisted sisters had puffed an exotic number not too long ago. I'm just not that funny; I know my limitations.

The gangling girl asks me if I'm Irish.

'How did you guess?'

Her friend, with the oak barrel shadow, says, 'I speak Gaelic: *póg mo thóin*, see.'

'No thank you, I prefer not. The only ass I kiss is my boss's and I won't be doing that any time soon seen as I'm currently unemployed.' *Sometimes I take photos of asses...*

'I've got Irish roots,' says the lanky one.

Jokingly, I study her bleached hair with strawberry

highlights while standing on the tips of my toes. 'Yeah, I see 'em from here.'

More laughs.

'Naw, I'm kidding. I've got a degree in genealogy,' rattling off the line. 'If you give me your surname and some minor details such as your bank account number I can put you in contact with your dead ancestors.' I'm on fire with wit!

'Spoooky!' says the butty girl and they roar with weakening laughter again. The tall one admits that she's just pissed herself and the concerned expression in her hooped and pierced face says as much.

'I'm writing my PhD thesis right now,' I tell them. 'This trip *is* my PhD thesis,' I say in earnest.

The girls scream and double over, bawling and heaving, 'No more! Jesus Christ! No more!'

Now I'm not joking and it seems like just a lack of respect on their part. Yep, they're high as kites, they have to be; they're not taking me seriously.

They call the rest of their buddies over. And before I know it, I'm surrounded by fellow-travellers. All I hear in the group is "Who invited him?" in hushed tones, "Where did he come from? I can't remember him from the faculty…? What did you say his name is??"

What I don't understand are all these perfectly symmetrical pearl-white chattering teeth. My mouth seems medieval. A purple bus pulls up to the kerb, all sparkling chrome. It bounces and hisses on its suspensions, *psss …whoosh*. The door swings open and a black man with an outstanding platinum 'fro yells, 'all aboard, yo!' He actually says "Yo!" First time I've actually heard it being used for real apart from in the movies.

I'm beginning to suspect something now as I'm swept up in the tidal rush to climb aboard. I yell out to the security guard to know whether I'm taking the right bus but he just waves back and smiles. Prick. I hold my balloon over my head out of harm's way as the crowd man-handles me onto the bus. I go to pay the driver and the bus itself skits and chugs with uproarious laughter. I try to join in with my temporary travel companions but I just don't find this process as funny as they do, sorry. When I get on-board, I notice that there are no seats but vast chaise-lounges, fibre-optic and ultra-violet lights everywhere. There is a cocktail bar at the back of the bus, advertised by a sloping fluorescent palm tree and a gay flamingo. I flop down into an empty chaise-lounge towards the back of the bus with 45's soul brother nestled tightly in my lap. These people think that I'm here to party. It's all falling into place now. They think that I'm one of them! It must've been the balloon and my earnestness, just like the girls said. Black semi-transparent panels drop to block the vast majority of what I can see through the windows and we pull away from the airport. Hip-hop pours out from the mega-speaker system. The group whoop and holler, popping open their backpacks to reveal thermos flasks and packed lunches. Maybe somebody could give me a cup of tea and perhaps a beef and chutney sandwich. I'm hungry despite having just eaten.

The thermos flasks and pack lunches re-reveal themselves to be six-packs, beer kegs, whisky bottles, red bull, vodka, home-brew galore. Somebody's passing around a bottle of Americanised poítín. It comes my way and I take a deep slug for old times' sake. I wish my balloon good health which finds more laughs. I find that offensive but I must remind myself that these people don't know that the balloon is not what it seems. I think of Jesus on the cross: Forgive them father for they do not know what they do. I'm not comparing myself to Jesus but the parallels can't be dismissed. Everybody's drinking like the Prohibition is coming back but nobody sparks up a doobie. I'm only too aware of the Rolled Gold in my money-belt. Charley's not going to believe this. I take my iPhone to call him but take a photo instead. No sooner had I the photo taken when the iPhone dies on me again. I hadn't

Jonathan Dunne *Balloon Animals*

charged it for long enough back at Sheridan's.

'Does anybody have an adaptor for an iPhone 4 or 4S? I call out to reams of laughter. Evidently, I'm still in character. 'Where am I?' I feel disorientated. It's not the drink in my system but the blacked-out windows.

The butty girl starts an impromptu belly-dance in front of me. Something she shouldn't do because she *has* a belly and it grows a life of its own under these disco lights. Jesus of Nazareth, she looks like a writhing grub.

She tells me that I'm aboard the party-bus celebrating a five-year reunion with the Iowa University dentistry faculty.

Of course I am.

Now I understand the wonderful teeth which look even celestial in the ultra-violet lights. 'Are we going to Anamosa?' I ask.

The lanky girl drags me up to my feet and starts gyrating around me with her crotch and rump, bumping and grinding to the beats. She swings off one of two poles that I now recognize as a stripper pole and nothing to do with the fire-service. She grabs my birthday balloon and starts to dirty dance with it, sending it in and out through the fork of her legs. 'I'm Lana, by the way.'

'Jesus of Nazareth,' I answer, not sure whether to leave 45 or save him from Lana's pubis bone. As usual, I bypass good mannered negotiations and snap instead. 'Be careful!' Cringe-worthy timing, I shout between rap songs. I've started so I'll finish. 'My dead grandfather is in there!'

Luminous teeth begin to disappear in the party bus as smiles drop from faces. People stop dancing ... lower their drinks ... put their clothes back on ... slide down the stripper poles to land in heaving heaps in the shadows.

'So you're not a persona,' says Lana's side-kick. 'You're not one of us and you're not an actor. So, who are you? I thought, well, we thought that you were some zany character with a ridiculous jacket and balloon.'

I tell them the whole story. I explain who I am and my

mission to release 45 amongst the corn. I realize now that there is no corn, only flat plains of snow and ice but it's the thought that counts and the roots are still alive in the ground which is a metaphor for my quest.

People are collectively dumbstruck. I can see that they're not sure how to react. The fibre-optic lighting and neat alcohol lacing their bloodstreams is playing with their sense of reality but this is *my* reality, surreal as it has become. I tell my audience how 45 and I have become closer in death; how I love him more every day and how sometimes I just want to stick a needle in my balloon and set him free. But I know he won't be happy until I contact this Candy character, it *was* in a way, his dying wish. At this point, I take Candy's image from my little backpack and ask the group if they recognize her or if they could shed some light on the 1010 that 45 spoke of. The photograph gets passed around to a Mexican wave of head-shakes and furrowed brows. The group, now sitting around my ankles like children around a storyteller, asks me where I had gotten the photograph.

I think hard about that. 'I cannot give you an answer to your question because my method of gaining this photograph is something that I'm not comfortable with. I still haven't accepted what I did and not so sure you would understand if I told you. Let's just say that I went to extreme measures to get it but with good intentions. I need as much help as I can get to reunite this Candy character with 45's ghost. So, if you don't mind, I'd like to keep this part of the story to myself.'

They accept me and my story though the atmosphere has changed, not soured just different. Few words pass between us after that. People don't feel like dancing anymore but just look at us (my balloon and I) curiously and smiling with, I think, admiration. They know that they've witnessed something special and a special person (in a good way) here today. I'm somebody who they never thought that would meet on their party bus.

The bus pulls up and the driver declares, 'Anamosa, yo!'

I gulp. Everything is happening so fast. People hug me and the girls gravitate towards my balloon and some of them kiss and caress it. The guys, on the other hand, fist it gently and wish us the best of luck.

As I get off the bus onto the side of a secluded road, a petite woman of Chinese or Korean persuasion with glasses calls me back. She leans out of the party bus to be out of earshot of the others. I remember her as one of the few drinking who was drinking pop.

'I think I know where you can find "Candy"'.

I can't believe what I'm hearing. 'What's with the finger-commas?' I ask. 'I'm not deaf.'

'I'm from Anamosa – though not originally,' she smiles and gestures to her general face. 'My family from Laos settled in Anamosa in the forties. I don't know if you know Laos.'

Just get to the point...

'I've looked at the photograph of the tattooed woman.'

'You know her?' I ask, unable to disguise the hope in my voice.

'No.'

'Okay.'

'I don't know her because she's before my time but she looks like she's not from 'round Anamosa. Everybody knows everybody in Anamosa. It's a close-knit community with great values and some astounding results in general. Candy's a stranger. At least, she looks like one.'

'A stranger?' I'm confused. 'I don't follow you.

What's a stranger supposed to look like?' My freezing breaths puff out in front of me.

'All strangers come from the same place in Anamosa. The kids who grow up there are told not to talk to strangers.'

Now I'm getting a little spooked and her sweetly prim manner isn't helping.

'C'mon, let's rock, biatches!' yells somebody from

inside the party bus. '*Yeee-haaa!*'

'Also, her 1010 surname is a number.'

'Yes.'

'You don't know her surname, do you? I presume Candy's a nickname.'

I've just gotten used to saying Candy 1010 and tell her so. Charley and I had never discussed whether Candy was a nickname and the relevance of 1010 sort of fizzled out with thoughts of photographing a freshly buried corpse's rear-end. 'That's all I know. Like I said; I'm just following what the note in the balloon told me – what 45 wrote.'

She's looking at me as if I should be putting two and two together by now…

'Do you ever think that 45 maybe left out some details on purpose?'

'Careful now…'

'You told us all just now that your grandfather was senile but he wasn't senile enough to include just the basics to get you to Iowa. 45 might've thought it was obvious but I doubt it somehow. I think he deliberately left out the important stuff because you wouldn't have come if he included Candy's full address.' She pushes her fashion-statement white spectacles up onto the bridge of her button-nose. Those hideous glasses detract from her porcelain finish.

'What do you mean?' I've started glancing at my balloon. A nervous energy is escaping from my solar plexus chakra, feeling a tinge of betrayal, that's how I feel.

This stranger seems to know 45 better than I do. I'm starting to wonder if private investigation is my calling.

'Well, what does 1010 mean?'

'1010 is Candy's number.' She's rolling her wise oriental eyes.

'You're not giving too much away here. So what part of the address did 45 leave out if you're such a smarty-pants?'

'Anamosa prison; 1010 is Candy's cell number. The prison's ten minutes from here.'

19.
Roadside Musings

Candy is a jailbird and she's ten minutes from here …?

I look about me, every point of the compass, fascinated that this Candy character is so close. I'm half expecting to see her peer out at me from beyond one of those naked trees that line this roadside. I'm not sure how long I've been sitting here on the road-side in this neat little town called Anamosa that hides more than it's letting on. The party bus has long since driven off towards Dubuque to a chant of admiring glances and goodbyes through the bus's rear-window (they had raised the black-out panel on my behalf), leaving me sitting on my back-pack in an utter state of freezing numb incomprehension. My multi-colour weather-beater may as well be the flag of Jamaica in this Iowan winter. With numb hands, I search for the Rolled Gold bumper-doobie Charley had so lovingly prepared and smuggled on my person, spark up, and inhale all things good until I feel that I'm back at the bong-house 128. I need solace now and would give anything just to sit in the Cortina seat and listen to Charley's drunken and stoned musings and maybe watch Brillo molest Molly. Or, dare I say, even some sweet succour at the hands of the Mistress. Some TLC from the Reiki Mistress would be great about now. Never thinking that I'd need to hear Charley's voice, I whip out my iPhone 4S and speed-dial…

'Charley?'

…before I see the blank screen and remember that my battery's dead I check my gold Casio calculator watch. It's after 4pm. The afternoon has begun to creep away on me. I'm tired and hungry and not sure if I'm mentally ready to visit a prison, not today. Prisons scare me. Tomorrow, crack of dawn, I will be ready to come face to face with the unknown but right now I crave a hot meal and a lengthy siesta. I need to locate a B&B and put my ever-decreasing dollars to a good cause. What if the girl on the party bus is wrong? I'll have to go to the prison to find out. There's no other way. If it turns out that Candy is an inmate then I will deliver 45's note to her personally. Who would've thought that I'd have the luck of finding a lead on Candy in the first hour on Iowan soil? I'm convinced that it comes down to some good P.I. skills and not simply luck. I had had the image of me walking aimlessly along the streets of Anamosa, stopping people on the street and showing them the photograph of 45's rump. At least I've saved him that degradation (if the oriental orthodontist is right in her assumption).

What kind of idiot doesn't make the connection with a prison when the lady in the tattoo is obviously *in* a prison cell!? I thought that those lines or *steel bars now* had been a metaphorical symbol for her unwillingness to dumb down; a rebel without a cause. Yes, I had been right in thinking that Candy had been a tough old bird but I presumed this from her bedraggled bleach-blond hair running black-at-the-roots. My gut had never suspected a thing and for that, I have not forgiven it. But the thing is that 45 hadn't known then that I would be digging up his ass (God forgive me) to get to the tattoo that he had hinted at in his final message. If 45 had written Anamosa Prison instead of Anamosa then he might have thought that I wouldn't have come, just as the orthodontist had said. Would I have still come if I had known that Candy is (was) a jail-bird? Yes, probably. Only now it's starting to shed a different light on 45. Maybe I'm being judgmental here but it takes a certain kind of man to get involved with a woman known to the law. It takes me back to our duet together in my patio.

Take me back home when all this is done. I'd do it myself only I'm afraid they might turn me in.

I had dismissed his words of paranoia as addled senility but now this craziness is starting to show chinks of logic and a pattern is coming through to the surface and I'm not sure I like it. I don't remember any guerrillas or spies at my birthday that could turn the old man in? *I never belonged here since I lost your Nan. My heart's somewhere else.*

Now, the blatant truth is staring me in the face: 45 had never loved Nan, at least not in the way that he'd loved this questionable Candy character. Why would he after she two-timed him? I'm beginning to know Candy better than I knew my own grandmother, Nan; not that I ever knew her, just hand-me-down memories.

I won't be safe until I'm outta here for good, the whole goddamn show, hoop-la.

I try staring down my balloon but it just looks back at me in defiance and not giving too much away. 'Safe from who or what, old man?' I demand. 'You in there? Anything else you've decided to keep from me?'

Is it possible that I'm in over my head here? Clinical Dad, aka Ronald McDonald, had told me – *warned* me –not to come here. Why? Because he's known something all along? If that's the case then Vera knows more than she's letting on. I cry at my birthday present in anger and bereavement. 'Who the hell is in there!?'

Traffic slows down to watch the lunatic screaming at a defenseless balloon on the side of the road in Anamosa; a town that had been anonymous to me until a few days ago.

'Why didn't you tell me the truth? I would still have come…' My birthday balloon, withered somewhat now, seems to be growing a head of its own.

The Rolled Gold, coupled with jet-lag, is starting to draw three-dimensional features on its rounded wrinkled face. The balloon bares a striking resemblance to 45 now but it's different at the same token. 45 and his soul-brother are in cahoots. They've led me here under false pretences and that scares me a little now. Again, I make a conscious effort to separate us from fusing into one person: Jonny 45. What's also becoming apparent is that I'm slowly shaking off my sense of identity loss but now, to my horror, 45's identity is taking over: *I'm* becoming the ghost.

This quest had started as a two-prong wish-bone affair: release 45 in some corn (but now I think that general Iowan territory will have to suffice) and find this Candy character to relay 45's love message to her. But now I just might be able to discover a little about 45's past which is something I hadn't hoped for or thought about because my aim was to simply find Candy. Charley was right after all: Candy will lead me to the real 45.

I top my doobie and place it into a discreet pocket of my multi-colour weather-beater and walk towards town in search of lodgings for the night with my flabby balloon. Dusk is setting in. We're tired, cold, and ragged. In my heart, I know that it's a race against time as 45 continues to seep through my birthday balloon's semi-permeable membrane.

I have the unsettling feeling that I'm being watched.

Is the town watching me? Has it been waiting for me? But I can't allow that factor to consume my quest.

As I walk towards the lights of town, I see 45 through my sepia-tinted mind's eye view fifty years back. I wonder if he had taken these very steps before he had come into my life? Candy had brought him to Anamosa ... or had he brought her? Just because he knew her doesn't mean to say that they met in this quiet little picturesque town in Jones County. It's strange to think that 45 had once been an individual with a life before he met Nan; a free-thinking man who didn't confuse the cheese knife for the remote control.

I locate a McDonald's on the outskirts of Anamosa, spotting its promising golden M from a way off. When I get inside to the warmth I check for suspicious clowns and find a quiet corner for us in a comfortable booth. For once, I blend in nicely because several children are chowing down on Happy Meals and surrounded by celebratory red balloons because Ronald McDonald is celebrating his 200 year anniversary or something like that – he didn't look it in Vera's bed this morning but it's amazing what make-up can do.

I order a McWrap meal, large all round.

What about the blonde bombshell with the chassis of a Lamborghini (or was it a Ferrari?) that 45 had promised me in return for his safe passage home. Maybe it was that air-hostess Ruthy but she was clearly a Mediterranean brunette though she did have the chassis of a luxury sports car or a new mini perhaps is closer. Alas, I'll never get a chance to service it because she'd done a blonde thing and had forgotten to give me her number. Anyway, why worry? We come from different worlds. We met over the Atlantic Ocean and there our spirits will stay. I'm prone to melancholic asides while dining at McDonald's.

Suddenly, I poke myself in the eye with my straw and my ketchup ends up on my wrist bandage, not on my chips, and the more I try to wipe it off the more it looks like congealed blood.

Some of the children are gawping at me now, then comes the inevitable pointing and asking mommies and daddies about the demented person sitting alone in the corner with a balloon.

I'm a nervous-wreck. I've been trying to keep my visit to Anamosa prison on the back-burner but it's getting the better of me. Unable to control myself, I leave McDonalds, disgusted and jittery. I have to stop this habit of running from McDonald's. My passage to

Iowa has left me distraught. The constant worry of having my balloon safe by my side has taken it out of me. I owe it to 45 to meet with his past, fresh-faced and eager. Maybe my chakras would benefit from a half an hour of transcendental meditation. I feel low on Qi. I must find an adaptor for my iPhone so I can text the Reiki Mistress to top me up remotely. I gave the Reiki Mistress one of my molars that had been knocked out in a horse-riding accident back in '99. Any personal relic will suffice.

Like a couple of wearisome vagrants, we walk and float the streets of Anamosa until we find suitable lodgings for the evening in an overly-priced, slightly grubby hostel called The Locker on Cedar Street and happy to be here.

We retire early to catch up on some jet-lag. Lying in my single bed in my minimalist rented room, I dream of a woman who I seem to have known all my life but every time I see her it's for the first time. In the middle of the night, in a dingy room far from 128, I wake up to the crazed notion that Candy is jailed for life to 45's ass ... and 45 to her anonymous ass.

Charley would laugh if he were here. *If* he were here...

20.
Anamosa State Penitentiary

The following Saturday morning I wake at 7.30am with the same feeling of dread in my waters that I had woken with on my birthday a few days ago.

I take a warm communal shower while thinking about my impending meeting with Candy at the prison here in Anamosa. Let's hope the oriental orthodontist is right. At this point, I'm kind of taking her word for it as my time is limited and she seemed to know what she was talking about yesterday. I can see her logic, taking everything into consideration.

Seen as my hostel isn't the kind of place that serves buffet breakfast, 45 and I bid a quiet farewell to The Locker: a title that works on so many levels. We cross the street to a café called Jacks' with the apostrophe in the incorrect position but the woman behind the counter has an iPhone adaptor. I order home-made scrambled egg on toast with black watery coffee and avail of the free electricity. I surreptitiously gaze at the diners, half expecting to see 45 or Candy sitting at a table with the same face they had decades ago. I wolf down half of my breakfast before deciding that I feel ill due to nerves. I order the pie special and another watered-down coffee and ask the woman for my iPhone. I try to ring Charley for a long overdue update but the battery is still dead. I ask her if she'd mind plugging it in again for me which she does but with a grumble this time, something about having to feed customers. I need to speak to Charley (never thought I'd say that) so I compensate by leaning in over the counter while leaving my iPhone charging.

'Charley?'

'Jonny!'

'Just thought I'd check in with you and give you the latest –'

'Jon, can you hold the line while I kill somebody...'

I know by his distracted voice that he...

'Take that you warped fuck!'

...must be on Gears of War, playing against an anonymous cyber-net opponent.

'Yea, Cha, course I can hold the line for a killing, Cha, I'm just calling you from Iowa, that's all.' I realize that everybody sitting along the counter is listening in on my conversation. I turn my face into the sink.

Charley screams victory down the line. 'Sorry, Jon, continue. I got distracted there. What's happening? I was worried about you.'

'Not that worried – I don't have any missing calls from you. Where are you, by the way?'

'Sitting in the throne of Cortina at the bong-house. Where are you?'

In the bong-house? That doesn't make sense. 'What? Since when do we have computers and internet at the bong-house?'

'Jon, I told you that I'm gonna be here, just hanging 'round 'n stuff. I brought my laptop and suckin' up your Wi-Fi.'

Charley has his faults but loyalty isn't one of them. I quickly fill him in on my quest-PhD thesis, right up to the house special pie.

'You can be thankful that Anamosa's not a big place. You've been lucky. Candy's no longer in a haystack my friend...'

I agree with Charley. 'How're things there?' Deliberately keeping my clown-in-the-bed syndrome to myself for now. 'Vera? She's okay?'

'All good.'

'Uh-huh. Sure?'

'Why?'

'Well, y'know, now that Clinical Dad is working at McDonald's...'

'I'd have spotted a six-foot clown with an orange

213

'fro wandering 'round 128, Jon.'

'The 'fro's natural.' I recognize that I'm defending my runaway father. 'You haven't seen him around then?'

'Like I said…'

A bitter wave of sadness rolls inside me. Sure, Clinical Dad's a confirmed loser (borrowing my savings confirms that) but I thought that he might've stuck around … but I hate his guts. I don't know what to think right now so I bid Charley farewell and tell him to stay by his phone for further updates.

'Jon?'

'Yeah?' Charley's tentative voice tells me that there's information coming my way. He always leaves whatever is on his mind to the last.

'Vera is, well, acting kind of weird.'

'Expand.'

'She's got the mole syndrome.'

'What?'

'She's diggin' 'n rootin'. She's got the mole syndrome, got it real bad. She just digs at 128 when she's not at the airport. You think she might be looking for something?'

I'd forgotten about Vera's curious behaviour before leaving on my quest because I've more important issues at-hand. 'That started the day of the wake, when we were in my room, remember? The front lawn? Keep me posted.'

'Oh, Jon?'

I hear voices in the background, sounds like Brillo's dulled tones. 'What?'

'Brillo tells me that you're …' Charley's voice wanders away from the receiver, 'in grave danger.'

I thank Brillo through Charley for her deadly advice and pay for my breakfast (noticing how my funds are depleting rapidly) and ask the other person behind the counter, an old boy with a handlebar 'tache, for directions to the prison.

'It's normally the opposite,' he smirks, 'tryin' to get away from the place…'

214

This ominous comment doesn't help my growing fear of the prison.

'Who died?' he asks with a nod at my balloon trailing behind me.

'Not sure yet,' I answer back.

He nods as if he understands. 'Anamosa state penitentiary's on North High Street, ya' can't miss it. If you find the court-house then she's tucked in right behind that. Keep yer back to the wall.'

Other diners, truckers and such like sitting along the counter, chuckle into their blueberry pie.

I curtly ask for my iPhone back, flash my embarrassed face, and leave Jacks'. I feel them watching me and my balloon leave the premises with speculation. Before the door shuts, I hear one of them say, 'That fellar's a looong way from home...' in a resigned way.

It certainly feels like that.

I follow the directions the old dude had given me, crossing town from Cedar Street onto High Street.

Within fifteen minutes, I locate the courthouse and behind it...

Jesus of Nazareth...

...the sandstone walls of Anamosa maximum security penitentiary. My palms begin to sweat despite the freezing cold and I notice that nerves have grip-locked my fist around my balloon's streamer. My heart's pounding harder in my chest and I keep trying to clear non-existent phlegm from my dry throat. A feeling of sudden horror accosts me as I pass through the gates. I've never seen such a beautifully ornate prison. The front façade could easily be a museum of some sort. Back in Limerick, the city prison is grey drab limestone and spells all the darkness and desperation that might be expected of such a place. Security is crawling all over the place. I suddenly question the reason for my being here in this alien place. I'm in over my head again.

I make my way to the information office which

is clearly signalled to visitors to avoid anyone straying off. There I meet a hefty African-American woman, sitting hunched behind a desk.

'Can I help you, sir?' she asks with a genuinely warm smile though eyeing my balloon. 'Sir, can I ask you to leave the balloon outside the confines of the building.'

'Where should I leave it?'

'Tie it to a tree or the pedal of a bike or the side-mirror of a vehicle ... I don't know, sir.'

'No, you don't understand. This is my grandfather ... cutting a long story short.'

With comically raised eyebrows, the woman looks at my bedraggled birthday balloon that had once been scarlet but now running to watery shade of pink. 'He doesn't look too good. How about you cut your short story a little longer, sir?'

So, for the hundredth time, I explain yet again, the reason for my relationship with the balloon – not that I should have to explain myself. I also tell her that this quest is to become my PhD thesis for my Master's degree in Genealogy. I'm doing well until I tell her that have aspirations of opening a private detective agency.

She heaves a sigh. 'I can help you from here sir but you won't get inside the facility with a balloon whether he's your dear granddaddy or the pope.'

'Well, I don't actually want to get inside the, uh, facility and I don't really want to if I can help it. I
would like to know about a prisoner who once, perhaps,
stayed in one of your cells. Maybe she's still here? Why I would think that Candy might still be locked up escapes me. She's probably in her eighties by now. What kind of crime had she committed to get so many life sentences? Do you have death row in Iowa? If you do then that sort of defeats my purpose. What are the visiting hours?'

'Sir!? *Relax*. Please give me the name of the inmate – past or present.' She purses her lips into a kiss and looks at me.

If I could only take a photo of her face and send it to Charley.

'Sorry, I tend to waffle. I've just realized that I've been living in the past.' And I have. 'Candy – the prisoner's name is Candy.' I loosen my strangling hold on 45's soul-brother.

'Candy?'

'Sorry, Candy 1010. I think the 1010 might've been Candy's cell number.'

'Candy sounds like a woman's name. You take a glance at any one of these guys we've got caged up in here and you won't find a Candy, let me assure you of that, sir. And if there is, then I pity the poor bastard after lights go out, sir.'

'Candy is a woman.' I produce the photograph from my backpack.

The warden holds the photograph out at arm's length and up to her scrunched nose then raises and drops her eyebrows in dramatic fashion. I'm getting dizzy just looking at her, there's so much going on. 'What am I looking at, sir?'

'This is the only visual evidence I have of this Candy character.'

'This is a woman.' She inflects her voice to a question. 'Look at her hair.'

'Yes, black at the roots, that's correct. The tattoo artist didn't miss a trick.'

She looks out the window. I follow her gaze thinking that Candy might be looking in but all I see is a flurry of snow. 'This is a men's facility, sir.'

'Huh?'

'What's your connection with the woman? Sir?'

'Huh?' She had lost me when she mentioned "men's facility." The oriental orthodontist on the party bus didn't know her arse from her elbow, as 45 used to say, hoop-la.

'Let me rephrase myself: how do you know this Candy character?'

'I'm trying to contact this Candy character on my grandfather's behalf. It was his dying request, although he had asked me before he died so I don't know if that actually constitutes –'

'Anamosa penitentiary has been woman-free since the early 20's I believe – or even earlier – though a few woman stragglers were kept on to finish their sentences and work in the kitchens … laundry etc. And before you accuse me of being sexist, these women didn't know how to exist on the outside. They were given a paying job inside the walls of the facility. A handful of ladies made it into the '30's I believe.'

Candy in a haystack … Candy in a haystack…

'Maybe Candy was one of these women?'

'Sir, our records don't date back that far…' She turns and asks a young man at a computer if Candy 1010 rings any bells. The man, no more than a teenager, shakes his head without taking his face from the screen.

'However, there's a woman in town, self-professed historian on our facility and reclusive stage actress, goes by the name of Sooty LeDanse.' She sees my reaction, 'Yeah, I know. Dramatic, right? Sooty's a little eccentric but she knows every rat that's ever been through the facility … and inmate,' she chuckles, her heavy bosom heaving up and down which I cannot help but wonder at. She wags her head and slugs from a polystyrene cup. 'Sooty's got a little theatre called the Red Herring.'

Interesting. I'm starting to think that this whole trip is becoming a red herring.

The heavy black woman continues. 'I like to be seen near her cos she makes me look like a cucumber next to a pumpkin.' More giggles. 'Only problem is that I never get to be in her presence – *nobody* gets to be in her presence. Are you familiar with Miss Havisham, sir? Dickens?'

'Yes.' Charley and I read (*had* to read) *Great Expectations* in high-school, though I've come to love Dickens over the years. 'Nobody ever sees ole' Sooty so you will have to be granted a visit with Miss LeDanse. Rumour has it that she's grown too fat to leave the theatre but that's not for me to say.' Slurp, slurp.

The pimple sitting at the Dell snorts a giggle and shakes his head but his face doesn't leave the screen. This gives me the impression that they might be winding me up because they're bored.

With no other options left, I ask for directions to The Red Herring.

'Davis Street, that's where you'll find her; just off Main Street.' I bid them good day and quit the penitentiary.

As I walk back out through the entrance gates, a biting gust of wind snaps my balloon from me and whirls 45 back inside the confines of the penitentiary as
if he was intended to stay there which my waters
understand as an ominous sign.

Jesus of Nazareth!

The balloon backs up against the front wall of the reception building and the wind catches it, whipping it skywards. *'45! What are you doing?! Get down here
this instant!'*

So addled in the moment, I'm not sure if I say these words in my head or for real. My balloon clears the barbed-wire walls by inches (my heart going with it) and soars high, five … ten meters upwards with the breeze, disappearing somewhere inside the belly of Anamosa.

A weakness overcomes me as 45 floats away out of sight. Within seconds, a shut-down siren is wailing out across the yard and through Anamosa town. Now, I'm having flashbacks of that fateful day when the ambulance arrived to pronounce 45 dead on my patio, no more life in him than the hundred garden gnomes Vera has taken a shine to. I chase my balloon but am stopped by a swarm of guards with raised weapons. 'My balloon! 45!' Through an arched gate, I see 45 suspended high above an exercise yard full of medium and maximum security inmates. I can see them from my vantage-point, gazing up at the red balloon as if it's some kind of strange god looking down on its subjects. The next few seconds seem to blur into a line between fantasy and reality as I wish my birthday balloon to blow away, once and for all. It would seem fitting. And, just as I'm thinking this, the breeze drops and 45 alights amongst the prisoners like a child falling into the lion enclosure. Jesus of Nazareth! I want to save him from certain death but I've got prison guards in my way. Over their shoulders, I see the inmates gather around my balloon and look at it inquisitively; an alien that just fallen from the sky. Like savages, a butch skin-head slams another inmate's face into the concrete to get to my balloon first, then a weedy terrier of a man trips up the hefty skin-head with an iron bar that he produces from who knows where. He grabs my balloon and hollers, 'Victory!' I hear him from here and I don't know why but I cannot wipe a black and white image from the *Lord of the Flies* film from my mind. Another goon swipes it from the terrier while he's waving my balloon above his head. His guffaw stops short and comically looks over his head with his hands still in the air but empty now. Others gather around and ogle 45's urn with fascination and curiosity. Without wishing to be condescending, I've seen similar reactions in experiments with baboons on the Discovery channel. Still, a balloon alighting in the exercise yard must be a metaphor for 'The Outside' for these prisoners – a sign of hope – and I'm sure such a simple thing as a balloon landing from the outside must be an exotic occasion for these caged men living strict routines. I think I would look every bit as gobsmacked by a stray balloon as they are now. With an acute sense of pride for what I have done for these men, I wet myself as five gun barrels point in my direction.

'What's in the balloon, sir?' asks one of the guards straight out of a cop movie.

'My grandfather.'

'Sir, no funny business! Tell me what's in the goddamn balloon or I'll pump it full of lead! Blow it outta the skyyy!'

'Oh, you wouldn't want to do that. There are rules and regulations.' Shut up, Jon, my gut whispers.

The guard, taking this as a direct threat, gets on his walkie-talkie device and I witness more than twenty guards raid the exercise yard and gain control over my birthday balloon. At what point do I forget the birthday part? What the American Air representative had potentially accused me of comes to mind. 'No, don't get me wrong! I don't have anthrax in there!'

This sets them off again, panicking like a flock of geese on Christmas Eve.

Another voice comes at me. 'What happened to your hand, sir?'

I'd forgotten all about that. 'Oh, uh, a Reiki master twisted my wrist and tomato ketchup is what you think is blood.'

Triggers are cocked in surround sound.

One of the guards back-answers me, 'Reiki is a hands-off holistic medicine sir.'

Thanks Wiki, I feel like saying. 'My Reiki master is a hands-on kind of woman.' I inflect my voice for the benefit of the guards. They exchange just the kind of looks that they think they would. I take a deep breath and yet again, I explain, to a bunch of nonplussed faces, the reason for the balloon. Their reaction is just as the same as everybody else. They just don't understand and I forgive them for that. I tell the ring-leader to contact the woman who I had been speaking to and she will verify my story. She should be out here already, owing to the commotion.

I glance around to the back window of the information office, gun-barrels following my line of vision, and spot the black woman standing there, jiggling like a jelly with laughter while spilling coffee from her polystyrene cup down her uniform. She ducks out of sight when she knows that she's been spotted and comes up a second later. She casually opens the window as if throwing crumbs to the birds and calls off her boys.

With some reluctance the ring-leader, Wiki, does this and with equal reluctance, instructs his men to put down their weapons.

A warden, hydraulic in nature, returns from the exercise yard with my balloon and I cannot help the tears of relief that stream down my cheeks. We've been through so much together. It would've been a dramatic
send-off but I wouldn't wish such a second death
on the old man. My balloon is returned to me and I'm kindly escorted off the penitentiary grounds but not before being frisked first and my passport and plane ticket photocopied.

Thankfully, they don't find Charley's butt of Rolled
Gold in my garish weather-beater which I think
probably helped somehow. I'm warned not to bring
anything suspicious into the prison again and I promise him though I think he's being a little dramatic. I also get the distinct impression that I wouldn't be welcome either.

Disheartened but with a rekindled flame of excitement, I make a bee-line for The Red Herring theatre. It's my last chance to grant 45 his last wish.

Why is my new image of 45 becoming darker and darker?

21.
Slap me, Sooty

'Red Herring Theatre.'

I repeat it again to myself, reading the Gothic letters above the front door of the tiny theatre (more of a town-house) down a dead-end alleyway off Davis Street. It had taken me just a few minutes to find the place from the prison using the GPS on my iPhone.

'The Red Herring is down a dead end?' I hint to 45. 'Is somebody trying to tell me something?' I know this is another seminal moment I will cherish for the rest of my life. My waters are telling me that everything up until now has been foreplay: digging up a corpse … swelling on a flight … smuggling my balloon into the US … eating at McDonald's with other balloons … near-death experience at Anamosa prison: all just fingering me up for the grand finale.

'Should I go inside?' I ask my ailing balloon. Just looking at its ever-decreasing wrinkles tells me that that's probably a good idea.

A couple of schoolgirls giggle as they pass but it is water off a duck's back by now.

I need to compose myself, sit down and savour this moment of possible truth, and as luck has it, there's a bus-stop directly in front of the theatre. I cross the street and sit down. I gawp across at the red-brick building with old-style lanterns and stained-glass turret windows, almost tacky in nature. The Red Herring's current bill, going by the posters lining its wall, is a puppet-show from Prague which uses the elements of dark and light –

'You getting on or what?'

I hadn't spotted the bus that had pulled up and was waiting for me to climb on.

'Sorry, no. I'm just taking time out before –'

'Fucking *time-wasters!* The United States of America is full of fucking time-wasters!' The driver revs up the bus and belches smoke in my direction, temporarily obscuring my view of The Red Herring. When the fumes dissipate, it leaves a clear path to the theatre.

I take this as a sign...

With a shrinking scrotum, I approach The Red Herring with trepidation; as concerned about meeting Sooty as knowing the truth.

I climb three steps and push the entrance door but, to my inner delight, it's locked. I knock timidly and announce to my balloon, 'there's nobody in,' before I really give anybody inside a chance to answer. I bolt. *Be the Sleeping Dragon, Jonny...*

I can't outrun 45's voice inside my head. I skid to a stop, slap some sense into my face, and stoke the fire in my belly. I apologize to my birthday balloon for my moment of weakness and turn back.

I knock on the red stained-glass door again, regretting now not to be wearing fresh underwear for my epiphany but the communal bathroom of The Locker wasn't a place to go changing underwear. I make a mental note to stop off for some boxer-shorts.

A bothered female voice comes from within the theatre. 'Who's out there?'

I frown to myself and look at my balloon. What? Does it matter if I give her my name? I'm sure the owner of the female voice doesn't know me. 'Um, you don't know me. I'm Jonny.' That's a waste of information right there. My gut and waters tells me to hold out on my surname. 'Jonny Garfunkle.' Garfunkle? Jesus.

A brittle face comes to the stained-glass, changing from red to green to blue each time she moves. 'You're not violent, are you Jonny?' She could be pale for all I know.

I look at myself. 'No, I don't think so.'

No answer is coming back. I try to coax my right

hand into a half-fist to knock on the red stained-glass door again but fear has ceased me. Angry with myself, my nerves take over, co-ordination leaves the driving seat and I'm left drifting. I let fly with a left swing that catches me under the chin. As my fist grazes and rockets passed my chin, the person opens the door of The Red Herring ... and ducks when they see a fist coming fast in their general direction.

'Jesus Christ, are you cuh-razy, dude?! Anger Management!' The girl with fragile features homes in on my bloodied wrist bandage immediately. I'm right; she *is* pale. 'Are you one of those maniacs taking over our beautiful town? I bet you'd climb that tree across the street if I gave you a dollar.' She reaches into her pocket while I try telling her that it's just ketchup from McDonald's but she just goes, 'Yea, yea,' kind of like my brother Tommy in his karaoke act. She isn't having any of it, telling me that her daddy told her the same when they used to watch over 18 horror flicks together. 'You look crazy. Did you just try and hit yourself?!'

'I'm nervous.'

'Well, join the club!' She sparks up a cigarette and sucks down half of it.

'I guess I just froze up. It's literally a matter of life and death. You see, I'm about to unearth my grandfather. He left me a note in my birthday balloon...' I fill in all the blanks in a nervous rush, leading right up to an hour ago at Anamosa prison.

'I didn't get a word of that? What?' She eyes my balloon. 'RIP? Who's dead? Where did you say your grandfather is?'

The pretty girl with the fringe is confused. I can't go through all that again.

'In here.' I present 45 to her.

She raises her eyebrows in disrespect. 'Oh, here we go, one-act play, Jesus Christ. Let's take the piss of the arty-farty folk cos they're away with the fairies. We do puppet shows and Aladdin's Lamp when we're hard-up but existentialism isn't profit-bearing, Jonny. Intriguing pitch but please take your act elsewhere. Sooty would cack her 'tards if she knew what was going on here, s if we don't have enough problems. You're probably a good guy but we can't afford to back another show.' She makes to slam the door in my face but I slap my palm to the green pane and speak from the heart like a caged bird, just like 45 had always told me to do.

I can't help but notice that the young woman is dressed in a black bodice and ballet tutu, so I literally put tu and tu together. 'You've got the finesse of a Siamese cat and can spit just as far,' I mouth edgeways through the closing door, 'but I'd love to see you do the Swan Lake...'

The pressure subsides behind the door. I push and it gently gives way. The woman is standing there, in what seems to be an empty exhibition room. She holds my gaze before suddenly breaking into a pirouette and a series of mind and toe-bending tricks. She swirls around the room like a dervish before coming to a stop. 'I did a season with Bolshoi,' she pants. 'How astute of you, Jonny.'

Does she wear her ballet costume on a daily basis? 'Only one season?' I ask, using my emotional intelligence now. I don't care about open or close season at the Bolshoi. I'm just buttering her up for information. All this hands-on experience is invaluable when it comes to my future work as a private investigator. I've learned so much already during my quest.

'My grandmother Sooty needs somebody to make her mid-day snack. She's old and she doesn't have any other family. She used to tread the boards but she's lost her muse.'

'Ouch,' is all I can manage as a response. 'Listen, um...'

'Tiffany, everybody calls me Tiff.'

'As in lover's tiff?'

'Well, um, yes, I s'pose.'

'Tiff, this is not fantasy nor am I an actor even though people do tell me that I act the bollocks quite a bit.' Nothing like frothy humour to break the ice but she doesn't understand the word bollocks, I think. 'I need to speak to Sooty LeDanse.

'I love your surname. Sooty loves Simon Garfunkle. She's got all his Greatest Hits. Are you related?'

'We can have tea some day if you like, and I can tell you where the name originated and how. I'm a genealogy student as matter of fact. My journey to discover my grandfather will be the thesis for my P –'

'You must be from Ireland. You've got a sexy accent.'

'Thank you. I made it myself.' I embrace her silly little throw-away comment. 'Listen, how about that chat with Sooty? I need to know about this Candy character and my balloon's deflating by the hour and you don't want a ghost in the theatre.'

'Oh, yes we do! Bring on Slimer! We could do with the publicity. I'll give you a hundred dollars for the balloon right now.'

'Please, don't downgrade my grandfather to Slimer who was just ectoplasm.'

'Oops, my mistake. Sooty's upstairs in her dressing-room. I've just brought her tea.' She pulls a walkie-talkie from somewhere inside her tutu. 'I'll radio you up.' Only it isn't a walkie-talkie but a baby monitor. 'Somebody here to see you, Soots.'

'I'm drinking tea,' a deep dramatic voice answers back. 'You know what happens when Soots drinks her tea, Tiffs.'

'Yes, but he's brought his grandfather in a balloon.' She winks.

A pause. 'Oh, that's wonderful! I've always wanted to see Iowa City from the air. He can take us for a ride?

Maybe we can convince him to take us over the airport? Hmm? Check the fridge for scotch eggs, Tiffs, we can have a picnic.'

227

'Yes, a hot air-balloon, Soots, just for you. I bet you'd like to see Anamosa again, hmm, babes? Even the street outside, hmm?' Tiffany dramatically covers the mouth-piece. 'It's my dying wish to see Sooty outside her dressing-room again.'

I bet this one would get on really well with the Reiki Mistress. I can just picture the two of them, engaging in lesbian tendencies on Guinevere's bed of nails. The baby monitor in Tiffany's hand is silent before a long slurp breaks me from my stream-of-voyeurism. 'Send him up at once.'

Tiffany leads me down a carpeted hallway that takes us to the box-office. Next to the box-office is a lush ruby-red stage curtain. This is where we stop. I'm wondering what I'm doing standing in front of the curtain until she pulls it back with flair, revealing a doorway leading to a stairs like a secret passageway. I tell Tiffany that we should be pen-friends when all this is over and climb the stairs. My curiosity pricked, I ascend the stairs in the darkly lit hallway while my heart thumps hard in my temples. I make a mental note to lay off the junk food. At my heels, my big red balloon bounces up the steps in great strides. It has come alive and has an extra spring in its step, by Christ. It's smiling up at me like an old friend and I experience melting warmth as my ducts release tears of jaded joy. Finally, *finally*, it's all falling into place. I realize that this is a bit of a long shot, especially going by what I'd just heard on the baby monitor – Soots does sound vague. I reach the top of the stairs and trot along another hallway which confuses me because the Red Herring looks smallish from outside. A lingering smell lingers on the stairs which I can't put my finger on: mildew, boiled potatoes, and sweet perfume to hide the stale odours. And butane? Suddenly, I want to vomit. I duck my head into the nearest stage-prop and heave a dry gag until my ribs ache, and without wishing to be crude, a jet of semi-solid mass gushes my back passage and rushes my underpants; it's just as well that I didn't change after all. I expect that 45 feels an urge of pride seeing his determined grandson shit himself. Excuse me for my baseness but shit like this is imperative for my genealogy PhD. It's these minor details that make a PhD thesis a seriously-considered academic study. Without defecation, we fail to exist. (I'm thinking now that my touch of looseness could've been attributed to the home-made scrambled egg at Jacks')

At the end of the hallway, I find a white door with a large purple star emblazoned onto it. In the middle of the star is the name Sooty in theatrical italics. This is probably Sooty's dressing-room, I deduct.

I knock with a definite sense of purpose. The ghost of 45 stands behind me now,nudging at my spine. *Sleeping Dragon, singe monster ass...*

I'm about to come face to face with somebody who might know about this elusive Candy character, my lack of clean underwear is affecting me more than I had anticipated.

'Enter.' As I open the door, I half expect to see a large antique dark room with yellowing fabrics and a family of squabbling rats going for broke on the stale wedding cake, just like that Anamosa warden had said. Instead, I'm greeted by a bright room, heated with a Super-Ser heater with enough fumes in here to raise the dead. I steal a peek at my red balloon. Where is Miss Havisham? And then I see her; it's hard to miss her. In *Great Expectations*, Miss Havisham is a frail thin character.

Sooty LeDanse, however, is not Miss Havisham. It's hard to put an age on Sooty LeDanse because she is *gargantuan* with a capital *G* and fatness itself seems to have taken the edge off her age. She doesn't suffer from wrinkles as my balloon does because fat has filled her out to capacity and she spills over the armchair she's flopped in. This woman is colossal and she makes Brillo look like a woman suffering from a wasting illness. She's slumped in a

balding armchair, delicately poising a cup and saucer at her humongous breasts hidden inside a black silken kimono hand-woven by Chinese silkworms. I'm not sure where her breasts finish and her pelvis begins. Her stubby pinkie finger is pointing north-east but it doesn't make her look any daintier. She's wearing a nervous coat of make-up and there's a clear line of face-powder beginning at her triple-chinned jaw-line. Black-pearl lipstick overshoots her lips in spectacular fashion as does her smoky eye-shadow which has left most of Sooty in the shade. It's clear that she has given up the use of a mirror and I get the impression that the Super-Ser's noxious butane fumes are keeping ole' Sooty alive. The black ankle-length wavy dress with a single colourful belt about her equatorial hips and a pair of wonderfully grubby pink rabbit slippers just add to the overall effect. It's the belt that makes me want to laugh at this tragic figure. But it's the rhinestone belt that seems to be the one last fashion compliment that could possibly camouflage Sooty's enormous mid-riff and the last hint that she still has a flicker of a conscience. The Reiki Mistress had often commented on how women might wear
something in a certain way to offset 'a bump here or a
dip there.' The belt is stretched to capacity, rhinestones no longer identifiable, and has had numerous new holes punched into it during the years. The buckle is hanging onto its last hole and that is stretched beyond recognition. Tragic.

'That's me up there.' With a marvellous New Orleans accent, Sooty speaks deep and husky wheezes into her baby monitor while gesturing at the signed pictures and photographs lining the walls, mostly grainy black and
whites. Sooty's in all of them, dressed in various theatrical costumes with her signature Goth black and white make-up. I could say that she was a beautiful woman back then but she was even uglier then than now if that's possible, but she did have a good figure. I ponder what roles she might have played in children's fairy-tale pantomimes and don't

rule out the monsters and goblins and the role of general grotesquery. Sooty slurps tea in spectacular fashion and heaves her colossal frame. 'I used to tread the boards.'

Tread the boards implies nimbleness but now Sooty would go through the boards. 'Have you been drinkin', boy? You've got the head of a vagrant about you,' she croaks into her baby monitor. 'There was a time when I starred in a new production every three months at the Red Herring. I've treaded the boards over a million times, each time a new show.' She clocks my big red balloon for the first time through her tight spectacles and her beady eyes stay there.

'A million times?' The fumes are getting to me. I feel lightheaded and almost giggle. 'I need to ask you about somebody who might've been at Anamosa prison a long time ago. Perhaps, one of the last women inmates.'

'I don't have a head for heights anymore.' Sooty gazes idly at my balloon.

'Hot air is one thing this balloon doesn't have inside it. This is the balloon your grand-daughter Tiffany spoke about. You see, I'm carrying my grandfather's remains back here to Iowa.'

'How dare you.' In the same breath, Sooty points to the tea-pot on a tray by the make-up mirror. 'Help yourself to tea and condiments.'

I nod and thank her but no thanks. Being a person of the arts, I thought that Sooty would understand the noble concept. 'I don't have him in here for some sick joke. His soul is in here.' I say it with the sure conviction of an astrophysicist on the Discovery channel. 'Not only his soul but his living-dead breaths.' Why is having my loved one's spirit in a balloon so hard for people to identify with? 'We're taking the whole show on the road, getting back to basics, back to corn. But I have a message I want to deliver to a woman on his behalf before I finally lay him to rest,' I proudly smile, thinking she might appreciate the analogy with the bohemian life of the theatre.

231

'That poor bastard should be free to roam the boards wherever he chooses. You don't keep a lady of the night locked up in your bedroom, do you? No, you set her free in the morning. You must do as you say, boy, and set him free in the corn stalks.' Sooty is obviously thinking about her own decrepit soul and I briefly consider its size and dimensions. I feel a twinge of pity for this obese barrel of a woman. I consider her wide frame and momentarily judge the frame of the door I'm standing in. I did some furniture-removal part-time work around Limerick city and county when I was younger and I've developed a keen eye for such matters. There's no way Sooty LeDanse is leaving this dressing-room. This is where she will spend the rest of her life; this dressing-room is Sooty's mausoleum. Sooty's grown quiet, nodding in a vacant way while staring longingly at her Super-Ser.

'Yes, corn,' Sooty mumbles into her baby monitor. 'Who is this lady-friend you speak of?'

Potential time-bomb...

A very hazy memory rises up out of the fog of my subconscious. Clinical Dad is telling Vera that he will never let a Super-Ser inside 128 Hydrangea Drive because it is a "potential time-bomb." The only time-bomb was him.

'Sorry, yes. I need to get in touch with a woman who might've been at the prison and who might've known my grandfather. That's a lot of ifs...'

Sooty flaps her great hands in front of her. 'That'll be difficult. Anamosa hasn't had any women for years.'

I reach for the photograph of my grandfather's dead buttocks and pass it to Sooty who struggles to focus, comically scrunching up her nose and frowning like the mother of all hobgoblins. She doesn't give me a chance to give the name of the woman in the tattoo because her beady black eyes open wide in shock. 'I've seen this snapshot before!' She gawps at me. '*Candy!* Poor, poor Candy Dufraine! Where did you get this, boy? *Where?*' she bellows.

'Dufraine?' I say aloud to myself, rolling around the name in my head. 'Are you telling me that you know her? Candy 1010 Dufraine? That was her surname?'

'Uh-huh, t'was her surname till she tied the knot then undid the knot and changed her name back when her no-good husband did a runner.'

The heat from the Super-Ser suddenly intensifies.

'Not personally, son, but my daddy was a guard over at the clink and he knew her. I remember him telling me stories at night while I sat on his knee in front of the open fire. Daddy always maintained that Candy was a good lady who just lost her way. Anybody who knows anything about the prison will have heard of Candy 1010; 1010 was her cell number and that's where she did it, of course.' She seizes me in her wily gaze. 'Where did you get the photo, boy?'

Looks like the oriental orthodontist's hunch had been right. I brace myself. 'Where she did what? What?'

Sooty LeDanse holds me in her stare. 'Why are you so interested in Candy?'

'I want to pass on a message from a man who once knew her.'

I point to my balloon. 'My grandfather as matter of fact. I'm not sure how they knew each other but the message is in here for her.'

'Well, you'll need a clairvoyant to read it cos ole' Candy's dead, son, gone the way of the truth.'

The silence that follows Sooty's revelation presses in on my ears. I'm utterly flummoxed and flummoxed is not a word I use lightly. 'You mean that I'm too *late?*' I think of that old crackpot who had approached me after burying 45 up on the hill. The one who asked me if I would like to speak to any of the cemetery's dead. I could use her services, right now. Maybe 45 would like to come forth and explain things over a coffee.

'Been dead for an age, boy. Long time before you were

born. She was one of the last women to be behind bars up at the penitentiary. For a finish, she served her time but was too afraid to live life on the outside. By that stage, the prison only housed male inmates so Candy was wastin' her time committin' any petty crime to stay inside the safe walls of Anamosa prison but the authorities had grown a likeness for ole' Candy down through her stint and gave her a payin' job in the laundry.'

'What was her crime?'

'She robbed banks and any institution that held money. Things got messy when they shot a police-officer in Dubuque and that pegged on the years for Candy. They raised hell, them two, whooh! You've heard of Bonnie and Clyde?'

I nod, unable to process Sooty's barrage of new information. Bank robberies?

'Well, Candy and her partner-in-crime were the original Bonnie and Clyde. They just weren't as well-known cos Hollywood didn't make a movie about their exploits. They should've done for the sheer originality of their crimes.' She flicks her baby monitor.

Tiffany answers on the other end. 'Yes, Grammy?'

'Tiffs, bring me some toast croutons to dip in my tea.'

'Why?' I ask.

'Cos I like 'em soggy.'

'No, why were these two an original couple?'

'Anybody can rob a bank but not everybody can get away with it, and they did, for six months they worked mid-America. But the genius of their rampage was not violence but how they went about it. It turns out that Candy's other half was a stage hypnotist, and he would lull bank-tellers into um, a false sense of security. Boy but the women did love him. He was no Jonny Weissmuller but he had a magnetic quality to him that drew you into him. He never chose a male bank teller, always women to put under his spell. He worked the stage most of his life though I never had the opportunity to have him perform here which is one of my regrets. In a nutshell, this guy was an A-list actor who just took the less conventional route. He hid inside more Russian dolls than a closet drag.'

Why now, do I recall how 45 worked the crowd as he sang *I Did It My Way* with such natural ease? I refuse to allow my train of thought to proceed down this lane. Pokerfaced, I ask, 'How did she die? Candy, I mean.'

'I was gettin' to that when you stopped me with your impertinence. Topped herself in her cell, poor dear. Get this: she ended her life in her cell but she was no longer a prisoner by then but she'd worked up a relationship with some of those wardens and they let her stay in her cell whenever it was free like some kinda stray. Candy was *that* afraid of leaving her cell.'

Candy committed suicide? Not for the first time on this quest I stare at my balloon and realise that I only know a small part of 45. I look for a chair to sit down on but there isn't one. I never knew Candy; a fleeting character in my life so I can't understand the grief that weakens me. I can't believe she's gone. She's still living in the photograph. It all seems like a terrible mistake. She took her own life in one deadly final desperate act. What had led her to such a sad end?

And then, as if reading my thoughts, ole' Sooty answers me. 'Candy finished her life cos she gave up hope after the man she loved never came back to save her. Candy worked the laundry – dirty sheets, etcetera. She took one of those sheets and hung herself out to dry in cell1010. That was the same cell where she married her man fifteen years earlier – partner-in-crime – and spent half a life-time waiting for him to never return.' Sooty stares into the Super-Ser, shaking her head gravely while idly slurping at her tea. 'They got married in 1010. They brought the groom over from the men's wing, surrounded by a wall of nervous guards. T'was in all the papers at the time; a regular celebrity couple for all the wrong reasons, after all, these people were law-breakers and killers, mistaken or

otherwise. Mama always said that you cannot be innocent
if you've got the gun that kills the man, no matter how the
bullet kills him. An Irish priest pronounced 'em man and
wife them in Candy's cell. The ironic thing is that her new
husband used those laundry sheets to scale the wall an'
have it off on his toes sheets; the same sheets that Candy
would hang herself off in time.'

'What was his name?'

'Father Mick O'Connor or something Irish – maybe just
Mick. How the hell would I know?'

I try to conceal my concern. 'No, I mean,' I falter,
close my eyes before opening them again and breathe
deep through my nostrils. The fumes go to my head and
maybe it's better this way, 'the name of her husband?
Candy's partner-in-crime?'Please, God, don't let it be –

'45.'

Somebody's just nudged me out over a cliff...

'Everybody called him by his nickname, 45. Denny
Rowe was his real name.'

The world slows down by five revolutions. I repeatedly
lip-synch the number that comes from Sooty LeDanse's
lips in a deaf void. The room grows washy. I lock against
my legs from running and manage to sit on the floor.

'I knew you'd been drinkin', boy!'

'Huh?'

'Well, d'ya want to know or not?'

'Uh-huh...'

'They nicknamed him 45 after the shoot-out; the
police knee-capped him with a bullet at a hayseed bank
over in Dubuque. T'was the same policeman that Candy
accidentally shot. She claimed that the sight of 45 takin' a
bullet had made her jump and accidentally sent a wild
bullet through the policeman's gullet. Uh-huh, some say
t'was God punishin' 'em for their sins cos every time 45
limped it was the scourge of that dead policeman's baton
upon his tainted soul. The papers played word-games with
her surname: Death Rowe and suchlike. Candy and 45 still

managed to make a get-away but that was the last of their shenanigans.'

Jesus of Nazareth. 'So 45 didn't lose his knee in some war?'

'Huh? 45 never spent a day in soldier's uniform. He wasn't the kind of chap to take orders. 45 was a stage hypnotist. *What ya' see isn't always what ya' get* was his line at the time. It became sort've a catch-phrase; everybody was usin' it.'

LeDanse pauses for me to respond but I'm temporarily out of order. Is this the same old man who used to shit in the acorn pot and sit on our back doorstep all day waiting for a non-existent bus? I recall 45 wandering aimlessly about the house but coming to life when he saw Brillo's pudgy ass doing the truffle-shuffle up our stairs. Had it all been one big hoax? Had the old man hypnotised us all?

'45 used his talents to, shall we say, remove money from whatever institution Candy and him had decided to visit. Technically, they never stole a penny. That's the tragedy behind all of this. It was brilliance but things came to a head when a police-officer came snoopin' 'round. She pleaded innocent in the courthouse here in town but was found guilty of manslaughter but the damage was done, as they say. Some say the police officer came to her at night through her cell bars and sent her into near delirium. Poor old Candy was in and out of the psychiatric ward more times than a trucker visits a whorehouse. 45 never came back for her and she lost hope but,' Sooty looks around the room with a hint of conspicuousness, 'I think it was the child that did most of the damage.' She almost whispers *child* for fear of being heard.

Jesus of Nazareth. 'Child?' I hear my voice, minute in the distance.

I drop my birthday balloon onto the linoleum floor, dangerously close to the Super-Ser. I quickly fetch it back and offer an apology. I'm struggling to take all this in. 45

was *Vera's* father and she doesn't have brothers or sisters. That's really narrowing down things. I hold my breath. 'What was the girl's name?'

And I'm already saying Vera's name as LeDanse confirms my suspicions.

'Vera...'

Now, any possibility of doubt has gone sailing out the window along with my rose-tinted image of 45.

Sooty nods, grinding her gums. 'They had a bouncin' baby girl during their bank-robbin' rampage – a love-child if ever there was one. She was taken up for adoption by a dodgy foster-house for homeless children in Iowa City. 45 kidnapped his own daughter the night he broke out of Anamosa and neither hide nor hair was ever seen of him or the girl again. Of course, 45 and the girl have been spotted in...'

Wait a minute, this can't be right. My mother, who battled cancer and won, is the love-child of a couple of famous outlaws? That's where she gets her feisty spirit? I come from a family of AWOL celebrity bank-robbers! I'm stunned, speechless, but Sooty LeDanse is an out-of-control freight train with a cargo of lost information. It seems as if she's been here all this time, waiting in the killing-fumes to relay this message to me.

'...New York City and Timbuktu – sometimes on the same day,' Sooty goes on. '45 and Candy have become the stuff that legends are made of.' Her face darkens and I'm sure I see a pin-prick of blush rise in her wizened cheeks. 'If I get my hands on that chicken-shit, I'd wring his scrawny neck. Okay, give him his due: he worked the banks beautifully but never leave a man behind as they say in the forces.'

I look at the meagre sickly balloon nestled between my knees. It's certainly pale in comparison, literally and metaphorically, to the corker of a story that Sooty's just spun me. I remain dumb and mute as Sooty LeDanse hits me with one killer final blow of information.

'I get some consolation in knowing that 45 never knew about his son.'

Bang!

'What?!' I steal a glimpse at my balloon and ask it the same question. Vera has a *brother? A brother?!*

Now things are really starting to get weird...

'Where are my goddamn croutons?!' LeDanse screams into the baby monitor resting on her expansive chest, startling me from my stupor.

Tiffany's meek voice crackles from Sooty's gadget.

'I burnt the first batch, sorry. Two minutes.'

'My, my, that girl. Now where was I? Oh, yes, Ole' Candy had a child in prison, exactly nine months to the day after they hauled 45 and Candy in for trial. Tests proved that the boy was 45's but 45 had up shot 'n left six months before the baby's head appeared.' Sooty LeDanse chuckles to herself, 'a regular telly-novella. Course, the baby was taken for adoption and Candy was left with nothin' but stretch marks 'n a broken heart.'

I find myself sneaking a peek at the lady in the photograph on 45's ass. The hint of anger in her face had dispersed and now I can see that it's melancholic. If Sooty's story is to be believed, this Candy character is my *grandmother?* Then who the hell was Nan? Did Nan ever exist? She conveniently fell on her lover's buzz-saw at the timber mill in Old Castle. A wonderfully implausible death to stop us asking questions about Nan because, sometimes, truth is stranger than fiction. I've never met her. Come to think of it, nobody has ever met her; like I've said: hand-me-down memories. Another word for that could be brainwashing.

'Is it any wonder that she lost her way?'

'Did the son disappear also?'

'No, sir, Denny Rowe Jnr runs a second-hand car dealership out on Cemetery Road – just up the road from where Candy lies in state. Look the opposite way if Denny Rowe Jnr tries to sell you one of his death-traps.

Unsavoury character; gotta chip on his shoulder. Kept the name of his father, more to sell cars than anything else but what else has he got? Certainly not the money. He's become something of a local celebrity cos of his connections.'

'Junior?'

'Personally, I think he kept the name and added Junior to convince himself that he's not a bastard child.

Kind've a psychological thing. He wants to feel loved by the man who ran out on him.'

Maybe this Denny Rowe Junior and I can swop notes. 'Does he know he has a sister?' My loss of identity is beginning to fill up big-time. I literally feel myself clicking into place like a human Tetris. But does it have to be so dramatic? I know more about my family now than I have ever done (if Sooty is to be believed and why would she lie when she doesn't know about my connection to 45) but this is exasperating because now it seems the more I know the *less* I know. For the first time, my findings seem to go beyond my PhD genealogical thesis. My PhD doesn't seem much to me now. This is blood and guts, not a piece of paper.

'He knows that he has a sister – *everybody* knows he has a sister as well as knowing that his crook of a father took her *and* the money and ran like a jack-rabbit on a dune. It's no good knowing you have a sister if she falls off the face of the planet. He'll never know her and she'll never know him and things are better that way in Sooty LeDanse's book.'

I have to get out there. I've got to tell Denny Rowe Jnr – my uncle – all about his long-lost sister. 'Wait a minute, what money?'

'The money.'

My vacant expression must be evident.

'Holy cow, the money, boy, the goddamn *money*. Isn't that what all this is about? You and your buddies want to find the treasure?'

'I've no idea what you're talking about. I just came here to ask if you know where Candy is so I can deliver her this message from, um, an old friend of hers.'

'Candy and 45's stolen money. Nobody ever found a dime. They stashed the cash but when 45 ran out on Candy she informed the authorities where the cash was hidden out of spite, in some hay-barn along the old Dubuque road, between here and Cedar Rapids.

Treasure-hunters searched the place up and down but nothing ever came of it. It became one of them, whatyamacallem, urban legends.'

I probably passed it on my way here in the party bus, I ponder through a vague haze. I have come here to complete my PhD thesis on my grandfather but I've discovered an unknowing species of family tree. I will be awarded special merit from Trinity College Dublin! These crazed notions flit through my mind with all the other endless possibilities and revelations. I stare at my crumpling red balloon for some time with eyes out on stalks. The more I gawp in disbelief, the redder 45 seems to become. I'll take this up with him later.

'Of course, 45 had taken the money: a clean sweep, the girl and the money.'

Vera!

Now it all makes sense...

Vera had been digging up 128 when I left. The money!

OMG! She was looking for the *money!* I have a cramping itch to ring Charley but now Sooty's regarding me with increasing suspicion.

'Now, for the last time, where did you get this photo?' She holds the photograph impossibly close to her nose. 'This looks like cleavage of some kind.' Sooty isn't as senile as she looks. 'Is that an ass crack or an elbow crease?' Her lips jitter as she studies the picture a little harder. 'This is a buttock! Boy, I know a buttock when I see one! The tattoos are well documented! She had a tattoo of him on her ass and vice-versa – his 'n hers – in some

warped way of declaring their undying love for each other.'
Sooty heaves herself out of her rattan armchair that I see
for the first time. The chair creaks and groans as she drags
herself upwards, pulling herself onto the worn-down heels
of her pink rabbit slippers. She crosses the room
under two warped walking sticks. The floorboards
creak as she shuffles passed me and pulls an old book with
a fading red cover from an expansive library which I also
haven't seen until now, so engrossed in LeDanse's story.
She picks out the book with some difficulty then jiggles as
she waddles back to her rattan armchair and drops back
into it. She heaves and pants as she beckons the photograph
from me. She holds out her hand and inflects her voice as if
trying to convince a toddler to do something he doesn't
want to do. 'Let's see how genuine this really is. Just stand
back and give us some light here.' Sooty comes alive
somehow and the eagerness in her flabby body-language is
frankly sobering. At first, I refuse to hand over the
photograph but, on the other hand, if I don't show Sooty
the evidence I will never know if my grandfather is the
same outlaw, despite the consequences.

Gulping down on a dry throat, I hand over the
photograph. She scrutinizes it with the photo in her book
which I see is a scrap-book, full of black and white articles
and photographs about Anamosa prison down through the
years. Sooty sifts through the pages with surprisingly agile
fingers despite their sausage quality. Her nails have been
chewed down to stubs. You can tell a lot about a person,
just by looking at their nails.

'Ah-ha!'

I angle myself to see a black and white mug-shot of
Vera only I do a double-take, realizing that it's *Candy* in
the photograph. How had I not seen the uncanny likeness
before now? Her face passes from my photo to the one in
her scrap-book numerous times before she gawps up at me,
all glaring and panic-stricken. LeDanse hauls her obese
frame closer to the Super-Ser. Something comes alive in

her bloated face and she searches her creases for her baby monitor. 'This is an *abomination!*' She tails off, shaking her head gravely, muttering gibberish. Fury and saliva unexpectedly unexpectedly burst forth from Sooty. 'A travesty!! This is the original buttocks! She had him branded to her ass and took him to her grave and he had her branded to his behind!' All the while, her fingers search her creases for the baby monitor. 'Where did you find this buttocks, boy!? Where has the chicken-shit been hidin' all this time?' she snarls. Now I see that her remaining teeth are tea-stained, adding to the overall effect. 'How did you say you know that son of a bitch?' There's a minute silence before her lower jaw comes unhinged. 'Your grandfather? That's what you said! You drunkard!'

I try confusing her but Sooty's been waiting for me all her life in her dressing room like a sleeping dragon spouting butane fumes...

'45 is your *grandfather?!*' She spits and hisses vehemently, covering me in spittle from a distance of three feet. Her turkey jowls all aquiver. She locates the baby monitor somewhere along her midriff. 'Tiffs? *Tiffs!?*'

Tiffs comes back on the line. 'On my way up, Grammy. I've buttered your croutons...'

'Hold off on the goddamn croutons! Bring a telephone, Tiffs!'

I try to intervene again. 'No, let me explain, he, he died a few days ago.' I don't go into how I possess a photo of 45's rump. (God forgive me.) 'I've got his remains in my balloon, look if you don't believe me.' I briefly hold up my balloon to the overhead lights,
showing her the vacuum inside and the outline of 45's hand-written message.

What happens next is difficult to word: perhaps a minute's silence or a shock-gap in time would suffice.

Sooty screams, 'reincarnation!!' then moans, stutters, and grunts as she gets to her feet that seem ready to burst from her pink rabbit slippers. Her blue varicose veins pop up like tributaries on a 3D map and her whole body wobbles like a human jelly, good God. I tell her to relax but she makes one thunderous jolt towards me, arms outstretched like something from a B horror movie. I swipe my balloon out of harm's way as her humongous frame shunts passed me, wheezing. Sooty straightens up and makes another desperate dive for my birthday balloon, going *'baaagh!'* bleating like a lost old goat as she comes billowing at me, all raised arms and jiggling chicken fat.

'Now, hang on a minute...' I take a quick step back through the doorway and into the hallway until my back is against the wall on the opposite side of her open door. I hold my big red balloon as far from her grasping claws as I can. She bears down on me, kimono billowing, and all I can do is squeeze my eyes shut and dream of having a simple life again, back at the bong-house at 128 Hydrangea Drive with Charley, even Brillo is invited. I await her wrath, soiling myself for a second time.

A hysterical series of grunts prompts me to peep, just in time to see the behemoth jam in the doorway. 'Ugh! You can't kill the devil! Buaagh!' Sooty LeDanse's chewed fingers reached out at me like tentacles, only inches from my birthday balloon. Sooty heaves her morose torso but the more she writhes the more stuck-fast she becomes. Ugly sinewy tendons begin to break out on her neck and her glasses slip down her nose and hang sideways on her face.

I know it will be the falling glasses that I will remember later, nothing else, just like 45's lop-sided party hat. Her tongue lolls in and out in crude sickly fashion as she inhales and exhales a tearing, agonizing cackle. Her calves stop pushing her forward and cave beneath her, lodging her giant trunk in the door-frame. To my astonishment, the doorframe keeps LeDanse suspended in some amazing trickery of gravity and physics.

I sit there on the hallway linoleum with my back against the wall, literally, and 45 clutched to my chest or I am clutched to 45? Sooty LeDanse lays suspended above me, held in a perpetual attack stance. Her uncanny long blue-grey tongue swings limp from the corner of her mouth like a dead trout and I morbidly imagine it touching the tip of her nose. It was probably one of her many party-pieces.

'Bravo!' My brain tries persuading me that she's just acting out an old routine she used to do at the Red Herring, terrifying the children as some grotesque genie in Aladdin's Lamp. I clap and ask for an encore with a demented smile but her dead eyes only gaze through me. Such a strong and convincing performance – a dramatic stage exit. My nerves encourage me to continue speaking to Sooty even though I know she's dead. She had saved her last dance for me. In a delirium, I go to grab 45's streamer but realize that it had floated back into Sooty's dressing-room during the fracas. What's 45 trying to tell me now? What oblique message is he sending me from wherever he is? I don't think that there's much left to tell. I'm yet to digest Sooty's information, God rest her soul.

I curse fluently in a whisper, knowing the only way back into Sooty's dressing-room is to go through the fork of her legs … and didn't Tiffany say she was on her way up?

There's no other way around it but through it so I fall to my knees and clamber through Sooty's limp colossal calves, grimacing as I squat and crawl commando-style. God only knows what lies above me. I edge on past Sooty's pink rabbit slippers caught in an eternal ballet dance. Life is a series of epiphanies and defining moments and this is to be one of them because I make the mistake of looking upwards…

I don't know why I peer above me, maybe deep-seated curiosity; I had once seen a giant pair of granny knickers at a street-market in Toledo, Spain, while on a cheap weekend away with Charley (Ryanair; no taxes). The image had stayed with me for months afterwards. I look upwards through the hem of Sooty's dressing gown to see her knickers, only, Jesus of Nazareth, she isn't wearing any. My stomach turns. At first, my eyes don't, well, work.

245

My gut's telling me to look away, Jon, for the love of God, keep your eyes on the deflating balloon but it's too late.

Not to offend, I sometimes resort to everyday idioms and expressions to sum up a situation where my written skills lack. My idiom of choice for this particular scenario is: *a close shave*. Sooty LeDanse's undercarriage genuinely intrigues me. I beg to ask the posthumous question to Sooty: why at this stage of your life when you seem to have left everything else go to seed?

I debate whether including this scene in my PhD thesis diary or pretend that it never took place. I could easily just relay how I go back into the dressing room, grab the balloon, and leave. I could erase the ghastly episode but on second thoughts, I decide that little details make up people's personalities and people make genealogical history of character. Taking this self-explanatory equation into mind, I have decided to include the horrible image which will never leave me.

I grab my balloon and, sick to the stomach, discreetly tip-toe back down the musty hallway while my brain tries to convince me that I'm not tip-toeing to flee the scene of a crime but being considerate of others who may have been sleeping at five or six o'clock or whatever it is in the evening. My waters say otherwise.

I sprint down the hallway on the balls of my feet, like I've invented a new Olympic sport. I get to the top of the stairs and trip myself up and tumble down the stairs, head-over-heels.

Of course I do...

Instinct takes over and prompts me into huddling 45's soul-bubble tight into m chest. I would've learned the same technique in the army.

As I crash down the stairs, Tiffany comes up the stairs to meet me. She screams but I tell her, as I roll, that I'm just going to use the bathroom, 'I've an upset stomach...' which is true, don't forget that I've already soiled myself twice. From my upside-down position, I notice that Tiffany is carrying a plate of croutons. Good, she hadn't heard Sooty's telephone request. That will buy me a minute or two extra.

I hit the bottom of the stairs hard and keep rolling three or four meters more before falling apart, splayed to the four points of the compass. I get to my feet and check behind me to see that Tiffany isn't concerned. She isn't; she's continued upstairs to Sooty. She has no leads on me. My waters had been right to introduce myself as Jonny Garfunkle.

I leave the Red Herring in a daze.

How has all this happened so suddenly?

45's roped me in to be his new partner-in-crime just by handing me a red balloon for my birthday. All alone in a strange old theatre in the middle of the United States, chasing a red deflating balloon beneath a knickerless dead obese woman lodged in a door frame. 'Where to next, 45?'

My balloon doesn't reply but it's leading me down paths I would've never ventured nor dreamt of while biding my time at 128, literally, I'm walking down a dead-end alleyway. Yet, my sense of identity has never been stronger. It seems that 45's identity is beginning to spill over onto me, somehow filling up my wanting chakras and Qi energy sources, plus how can I forget my astral projection. But I fear where my balloon will take me next ...

... but I already know where I have to go next.

22.
Two Juniors for the Price of One

I leave the Red Herring and flee down the dead-end alley, literally, realizing that I'd turned left instead of right when I exited the theatre's front stained-glass door. My waters had told me that the dead-end was ominous but initially I had supposed that it was a metaphor for not finding any information on this Candy character which has turned out to be a hilarious blunder on my part; I've gotten more information than I can deal with right now. No, the dead-end has turned out to be Sooty LeDanse's dead-end.

I skip fifty meters before the blank wall stops me. Cursing and swearing to beat the band, I grow sweaty and nervous all over again knowing that I have to pass the goddamn theatre yet again. I come to a halt like a regular idiot in a dead-end alleyway, wondering if anybody's watching me. I walk into the wall and kiss it before turning back because in a way, it is a day of wailing, and that has to be recognized.

Whistling and gazing everywhere except at the theatre; this is how I pass the building, trying to look inconspicuous but looking *very* conspicuous. So I fall back into my play-retard mode where I metamorphose into a physically disabled person and I hate myself for doing it and vaguely wonder why I'm even doing it. It's becoming a dangerous trigger-impulse in stressing situations. Cemetery Road is on the outskirts of town, about four or five streets from here. I contemplate taking a taxi but determine that it should take ten minutes or so to reach Cemetery Road. I need to save money. I still haven't bought my return ticket and my funds are down to no more than two and a half grand. How I have spent the guts of Clinical Dad's money is beyond me. The only solace I take from this is that this money is going to a good cause. I cannot think of spending it on anything else.

On the trot, I shake off my disability like Forrest Gump

and break into an all merciful power-walk down Davis
Street, passing Booth, Ford, Garnavillo, and Walworth
strats with an extra spring in my step and a crick in my
neck from constantly looking over my shoulder. I've lost
track of time but I know it is Saturday and the sky is
beginning to bruise. I carry my wilting balloon safely in the
crook of my arm. We are both tired and exhausted. By
now, my big red balloon is half of its original birthday
dimensions and, to my bitter-sweet knowledge, I know that
45 has left a piece of him *everywhere* we have passed
through on this life and death-altering excursion. Who
knows, maybe 45 and LeDanse are sharing transcendental
croutons right now. Yes, I can just imagine where Sooty is
shoving those croutons about now.

With a pounding heart, I ring Charley and tell him
everything. 'My quest had seemed so simple but it's
becoming complicated and *dark*. Then again, I've always
had a fear of second-hand car dealers after Clinical Dad
bought the sky-blue Cortina. The only thing that ever
worked was the seat and that sits in the bong-house right
now in another galaxy.'

Dead air eats up considerable phone credit by the time
Charley responds. He senses my fear coming down the line,
I know it. He tells me that he's actually sitting in the
Cortina seat. He also tells me off for having ditched the
relatively straight-forward programme of releasing 45
amongst ears of corn and finding this Candy character to
relay 45's undying wish. He finishes by telling me to, 'drop
off the damn balloon anywhere seeing as there's no corn
this time of year. I told you that the Jolly Green Giant was
a serious option and you wouldn't listen to me. The only
place you'll find corn now is at the supermarket, Jonny. Let
it go, Jon. Just like dropping off a dog.'

My God, Charley's lucid and has actually listened to me
for once in his life. 'Show some compassion.'

'Don't go near this second-hand car dealer, Jonny.
You've succeeded in finding Candy. You can't tell her

anything cos she's dead, ditto, so drop the balloon off at the nearest doorstep and come the fuck *home*. Quest complete, good luck and thanks. You've already said that Vera doesn't know that she's got a brother and this car-dealer guy doesn't know where his sister is so why open old wounds?'

'There's an old Chinese proverb…'

Charley complains, 'Oh, here we go.'

'… that goes something like: it takes a wise man to know when to let go a rising balloon.'

'Maybe now's the time to let go? Hint, hint. Break a leg, even two, but it's worth it in the long-run, Jonny.'

'Cha, my waters are advising me to strike while the iron's hot and tell Denny Rowe Jnr – my new uncle – about his sister this very evening; *I'd* want to know if it was me. If I mull it over in a strange bed in an even stranger motel then I'd probably let bygones be bygones and get the next flight out of Iowa but I'm in too deep now and I know that I will regret it for the rest of my life if I don't do the right thing and close this door before opening any others. I've come this far, Cha, and I intend to put all these ghosts to bed. Don't you think 45's son has a right to know about his father and long-lost sister? I'm doing this for 45 too. He hadn't known about his son.' I hadn't thought about this. I look at my pathetic balloon and tears well in my eyes. What a waste. Now it's too late. I'm just too late for everything, including the goddamn corn.

'You don't know this individual, Jonny. How's he going to react? Hmm? By the way, you're on speaker.'

'*What?!*'

'Say hi to the miss, to um, miss Guinevere.'

The Reiki Mistress's squeaky tones take over. 'What address did you say this second-hand dealer is at?'

'What are you doing at the bong-house?' frowning at my iPhone. 'What's the address got to do with anything?'

'*Where*, Jonny?'

Now I know what she's getting at. 'Cemetery Road.

Why?'

'Babes, you're going to Cemetery Road and you're putting ghosts to bed? Is this not a harbinger of doom, Jon?'

'No, it's just coincidence.' I must admit that I do sense the ominous signs. I don't mention that Cemetery Road intersects with Elm Street – that *would* be a nightmare. 'I'm coming to the end of my adventure and it's fitting that it should be on Cemetery Road.'

'Pardon my French but this, *this*, is a fuck-ing omen, Jonny, if ever I've seen one. *O-men*. Make sure you come back from Cemetery Road, that's all I'm saying, babe.' There's shuffling on the phone and I'm handed back to Charley. I know this because I've got silence save for a long hit and exhale into my ear from 5000 or something miles off. 'Get out before it's too late.'

'Cha, you're spending too much time with Brillo.'

'Oh, I'm not spending any time with Brillo. She was sent back to Eastern Europe.'

'What?'

'Vera presented her with a necklace from Claire's and sent her back to wherever she came from.'

I'd gotten used to seeing her around the house. 45 loved to chase her. Should I read that in a different light now too? He was probably enjoying the charade. I was just getting used to Brillo and I'll miss her in an odd way. 'Why?'

'Well, 45's not around anymore for one and I think Vera needs the money.'

I'd purposefully omitted the money side of Sooty's story. But now I don't see any reason to keep it from Charley or the Mistress so I tell them about the hidden treasure.

All Charley can muster up is garbled gibberish of excitement.

'This doesn't pass any one of us for now.'

'Why didn't 45 tell Vera where the money is?' asks the Mistress.

'Maybe the old man died before he had time to tell Vera where the money is.'

'But why hadn't he told her all along?' asks Charley. 'He had forty-something years or more to do it.'

And now the pieces of the puzzle are staring to fall into place. 'Isn't it funny how Clinical Dad turned up –'

'...as Ronald McDonald...'

'...just when 45 died? He asked me for a loan and suddenly he's at 128 with dirty red clown shoes and a muddy clown costume.'

'The bastard came back for the money. What a fucking low-life, Jonny. He knew all along. Sorry. Vera and Ron were digging for treasure while we were digging –'

'Stop!' Deep breaths. 'Let's not jump to conclusions.'

The Reiki Mistress opines that the money could be anywhere – if there is any money. 'Don't you think all of this is a leap of faith, circumstantial, like?'

'It's all I've got and Sooty wasn't talking through her arse because we've both seen Vera acting weird since 45 died. Digging holes where she wouldn't normally dig holes, etcetera.'

The Reiki Mistress butts in by commenting that the grieving process takes many forms.

'Digging holes in the front lawn?' I ask, repeating it again for emphasis. 'No, Vera's looking for the money that 45 and Candy lifted from those banks, cool 'n calculated.' I can't believe that I'm actually using these words in relation with my own mother. 'What sickens me is that she allowed that low-life into our house to dig with her in unison. I've got to sort this shit out and then sort out my home shit.'

There's a pause before Charley's frantic voice comes on the line. 'I'm gonna get my shovel! I left it in the bong-house after we dug up – '

That familiar prickly feeling of shame and embarrassment heats me up from inside again. I hang up before Charley says anything else incriminating in front of the Mistress. Despite the freezing cold, I take off my rainbow weather-beater because Vera had told me that I will never get lost wearing it. My objective now is just that, to mingle and merge as we say in the business.

'Why didn't you *tell* me?!' I yell at my balloon, crossing a zebra-crossing on Walworth Street. 'Fucking hell!! You let me walk into that place and you knew Sooty was waiting, didn't you! She'd been waiting for us all her life!'

A lollipop man asks me to curb my language in front of his children. As he does, an ambulance rockets right between us on the zebra crossing, going in the direction that I'd just come from. No doubt, to prize Sooty from her ethereal perch. Thank Christ I'd removed my weather-beater. I ask the lollipop man directions to Cemetery Road but he's too busy throwing his fist plus a barrage of obscenities at the passing vehicle. I let the lollipop man in peace and check my iPhone for directions on GPS instead.

* * *

Ten minutes out along Cemetery Road, I spot an enormous flashing sign rising high into the horizon. As I loom closer I see a couple of upended luxury cars on each end of a sign advertising *Denny Rowe Junior's Quality Second-Hand Cars* that looks more like it's advertising a local brothel. Fear suddenly grips me and sticks me to Cemetery Road. I'm at the entrance to the yard but my waters and gut are holding me back. *Turn back, Master,* they whisper inside my head, sounding a lot like Brillo. For the first time in my life, I decide to over-ride my instinct. That man in there needs to know where his sister is and Vera needs to know that she has a brother. I refuse to have this on my conscience. This reunion will also reunite 45's spirit with his estranged family. Thus, he will rest in peace.

I pass beneath the flashing sign Junior probably uses to dazzle potential clients. I see a kid, twelve or thirteen years old, wearing fluffy green ear-muffs and cycling around in circles on an old Chopper bicycle only he's got the big wheel on the front plus the trademark handlebars with the traditionally smaller front wheel on the back. The result is that the kid's chopping his ass around the yard. He catches me off-guard and I chuckle to myself despite impending circumstances.

'I'm looking for Denny Rowe Junior.' I've realized that I'm gripping my balloon so tight that it's being downgraded to a balloon animal. 'Is he around?'

There's no turning back now.

The kid pedals a few tight circles before falling off the Chopper and chopping his ass on the frozen yard. 'Which one?' he asks, kneading his buttocks.

'There are *two* Denny Rowe Juniors?' How can this be? Is that possible?

Sooty didn't mention anything about this.

'Papa and I share the same name only I'm Junior Junior or J.J. for short.'

The kid speaks quite well, too well to be surrounded by burnt oil and scrap iron. This is hilarious.

'Where do you come from, sir? You speak with a funny dialect. And what's with the balloon? Who died?'

With mixed feelings, I realize that this kid J.J. is, for want of a better word, my first cousin. Jesus of Nazareth, I'm discovering a whole new civilisation here. This quest has become so much more than presenting an academic work, to do that now would somehow cheapen my experience.

The boy cycles off at high speed, hollering, 'Papa!' so I decide to mingle and peruse the second-hand cars. I'm on my tip-toes looking into the dash of a hummer up on cinder blocks and wondering if I'll ever learn to drive when a voice from behind startles me.

'What can I get you interested in, sonny? How 'bout two vehicles for the price of one. That's a special offer that I'm running today, exclusively today, sonny. Wachya say, hmm?'

I turn on my heels to see an individual (without wishing to tar him with the same brush) who looks and talks like a second-hand car salesman though all of him that I can see is his face hidden inside a zipped up parka overcoat with a fur-lined hood. I know now that I'm looking into the face of my new uncle: Denny Rowe Jnr. I have no doubt because this man is the spitting image of Vera. Whereas Vera bares a strong resemblance to Candy, this man is a younger 45, make no mistake with those sharp features and dreamy blue eyes half-hidden inside his parka hood. And he's got that same wiry gait 45 had. My heart is racing and not for the first time I wonder if I'm cured of my identity crisis or complete loss?

'You look like a sedan man, would I be correct?'

He's doing what a lot of second-hand car dealers like to do: plain-day divination; a little party trick the used-car industry like to engage in. He reaches out his freezing hand to shake mine. I notice that he's wearing a bracelet laced with the solemn faces of Jesus and his apostles. Should I be worried? He's also got one wonky eye, not crossed just gone astray.

'Actually,' I say while shaking his hand, 'I've got something that you might be interested in.'

The car-selling smile drops from Junior's face and I witness a glimpse of a ghost in those cerulean eyes – the same ones Vera handed down to me. 'Be gorra, a leprechaun!' He vocalizes some deedle-dee music, taps his heels, and doffs his hat to me.

I could get used to this.

'Top 'o the mornin' to ya'!' he says in a bad actor's pseudo-Irish accent. 'What part of the Emerald Isle do ya' hail from, sir?'

I clam up as my waters tell me to keep my location to myself for now. Maybe I should've put on a French accent.

Junior sizes me up, checks out my balloon ... bloody

bandaged wrist … Technicolor weather-beater … and back
to the balloon like all the others who had gone before him
on this life-altering quest. 'You want to do a trade-in, isn't
that it.'

'Huh? No, no, not exactly a trade-in per say. Um,' get a
grip, Jonny, 'I wish it was that simple. Well, yes, maybe it
is a trade-in, of sorts. No, actually, it concerns *family*
matters, yes, family.' Holding my breath, 'your, um, father
and mother.'

'My runaway father and poor mama left to rot in hell,
ya' mean?' It's a rhetorical question. He's looking at me
nodding in his hood as if I should agree with him.

'And your sister…'

His eyes glare out at me from inside the furry folds of
his parka and I suddenly feel completely out of my depth.
Where is Charley when I need him?

'You know the score: grease my palm with silver then
you'll get your interview.' He takes a pouch of tobacco
from his parka pocket. I read J.D.'s Blend on the side. He
balls some tobacco to marble size then slides in between
his cheek and gum. 'I tend to insist on
seeing cash first for obvious reasons…' He demands and
masticates on J.D.'s Blend. Obviously he's used this line
before when speaking to reporters and journalists looking
for a scoop on his tired tale. He clocks the balloon lying
limp at my side. 'Whose party did you piss on?'

'I didn't piss on any party but my grandfather did. He's
in here.'

Junior half chuckles, unzips his face a little, and frowns.
'Sorry, I don't get it. Is this your technique? Sonny, I prefer
if you shoot straight questions and I'll shoot straight
answers right back at ya'. None of this fancy-footin' shit.'

He's got a few real gold clunkers on his digits. 'That's
the way the institution brought me up.' Junior lets fly with
a tendril of brown ropy spit that splats onto the slushy
ground six inches from my numb toes in my Converse
trainers. Of course, he is referring to the orphanage where

he grew up and he expects that I know that which I do thanks to Sooty.

As if walking over a cliff in the dark, I decide to let Junior know why I'm here. 'I have news regarding your father's whereabouts.' I've never felt more like a private detective.

Junior doesn't react at first but grows paler under the flashing lights of the second-hand car yard.

'And your sister,' I add.

Junior makes a point of clearing his throat. He opens down his park zip to reveal his full face and the shock that spreads across it gives the impression that he's just swallowed his plug of *J.D.'s Blend*. 'Step into my office.'

Reluctantly, I follow him into his shabby prefab and sit down in his draughty little office that smells like a mechanic's garage. Junior twists the blinds shut which makes me a tad nervous. Am I about to be interrogated?

He sits back in his chair and throws his feet up onto the desk between us for me to study the worn soles of his stunning cowboy boots. 'Repeat what you just said out there, sonny.'

Now, I'm genuinely cacking it.

Jesus of Nazareth, in my rush from the Red Herring to here, I've forgotten to change out of my soiled undies. Maybe it is written in the wind that I will cack myself for the third time today, *and when the cock cacks for the third time...* I am a disgrace and I want to go home now, please. 'Maybe this wasn't such a good idea.'

'C'mon, sonny, you've come a long way to get it off yer chest.'

I clear my throat and offer a quick prayer. 'To cut a long story short, I know where 45 is – *was*. I also know where your sister is – the one you never knew. She doesn't know about you, I think' I then go on to fill in some back-story and my quest which has led me up to this point. I tell him about Sooty LeDanse but I don't tell him that she had died before I left her dressing-room. I also leave out my exact

257

address: call it instinct. However, I do provide the black and white snapshot of Candy on 45's ass and hold up my lacklustre red balloon for analysis and it's this that seems to change things. 'Like I said at the beginning, 45's dying breaths are in this balloon. That's all that's left of my grandfather – *your* father. Why would I make it up? It's too crazy to be made up. I've spent my savings to deliver this message and other messages that will never be delivered because of death.'

Junior's blazing eyes seize me. I can't read what's going on beyond those eyes but I don't like the karma in the room right now. The Reiki Mistress could probably tell me exactly what this karma is but she's a long way from here. I'd gladly lie on her bed of nails right now. The freezing office feels too small and I feel like I'm getting in the way between father and son. It's crazy but I'm starting to feel like I've gate-crashed a party which I haven't been invited to. I place the balloon on the table. 'You've probably got a lot of catching up to do. So, I'll be on my way.'

No sooner have I gotten to my feet when a deep growl sticks me to my spot.

'Don't mess with somethin' you know nothin' 'bout, sonny. If you think that I'm gonna part with a single penny for my father's and sister's whereabouts then you're mistaken.'

'Huh?'

'Do I look as if I'm made of money? Don't think that I don't know what you're up to. Believe me; I know a con-man when I see one.'

I catch myself having a look out through the blind at the sea of rust-buckets and the quickest way out of here. 'You've got it all wrong.'

'I've had con-men come sniffin' 'round here before, full of empty promises. We all know 'bout the money, right? That information is in the public domain, *right?*'

Junior's nodding at me as if I should know what he's

getting at.

'You're gonna tell me now that you know where the money's at? Huh? You think that I'm gonna make a little investment by payin' you in return for my father's location and the blood-right he owes me.'

'Blood-right?'

'The money, son. The goddamn money that bastard stole and kept from me and my mother while we rotted in institutions.' Junior let fly with another angry globule of J.D.'s Blend into an empty polystyrene cup that turns my stomach. He doesn't believe me.

Everything Sooty had told me seems to be true. A deranged image of the fire service prizing the poor gothic cow from her doorframe with crow-bars comes to me and I blink systematically to wash it away. I try to think what else I can show Junior to convince him that I'm here with good intentions. 'No, I'm telling the truth. 45 – Denny Rowe – *is* my grandfather and your sister *is* my mother. That makes me your nephew.' I hold out my hand in what can only be described as silly innocence and tell him my name. 'Jon Rowe... Jonny to my friends.' I repeat everything again, how all this started out as simply taking 45's remains back to Iowa and possibly contacting this Candy character and relay his message to her. This prompts me to show Junior the message sitting in my balloon that has almost caved in around the message by now.

Junior reaches out for it but I hold it just out of his reach for now. I've grown very close to my balloon; we've been through a lot together. Junior gets to his feet and crosses behind me and makes a dive for the balloon when he thinks I'm not watching. I snap it out of his way. 'Hey!'

'Ha!' he exclaims, 'just checkin'!' He crosses back to his chair and takes up his same posture as before. 'So, you've grown quite an attachment to the balloon.' Junior holds me steady in his gaze. 'That tells me that what you're sayin' might not all be bullshit after all, unless you're a lunatic but you look too dumb for that. Where did you say you come from?' Junior's got a crazed look in his piebald eye now. He produces...

Jesus of Nazareth.

...a hand-pistol from one of the drawers of the desk and something tells me that it's not one of those fake gun lighters. I don't want him to pull the trigger to find out.

I search for my doobie and ask him for a light and he pulls a box of matches from his parka. I tell him to forget it and put away my doobie with a jittery hand. Where's Charley?

I haven't told Junior where I come from and he knows that. He's trying to cross-examine me and now I'm beginning to regret saying anything. 'Maybe, I, uh, maybe I made a mistake... I think I'll be on my way. I'm heading back tomorrow anyway.' It's true. I had promised myself that 45 would rise again on the third day (me in my plane home and him amongst corn or maybe just the nearest quiet spot to Cedar Rapids airport).

I get up to leave, growing dizzier by the second as my vertigo kicks in.

Junior thumbs his chest. 'My gut tells me that you're the real thing. Why don't you sit back down there and tell me everything. How has daddy been keepin' all these years? Hmm? And my sister, how is she doin'?' Junior's sudden sickly sweetness puts me right off my supper – wherever that will be.

I glimpse out the window and see that night has come and a coating of ice covers the used cars. A light flutter of snow has begun to fall but there's nothing Christmassy about it. I don't think I've ever felt as alone as right now. Maybe it's just coincidence or perhaps my brain is on overload but the handgun Junior had dropped into the conversation so nonchalantly is lying on the desk as it had before but now I'm looking down its barrel and the fingers of Junior's right hand are no more than an inch from the trigger. 'This has been one big muh-mistake. I'm sorry I

260

took up any of your time. You're right; I am a con-man and I'm sorry for praying on your vun... vur... vulnerabilities.' I leave my chair swiftly and make my way to the door with dread prickling the hairs on the nape of my neck. I've just got my hand on the handle when I hear moans
and sobs from behind me. I peer over my shoulder to see Junior blubber like a baby, his body jerking and heaving in deep mournful sobs inside his parka.

'I've waited my whole life for you to come to me.' He's got his face hidden in his hands. 'I just wanted to tell 45 that I still love him even though he did what he did. I know he did what he had to do.'

Without leaving the comfort of the door-handle, I read the message aloud from memory and paraphrase it for him. 'Your father had always planned to come back for your mother, Junior, but circumstances must've caught up with him. Don't forget that he took his daughter with him and I'm sure he would've rescued you if he had known about you. Don't forget: Candy is my grandmother and I never got to know her either.'

And hearing it said like this – my own far-away voice – makes it all the more real. I really have had a miraculously lucky break, discovering all this information from almost the very moment I landed at Cedar Rapids. My lucky streak had begun by getting on that party bus. I thank Hitesh Sharma, the Indian security-guard at Cedar Rapids airport, who had inadvertently and without a modicum of knowing, sent me on this amazing turn of events.

I explain to Junior again that I'm a student of genealogy and this re-uniting of lost family is inspiring but he doesn't seem to react to my heart-felt words.

'I'll never get the chance to tell my mama that I love her but I was sort've holdin' onto some vague hope that my papa would come looking for me some day and weave me under his spell like he did those lady bank-tellers.'

'Beautiful.' I have it said before I realize.

'That thought kept me goin', y'know. Some day an old

stranger would walk – limp – up to me lookin' for an automobile for a quick get-away, if you catch my drift.'

What do you mean? Just like I was doing two minutes ago?

'Those nights at the orphanage were lonely and very, very dark. You can't imagine.'

'I identify with you. I used to call out for daddy at night and all I had were glow-in-the-dark rosary beads to sail by. Clinical Dad had been too busy watching Philomena's tongue action: that double-timin' stamp-lickin' two-bit post office whore and I still stand by that.'

Junior stops bubbling and his stray eye peers out at me from behind his fingers.

Of course, Vera had always come to save her children from night terrors but now, Vera *is* a night terror because she was a stranger in my bedroom at night. I don't know Vera. Where does Clinical Dad fit into all of this? Maybe he just doesn't fit in.

'I don't blame my mama.' Junior insists on looking at his pistol rather than at me. 'She was locked up and mentally demented in the head,' flicking a thumb behind him. 'She was no Flo Nightingale but she was still my mama and that broke me up knowin' that she was just a few miles from the orphanage and I wasn't allowed contact with Mother Bird. It was all his fault but I'd have given anything just to see his face for five seconds and listen to his voice and give him a chance to explain himself.'

I can't deny the mirror that exists between us. 'We've got a lot in common. More than you think.'

Then I remember that Alba (I'm not sure if that's just my sister's nickname or the collective name of her group) had recorded our birthday duet on my iPhone so I whip it out and place it on the desk in front of Junior to see. His head turns in the direction of my phone and he leans into the screen slowly and just gazes. I also take this opportunity to watch ourselves play out the old duet *I Did It My Way* again. We both watch the video intensely but I notice that

Junior's good eye isn't on me singing or the old man but on the background, flitting through the crowd every time Alba pans around to see the guests.

Junior wraps his bony hand around my damaged wrist with a little more vigour than is comfortable. 'Which one is your mother, sonny?'

I try to take my hand back but he isn't letting go.

'Where was this video taken? Hmm? In Ireland? That's where the old man went? Back to his roots.'

His roots? I'm starting to wish that he'd kept them in the ground.

Junior's grasp tightens. 'Which one is my sister? I'd love to know what she looks like.' He's looking up at me now from the desk with a strange expression like he's trying to control himself.

Why do I feel like a child taking sweets from a stranger? I decide not to reveal the location of the video nor point out Vera in the crowd. I'm tempted to single out annoying Mary; Vera's boss at the airport cleaning company. I try to buy time by commenting on 45's singing voice but Junior is fixed on the screen, unblinking and asking the same question again: location and Vera. Then he gazes at me with a smile. 'Maybe I could visit some day. Get to know my sister and see the place where my father spent the second half of his life.'

The man's got a look of delirium about him which I don't like all that much. I don't know what it is but I know now that I should've left when I had the chance.

I prize my hand from his grip and very carefully reverse to the door while he watches me do it with anger seething in his reddening face. It had all been a hoax; a false show of love. But I haven't fallen for it.

I fling open the door and stumble out into the snow...

23.
Pop!

Junior comes bounding after me.

In a daze, I duck down and disappear into the sea of used cars. Where has all this gone wrong? Probably when I went against my gut's wishes.

'I'll find you, sonny, and when I do, you can help me find yer mommy too and we can sit down 'n catch up on old times. Ya' like coco? We can sup coco all night 'n roast marshmallows. I've been waitin' for this all my life but don't think for a minute that I'm interested in that old bastard who walked out on us or don't presume that I'd like to meet yer mommy just cos she's my long-lost sister. I don't have a SISTER! I don't have a FATHER! But y'know what else I don't have!?'

I almost answer back.

'The MONEY!'

Finally, the penny drops. Now I get it! This is about the *money*. It's always been about the money. He doesn't care about Vera or 45. Well, yes he does, but to lead him to the hidden stash. Should I have cottoned on to this earlier?

Junior yells blind into the night but I can barely hear him over the pounding of my heart in my ears. I feel like Danny running from crazed Jack Torrance.

'That's right! Not a single penny was left to me. What ya' don't have ya' don't miss, right, *SONNY?*'

Is he asking a rhetorical question? Surely he thinks I'm not dumb enough to answer.

'WRONG!! That fucking money's MINE!! I suffered for it and yer poor mental granny over in Anamosa eatin' flies off the goddamn window-sill.' There's a pause before Junior calls out again, his voice is closer now. 'Look, let's just sit down and talk about this. All I want is my cut. It's just fair. 45 took the money and disappeared with the sister I never knew. Try to see it from my point of view. All I want is what's rightfully mine.'

I desperately want to tell him that I haven't seen this supposed stolen stash and nor has Vera according to her recent digging excursions both inside and outside the house but he's not going to believe me if I tell him. It's a catch-22 –

A gun-shot cracks open the night air, giving me such a fright that I hop my head against the side-mirror of the old Citroën XM that I'm ducking behind. I fiddle with my iPhone, trying to get to Charley's fast-dial button but my fingers are frozen and my nerves are shot to smithereens and buggery.

'Come out 'n tell me where the money is, son. Come out 'n tell me before I've got to go lookin'. I know the layout of this place a lot better than you do. My son's got the I.Q. of a robot but I can't send him to a better school cos I don't have the dough. J.J. has been waitin' for this night as much as me. My wife divorced me cos she said I was obsessed with findin' the money I'm owed. She said that I'd lost her for the price of findin' my past. But let me cut to the chase here: it's the money I want. The old man's nothin' but bad breath in that saggy bag of a balloon and I don't need no sister at my time of life.'

Bad breath? I frown at my balloon. I've never thought about that before but I can honestly say that there's an element of truth in his logic. After all, my balloon has brought me nothing but scares, stares, revenge and bullets, however, 45 didn't have actual bad breath yet it is carbon dioxide. I peek through the glass of the Citroën and see Junior five cars ahead of me. He's flashing hand-signals at his son, J.J., who pedals his ridiculously modified chopper to the main entrance, tears his ass in the snow, then begins to quietly close the gates.

Jesus of Nazareth!

I whip out my iPhone, making helpless whimpers, and try to dial Charley's number again.

Another shot rings out…

I think I just manage to touch-dial Charley before I
flinch and send the iPhone into the air before catching it
again. I'm a ball of nerves. What would Jason Bourne do? I
actually think this; not what Jonny Rowe of 128 Hydrangea
Drive, Limerick, Ireland would do but Jason fucking
Bourne. Jason would creep into a car, wouldn't he?
Hotwire the bitch, of course he would. Then burst his way
out of here only I don't know how to hotwire a car – I don't
even know how to cold-wire. I don't even know how to
drive a car!! Why didn't I get up off my arse and take my
driving test at a respectable age?

Too many questions and too little time to answer, Jonny.

In sheer desperation, I call out. 'I don't know where the
money is! I didn't even know that there was money until
that fat old Goth Sooty told me about it a few hours ago!
My mother is a cleaner for Christ's sake!' Deliberately
leaving out where.

I decide to stick with Jason Bourne's plan. I look into the
Citroën and almost faint when I see that the key is in there
whereas Bourne would probably have to hotwire the
vehicle. Silently, I ease the door-handle open but it doesn't
open.

Of course it doesn't.

I sidle back to the rear-door on the driver's side and try
that one. It opens with a click. I've never been so happy to
hear a click in my life. I slip into the XM with the stealth of
an old-age pensioner and hop into the driver's seat. The
only other driver's seat I'd sat in is the one on the floor of
the bong-house where I would occasionally pretend to be
driving when nobody was looking. I've got one chance. It's
a simple equation: the Citroën splutters – I splutter. I
vaguely remember Clinical Dad telling me that the car must
be in neutral before switching it on. The clutch is on the
left, I know that much, so I press my foot but my foot just
hits the undercarriage of the Citroën. I peer down between
my legs. 'Where's the fucking clutch?? The *fucking*
clutch!'

It's an automatic. Of course it is.

From the corner of my eye I see Junior coming down towards me. His face hidden inside his parka hood and a glinting pistol in his hand. From my left comes a pair of green fluffy ear-muffs holding up J.J. on his modified chopper. I stick the gear-shift into D for Neutral and switch the Citroën XM 2.1 TD. The engine fires up first time and catches me by surprise when it levitates upwards on its suspension like a mantis. When I pass my driving test I will get one of these quirky motors, I promise myself. It's a glorious moment until the car shoots forward and slams into the rear of a rusty Beetle. 'Fuck!!' I check to see if 45 is ok in his balloon and throw the gear-stick into P, N, D and then X, Y, and Z before flooring the accelerator as Junior and Junior Junior come at me from both sides like characters in a demented Christmas play. The Citroën fishtails but I manage to keep it moving forward along a snowed-up path cutting through the mass of snow-capped motors.

I aim the Citroën's snout at the fence gate and close my eyes…

For a moment, nothing happens before the cabin is filled with the sudden scraping crash of metal on metal.

I open my eyes and see that I'm doing a doughnut on Cemetery Road, just like riding the Octopus at the carnival only free and unregulated. Again, pulled from the files of childhood, I remember Clinical Dad and me driving into Limerick city on a freezing January morning. Without warning, the sky-blue Cortina slid into a spin and was heading for an innocent wall
bystander. Clinical Dad took his foot off the accelerator and, defying all logic, leaned the steering wheel *into* the
direction the Cortina was sliding, never once hitting the brake. I'll never forget it. In a flash, I do the same, easing off the gas and steering into the doughnut…

The Citroën's front wheels find traction on the snow and I drive towards Anamosa town with my heart literally in my mouth. In my rear-view, a double-beam of light appears from the left, juggles, and straightens up fifty meters behind my exhaust pipe. Junior's on my tail and maybe Junior Junior is riding shotgun. I speed up but careful not to lose control on the icy surface of Cemetery Road.

Jesus of Nazareth.

'What do I do now?' I ask my birthday balloon rolling back and forth in the passenger seat. 'What the fuck do I do *now?!*' The balloon is content in letting me figure my own escape. I have to speed up to get some distance between us, that'll give me time to pull up and hide out somewhere in the urban setting of Anamosa. That's what Bourne would do so I stick with him because he seems to know what he's doing.

'Thanks for nothing!' I scream at the balloon. 'It's true for Uncle Junior! You're nothing but *baaaad breeeeeath!*' I lose control of my speech pattern as a direct result of losing control of this two-timing French beauty. Just ahead, there's a roundabout and judging by my present trajectory, I'm going to go through it, literally. I pull hard to the right on the steering wheel, too hard, now I'm going for impromptu supper in someone's living-room but I don't have time to ring ahead, sorry. I compensate by pulling to the left and ... here we go ... skating free-form and slow-motion down Cemetery Road and I'm heading for a three-story building right in front of me. All I need now is some classical music to top off the effect. Somehow, I

manage to get the car under control just as the Citroën's

long nose finds the ostentatious gates of the building. I brake...

Here comes the moral of the tale...

The Citroën has no brakes.

Of course it doesn't.

I guide the car through the open gates of the building at a steady fifty-two miles per hour and now I'm beginning to regret my decision because I see a large luminous room ahead of me full of sitting people and I cannot stop this runaway Citroën.

I let go the steering wheel and reach for my balloon and clutch it to my chest as I realize that I'm not wearing a seat-belt. I had forgotten the most important part of Clinical Dad's driving lesson from the past. And as my Citroën's nose crumples into solid wall and shattering glass I remind myself that I've found some closure: I know who 45 is, more or less. I tried to tell my grandmother Candy but, alas, I've been too late. I don't know where the money's hidden and never will now but that's fine with me. I'm okay with that. I've completed my original quest: find this Candy character and set 45 free.

I'm thrown forward like a rag-doll...

That's when I hear *POP!*

24.
Rip Van Winkle

'45? Where's *45?*'

'Jon...'

'My balloon? I can't find it...'

The first thing I do when I wake (not that I know that I've been asleep) is scramble for my balloon but my old sidekick isn't at my side. A hand meets my shoulder and eases me – or pushes me – back onto where I lay but all I feel is acute dread. I try to sit up but stars explode in front of me and feel the need to puke more than any morning after drinking dodgy alcohol at the Old Quart with Charley. I call out for 45 into my bloody blurry world, unsure where I am but my eyes have landed on the misty outlines of, Jesus of Nazareth, two faces and I just know that Junior and J.J. are sitting two meters in front of me (three J's, a chopper, and a cocked pistol). I'm being held captive by the devil and its spawn.

'Don't hurt me.' I sound like Little Red Riding Hood and there's not a lot I can do about it. 'My mother Vera doesn't know that I'm here. She'll never find me if you *do* something to me. I love her ... I should've told her that I was coming.' I mumble incoherently to the unseen people in the room. 'I should've listened to the clown but I'm the clown for coming here.'

'Jon, shush, listen, everything's okay...'

My eyes gain some focus. I'm in a strange room that washes back and forth like looking down a kaleidoscope. 'I dunnooooo,' I moan, only vaguely aware that I've even opened my mouth or am I speaking in my head? 'I dunno where it is. Please, just gimme what's left of 45 – my balloon, I mean – and I'll, and I'll be on my way. All I wanted to do was an act of good: release 45 in the corn or wherever and tell Candy that he had loved her to his dying day...

270

Where's my balloon?'

One of the faces draws up near. I flinch and cover my already aching face from the blow in slow-mo but a pair of soft warm lips pecks me on the cheek instead of a baseball bat. The second face homes in and suddenly I'm wrapped in a warm hug that consumes me and I feel safe though I've no idea what's going on. All I know is that I've come to the end of a long cave to come out into the bright light, fresh air and blue skies...

So I'm surprised to be greeted by Vera and Charley at the mouth of the cave that has just materialised into my bed-side. I sit up slowly and wince as my world comes back into focus and slips away again. They're here, they're actually here! Emotions disable my tongue and all I'm able to do is blubber like a baby while Vera holds me tight and Charley pats me on the head.

Eventually, the wave passes over. I'm in a hospital room, all for me apparently, with a TV and DVD, pleasant pastel curtains and a vase of – if I'm not mistaken – daffodils. Vera's crying and Charley looks as if he needs a drink or a puff on something to put him to sleep for an indefinite period. I'm confused. Vera and Charley are here but seeing them in this strange hospital room is just as weird and out-of-place as being greeted by them at the entrance of my make-believe cave. I ask Vera where I am but all she manages is to blubber back at me and now Charley's getting into the spirit and that gets me going again and we cry together, over and over again, though why we're lamenting is beyond me. I'm alive!!

'Jesus, Jonny, you're alive,' Vera rejoices as if confirming my suspicions. 'Thank *Christ*, oh thank Christ.' She reaches over and hugs me. 'You stupid boy. Why did you have to come to Iowa? You just couldn't let the past die with 45?'

'Huh? I'm still in Iowa? What are you doing here? What day's today?'

Charley tells me that it's Sunday.

I must be out cold since last night. 'I'm going home today. My work here is done.'

Vera and Charley exchange worried glances.

'What?' I ask. 'What's going on?'

'You're in a private hospital in Anamosa.' Charley throws his eyes heavenwards and shakes his head in a way that confuses me and repeats "private" with inflection in his tone. He then asks me if I've seen Michael Moore's documentary on the health system in the USA.

I answer that, no, I haven't seen it and he just comes back and says, 'Good.' I scan the room. 'Where's Junior?'

Charley scrunches up his face while Vera looks up at me, her face blotched and wet with tears and snot.

'Junior Junior? Is he waiting outside?'

Charley whispers to Vera as if I'm not in the room. 'Will I call the men in the white coats?'

'I can hear you,' I tell him.

'Sorry,' Charley apologizes, 'habit.'

I tell him that I'm not mental either. 'There were two of them: Junior and Junior Junior or J.J. for short. He cycled 'round on an upside-down chopper and had green ear-muffs.'

More fretful glances and Charley's eyeing the button for some nurse attention.

'Who?' Vera demands. 'Jonny you've been in a coma for almost a month.'

I seem to go deaf for a moment. There's a lapse as this information sinks into my aching brain. I look around the room again. I must admit that I do have a settled appearance about me, longer-than-usual nails which my nerves usually keep gnawed to the bone and a genuine beard that has migrated willy-nilly from my designer goatee look. 'How long?' I ask again, just to be sure to be sure. 'But Charley just told me that it's Sunday.'

'Yes, it's a Sunday in March.'

'A month tomorrow.' Then Charley adds, 'Head

272

injuries,' as the root of my existence in this strange room.

Vera looks as if she's about to say something but cannot bring herself to say it so Charley intervenes again. 'You could've been killed in the crash. You're a lucky man, Jon.'

Vera snaps, 'Why the hell would you sit into a car without brakes and not wear a seat-belt?! Did I bring you up to be a *moron?!* On an icy *road?!*'

Vera's glare is enough to put me off my food (I've just spotted the steaming steak fillets and buttery mash on the tray on my bedside locker). It is typical hospital food but more wholesome.

Charley emphasises '*Cemetery* Road.' He stares at me and I remember our telephone conversation after leaving Sooty's place on Davis Street – a *month* ago. It feels like yesterday.

'But I wasn't killed.' I try to make light of the situation and smile the smile of the rictus-dead. But the exhaustion in Vera's face is nothing but sobering. I've never seen her look so worn out. She looks now as she had then when she was undergoing chemo.

'Yeah, thanks to your balloon...' Charley keeps his eyes fixed on mine. Still not in my complete senses, I find my hand reaching out to touch the reassuring feel of my saggy balloon buddy but it's not there. I question Charley and Vera with a look and they know something that I don't. If pauses can be pregnant then I would describe the silence in the room as a pregnant pause. Vera and Charley look at each other. A look that says something's happened while I've been away.

'The bubble's burst, Jon.'

What's she talking about?

Vera looks at me with a tired smile. 'Your balloon acted as an air-bag. It cushioned your skull in the impact. It saved your life.' She sniffs and bats her eyelids and gives in to another bout of tears. Vera's not one for melodrama so I take her at word value.

Now I remember that single pop when I went through

273

the gates and hit the wall of that building.

Charley reaches over, opens the drawer in my bedside locker and from it takes the remains of a shredded balloon. 'I kept it for you as a souvenir,' he says almost apologetically and holds up the pathetic strip of burst balloon, all that's left of 45's soul bubble. He places it in my hand and closes my fist.

I know it's dumb but I cannot help the chill down my spine and the constricting feeling in my gullet. I turn to Vera in a haze. 'Now, I get it,' I muse. '45 saved my life.' I'd made a promise to myself in Tesco Express back in Old Castle that I'd write 45 under the balloon's RIP when I discovered the real 45. I still don't know the real 45 but I think he's earned his stripes. 'Do you have a pen?' I ask Vera.

She gestures to my bedside locker and I see my Sheaffer pen. I'm delighted to see that I haven't lost it but I need a marker or something that will write on rubber.

'Here.' Charley digs in his inside pocket and pulls out a permanent marker. The smirk on Charley's face tells me that it's the same one that I'd bought in Tesco Express. 'You left it on the street. I didn't think you'd need it again so I pocketed it, sorry. I was wrong, sorry again.'

He hands me the marker and I carefully scribble 45 onto the balloon remains while I hyperventilate uncontrollably. 'Rest in peace, wherever you are.'

Charley nods, adding, 'Went out in a blaze of glory.'

'Maybe it was his way of thanking me for the pledge I had taken.'

'We'd be at your graveside on Cemetery Road if it weren't for your goddamn poxy balloon!' Vera hides her face in her hands and cries again. 'We wouldn't be in this precarious position if it wasn't for your fucking balloon!' She glares into thin air.

'Steady on. 45 saved me,' I reflect. 'His one last noble gesture.' I hold Vera in my gaze and take her hands in mine. 'Is it true?' My heart's pounding all over again and now the moment of truth has arrived. It has all been speculation up until now.

'Is what true?'

'Everything,' I blurt out. 'That Candy's your mother and 45 was a bank-robbin' hypnotist on the run?'

Vera nods. 'Your grandfather was a fugitive, yes.'

Charley sits forward while my world seems to slow down even slower on hearing this final home truth. There's no doubt now.

'Well, why didn't you tell me?'

'I couldn't afford to tell you, any of you. There was too much at stake – plus dad could've been extradited back here to the States. Your grandfather had to lose himself when he went to Ireland so the best way, we figured, was to get lost mentally but first we had to get lost physically. He knew a guy who knew a guy in Boston who got us false passports and complete new identities to get us out of the country – for a price. That two-timin' Boston bastard later blackmailed us for double the price we'd already given him; either we hand over the money or he goes to the cops.'

Am I still unconscious?

'So this explains your rejoicing after his death?' Something clicks in my head and it's not the tubes and cables. 'Now I understand why you said "Tying up loose ends" that day of the wake.'

Vera flashes a consolatory smile. 'It was the sheer relief of his death, Jonny. Finally, dad didn't have to look over his shoulder anymore.'

The Juniors flash in my conscience. 'And that also explains why you were in such a rush to get rid of any hint that 45 had ever lived at 128.'

'I've done it all out of love, Jon. I loved – still do – 45 more than you can ever imagine. We shared a special link just like you had something special with him.'

Charley decides to speak, finally. 'You say "we?" Whose "we" exactly?' Charley speaks like a courtroom drama.

'I was a young girl who could think for herself when 45 kidnapped me from the orphanage in Iowa City. He'd done a few years by then in Fort Madison, don't forget. They escorted him from Fort Madison to Anamosa for the wedding. It was in all the papers at the time.' She holds up her wedding finger to me with a smile of pure relish and now Vera's beginning to come into herself and enjoying this release. 'This is my mother's wedding ring. This is the only thing I've ever known of my mother Candy Dufraine.'

In my weakened mental state, I almost make the terrible mistake of telling Vera that it's the same ring that's in the tattoo on 45's ass.

'Dufraine?' repeats Charley suspiciously as if he had once known a Carterwell.

'He didn't have to answer any questions by letting on that he had some vague mental illness and, even if he did, nobody would take much notice of a senile old man.'

But the timeline doesn't add up. '45 must've been a youngish man when he escaped to Ireland?'

'Yes, he was in his forties but at the time he was just an ex-American soldier with his daughter. That's
the story we circulated. 45 made it known that he didn't want to talk about his past. People being people jumped
to the conclusion that it was the horrors of war that he didn't want to be reminded of so nobody asked questions. We just played the roles of the fictitious people we'd invented. It just seemed like the easiest thing to do at the time. He found a low-key job shelving books at a library in Limerick city where nobody bothered him while I went to school there.'

'I left for Iowa wanting to know who I was but I'm here now wondering the very same thing. It's hard to wipe away a life-time lie.'

Charley thumbs in my direction and exclaims with comical gravity, 'He suffers from identity crisis,' as if this is partly the reason why I'm in hospital and maybe it is.

'How do you think these revelations are going to make him feel? Wasn't it Willy Butter Yeats who said "I wander lonely as a cloud"? That's Jonny right there, a cumulus adrift.' Charley's getting flustered now, so much so that he's tucking his dreads behind his ears. 'Pardon me Vera but you've really mind-fucked your son and I say that with good intentions.'

'He's right. Charley's actually correct.'

'Look,' Vera points out, 'you are who you are. Your family tree is not going to change that.'

'That's where you're wrong,' I contradict Vera, 'Susan or Alba, whatever she's called, and Tommy, they've got a part of you. We've all got a little part of you and the clown – Fictitious Mom and Clinical Dad and we've also got Candy and 45 flowing through our bloodstreams. I hadn't known that Candy even existed until yesterday – or last month, sorry.'

'No, son, you're not right…'

'Clever way of not repeating that I'm wrong.'

'You are an individual, got it. You are Jonny Rowe who lives at 128 Hydrangea Drive, got it. You are the person you have grown up to be. It's the same Jonny Rowe who decided to come to Iowa and spread 45's ashes in his homeland and tell Candy Dufraine that he still loved her.' Vera's voice quavers. 'If you don't know who you are then who does?'

This is getting confusing. My brain aches.

'I never got to know my mother,' Vera says, 'and y'know what's worse?'

Reluctantly, I shake my head.

'She never knew what happened to me. I don't even know if she's alive.' She blinks and seems to come back to herself. 'Wait a minute, how do you know about her? What do you know about my mother, Jonny? All you had was the note.' Vera reaches into her handbag and takes out the note that had travelled with 45. She hands it to me. This is the first time that I touch the paper and I find a sense of

277

comfort in this and an inexplicable closeness. 'That's all you know about Candy, isn't it?'

Vera looks at me with the optimism of a child and in a Freudian way, I feel like her father. Jesus of Nazareth, Vera doesn't know about Candy.

'All I know is that she was dad's accomplice. They were caught after I was born. She did time in Anamosa and that's all I've heard of her and that's all 45 knew of her. This note is all truth, Jon. You must know that. 45 lamented every day, the thoughts of his beloved Candy alone in prison. It tore him up but he didn't turn himself in. If he did, well, we would've been separated and God knows what else. He had always planned to go back to get my mother but time caught up with him and after a while, we began to become our fictional people.'

Would he have gone back if he knew that Candy had his baby a few months after you two went AWOL? I want to ask this question but something inexplicable is stopping me.

'I've always been afraid to come back to find my mother, in case I speak to the wrong people. That money they stole is still stolen, don't forget that. Technically, I'm still an accomplice.'

For a moment, I play with the idea of not telling her about Candy's sad demise but it would be nice to have closure. 'She ended her life.'

The silence in the hospital room is palpable. I'm almost afraid to speak again but hold my ground. I find myself looking for the comfort of my balloon but all I've got now is a strip of rubber. I try to take strength from the idea that 45 is finally back in Iowa though he literally did go out with a bang or a *pop* in this case. 'Ever heard of Miss Havisham?'

'Hmm? Uh-huh, that was the one with the cake for the rats.' Vera nods but is gazing through me. 'They ate the cake,' she says in a meek distant voice. 'Some of Candy's cellmates organized the cake though security broke the

278

little groom's legs and snapped off the bride's veil which could have been used as sharp or blunt objects. All they found was strawberries.' Vera speaks in a small voice. '45 and Candy swopped the strawberry 'n cream sponge through their bars. They even shared it out amongst the other inmates and wardens. People forgot where they were that 23rd of September. The priest who married them was an Irishman, just like in the movies; Mick O' Connor was his name.' She gazes off into space. 'That's all I know.'

I hadn't known of the date but it all seems a little superfluous now. And then I relay her late mother's story and how she had lost faith in 45 ever returning which sent her into a spiral of depression that ended with her own self-inflicted death by using her work tools (sheets) in her own rented cell.

Vera takes this information on-board and keeps quiet still before speaking. 'Finally, the hiding is over. That's what I was celebrating after dad died. I was celebrating the fact that he could rest once and for all because he slept with one eye open.'

'The Sleeping Dragon,' I muse.

Vera smiles, obviously being familiar with the Sleeping Dragon but I can't find it in my heart to return the smile. After all, the hiding isn't over: The Juniors are out there and they know I'm in here but are keeping a low profile and hoping that I won't go to the police. As long as I don't go to the police I think they'll be wise enough to stay away. I decide not to tell Vera about her brother. She doesn't need to know for now ... maybe I'll never tell her. It depends if Junior and J.J. decide to turn up at 128 someday looking for the treasure, then I'll have no choice. He doesn't know where we live but he does know that 45 went to Ireland now all he has to do is check the yellow pages for the name Rowe. Oh, now I remember that we're ex-directory, always have been, probably measures taken by Vera and 45 to make their lives a little easier. With an ominous sinking feeling, it dawns on me that the only thing that 45's really handed down to me is this new habit of sleeping with one eye open. I'm going to be looking over my shoulder for the rest of my life. If I could just find that damn money, I'd gladly hand it over to my new lunatic relatives. I would do that just to live in peace. We've never been rich but the Rowes, ahem, are survivors. Maybe someday I'll find the right moment to broach the subject with Vera regarding her brother.

I decide to change the subject. 'What about Clinical Dad, aka, Ronald McDonald? Where does he fit into all of this?'

'Into the tightest corner as possible where I can kick him where it hurts. He's a loser, Jon, always was and always will be. A charismatic bum. There's no happy ending when there's a charismatic bum concerned.'

I sense Charley's about to crack an ill-timed one-liner even before he says it...

'I once knew a charismatic bum...'

I glare Charley right the *fuck* down. Vera doesn't know that he's talking about 45's tattooed behind. She will *never* know about the goings-on at the cemetery on the hill just as she will *never* know about her vengeful brother. She has enough on her plate.

Vera can never know about what we did at the cemetery on the hill.

'We won't be seeing him again.'

There was me thinking that I might've had a chance to get to know him. Sometimes unhappy endings are as much a part of life as happy ones.

'Didn't you notice how he started sniffing around when 45 died?'

I had actually. I remember now that I had had a conversation on this very topic with Charley and the Reiki mistress before I made the mistake of visiting the Juniors. Charley had also warned me about that and I make a mental note to thank him later.

'He knew about the money just as I did. That's why you saw him in my bed the morning you left. We had both

Jonathan Dunne *Balloon Animals*

been out all night looking for dad's stash and one thing just led to another. It was a mistake, Jon, but like I said to you, some things just cannot be explained. It sort've seemed like the good old days as we dug up the foundations of the house.'

'Yeah,' I answer vaguely, 'I know what you mean, the old house foundations and the good old days.'

'And Brillo?'

'Well, we genuinely got her in for some home-help because your father had committed suicide and I was working twelve-hour days at the airport. We got talking a little – dad and I – while you lot were out playing in the back-yard and decided that keeping Brillo on would just make our illusion even stronger.'

'But 45 chased Brillo around the house and you didn't care ...?' My heart starts racing and I feel queasy again.

'Jonny, when you've been pretending for half a lifetime,' Vera stalls and looks for the right choice of words, 'the boundaries between reality and fiction become hazy. It just became part of the game until we, 45 and I, had convinced ourselves of a life completely invented.'

'And Nan?'

'Who's Nan to you?' Vera's question is another way of saying: You *know* who Nan is. 'Have you ever met Nan?'

I shake my throbbing head.

'Have you ever seen her in any photographs?'

Again, I have to admit that I have never seen the woman. I'm starting to feel a little stupid and naive.

'We invented her after you were born, to avoid awkward questions. 45 told me about her one night when nobody was at home and how she had had an affair and fell on her lover's buzz-saw.'

'You couldn't make it up if you tried,' interrupts Charley.

I throw Charley some looks. '45 did.'

Vera adds, 'It was so outrageously unlikely that it became reality. Things like this do happen in real life. All

281

you've got to do is surf the net.'

'Kind've like fact is stranger than fiction,' adds Charley.

'You lot grew up believing in a woman who didn't exist. It still amazes me how none of you suspected a thing. Nobody ever told you that they'd never heard of Nan and the buzz-saw incident. You just took it as gospel.'

My head hurts with unanswered questions bottle-necking in my lobes. 'Why wouldn't we? We're not expecting our mother to be lying to us.'

'45 was just lucky. He had me and the money out of the country and into this one before ports and airports were notified. They didn't have the internet back in those days. By the way, your father told you not to come to Iowa and you didn't listen to him.'

'Why should I?'

Vera falters. 'Cos he's your father, Jonny.'

'Clinically, yes, but he's a clown in real life.'

'Can't argue with you there,' snorts Vera, 'although apparently he hung up his clown gloves and walked right out of McDonald's without a word. Maybe he'll come 'round again maybe he won't. Who knows? He started sniffin' around when he heard about dad's death but he's done another disappearing act.'

I actually thought that there might've been a happy ending with that end of the story. Having him around again might not have been such a bad thing despite his past wrong-doings. 'Where is he? Wait, how do you know that he'd told me not to come?'

'He told me.'

'What? You mean you've known all along? You knew that morning when you waved us off? I asked him not to tell you because, well, because I didn't want to worry you.'

'He was just looking out for you, Jon.'

Charley pipes up. 'Look, he's a bad penny. He'll come 'n go every now and again. Let's get back to the money?'

'Well said.' Vera nods along with Charley. '45 never told us the location of the money to protect us. Things of this nature are always best kept in one head. I see that now but I never understood it when I was younger. I guess it's all tied up now with 45 gone and Candy too. Maybe they will catch up on old times in the next life. The money's gone and now we can forget about ever finding it. It's a relief.'

'You didn't have that attitude when I last saw you at 128.'

'Jonny, I admit that I did hold onto the idea of finding it but those holes in the front lawn was pure desperation after 45 had died. I was kicking myself –
still am – that I hadn't forced him to tell me. Then he went and died on me and I was just crazy with the thoughts that the money was so close yet now so far. In a strange way, my grieving mind was telling me to find it quick because he's just died; there was something *fresh* about the loot.'

The Reiki Mistress had been right, blaming Vera's digging on the grieving process. It's true; it takes many forms.

'In my twisted logic,' continues Vera, 'the longer I left the money go the further away the chances of ever finding the money became.' She throws a glance at Charley. 'Boy but could we use it about now.'

I'm itching to tell her about Uncle Junior.

Vera breaks me from my thoughts. 'Every ending is bitter- sweet. The sweet ending is that you managed to track down my mother and return dad to his homeland...'

'Blaze of glory,' Charley triumphs, bowing in reverence.

'But the bitter ending is that we never found the money. What makes it twice as bitter is that I will have to remortgage the house.'

I sit up but my head pitches and rolls and my stomach begins to wallow. I ease back down onto my pillow which, I think, might be of the orthopaedic variety. 'What are you talking about?'

'Y'know how the States is famous for stitching up its own wounds if it doesn't have private insurance?' asks

Charley with a raised eyebrow.

'We're talking thousands of dollars for medical treatment, Jon, *your* medical treatment. You don't have private insurance but we are in a private hospital – the hospital you crashed into.'

'You could've crashed into a public hospital, at least,' Charley scorns. 'Now look. We're living it up at Woodview Heights.'

'This was Christmas come early for Woodview Heights when you came crashing through the window. Three liberty bells!'

'Why were you driving a car without brakes?'

I look around the room in a mild state of shock. I can do without the portable telly and DVD player and who needs real flowers? Plastic would do. 'Obviously I wouldn't have gotten into the car if I'd known about the brakes.'

'But why the rush, Jon? Y'know what some people are saying? Some people are saying that you were running from somebody. Some people say that they heard gunshots the same time you came through the wall.'

Feeling sorry for myself, I'm on the point of telling Vera everything but my waters are telling me to hold my tongue and invent an excuse. Now, Vera *definitely* doesn't want an extra headache. 'I bought the car for 1500$ off a second-hand car salesman who chews J.D.'s Blend tobacco. I just wanted an old crock to get around while I was here.' Although I still have ambitions of owning a Citroën XM someday.

'Uh-huh.' Vera eyes me up. 'Even though you were returning to Ireland the following day after buying the car?'

I can feel Charley's eyes on me. He knows I'm spinning porkies.

'We owe the guts of 50,000$ treatment expenses and every day more is another grand or two plus damages. I don't have any money, Jonny. How much do you have left? Oh, that reminds me, we still owe Jim O'Connor for dad's headstone.'

'Two or three grand max.'

Vera looks to Charley with some hope. 'Do you…, no, forget it you.' She takes one look at him and abandons the idea.

'What are we going to do?'

'There's only one thing for it.'

'And that is?' asks Charley.

'None of us have any money and I'm not prepared to spend a few nights in Anamosa penitentiary… ironic.' She's looking at us both now as if the penny should've dropped. 'Jonny, you feel up to a walk?'

Jesus of Nazareth, is she suggesting what I think she's suggesting? 'You're going to smuggle me out of here? Who are you again? You're Vera, right?'

'They called me from your iPhone.'

Charley admits, 'They called me first but I pretended not to know you.'

'I told them that I would take care of it. We're kidnapping you tonight and getting you out of here and out of Iowa.'

'What?' It just dawns on me that I haven't seen a lot of Iowa. I've had a brief sojourn with Anamosa but that's it. The party bus had been more or less blacked out and I've been in a coma since then which limited my sight-seeing.

'Stop being such a Goody-two-shoes, Jon. We'll figure out a way to pay them back but just not tonight. I've our return tickets bought. We leave from Cedar Rapids at midnight.'

Jesus, it would have to be midnight. I tell Vera that she's finally flipped.

'V,' says Charley, 'maybe Jonny's right. Y'know that I'm open-minded but even this seems a little extreme.'

Vera's got a wild look about her. 'I've wanted to do this ever since I was cured of the Big C.'

'You knew about this?' Charley asks incredulously.

'No,' Vera throwing her eyes heavenwards, 'Us Rowes never wanted to draw unwanted attention so I

285

suffered and celebrated in silence. I've been waiting for an opportunity like this. I've kept my head down all my bloody life because of 45's past. I got over the cancer. I want to live life on the dangerous side.'

'Are you for real?' I ask Vera. 'Then what have you been doing all along?'

'I'm sick 'n tired of being careful.' Vera says in such a breezy tone which makes me think that she's definitely lost her sense of reason.

Before I know what's happening, Charley and Vera are levering me up from my bed and extracting me from various gadgets. 'What? Now? Right *now?* But I've only just arrived! Or it seems that way…'

'*Right* now, Rip Van Winkle!'

25.
A.W.O.L

Not having Harry Potter's invisibility cloak at hand, I make do with my paisley pyjamas that Vera had brought across the Atlantic Ocean for the break-out. Apparently, my pjs had been the first thing that she had packed when she got the call that I had driven through Woodview Heights' waiting-room window. Talk about trying to jump the queue.

'How do you s'pose we get out've here?' I ask, still unable to believe what I'm about to do. By now, I've managed to sit up and heave myself to the edge of my bed where I sit out another dizzy bout as Vera frantically pulls on my pyjamas. Where is my dignity? I still haven't gotten used to my hospital bed and feel a little cheated that I've been asleep for the last month and haven't fully availed of the costly facilities.

Charley suggests that we should climb out the window but Vera opines that using the door would be easier, 'cuts out a lot of unnecessary pain and stretching. Besides, the two-floor jump could make this all but completely pointless.'

I pack essentials and what's left of my balloon into the deep pockets of my red and blue dressing-gown complete with tassels (also brought from 128). We leave the room on the arms of Vera and Charley only I forget that my John-Thomas is strapped to a piss-bag and apparently I've got another one strapped to my ass. Charley gets a wild fit of laughter when they pull me away from my bed while my ass and J.T. tug me backwards to the bed.

I manage to set myself free, cursing Charley as I do, and we walk-slash-slump down the hallway, my wobbly legs occasionally giving way beneath me. Vera repeatedly tells us from the corner of her mouth,

'This is going to work … This is going to work…'

Charley and I look at Vera who seems as if she makes a livelihood out of getaways. In a way, she has. She's enjoying every minute and has obviously put some thought into my great escape.

'There's one security guard at the gate and he was losing to a game of solitaire on my way in here. I'll distract him and you two just wander out onto the road. It really is that simple. If any questions are asked, just say that you're going for a smoke because smoking isn't allowed on hospital grounds.'

'Aw, sweet!' Charley starts rolling right there in the hallway like a possessed man while propping me up with his shoulder. His ankles pop. Vera clocks this and somehow manages to get her hand behind me and thwack him across the back of his head when nobody's watching.

As we pass the nurse's station, the matron ogles us over the tops of her spectacles. 'Dear Jesus, where are you taking him? That young man's just woken from a four-week coma. He shouldn't be out of bed.'

'He's dying for a smoke.' Vera's acting skills leave me speechless. 'Four weeks without a cigarette…'

The matron answers back curtly, 'Now might be a good time to quit then.'

'Oh, he'll quit all right,' Vera answers back readily, 'quit Woodview Heights,' she mutters from the side of her mouth as we traipse passed the station.

We keep walking towards the front entrance and I'm beginning to sweat, feeling like I'm walking through airport security again with my balloon hidden on my person. I miss my balloon dearly, as if part of me has been severed.

We pass through the doors out into the freezing night, me in my paisley pyjamas.

'I'm freezing! I don't even have a pair of boxers on!'

'His nut-sack's freezing up into a walnut, Vera. We should've brought proper clothes for him.'

'Charley's right.' I shrink-wrap when I hit the night-air

288

and there's nothing the paisley pattern can do about it which would accentuate my manhood on any other day.

'How could we dress him up in proper clothes?' Vera points out. 'The nurses would cop immediately. By wearing pyjamas it tells the nurses that we're just taking him out for a quick stroll.'

'In the snow?!'

'Jonny, I hadn't planned for this weather.'

I tell Vera that *nobody* had planned for this weather. I had come here expecting to find three-meter green corn stalks.

'Nobody walks out the front gates in a pair of pyjamas.'

Vera's plan seems overtly childish. 'Couldn't you have brought me clothes for *after* our getaway?'

Vera's expression tells me that she hadn't thought beyond my escape. 'He won't have a nut-sack if this security guard gets suspicious,' warns Vera from the opposite side of her mouth this time.

And so on, the conversation crosses my face, back and forth, forth and back.

'Could we stop talking about my nut-sack, please?' The real cold fact of the matter is not the weather but I'm expecting to see a couple of Juniors come at me with a car-jack any second. I'm proud of Charley for not mentioning them.

Under the yard lights, I see how much damage I had caused. A new window had been put in and the wall had been reconstructed but had yet to receive a lick of canary-yellow paint to blend in with the rest of the building.

'Charley,' Vera mutters, 'whip out a cigarette and make as if you're anxious to spark up.'

The security cabin comes up five … four meters ahead of us.

'I've only got doobies.' Charley's cool exterior is beginning to crack.

Vera snaps back, 'What?'

Charley's falling apart, wildly tucking dreads behind

289

ears. '*Doobies*, Vera.'

'What the fuck are *goobies?*'

'*Doobies*: exotic smokes from the Highlands.'

'Oh for fuck sake, Cha, just take one of mine.' Vera reaches into her handbag, throws a Silk Cut blue at Charley, dropping me in the process. I hadn't realized just how weak I am.

The security guard's head pops out from the security hut's interior. 'Everything ok? Do you want me to call somebody to take you back in? I'll call for a wheel-chair.'

'That won't be necessary,' declares Vera and breaks into the same smoking story she had weaved for the matron. She urges Charley and me onwards towards the main gates. 'You look Irish,' presuming she's flattering the security guard, 'would I be right?'

Vera sidles up to the hut. The security guard is momentarily confused and chuckles. He doffs his uniform hat and side-parts what's left of his receding hairline. 'Dublin's fair city where the girls are so pretty…' he chimes, 'you must be from Dublin yourself?' The security guard flirts with Vera and laughs hard but Vera's laughing harder as we make our way nervously through the front gates.

As a result of nerves, my mechanism is threatening to fall back into retard default mode while Charley twists, plaits, and flings dreads in my face.

We make our way onto the icy road.

'Now what?'

At first, all I see is a flashing pair of headlamps a little way off. Charley signals back and an engine rumbles into life … then I spot the taxi plate.

Stunned, I direct my attention at Charley for answers. 'She had the whole thing planned?' I have to remind myself that I'm not in a spy movie.

Charley takes me in with one of his mildly lost expressions and says, 'I'm not sure who *Vera* is anymore, Jonny. We were taking you out tonight asleep or awake.'

We sit into the warmth of the taxi. I'm half expecting to see Dennis behind the wheel but a little disappointed to see just a taxi-driver.

'C'mon Vera!' Charley's a ball of nerves. 'This wasn't in the rehearsal!'

Charley suggests driving up a little closer to the gate so the driver does as he asks, slipping into D and his role as getaway driver with equal ease. Though he keeps only his side-lights on for now and we sit in the relative darkness.

Vera appears ahead of us in the dim light, laughing her best belly-laugh she can muster and looking as if she's about to spark up a Silk Cut blue before suddenly bolting towards us. The eager taxi-driver takes this as his cue to rev up and throws on his full beams. Vera is suddenly blinded and she runs at our bonnet with outstretched arms before smacking into our bumper.

The driver recognizes his error and flicks back into his dims and apologizes to us in a strange English accent.

Charley opens the door, a whoosh of cold air rushes in with Vera who slides into the backseat and we're gone baby, gone, Vera screaming, 'Fuck! Prick! Fuck!' while kneading her shins. As we race passed the gates of Woodview Heights, I'm not bothered by the screaming security-guard flapping his uniform hat at us; it's the unseen face inside Junior's parka hood that's more worrying.

Epilogue
Home Truths

My sleep pattern doesn't have a pattern these days. My
nights are restless for good and bad reasons. The bad
reason is that I see the silhouettes of a man in a parka and a
kid on an upside-down chopper standing at my bedroom
door every night. I would love to have the egg 'n spoon
dream back again, just once. I haven't spoken of Vera's
brother or his son and don't intend to until they show up
here … if they ever do.

I thought all the cards were on the table when Vera had
poured her heart out at Woodview Heights back in March
but a few nasty surprises were still to come in May.

Last Friday, we received a bill in the post for the
princely sum of 62,000 dollars including VAT, that or court
proceedings. But to be honest, we never doubted for a
minute that the private hospital hadn't gotten my address.
They had taken my passport number and traced it to here
even though Vera had given them a false address back in
Iowa, up to her old tricks. There was a moment there when
we actually thought that maybe we had gotten away with it.
But I always pay my debts and would've returned the
payment even if Woodview had never tracked me down.
How? Dunno, but rest assured, I would've found the money
somehow.

As a result of my actions in Iowa, I had brought the
Rowes to financial ruin. 128 had been up for sale: Vera had
decided to auction off our memories, really she was left
with no choice and all of this was of my doing in my bid to
set 45 free.

Clinical Dad? He hasn't been seen since his stint as
Ronald McDonald. I don't know if I'll ever see him again
and it doesn't bother me either way. He is who he
is. On several occasions I've thought about asking Vera
his real name but I prefer not knowing the name signed at

the bottom of that hoax suicide-note. It just feels better that way. What can I say? I'm a creature of habit.

But Vera says that every good story has a bitter-sweet ending so here goes, we've crossed the bitter border and now we're into sweet territory.

I mentioned that I've got restless nights for a good and bad reason. You know the bad reason: nightmares. The good reason I'm having restless nights is because I've got a woman in my life. Remember that little forest pixie? Ruthy, the air-hostess? Yes, that firecracker who joked by asking me if I was happy to see her or was that an expanding balloon in my pocket. Fate had decided to bring us together as fate had decided that it was to be me who would give 45 his final parting. She had been on my flight home. What are the chances of that? A full month later! This time she gave me her full number (I even handed her back the napkin which I'd kept) so she could fill out the rest. It turns out that she lives in Limerick city when she's not in the sky. I've spoken to Guinevere the Reiki Mistress and we've mutually decided to keep our Reiki strictly Reiki.

And here comes the icing on our sweet cake…

Just this morning, I was sitting on the back doorstep where 45 spent most of his time waiting for the one-way bus (but now I know he'd been sitting there for a very different reason). I was looking onto our patio and re-enacting that fateful day when 45 and I sang a dreadful duet before part of my life died and a new one was born for 45 inside my birthday balloon. I was gazing sadly at the For Sale sign which led me to Vera's mole impression in the lawn which she had done while looking for 45's handsome ransom. Then my memories go way back to the days when Tommy, Alba (then Susan), and I played whatever our imaginations came up with. And all the while, 45 was watching over us from his step. In an existential kind of way, I felt that 45 was looking through my eyes just then. This isn't so far-fetched considering the amount of time we'd spent together on the road, just one man and his balloon.

I was savouring all these memories and emotions, soaking it up; a young couple put an offer on 128 just yesterday evening and it looked like Vera was going to accept. But 45 wanted me to see beyond memories and feelings. Maybe he had hypnotized me before his death and had timed me to really open my eyes on this very day.

It was while I was sitting on the back doorstep that I realized that I'd been absentmindedly picking away at the cracked cement that joins the three tiled steps leading down from our back door. The country had virtually flooded with rain while I had been in Iowa and I guess the water had dislodged a part of the step and the freezing nights on top of this had cracked the cement.

Now, you know what's coming, don't you?

Are you sitting down? I haven't been able to sit down since my discovery.

If you've stayed with me and my quest diary up until now then you'll know that fate has a strange way of working.

When I tried to fix the tile back into place, I noticed something stuffed into the space beneath the steps. I stuck my hand through the space and pulled out a dusty and cobwebbed leather bag, just like a doctor's valise in those old films.

Mildly amused, I undid the clasp and opened it.

What I first saw didn't register, just a blur. I took my eyes from the contents of the bag and looked about the back yard again but everything seemed to have changed in those intervening seconds. With 45's eyes, I peered down into the bag to see what seemed to be a million sly Benjamin Franklins staring back up at me.

The money! The treasure!

The old man had been watching over his stash all these years.

With bolts of electricity popping and fizzing inside me, I snapped the valise shut. I stumbled into the kitchen, threw the bag onto the table, and paced the room, my eyes never leaving the leather bag sitting ominously on the kitchen table. Vera returned from her twenty-four hour shift at the airport like a bitch in heat as Charley would say. She wet her knickers when I told her what that "filthy thing sitting on our kitchen table" was.

We sat down and simply gazed at the bag and all its implications before cautiously opening and counting the money.

It's here where we slip momentarily back into a bitter aftertaste because what had been a lot of money in the 1930's turned out not to be a lot of money in 2012. Once we'd done our conversion rates on my Casio calculator watch, Vera and I discovered that we had just enough cash to pay back Woodview Heights for treatment and damages. Still, 128 is saved and already off the market.

Where do I think 45 is now? Well, I know that he's left a piece of him all along our journey together but my heart tells me that he's back there now, in Anamosa, hovering at the side of Candy's gravestone on Cemetery Road: one ghost mourning another. I think they can work it out over time.

Even though I finally got to write 45's name on the remains of my birthday balloon, I still feel that I never got to know the real 45. As I sit here on the back doorstep, writing these words in my diary, I've come to the conclusion that my noble grandfather 45 had put us all under his spell, not only the lady bank-tellers. The old man had been a magician of sorts who had toyed and moulded us all into his own creation that you see before you today: we are his balloon animals.

THE END

The Author

Admittedly, Jonathan has done things arse-ways most of his life, from completing a BA in Literature in his thirties to fitting teeth brackets (30's, porcelain). During this general confusion, Jonathan has written and published a variety of short stories. He suffers from photophobia though has a tendency towards fireworks. Originally from Limerick, Ireland, he now lives the reclusive life in Toledo Spain, as a bearded hermit, with his wife and two daughters. He can be found strolling the cemeteries of Toledo on a Saturday afternoon.

Contact: Twitter @ WriterJDunne
Blog @ jonathanwdunne.wordpress.com
Facebook @ jonathan.dunne.505

Jonathan's second novel *Living Dead Lovers* Autumn 2013!

Living Dead Lovers preview

Synopsis

She's alive but he's dead...

Living Dead Lovers follows the life and times of famed psychic-medium half-Romani gypsy Valentina 'Cabbage' Moone, from her mute infancy trawling the roads of Europe to a fiery-tongued, hard-drinking, speed-loving clairvoyant with a complete disregard for human life, including her own of late...

Psychic medium Cabbage brings forth more than she can chew with a womanizing dead racing-car driver, Marty 'Magma' Molloy, who doesn't want to give up the chase. Unfortunately, Cabbage has always possessed a sick fascination for deviants and perverts which she blames on her unconventional bohemian quasi-gypsy upbringing.

A twisted love-affair never meant to be. Necrophilia: that's what the skeptical call it. Romantics call it the yin-yang love between being and human being, light and oh so very dark.

Cabbage wishes to be with her dead lover but it's not fair because she must take her own life, it's not as if Marty 'The Magma' can come back to life – that wouldn't be believable. However, a life-time of snooping around in the after-life and conjuring up old ghosts who never wanted to be conjured up has left Val with a predicament: she isn't allowed to die ... she isn't allowed to be with her other celestial half. The vengeful powers-that-be don't want Valentina the spy on their cloud because she'd spent a life-time hauling ghost-ass to the living. The motto of the Dead is: *Don't Call Us; We'll Call you.*

Cabbage resorts to suicide which becomes a morbidly sick failed pantomime. This is the most original right-to-die case the country has seen and all for the love of a man.

The impossible love story becomes a national scandal... And her guardian angel Mr. Brick Shithouse makes it even more complicated...

Living Dead Lovers chapter 1

My Predicament in 2013

Reader, would you care to join me on the edge of this cliff?

'Honey, I love you, but for the love of *Jeeesus*, hurry up 'n jump before the cliffs erode... It's not all my fault.'

'I need time to think, Magma!' I don't have a Facebook page but if I had I would choose 'It's complicated' from the drop-down menu regarding my love-life.

'That's your problem: you think! This is not something to think about, Val. What's there to think about?! Your approach to the cliff-face? Your mid-air sequence as you fall to your death? It's mechanical: one foot in front of the other... and fall.'

Reader, I ask myself how I have ended up here on the side of a cliff but I know the answer: I speak with the dead. I *am* Valentina 'Cabbage' Moone, renowned psychic medium. Naw, I don't care all that much for that half-hearted term *medium*: I'm a BIG-ASS psychic in every way because that's how I roll. If you've seen my ass then you'll get the in-joke. My ass is not something I tend to flaunt in public, but considering immediate circumstances, who cares? It's that ironic fact of being able to make idle chat with the non-living that has brought me here to the highest cliffs in Europe – Cliffs of Moher on Ireland's west coast – to end my life as I know it. I chose the highest cliffs in Europe just to be sure, to be sure. If you're aware of my recent and very public debauched attempts at ending my life, you'll understand that I *need* the height. There's nothing worse than a failed suicide attempt and believe me, *I know*. I've had a string of them just recently, one series of misfortunate events after another which I will go into later in my autobiography but now is not the time for such trivialities – it has become trivial.

'Cabbage?'

But, Reader, y'know what's worse? The morning-after effect: the embarrassment of failed suicide, plus I'm finding it difficult to finish anything that I've started, losing interest halfway through. My will to live has gone and you can tell that by looking in my cutlery drawer. You will see how I started allocating the knives, forks, and spoons into their respective sections from the cutlery basket of the dishwasher but halfway through I just dump the basket into the drawer and shut it. No interest. Also, nobody wants to ask my opinion anymore or start a conversation with me because I probably don't care about the outcome. I decide to make a blueberry cheese-cake but I don't bother with the cheese ... or the blueberry: what's the point? There's a robot taking photographs light-years away on Mars: what's the point? I won't be going on holiday there, certainly not in my life-time – I won't make it to Trabolgan holiday centre at the rate I'm going. Even the porcelain upper and lower teeth brackets that I've had fitted seem costly if I break down their price into my remaining time on this planet: something the insurance company took into consideration when I financed, I'm sure. The porcelain version certainly seems outlandish at this late stage of my mortal coil.

But I *would* like to taste that blueberry cheese-cake, see what I'm saying, Reader? I don't feel suicidal yet I have to commit suicide if I want to be with my dead racing-driver lover, Marty 'Magma' Power or simply Magma as I've come to know him – he prefers Power.

Magma says, almost a plea, 'Don't you love me enough to jump?!'

'Aw, get a life!'

'Jesus, Cabbage, I *love* you.' Magma finishes his childish tit-for-tat reasoning while trying not to look at him/her/it looming not too far off in front of us, maybe five meters over the edge of the cliff, black and floating. All I see from here are the feet sticking from beneath its billowing cape, only the feet have no flesh.

Magma pipes up. 'Look, um, how 'bout a little privacy? It's like being in *Big Brother* over here. I can't even enjoy the view...' Magma checks his voice before he loses control. He controls himself because he's speaking to Death but Death never answers because it's above that. I still can't get used to Death's presence, ironic, seen as I'm a clairvoyant. It's the feet and face that unnerves me. Beneath that drooping hood (and that's not a cliché either, it really does have an ominous drooping hood) he/she/it (let's say 'it' for the sake of argument) has got the face of a rascal child who has aged horribly and prematurely. Clearly, this creature was never man, woman, or child but something in-between that lurks in the dark recesses of our fears and phobias. I've seen the face quite a bit this last week during my suicide bids and for some reason, I see this creature as getting younger rather than older.

I snap back at Magma, 'Would you stop laying on the big lines; its' all or nothing with you, isn't it? Hmm? Of course, I love you. I'm not about to throw myself off a cliff because I find you cute!!'

'But...'

'By the way, would you STOP reading my mind. You're making me anxious – a girl needs her secrets.' Deep breaths, Cabbage ... Nice n' easy does it. Be careful because he's the only man – dead or alive – who ever loved you apart from Papa the romantic and Papa once fell in love with a talking parrot.

Magma answers back, 'I can't help reading your mind. It's one of the perks of being dead. I didn't sign up for it. I didn't sign up for any of this, Cabbage.'

Magma knows that I'm having doubts about my reasons for throwing myself to my death. He can see the enormous cerebral Times Square bill-board of PRO's and CON's for jumping. I'm stalling my own death and my other celestial half knows it.

'No,' he reflects, 'love is too simple a word for what I feel for you.'

Here we go... Would you gimme a break... Magma has always been a bunch-of-flowers kind of guy, God love him.

'What I feel for you couldn't possibly be captured in a dictionary, especially an English one.'

Let's get one thing clear, Reader, before you go reading between the lines: my lover was a racing-car driver not Dickens. He's sitting next to me now, perched on the cliff-face at an impossible angle. His undying words of love come at me through the visor of his battered helmet which he hasn't removed since his tragic death along with his eternally singed and smoking racing cover-alls. His helmet has become a metaphor for our future together (should there be any students reading this on an educational syllabus). Marty will only remove his helmet when I remove my heavenly knickers in the afterlife. I think I will need a back-up pair by the time today is over, ha ha. I have never seen Magma without his helmet. Love is blind or what, Reader? They say opposites attract, well, *they* were right. Logistics and metaphysics mean that our relationship hasn't been consummated so when I say *lover* I mean it in a loosely-binding way. Oh, don't get me wrong, we've messed around, experimented, yes sir, but I don't know you well enough to kiss 'n tell just yet. Perhaps we will know each other better by chapter 10 (I mean no disrespect; I've got to say this if I want to sell copies). Let's just say that for all the Viagra in the world, a male ghost needs to summon a lot of energy, a lot, just to, um, maintain. And even then, would I even notice it, Reader? I've heard about drunk girls not even aware that they had, y'know, the night previous, but I think this is different. I guess i will find out in the next life, bah humbug.

The only consolation prize in all of this, Reader, is that I'm not allowed to die.

Let me repeat that for you... *I'm not allowed to die.*

See, this is my predicament: Death (sourpuss standing

behind us right now) is bitter at me for having conjured up his 'clients' without his permission for so many years. Whenever I try to do myself in, Death is standing not too far off, just waiting to save me from myself. The other side doesn't want me on their cloud. I've spent my years conjuring up spirits for grieving families when those poor souls never wanted to be conjured up in the first place. I've been spying on the dead all my life, giving away secrets that the Dead had supposedly taken to their graves (oops). Being summoned by Valentina 'Cabbage' Moone is like being summoned to jury-duty, I imagine. The poor souls prefer to, quite literally R.I.P, but I wouldn't let them in my blissful ignorance. For the Dead, the living is nothing but one big spamming insurance company dropping propaganda in their celestial letter-boxes. They just want a normal conversation with a stranger because it's easier to talk to a stranger without getting sentimental, being dead, and all. Not only that, I'm slightly embarrassed to say that I've been pocketing vast sums of money from vulnerable people who are desperate to know that their deceased loved ones are still with them. The spirits have a motto and that is: *Don't Call Us; We'll Call You.* Now, it is payback time and long-face over there won't let me lie with my lover in the after-life. Childish.

But y'know what, I think that it's probably enjoying this little game. I've brightened up Death's day considering that it is normally swiping people off the face off the Earth, not acting as a bouncer at Club Afterlife.

But y'know what's worse? And this is the part that you *have* to know now, Reader: I don't feel suicidal (I want to taste that blueberry cheese-cake) and yet I've made eight failed attempts this week – twice on Tuesday which I had actually pencilled into my agenda. It'd be a comedy if it wasn't so tragic.

'Cabbage, either you jump or I jump!'

'You're already dead, Magma. I'm not an idiot.' I'm suddenly overcome by a confusing well of emotion. I bury my face in my hands and my body screams at me but I can't, I just can't hear *me* any more – where are my hardy gypsy roots!? Mama's roots that would find purchase in the North Pole or the Sahara? Mama who was legally blind and illegally deaf and vice versa when it suited her.

'Are you laughing or crying, Cab?' Magma enquires. 'I don't like it, whatever it is.'

'I dunno, Mags. I'm desperate because I haven't found a way to finish this mortal stage of my journey to be with you. It's so frustrating.'

Below my steel toe-capped anti-corrosive maroon Doc Martens stands 213 meters of sheer jagged black rock. It hurts just to look.

'Cabbage,' Magma turns his shoulder to Death, 'what's there to think about? Our love breaks all barriers.'

'Yeah, it was breaking a barrier on the last lap of Donington race track that put you in the category that doesn't need life insurance.' I regret saying it even before I've finished my caustic line. See, Magma doesn't like to be reminded that he's dead. It's a sore point.

With a tremor in his voice, Magma admits that he never felt this kind of love when he was alive. 'D'ya hear me? I feel more alive now that when I was alive!' he rejoices, slapping his smoking chest. 'I've played around, I won't deny it, but you jump my bones, woman. Do you realize the power that that must take to jump *bones?*'

I'm almost sucked in until I see him lying horizontal to the cliff face. I have to remind myself that he's dead, never mind reminding him that he's dead.

'We've been through this a thousand times: it's the only way we can make our undying love work.'

'Only it isn't undying,' I answer back, 'because you're already dead and I *have* to die. I know love is blind but, Christ, I feel I've been *blinded*. At least, your death came as a surprise to everybody, including you. But I've got to think about it and there's nothing worse than having your own suicide on your mind.'

I've learned that relationships are all about give and take but it isn't as if Magma can come back from the dead, Reader. It's up to me to purchase that one-way ticket, albeit at a higher price. I've come here to end my mortal life to be with my dead lover; that much is easy to understand. And for the last time, it is *not* necrophilia – I've no intention of digging up Magma's dead carcass in the cold ground and lying with him in his coffin. Besides, he was cremated which sort of works nicely with his smouldering charm.

Magma's getting restless. I can see it in his eyes through his helmet's visor. He gets this annoying blinking tic. 'Till death do us part, my arse...' Magma sulkily contemplates the rolling Atlantic stretching out below us. The wind would probably be in his hair now if he didn't have his damn helmet on. 'On a clear day you can see New York,' he admits before trailing off. Like I said, he's no Stephen Hawking.

'Part my arse?!' I back-answer, 'I don't *love* you?! Eight attempted suicides this bloody week! My nerves are shot! Will this week ever end? It's not as if I've chickened out of death,' adding as an afterthought which is a distressing side-effect of suicide. 'My gypsy blood won't allow it, Mags. I'm fighting against my instinct here! Y'know what, sometimes I really regret conjuring up your spirit ... don't look at me like that, it's true. I wouldn't have fallen in love with you and I wouldn't want to take my own life to be with you.'

'Aw, Cabbage, c'mon, Death'll come 'round eventually.'

By the way, the world has been following my bitter-sweet love story. RTE, BBC, and Channel 4 are transmitting my impending death to the world and even Fox News. I've become the ultimate *Big Brother* star and viewers with morbid fixations wait for my next macabre stunt. From tropical monsoon shanty-towns where I've played middle-man between the living and the dead ... to

Scandinavian imperial palaces where I have also acted as go-between on behalf of a closet-gay prince and his dead king father ... to the local bars of Brooklyn and across the Atlantic to Limerick, the world has come to see Cabbage off with a collective tear in its eye; my fond farewell to be with my man forever in eternal happiness. My unwillingness to compromise has come from my gypsy blood and it has won (and lost) me fans across the globe. The only compromise I have ever made is one of love – the ultimate sacrifice.

'Just throw yourself off the damn cliff and be done with it, woman. Just put one foot in front of the other. It's easy, look.' Magma steps off the cliff ... and out into nothing and hovers there.

My stomach lurches.

I'm sure he's got a smug face inside that helmet. He's looking at Death for some recognition but Death has that ethereal face.

I'm scared and desperate. Just to prove it, I come out with, 'Lose the helmet, Magma, and gimme a big sloppy kiss just to remind myself why I'm making this, um, leap of faith.' I reach out, pout my lips, and lose my grip...

Behind me, the television crews gasp... My anti-corrosive Dr. Marten souls slide six feet before the clunky silver gypsy rings on my fingers hook on a rocky outcrop. I begin a gentle swinging motion in the wind and to think that I loved wind-chimes as a child! There is complete silence. I hear DeVotchka's *Exhaustible* coming from a radio car somewhere ... or has Magma put it in my head? Are you kidding me! It's our favourite song, Reader. How many times has Magma sang this song to me through his helmet visor.

Magma snaps, 'Just let yourself fall, woman!'

I take the silver flagon of Templeton Rye I was given as a gift during my tour of Iowa in '07 from my inside pocket and down an all-merciful gulp. I admit that I've developed a fondness for drink but purely for medicinal purposes: to sober up and rid myself of my ghosts that have haunted me since my childhood. I desperately crave a hug from Papa, the only true romantic I ever knew (he married Mama, didn't he)...

No, Reader, do you know what would be extra special right now: to feel the warm embrace of my guardian angel that goes by his stage-name, Mr. Brick Shithouse...

And suddenly, as if by providence, I see an angel of death riding in on an Atlantic thermal. *'Finally! It's gonna happen!'* As I bawl these words to the heavens, I see that my angel is nothing but a hang-glider being piloted by a cameraman looking for the winning scoop... sick.

Suddenly, I hurtle head over heels down into the void. Have I slipped or have I just been shoved? I've been shoved!

Does it even matter now?

I see my anti-corrosive steel-capped Dr. Martens somersaulting on the end of over-stuffed puppet legs and vaguely ponder the fact that I've never had the opportunity to drop an anvil on my toes or walk in a bath of acid – just to try out the claims written on the souls of my maroon boots.

My life flashes before me in the form of this official autobiography: *Living Dead Lovers...*

Printed in Great Britain
by Amazon.co.uk, Ltd.,
Marston Gate.